GUEST EDITORS OF
Scribner's Best of the Fiction Workshops

1997 Alice Hoffman

1998 Carol Shields

1999 Sherman Alexie

Scribner's Best of the Fiction Workshops
1999

Guest Editor
Sherman Alexie

Series Editors
John Kulka and Natalie Danford

SCRIBNER PAPERBACK FICTION
PUBLISHED BY SIMON & SCHUSTER

For my niece and nephews:
Giorgia, Giulio, Jake, and Luca
N.D.

CONTENTS

PREFACE

IT'S STARTLING TO THINK that the first creative writing program was founded in 1939—only sixty years ago—in Iowa City,
at the University of Iowa. Since then much has changed. In the
immediate aftermath of the Second World War, other American universities set up workshop programs as schools found
themselves suddenly flush with federal money. And by the
1970s as many as a dozen new programs were being established
each year. That growth has continued in recent years—though
at a less torrid rate. Today *The AWP Guide to Writing Programs*
recognizes 137 schools offering the Master of Arts degree
in writing; and another 49, the Master of Fine Arts degree. This
incredible proliferation of workshop programs has meant nothing less than a complete reshaping of American literary culture
and life. After the Second World War, the American literary
establishment would forever be associated with the academy. In
his book *Writing in General and the Short Story in Particular,* Rust
Hills, fiction editor at *Esquire,* observes this remarkable trans-
formation: "If one but stands back a bit and looks, one sees
that it is no longer the book publishers and magazines, but
rather the colleges and universities, that support the entire
structure of the American literary establishment—and, m̄

authors. The programs represented by these writers are diverse and this year the names of a few schools appear for the first time in our table of contents. There are some awfully good stories in this anthology, and we can say with confidence these emerging writers will also go on to bigger and better things. *Scribner's Best of the Fiction Workshops 1999* is a sneak preview of the first generation of writers of the twenty-first century. This is indeed a promising beginning to a new century.

We would like to extend our thanks to Sherman Alexie for his close reading of these stories and for his editorial suggestions. We would also like to thank, of course, all the people affiliated with the workshops who are truly responsible for making this series a continuing success: the program directors, teachers, administrators, and students. Our editor Penny Kaganoff, who has since left Simon & Schuster, once again provided valuable assistance—and for that we thank her. We also thank Caroline Sutton, our new editor at Simon & Schuster, who stepped in to pinch-hit at critical junctures, Jeff Wilson in the Simon & Schuster contracts department, and our families.

—John Kulka and Natalie Danford

INTRODUCTION

by SHERMAN ALEXIE

1.

I DIDN'T WANT to be a writer. Don't get me wrong. I have always been a voracious reader, but I never once considered becoming a writer. The whole concept existed outside every single one of my possibilities. Sure, I was a bright Indian boy, exceptionally so considering the quality of reservation education, but reservation Indian boys simply did not become writers. I had no role models, no examples of American Indians who had wanted to become writers, then wrote the book and/or books, and became writers. I mean, I was twenty-one years old before somebody, *anybody*, showed me a piece of literature written by an American Indian. Prior to that, I'd read the same buckskin-and-loincloth garbage still commonly referred to as Native American literature. Disgusted with all of that work, I immersed myself in the classics of Western civilization, reading the same books that every bright white kid reads: Hemingway, Faulkner, Steinbeck, Melville, Brontë, Austen, Fitzgerald, Dickinson, Whitman, Donne, Keats, Yeats, Frost, etc.

Looking back now, I realize that I didn't read a book written by a non–white person until I was nineteen years old. The book?

Adam Marshall Johnson
Florida State University

THE DEATH-DEALING
CASSINI SATELLITE

Tonight the bus is unusually responsive—brakes crisp, tires gripping—jockeying lane to lane so smoothly your passengers forget they're moving as they turn to talk over the seats, high heels dangling out into the aisle, teeth bright with vodka and the lemon rinds they pull from clear Baggies in their purses. Some stand, hanging loosely from overhead handles, wrists looped in white plastic straps, smiling as their bodies lean unnaturally far with the curves. Off-balance, half-falling, this position has its advantages: hips flare and sway behind you, ribs thumb their way through fabric, and this, it seems, is the view you've grown used to, daring you to touch, poised to knock you down.

You don't even know where you're driving yet, but through breaks in the trees, you can see red-and-blues on the parkway and know traffic cops are working the outflow of an I-High baseball game. The school is not a place you want to be near tonight, especially bumper to bumper with old teammates, especially as a nineteen-year-old go-nowhere who drives a charter bus for a cancer victim support group on Thursday nights. So you're banking a turn onto the Cascade Expressway

ing in your face. When she's composed herself a little, you give the BlueLiner a quick burst of gas and watch the tip of that catheter circle into a tight orbit below her hem. Cassini smiles sideways at you.

You two've done this routine before.

The *Blue Danube* kicks into gear, and across the women's faces in the mirror comes a certain serenity, like they're all picturing the slow-tumbling spaceships from *2001: A Space Odyssey*, a movie you thought was pretty sexual—all that docking and podwork—and which your dad said was a coded history of existentialism.

She lifts her flask high. "For my husband," she says into the mike, addressing the bus like a lounge singer. "Scholar. Diplomat. NASA scientist of the year." Here she whoops loud, and the women are swaying to the music just enough to make the bus woozy between lanes.

"He has a permit to buy weapons-grade plutonium, reserved parking at JPL. He wrote his name in the wet cement of Cape Canaveral's launchpad, but it's Thursday night, and he can't come within five hundred feet of his wife for four more hours."

The bus explodes, the women are in the aisles, some with their arms in the air, dancing and pirouetting homages to both the famous Cassini satellite and the weekly six-hour Cassini restraining order.

Mrs. Cassini tosses the mike into your lap, and from her glowing abandon you're trying to guess the destination this week: shocking the tourists at the Idanha Hotel? Maybe scar-strutting with the black ties at the Capitol Club or lobbying complimentaries from the Westin convention staff.

Cassini moves closer, her lips just brushing your ear, and you want to close your eyes. "To the Cove, young captain," she mouths and you know there's both a difficult U-turn and some slumming ahead. But your shoulders start to loll to the music and soon you have the old BlueLiner waltzing through the back roads of Boise, a little too fast perhaps, though none of your passengers are very worried about crashing because they've all had cancer, and the motion of their bodies tonight seems to confirm both *Space Odyssey* theories.

the stages of grief, and there were no surprises. Mom even died on schedule. Those doctors were amazing; they called it within a weekend.

Dad joined a support group and took up woodworking. He bought you a brass trumpet and a punching bag. Now he comes home from work, checks the Weather Channel—he's crazy about the weather—puts on a shop apron, and goes into the garage to build the look-alikes of Colonial furniture that fill your house.

Sometimes he gets nostalgic on Sundays or has a few too many beers over dinner and tells you things about Mom when she was young. You've heard most of them many times, but once in a while he says something new, and you feel close to him for that. Your mom had a pony named Applejack when she was girl. In college her favorite movie was *The Andromeda Strain*. That, pregnant with you, she was in Albertson's supermarket when her water broke, and she calmly took a jar of pickles from the shelf, dropped it over the fluid on the floor, and moved on.

But even these moments of disclosure from your father seem expected in a way, and his power tools never seem to rattle him the way you'd think they might, the way the BlueLiner's big diesel can vibrate something loose in you that makes you forget where it is you are driving, makes you check and check the overhead mirror for her in row six. You think if Dad could have seen her on this bus one time, bright-eyed and destination-bound, all those pieces from his replica projects wouldn't fit together so well.

You hear the thump of the red door and look out the windscreen to see a kid your age cross the lot with a white bucket of beer caps. He cuts around to the back dock, where he starts dumping them in the lake. It's dark and a long way off, but you think you know him from the baseball team, from before you quit. He leans against the rail and he pours slowly, watching the caps go down like all those green innings in a near-championship stadium. His name might be Tony. Finished, he spits on what is probably his own reflection and goes inside. When the door closes, though, there is a woman standing beneath the blue beer sign.

She crosses the lot, circling wide to avoid the floodlight. With calm, measured steps she walks around the far side of the bus, where she grabs a sapling with both hands and stares at her feet.

She's in trouble, about to be sick, but there's something about her shoulders, the way her ribs flare and trim toward her waist. She's younger, new to the Club, and caught your eye in the mirror on the way over. You could tell she was drawn to the mood on the bus, the abandon, the acceptance of being out without her wig. For everyone on the BlueLiner, the worst has already happened, and this is how they can laugh and talk to one another across newly emptied seats. This is what your mother wanted: for everything to race on without her.

Now the woman retches, the thin branches shaking above her. When her shoes and ankles get wet, you know you should look away, but there is something necessary in the sight. It makes you wish your mother could have shown this side, the alone-and-sick, slipping-outside part of the deal, because all her strength, like your father's adaptability, did nothing to brace you for after.

Her heels shift in the gravel again, heading for the bus, where she shakes the locked doors. You find her seat, her purse, and at the cab you strip the towel off your captain's chair before levering open the door. With the bright lights behind, she is more than alluring. She is here and real.

She takes her bag from your hand. "Jesus," she says. "This stuff I'm taking."

"I'm Ben," you tell her. Inside you're feeling that pulse, and don't know what to say because somehow you're already beyond small talk. And even just talking means you're making an investment of some kind. It's like standing before a brass trumpet or boxer's bag: they promise to show you a lot more of yourself than a red face or sore hands, and you're unsure if you want to touch them because of that.

You climb down to the last step and sit, so she's taller. "Here," you say, holding the towel in the air before her, and there's this thing between you so clear that she grabs the door molding for balance and places a foot in your hand. You begin with her calf, stroking down to the heel.

"Do you feel better?"

"Sue. I'm sorry, Sue."

"Do you feel better, Sue?"

"No, not really."

She has a Hickman port in her chest, a sort of gray button connected to a white tube that disappears into the skin below the collarbone. You know your cancers pretty well, and the Hickman's a bad sign. It's made so they can inject really strong drugs like vinblastine, chemicals which will burn out the veins unless they're pumped straight into the superior vena cava, straight into the heart. You can feel the slim bones of her foot through the towel. Vinblastine is made from the purple blossoms of the periwinkle plant. You want to push that button.

"I mean you're nice for this, but this medicine . . ."

"Ben."

"This medicine, Ben." She shakes her head.

You take her other foot when she offers, wanting to make her legs dry and clean. You want to tell her you understand, that you've tasted Cytoxan, that it made your fingernails loose and teeth hurt. The feeling like your molars have been pulled returns: platinum spark plugs have been screwed into your jaw, and for a moment, it's like when they'd crackle to life in the middle of the night, making you see blue on the inside of your eyelids. "It's okay," you tell Sue.

"What's okay?"

"Everything. It feels pretty bad now, I know, but it'll all work out."

She pulls her foot back.

Your voice is thinner even than Mrs. Crowley's, but still you say, "Things'll be fine."

"I'm pretty fucked, thank you. I'm screwed."

She says this and hops once, slipping a shoe strap over her heel before walking away.

From your wallet you pull your entrance ticket to the SAT. The picture you glued to it doesn't look anything like you. You cut it out of your sophomore yearbook, a dull-faced goofy kid who has no idea what's coming, who doesn't suspect that no one in his family will take a photo for the next three years.

You follow the route Sue took through the cars, into the Cove.

Inside, things are about what you'd thought. Several women have corralled two wrecker drivers into a group jitterbug that has them spinning off-balance from woman to woman, their eyes unsure where to land—avoiding chests and hairlines—while their hands clutch at waists as if for emergency brakes. Oblivious to the fast rhythm, Mrs. Boyden dances with a small, older gentleman in a brown jumpsuit. They move like strangers on liberty, her fingers hooked in his collar, his hands gathering the fabric of her emerald dress like parachute cord, a gesture which smoothes where his head lay sideways on her sternum, listening, as if to the source of the softer music they seem to move to. There is no sign of Sue.

Nothing seems to involve you. You sit at the bar wanting ice water while the bartender watches the *Tonight Show* on a soundless set. The music and laughing seem to sweep past, and it is as still on this stool as afternoons when you pull one of your father's pine Louis XIV chairs into your mother's cactus garden and contemplate in the half-light where it was she dug her holes. Lately, though, this is a riskier proposition because after only a year, you're no longer so sure of what she hoped for and feared. If you wrote it, this is what your college essay would be about: Feeling for divots in a dark lawn with your toes. Renting movies like *The Fighting Seabees* with your father. Living all winter in a house filled with cactus, sleeping in a room made small by jade-green ribs and spines while the smell of hot saw blades from the garage blows in through the heat vent.

Sue takes the stool next to you, and she also is ignored by the bartender. You ignore her, too. In front of you is a wall-length mirror littered with business cards, snapshots in cheap plastic frames, and several yards of dollar bills signed with red marker. There is a crisp five-dollar bill that says *Work-Battle-Battle-Win* in beautiful script; it was the motto of your I-High baseball team, and in a stupid ritual you chanted it before every game.

At the end of the bar, Judge Helen smokes and chats with a woman who has rad-therapy lines tattooed on her neck as if they were sisters. If you catch her from the other side, where they

"That's my Benny."

The bartender pours the tequila without limes or salt and when he changes the TV to the late news, Mrs. Cassini yells, "What time is it?" She turns to you, excited, and runs her hand through your hair, shaking your head with your earlobe at the end. "Come on, young captain. It's time."

Waving her hand to the bar, she yells, "To the satellite!"

With that great pull of Mrs. Cassini, you let yourself be swept. Reaching for the bar, you barely manage to grab the portrait of your mother and down the shot.

Outside, the patrons empty onto an oil-planked T-pier and, drinks in hand, stroll above black water lightly pushed from a breeze farther out. The clatter and footsteps of those moving ahead seem to echo from landings across the lake a pitch higher, like the tinny sound of old wire or metal that's been spun, and it feels good to be part of a group moving together to see a sight.

Mrs. Cassini is only a strong voice over the others, Sue a glimpse through the shoulders ahead, and you follow at the edge, skeptical about what you'll find, even though you get that feeling like you're safe behind the BlueLiner's wheel, like nothing bad can come within fifty-six feet.

At the end of the pier everybody looks up. You hear the soft thunk of a wrecker driver's Zippo, his eyes scanning the night above the hands that cup his smoke. Mrs. Boyden and the older man are together again, each with a hand to the brow as if the stars were too bright to consider straight on. Even the boy who might be Tony squints into the night, and the way he absently wipes his hands on his apron makes you see him as an earlier version of your father, thinking of policies and premiums as he looks to the future, though covered each way for whatever comes.

"I told my husband I wanted to see the new satellite. Then this morning, *over breakfast,* he changes the sweep of its orbit with his laptop," Mrs. Cassini says, and guides us across the sky with her hand. "It'll be coming from Seattle and heading toward Vegas, with enough plutonium to make a glass ashtray of Texas."

Judge Helen coughs.

You look at everyone's face and you know this is stupid. You can't put a restraining order on a satellite the same way you can't change the path of a tumor. It's stupid to think you can just wave your hand and summon up something that doesn't care about any of us.

"There," Judge Helen says and points back and away from where everyone was looking. They all turn in unison but you.

"Yes," says Sue.

"Of course," says the kid in the apron, with all the battle-battle-win optimism of a near-champion, and you look just to prove him wrong, because deep down you want to believe.

Twenty fingers guide you to it. At first it's too much to take in, all those stars. You wish your mother had thrown herself into something the last year of her life, like writing a cookbook or sketching cloudscapes, so that you could make some of those recipes and see how they tasted to her, so you could look up and see what she saw. Overhead, though, is a sky splattered as laughed-up milk, about as shaped as the mass in Mrs. Cassini's belly. Until suddenly you say *of course*. It's that simple. You see it: the green light of the Cassini satellite ticking its chronometer path toward Vegas. You remember the earth-shot on the Weather Channel and the thought that a satellite can't see you but you can see it feels pretty damn good. It makes you want to write *of course* on a ten-dollar bill in red ink.

Mrs. Cassini dives into the ice-cold lake and begins back-stroking.

At the end of the pier, you hear Judge Helen whistling the *Blue Danube* and look up to see her balanced on a tall shoring post. She launches, extending, and executes a thunderous jack-knife, the crowd throwing up whoops as people begin diving in.

The kid in the apron stands in disbelief, and you walk to him. It's not your father he looks too much like, but yourself. In his hands you place the picture.

"Hold this for me," you tell him. "It's important."

He angles the glass against the light off the lake to see. "Okay," he says.

You slip off your shoes and, barefoot, hop up to balance atop a post. From here you can see no more of the lake, but the women below are clear as they stroke and stretch as if doing rehab exercises. There will always be a reason not to jump into a cold lake, thousands of them, and a certain sense emerges from this. It's like the logic of getting a court order against a husband who spends his evenings watching TV in the basement. It's the desire to control anything you can.

Mrs. Cassini floats on her back in the cold water, facing the sky. She looks at you, then closes her eyes, floating. "I'm twice as alive as you are," she says softly, her voice so vital she almost sounds angry. Some women clap water in the air while others backstroke into deeper water, their arms lifting in graceful salute to a satellite that cannot see us, that for tonight at least, just passes on by.

You jump. One slow tumble in the air that unfolds into a sailor's dive, and you enter with your arms at your sides, chin out, barreling toward the beer caps waiting below. You hadn't planned on hitting the bottom, but it's somehow not a surprise. The muted rustling of tin, when you make contact, is the exact sound of the BlueLiner's air brakes—the *shh* of compressed air releasing—and the flash of pain in your eyes is bright enough to fire your irises white.

Surfacing, you can feel the flap on your jaw and the warmth on your throat. You swim to Sue and kiss her, awkwardly, half on the nose.

"Easy there, bus driver," she says and has to smile, just her slick face showing.

"You shouldn't swim with a Hickman port," you say. "You could get an infection and die."

"And that kiss was any safer?"

"I suppose it wasn't much of a kiss."

"I think you gave me a fat lip."

"I can do better."

"Another one like that and I won't need the zoo pass."

"The fishing pole, then."

"Maybe it was the satellite," she says. "All that pressure to perform."

"They're watching us on the Weather Channel right now."

Sue gets a conspiratorial look on her face. "I saw at least three satellites up there. How many did you count?"

You're both treading water, breathing hard between phrases. "They were fucking *everywhere*," you tell her.

"That Mrs. Cassini. I think the satellite she's talking about is halfway to Saturn."

Sue's treading water with you, and that's a good sign. You know you're going to kiss her again. You have a photo of your mother safe with a friend and a mild case of shock. You're immersed in ice-cold water, losing blood fast, and still you feel an erection coming on, the kind you'd get when you were sixteen, appearing out of nowhere, surprising you with its awkward insistence on the terrifying prospect of joy ahead.

Bich Minh Nguyen
University of Michigan

IMMINENCE

"**R**ice paddies," Andrew says. "Is this the Mekong Delta?"

The red earth is sodden, shaped by brown strings of water. Smoke smudges rise from squat shanties. Ho Chi Minh City begins suddenly, all concrete houses shoved against each other, colliding in rust.

"What about dengue fever?" Andrew says. "Did we get those pills?"

At the airport terminal, a row of women stand outside in turquoise *ao dai*s. "Welcome to Vietnam," they say in English. They are pretty. Their bright gowns flutter. They direct us to customs, stern men in hard, dark khaki suits trimmed with red, whose faces do not move as they inspect the passports and visas. I'd been worried about how they would see us, Vietnamese girl and white man, but no one cares. No one opens the suitcases, no one inquires about the family-size packages of toothpaste, soap, detergent, M&M's, these gifts my grandmother has made us bring. "Good in two ways," she had said. "Not only to use, but to sell." Bufferin, Centrum, University of Michigan T-shirts. She believes in the strength of the black market.

My grandmother had said there might be dozens of relatives waiting outside the airport, hands entwined in the tall iron fences, waving chrysanthemums. There could be dozens, she said, or just one. When Andrew and I step outside into the haze and heat, taxi drivers call out to us. They're leaning against the cars, their long sleeves rolled up, flashing cigarettes. All around us people are standing on the sidewalk with flowers in their arms. I realize I have no idea where to go.

When I hear my name, the high quick accent, I see two old women waving at me, their hands filled with gladiolus bouquets. Dressed in fancy *ao dais* of pink and gray shimmer, they push toward me. One of them holds a picture of me in her hand; it's my graduation photo—my grim face, hair hidden by the awkward cap. They tell me they are my great-aunts, my grandmother's sisters. Their hands cup my elbows as they peer directly into my face. One of them, the one in pink, lifts a hand toward my face. She doesn't touch me; her hand stops near my left ear, as though she is trying to frame me within her own comprehensible vision.

It is like naive magic, trust, the way we follow them to an old green minivan. The aunts are chattering too quickly for me to understand, and I worry that they're exchanging remarks about this white boy I have brought. Andrew, who has no idea, remains silent. We drive through a maze of tin and stucco houses and overrun streets to a neighborhood of narrow red earth lanes, rutted and muddy, where the aunts share a small concrete house.

My father sometimes brought jackfruits home from the Saigon Market. He'd lay them on the cement deck in the backyard and hack them open with an ax. Now I see them hanging from the huge tree in the little courtyard at the front of the house; the massive fruits hang down repulsively, swollen, a bruised and heavy green. Strewn around the tree are bicycles, chopping blocks, and motorcycle parts. The world is a daze of heat.

The front of the house is open to the air, the sliding metal doors pushed all the way back. Over the windows, iron grates make leaf and flower patterns. We sit on flat mahogany chairs and sip green tea from cups so small I could close one inside my fist. The room is partitioned off by curtains, but we can see the mahogany beds, the straw mats unrolled upon them. Andrew keeps staring at the ornate altar, incense, photographs, fruit, and flowers surrounding the bronze Buddha. On the bottom shelf, a Vietnamese basketball game is playing on TV. On the walls, scroll calendars feature glamour shots of female singers or landscapes of Vietnam. Andrew nods toward them and whispers, "It looks just like the one you gave me." If it's sweet, I don't know. I smile dumbly.

My aunts ask questions: How old is he? Are you tired? Are you going to be married? How is the family? How much does a pound of beef cost in America?

When the uncles come home, the aunts serve French bread, tofu soup, *cha gio* egg rolls, shrimp sautéed with green onions. I know that my grandmother has written: *she and her friend do not eat beef or pork.* The *cha gio* are always stuffed with pork. I pluck one after the other and deposit them on Andrew's plate. One of the uncles shows him how to use the chopsticks to sever the egg rolls and roll them with lettuce, cilantro, and cucumber shreds into a sheet of rice paper. Andrew eats messily, spills hoisin sauce. There are green bottles of 7-Up, long slabs of ice in each glass. "*Cam on,*" Andrew keeps saying, smiling and nodding. *Thank you.* I taught him on the plane. Also *ngon qua* (very delicious) and *xin loi* (I'm sorry). His pronunciation is terrible. One of the uncles taps out a Winston and says, "I guess he can't speak any Vietnamese." Andrew looks up as though he's been asked a question. "No Vietnamese," I say. I am this middling translator, making up half the words both ways. I tell my relatives that Andrew and I both love school. I try to explain that we are both going to go for doctorates, but they end up thinking we are both going to be doctors. The aunts are especially impressed by this. One of them makes sure: "Doctor instead of nurse?" I say yes. She brings plates crowded with mango slices and lychees, sets them in front of Andrew and me.

By the time blue twilight begins I am exhausted. My aunts and uncles press us only a few times to stay at the house; I know that my grandmother has explained *they want to stay in a hotel.* It is against all protocol of tradition and hospitality, but we are young and American and with Andrew I can get away with not knowing. What worries me is the gift giving. There is a proper way, proper words, but in the end I just take out all the packages and leave them on the floor while the uncles are outside waiting for the taxi and the aunts are washing the dishes. Between the bars of Dial I tuck the envelopes. They are filled with U.S. money, one hundred dollars in bills.

The taxi is a little Mazda that fills up the entire road in front of the house. The aunts scold the uncles to help the driver put the suitcases in the trunk. They press a foil package of *cha gio* into my hands. They shake Andrew's hand with a great politeness, leaning in to see his smile. As soon as we're in the taxi, he says, "They're so nice!"

The Luong Luong Hotel is on Le Van Sy Avenue, near downtown. It's a minihotel, a vertical five-floor French Colonial building. We have reservations for three nights later in the week at the Hotel Continental, which is $125 a night. The Luong Luong is only fifteen bucks including breakfast. Our room is on the fourth floor, with a wall of windows looking out onto the street. Bicycles, mopeds, pedicabs, and cars stream past one another, beeping horns, without the directives of traffic signals. All the stores are still open. I think about going down to browse in the shoe stores displaying stilettos in vibrant pastels.

"*Luong luong.*" I try it out loud. *Always.*

Andrew keeps saying, "I can't believe we're here." He turns up the air-conditioning. He talks about the bathroom tub that doesn't have a shower curtain. He marvels at the tea set in the room, the carved wardrobe, heavy chairs. I supply the right words: settee, chaise, valances. The carpet is a rich flowered burgundy, the curtains a celadon velvet.

It is our first night in Vietnam and we will have to make love. We take a shower together. When he washes my hair, he presses his body against mine, pulls my head back to look into my eyes. Later he throws the bedcovers back with dramatic flourish and says that he loves this, he wouldn't want to be anywhere else but here, with me, right here and now, exhausted together. He kisses me. He says, "I want to make love to you in this city you were born in."

■

WHAT'S THE spring song?

Xuan la ve, xuan la ve. Spring has come.

How do you say I love you?

Boy to girl: *Anh yeu em.* Girl to boy: *Em yeu anh. Em* is also the word for baby, child, younger sibling, younger person.

Xuan di roi: Spring has gone.

Xuan la ve, xuan di roi.

■

WHEN ANDREW and I first got together, we realized we'd been living two blocks away from each other for two years. "Maybe we saw each other dozens of times and never knew it," he said. "Maybe we were subconsciously looking for each other." Sometimes he said things like that in bed. He needed darkness. In the daytime he was just a guy, making conversation. In the darkness he tried to woo.

We met in a cultural studies seminar. At the oblong table he would sit directly across from me. He seemed to take notes at mysterious times. When he spoke, he addressed the class instead of the professor and would often lean forward, one elbow on the table, to make some point. I remember he used the word *matrix* twice in one day. He didn't always take off his jacket—it was a cobalt blue, sort of L.L. Bean looking—and it was a little small for him, so that sometimes his wrist jutted out of the sleeve. Like a boy. Growing up. Sometimes I walked behind him down the hall, leaving class. I liked his thin body, his blond curls tending toward unruliness.

On the day we were going to watch *Metropolis* I walked in and saw him sitting in the chair I usually sat in, the corner seat nearest the southeastern window. I sat down next to him. The professor came in and shut the door and just before the movie started Andrew turned to me and said, "I've been writing about you." I was easy to convince. He was staring down at his notebook, aligning his pen against the left margin.

Andrew's parents live in Manchester-by-the-Sea, not far from Boston. What I love about their house is the refrigerator: industrially large, stocked with family cartons of orange juice, three-bean salads, long trays of cold cuts, and four flavors of cream cheese. When we visit his parents, Andrew brings up the subject of marriage. He always wants to know if I'd wear a white gown or a traditional *ao dai*. He is sentimental about the idea of Asianness. He asks a lot of questions about my history, my community. He uses those words genuinely: *community, your history*. In concerned tones he asks about my family, about our emigration from Vietnam in 1975. He likes to hear the stories my father had told me, fantastical tales of Saigon on the verge of ruin, families flung apart and hurtling toward escape. "That's where you were born," he said once. It was in the bookstore, among the atlases. He was pointing at the Mekong Delta. "I was born in Saigon," I said, moving his hand away. He traced the path of the Saigon River. He had a way of saying things I couldn't respond to. He said we could have a crazy Buddhist atheist wedding, with a monk and a judge, incense lighting and document signing. He said he'd like to see his whole family lining up outside my house, bearing red-cellophaned gifts.

We slept a lot. A month after we met, we were sleeping together every night. We slept through spring and summer and fall, all the transitions. That next year I kept my computer at his house and worked at his desk while he studied, sitting up in bed. He wore reading glasses that slipped down his nose. The desk faced the window and I could see our separate faces in it, mine blurred out by the lamplight and his illuminated by it. Sometimes he caught me looking at him. Other times he tossed balled-up socks at me to get my attention.

When we started applying to grad school we had a discussion in which we agreed never to try to hold each other back, and not to follow each other for the sake of following. It was healthy and mature, we agreed. I knew this was so, even late at night in my own apartment. All winter, each night as I walked to his apartment I looked for Venus, ungainly and bright in the low sky.

■

WHEN DID your mother die?

She died soon after I was born.

What happened?

She'd been very ill.

It must have been a difficult birth.

I don't know.

What did your father do?

I don't know.

What happened next?

I don't know. We left the country.

Darling.

Darling? That word—I've never understood that word.

Come here.

But *darling*?

■

IT IS MAY NOW, and we have been together fourteen months.
In the fall Andrew will go to New York and I will stay in Michigan. After I knew that this was going to be so, I spent a lot of time sitting in my apartment, looking out the window. I followed the double lines of the electrical wires slanting upward from the ground, running through any tree in their path. After rain every tree glowed brighter, a fierceness of sight making sound so that the trees seemed to clamor, their heads in shock, every splinter of bark steepened. One day I took out the scroll calendar I'd never bothered to hang up. It was from the Saigon Market in Grand Rapids, where my father gets the calendars for free. I held it in my hands for a moment, trying to picture the landscape the calendar would feature. Slate sky, surely, holding between rain and nightfall, mountains and ocean and an ox or two standing stalwart next to a rice paddy. I went to my desk and took out a spool of leftover holiday ribbon. I tied a red bow around the scroll and took it to Andrew's apartment.

People were always asking me if I'd ever been back to Vietnam, but Andrew was the one who repeatedly urged me to go. He couldn't understand why none of us—my father, my grandmother, and I—had ever gone back to visit. I couldn't explain it to him. I said, "My dad's afraid of flying." But it was more about my grandmother's plants, the sixty-four she kept in the house and the gardens in the backyard. It was about the two nameless cockatiels my father kept in bamboo cages in the living room. After I left for college he decided he had no need for so much furniture in the living room because he never sat there. He gave the birds the center of the room, beneath the skylight and ceiling fan. They faced each other, level-eyed, on tall glass tables.

When my father and grandmother and I arrived in Grand Rapids in 1975, we had a sponsor, Mr. Vanderbeek, who set us up in a run-down house and gave my father a job in one of his feather factories. My father would come home dusty with feathers, sometimes bringing a pillow from the defect pile. He'd bring Pringles for me, dried squid for my grandmother, and, occasionally, cognac for himself. In the summer my grandmother and I would walk to the farmers' market. She handled the produce with an economical certainty, bargaining silently, with nods. When she gave me a whole pear to myself, I'd save it, carrying it around the house like a doll.

My father is in computer software now. He works out of the house, the one we moved into when I was ten. His desk is spare, rarely used, lined with geode paperweights. The house is too big for us, and my father never remarried. His girlfriends were always already married, usually to his friends. He never brought them home, but they called. When my grandmother answered, she'd tell them in a rude voice not to bother us. When I answered, the women usually spoke in English: "Is your daddy home?" Voices that bore the weight of lipstick. In warm weather my father was almost never around. He loved parties at other people's houses. My grandmother would harass him about his girlfriends, his drinking, his gambling parties, but my father always walked away with both hands in gesticulation, as if shooing insects. He'd say "Aghh." He'd say *"Khong co di." It's nothing.*

"It's not what I expected," he said once. Every couple of years he would tell me that I should have had brothers and sisters. I always told him I liked being an only child.

"You didn't even consider joining the Vietnamese Students Association," he said. Some of his friends' kids ran the association, had reported me missing from the meetings. "You think you are not like anybody," he said. "That's the problem."

I don't think he failed to remarry because of any grief over my mother. I think it was laziness. He didn't want to explain anything: where he'd been all day, when he was going to change the lightbulb in the bathroom, what he was going to do the next day. The only thing he explained was the night we left Vietnam. The story is his. In it I am a baby in my grandmother's arms, both of us riding on the back of the motorcycle my father was driving in spite of the twenty-four-hour curfew in Saigon. I never touch the ground, never pick the way through barbed wire to reach the last U.S. naval ships leaving the country.

My father says that the thing he did right was wait for other people to get distracted. On the crowded ship, he played poker for milk. When we finally reached the U.S., we had to wait for several months in a refugee camp before our turn for resettlement. Then we were given two choices: San Jose, California, or Grand Rapids, Michigan. My father said California. My grandmother said Michigan. She got her way, my dad said, because she'd heard California was filled with crazy people and volcanoes. She said she needed something quiet.

I grew up believing that rain mattered, made larger implications. When it rained, my grandmother opened the sliding glass doors in the dining room and stuck her head out.

There's a scene in *Metropolis* in which clouds swim dizzyingly overhead. In my mind it has become connected with Andrew, the way images lock onto a person, so it seems I cannot ever think of fast clouds without also thinking of him. I can see him sitting in that classroom, the new March sunlight pushing against the window blinds, reaching toward his body. He looked back at me and just like that, *like that,* his face. A more imagined sky, a mirage of blue in his jacket. Clouds racing and tumbling overhead.

Andrew had given me his textbooks from the History of the Vietnam War class he'd taken freshman year, saying, "I can't believe you don't know your own history." He'd say things like "You have to go into your past to know the present."

I thought ahead to May, graduation, to the way the spring would lose itself to summer. I didn't want to see him getting into his car and driving home. So when Andrew untied the ribbon and unrolled the calendar and regarded the landscape of mountains and oxen, I pointed at May 10. I wanted to say something dramatic, like "This is the day you can come with me to see what it's really like," but I ended up saying, "Want to come with me?"

■

IT IS NOT scandalous to be unmarried, in a hotel with a white man. It is not scandalous to walk hand in hand downtown, beneath banners advertising the new production of *Miss Saigon* in Saigon.

On Nguyen Hue Boulevard geckos roam the surface of the ornate yellow and white Hôtel de Ville, which is now the Ho Chi Minh City People's Committee Building. Andrew and I take pictures of each other posing with the statue of Ho Chi Minh. We eat French ice cream. At the Ben Thanh Market, I bargain; Andrew refuses, saying, "It's little enough money as it is." We walk through the big warehouses, among sheets of hanging silk, yards of jacquards and damasks doing nothing but showing off—beauty raw and protean.

Only tourists shop in the one o'clock afternoon heat. I carry a swatch of my grandmother's white silk, to find a match for her *ao dai*s. In the fabric stalls women are finishing their long lunches; younger girls sleep on great stacks of fabric, gabardines and heavy polyesters, flannels and tweeds. Plastic fans whir uselessly. Women call out, "Special price, just for you." When I find what seems the right match to the silk, two ladies unroll the bolt between them. The fabric, taut and suspended, is a dizzying shine. One of the ladies brandishes shears. Andrew stands to the side, silent and polite, smiling as if on cue when anyone glances his way.

One of the ladies, rolling the silk into a soft little package, asks, "Are you married?"

I have the urge to say yes. In this country of no wedding bands, the ladies could never tell the difference. Andrew couldn't either. I glance at him; he is lovely in his inability to comprehend the words.

■

I DON'T SEEM to be attracted to Asian guys is how I explained it once to an Asian guy who afterward stopped sitting next to me in astronomy lectures. He said, "It's girls like you who promote stereotypes of Asian women."

It's true that I have long hair. Andrew likes my long hair. In the shower, he sometimes washes it slowly. He once said that my aversion to Asian men was a form of self-hatred. I didn't bother explaining how I disliked seeing Asian women holding hands with white men; it was like that feeling I got when Andrew and I played around in bed and he sang *I've got yellow fever, she's got white-boy fever, we're in love* into my neck.

There was a warm evening in which all the electricity for several blocks went out for hours and he said, "Let's make use of it." That darkness had seemed more factual in its apparent irreversibility. He had pulled my hair away from my face and kissed my earlobes, saying, *mine*.

■

I AM STUDYING a map of the city, trying to measure the distance from the hotel to my grandmother's house, but I can't figure out where my grandmother's house is. Andrew is reading the same pages in the *Lonely Planet*. His mother gave us three guidebooks. She bought us sacks of insect repellent, eye drops, first-aid kits, vitamins, Pepto-Bismol. She bought in bulk, at Sam's Club. His father thought up itineraries. *We're playing it by ear, Ray,* Andrew had said. He called his parents Ray and Babsie. *By ear?* His mother had said. *How can you go to the other side of the world and play it by ear?*

On the morning we are supposed to visit my grandmother, Andrew takes a bite of the French bread I'm buttering and says, "Maybe you should go see her alone."

Before I can say anything, he says, "Don't get upset. I do want to go with you. I just think this is something important for you, and I don't want to get in the way." He nudges the coffee cup in a slow spin on the saucer.

I am distracted by his face. I have this urge to graze the surface of his wet hair with my whole hand but I just sit there, thinking of the right thing to say. He says, "If you want me to come with you, I will."

I picture Andrew tripping over the family altar, upsetting the Buddha, Andrew sitting with his knees bowing in. Now I picture him sitting on a stool at the Q Bar, where all the hip expats are said to hang out; I picture the violet lights around the bar catching in his curls.

What I say is "You haven't touched me all morning." It is not that I want it.

He runs the back of his wrist down my arm. "There."

I go to my grandmother's house without him. I have the address on a slip of paper and hand it to the taxi driver, who promptly asks how old I am and if I'm married. He keeps glancing at me in the rearview mirror. The seven-mile drive takes almost half an hour. On a crowded bridge over the Saigon River, we stay still in traffic for ten minutes. Men on bicycles thread their way among the cars. Deserted buildings flank the banks of the river, keeping time with cobwebs of rubbish and remnants of metal. The car's air-conditioning is too strong. The taxi driver pushes a cassette into the tape player and starts humming along to the impossibly high voice of a woman singing Mariah Carey, Vietnamese style. The taxi driver asks me where I'm from.

"United States."

"New York?"

I decide to agree. "New York."

The car stops perpendicular to several narrow lanes of row houses, low-roofed and dusty. The driver asks me if I know which house it is. I don't. Several people are watching us from the low stoops. A few feet away, a vendor offers small fat ducks roasting on little spits within a grease-fogged case. The driver rolls down the window to ask her help when two bright-clothed women step from a lane and peer at us. One of them starts waving.

"You want me to wait?" the driver asks in English. He points to the meter and makes a show of turning it off. "Half hour?"

"Half hour," I say. I get out of the car, awkward with my camera and my shoulder bag. When I reach the two women, they clasp my hands and squeeze my arms. Both wear delicate bangles of hammered gold. The one who says she is my mother's sister has plump elbows, big dimples, and permed hair. The other woman turns out to be her neighbor. They guide me, one on either side, to the row house. The living room is open to the air, and just across the threshold a little girl—my aunt's daughter, my cousin—sits on the linoleum next to a hefty sack of rice. One little arm slowly pulls out of the sack as she stares up at me. She can't be more than three years old. She pushes several grains of rice into her mouth. Her mother pushes her away from the sack, rolling down the top flap. "*Thoi. Di, di.*" Enough. No more.

She picks up the little girl, who also wears thin gold bangles, and I follow them through a windowless room, a dingy, shined concrete space that I realize must be the kitchen, to the room at the end of the house, which is also open to the air. A carved altar takes up one wall; it holds candlesticks, incense, and the requisite bronze Buddha. Facing it is a heavy oak coffee table and brown plaid sofa. On one end of the sofa my grandmother is sitting, her hands in her lap, her thick glasses held in place around her head with a wide elastic strap, her white hair cropped short as a schoolboy's.

"*Ngoai,*" my aunt says. *Maternal grandmother.* With a big smile she nudges me toward the sofa. If my father were here, he'd have the video recorder out, taping the whole thing.

My grandmother turns to me as I sit down. She says my name as though I have only returned from a trip to the market. She pats my knee. It is a possessive gesture, an unsureness mixed with tangible proof. She says, "*Em ve con ai?*" She is asking me whom I came here with; the verb, *ve,* implies both an arrival and a return. I tell her I am here with a friend, who is at the hotel ("District One," the ladies murmur), and I tell her that I cannot stay long today but will visit again in a few days. I know when I say it that I am lying.

She points in the direction of the altar and tells me that when my grandfather died in 1980, he had been very ill for a long time. She says something to me that means either *I miss you* or *I long for you.* Her eyes never stop moving; they are trying to halt an image, to cease the blurriness, the distance and bend of glass. When she smiles suddenly, I see a dark red upon her lips, a dark red stain on her teeth. For a moment I see it in terror, her blood, until her mouth moves and I realize she has been chewing betel nut, that the black-red color has seeped into every part of her mouth.

My aunt brings me a glass of 7-Up. My grandmother still has her hand on my knee. We make small talk about the little girl, Bien, about how hot and bright it is today, every day. After we take pictures of each other, and I set up the self-timer to get a shot of all of us huddled around my grandmother, I start thinking about all the one-hundred-dollar bills in my bag, the money I must give her with the right words. *Ngoai, em cho ngoai . . .*

I'm wondering how to take the money out of the bag, and what they will do with the money, and if I should give some to my aunt or all of it to my grandmother. I think about the taxi driver waiting and about the dirt lanes matted down with rain, layers of mud, and wear and I think of the way my aunt looked when she emerged suddenly from the row of houses, her fuchsia dress too vivid against the brown walls.

There is a picture of my mother on the family altar. I don't move closer to see it: a young woman standing in the lane just outside her house. Her bouffant hair matches her puffy skirt. Her arms are folded, each hand cupping the opposite elbow. She is not smiling, as though she's been caught daydreaming something not necessarily pleasant.

I reach inside my bag as if to put away the camera and quickly pull out the envelope of money. I take my grandmother's hand, the one that is on my knee, and fold her fingers around the envelope. I forget the words I am supposed to say when giving a gift. "*Ngoai, em cho*" is all I manage to remember. *Grandmother, I give you . . .*

"*Cam on, em,*" she says. It is the rule of hospitality. She neither looks at the envelope nor moves it. So I leave it in her hand and touch her thin shoulder, papery beneath the rayon shift she's wearing. I want to be back in the dirt lane, feeling the dust around my ankles as I walk to the road. I'll find the taxi driver lingering over coffee and conversation in a makeshift café. I'll have my sunglasses on, the car will be hot inside, and I will cross the same bridge over the Saigon River, going out of District Six, heading back downtown.

Later in the hotel room, Andrew says, "I should've gone with you, right?"

"Yes," I say, but when he lies down next to me his body is like a shutter framing a window. Slatted, prepared, but still.

■

"NO ONE could imagine this kind of heat," Andrew says. We are standing on the corner outside the Hotel Continental, and he is pushing a damp layer of hair away from the side of my face. It is slow, his hands resting on my shoulder. I know he means to kiss me, here in front of doormen and tourists and people looking out of their stores. I remember kissing him while waiting for lights to change, kissing over dinner tables, in the stacks of the library, in grocery store checkout lanes. I wanted the world to see; I didn't care if the world did see. I had flaunted. I was careless.

He says, "Why did you bring me to this country if you're going to be like this?" The way he's holding my shoulders makes me think of the word *throttle*. He says, "Look, I'm here, you can kiss me."

We go gift shopping at small boutiques. We buy lacquer jewelry boxes and canisters carved out of cinnamon bark. In a silk shop Andrew buys pajamas for his parents. He unfolds the dark red ten-thousand dong notes and the green fifty-thousand notes, handling them like play money. All of the bills bear Ho Chi Minh's face. His fatherly portrait on one side, a rice harvest scene on the other.

Outside Andrew takes my hand, holds it a moment, then lets go. He says, "What's wrong with you?"

Across the street, the giant marquee of the Rex Hotel is lit up, spitefully, in the heat. I can't think of anything to say.

He says, "Let your hair down." He tries to undo my knot of hair, but I dodge his hands.

"My hair is off-limits."

He swings the bag of pajamas in an arc around his body. It

bumps my hip once, twice. "I used to think when you were silent you had a reason. Now I think you're just full of refusals. You won't do anything. You make things seem useless."

"I don't know what it is you want me to do."

"This is what I mean. You never used to say things like that." Now he turns as if to walk away, as if to just disappear. I project his imagined body crossing the street and vanishing by degrees; I imagine an entire day without him, shopping and eating alone, finally meeting him again, silently, at the hotel late in the evening. It could happen. We could walk in opposite directions. But he needs my language, however much I have of it. He needs the physical accompanist. I used to wake up in the night and feel immense relief at the presence of his body. His thin, agile body. I can see the shapes of his shoulder blades beneath his T-shirt.

I say, "You're wrong. You just have to let me figure things out, let me figure out this whole country—"

"The country is an excuse," he says. "Why did you bring me here?"

And I don't know; I can't remember. It had something to do with his face, his waking face, the one I am sometimes afraid of. It had something to do with that which could be kept.

If we walked in opposite directions, who would leave first? Who would be the lover, the one left?

■

WHEN WE emerge from visiting the dim and silent Giac Lam Pagoda, white sunlight on the stone steps makes us dizzy. Clusters of children approach all the tourists, holding their hands held out in a cup, their eyes large, intent. They chant in English, "Please, please, please."

They can sense our hesitation. They crowd around us, throwing out phrases in English. "American tourist," one little boy says. "You are rich," says another. "Please." They say everything in the same rising voice, following us as we walk down the steps and into the square.

Andrew says, "I think we should give them something."

I look at the taxis lined up on the street outside the pagoda.

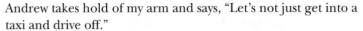

Andrew takes hold of my arm and says, "Let's not just get into a taxi and drive off."

"You think it's helping, but it's not really."

"It *is* something." His hand feels rough. "Where's your sense of compassion?"

"Compassion? I have compassion. I have lots of it."

Andrew says, "You're not making sense." When the children see him reaching for his money belt they fall silent; they push each other away to get closer to him. He manages to extract a few bills and in a moment the crowd of children is doubled, hands waving. I walk away. The children don't follow me. I watch Andrew pass out five-thousand dong notes, which are worth about forty cents. He is smiling and the children smile back at him. His hair seems so blond, his face ablush with freckles.

Of course, when he tries to walk away the children follow. I say, "Should we get into a taxi and drive away now?"

Andrew says, "Let's take one of those." He points to a row of pedicabs, the drivers idling on the bicycle seats. As soon as he points, a man appears at our side. Like all the pedicab drivers, this man is gaunt. He wears a ratty CK baseball cap and keeps a toothpick in his mouth. In Vietnamese, he shoos the children away. In English, he says, "You want to go? Cyclo?" It sounds like he's saying "sick, low."

"Yes," Andrew says.

"It's too far," I say. "They don't even let pedicabs go downtown."

"Then we'll go as far as we can."

"Andrew—"

"Can you do this? Can you do this for me?"

I ask the driver, "How much?"

Andrew gives me an annoyed look.

"I *have* to ask," I say. I ask how far he can take us toward downtown.

"*Hai nguoi,* thirty thousand dong," he offers. For two, thirty thousand dong, $2.50 U.S.

So Andrew and I end up wedged together in the hot pedicab, our legs splayed out. The driver flips down the canvas top, a futile attempt to shade us, and pedals into the street. Andrew takes out his camera. "This is an amazing angle," he says. He takes pictures of street life. We move slowly. The sound of the pedaling is like a sigh, each wheel's revolution pushing out a breath.

Andrew says, "Sometimes I don't understand you. This is your country, your people. Don't you care about helping them?"

"I care! It's not about that."

"What is it, then? We have so much. They don't. It's that simple."

"It's embarrassing."

"You're not helping anyone by just ignoring their begging, or ignoring the fact that these pedicab drivers need business."

I would like to say something searing, something invoking the word *colonialism*. But I don't want to talk to him. He's right and he's wrong, and I can't have both. I want to tell him that who he is exonerates him from a thousand considerations in this country. I don't know how to explain the idea of shame. That which begins early, in the mimicking of sounds, in the squinched-up faces laughing in the playground. Obligation, shame, the body, the self. The words are too strong to be spoken between us.

What I end up saying is "You don't understand."

He says, "I know your history better than you do. But if you think I don't get it, why don't you try to make me *understand*?" He tries to turn away from me, but he can't. Our bodies touch damply. He puts his sunglasses on, refuses to look at me.

It is raining when I wake up from a nap. I extricate myself from his sleeping embrace. I look out the window. Down the avenue, the café owners are hurrying tables into houses. The rain is turning into a storm. Andrew doesn't stir. I pull my bright blue raincoat out of the suitcase.

Outside the raindrops come down straight, steadily. I walk past the shoe stores. I find myself in front of the plush pink-stone Amara Hotel which sports a banner advertising MALAYSIAN FEAST ALL THIS WEEK! So I go inside. In the empty restaurant, I order hot cocoa. It tastes like Swiss Miss and costs $1.75 U.S.; the price comforts me. The only other customer is an Australian businessman who is eating a full dinner; I cannot tell if it is the Malaysian feast. One of the waitresses attends to him closely, asking several times if everything is all right. The man says, "Ah, yes!"

It is still storming when I leave. Everyone is wearing ponchos, wide flaps of plastic draping over their bicycles. People stand just inside their houses, leaning. I walk past stores devoted entirely to men's dress shirts, blenders, or bicycle wheels.

All along the streets—all over the city—elegant twists of trees arch over sidewalks and streets, bearing masses of orange-fire petals, spilling color like maddened goblets. The brightness disintegrates into the ground, curling up in the heat. The trees stand as if in wildfire, spreading red glow to each other, spreading indelible stain.

When I return to the hotel room and close the door, Andrew rolls over in bed and looks at me.

"Come here," he says.

I remove my raincoat and touch my wet hair.

In bed he kisses my forehead first.

■

ON THE overnight train from Saigon to the coastal resort town of Nha Trang we share a couchette with a tired-looking woman dressed all in denim. She smiles politely, hoists herself up on a top bunk, and sleeps there for the rest of the journey. There's no air-conditioning, no screens on the windows. Before the train leaves, a brakeman stops by to hand around cans of Coca-Cola and loaves of plastic-wrapped pound cake. "Hey, is this first class?" Andrew asks. I tell him there is no such thing.

All night the insects keep me awake. I nibble on cake and watch Andrew sleep. Just outside the door is a large open window and it is there I decide to stand for most of the night, waiting for dawn. The train cuts through grassy fields and through bloated expanses of paddies. Precarious shacks stilt just above the water, fires burning silently within. The train brushes past heavy foliage, small cement-building villages, and wide ponds choked with lotus blossoms. Occasionally the train stops in the middle of a field for an hour. Cloud-haze obscures the stars.

Finally I notice light in the shape of the mountain range that follows the coastline of the country. The dawn emerges slowly, revealing women working in the rice paddies. Already they are wearing the cone-shaped hats; some of them glance at the train. Their hands never stop moving. There are no men in these fields. The men are somewhere near the fires in the shanties or somewhere with the water buffalo, maybe. Or maybe they're still in bed, dreaming the last dreams for the night.

I can hardly believe such words are true: *paddies, water buffalo, rice.*

Now Andrew is beside me, touching my shoulders, massaging them, making both my body and his hands feel old.

"We're almost there," he says gently, as though breaking bad news.

The train passes open cargo loads filled with great slabs of marble standing in a field.

"If you wanted to watch the dawn, you should have woken me up." His hands travel down my back, find a hold on my waist. "You should have woken me up."

■

ARE YOU glad I'm here with you?

Yes.

I don't want to go back to school.

I don't want to be without you.

■

SIX IN THE morning and gray when we reach the Hai Yen Hotel. Our room overlooks a strip of beach—palm trees, coconut trees, colorful umbrellas. I stretch out on the bed while Andrew goes onto the balcony. I can hear him singing something to himself.

"I'm taking a shower," he announces, coming back into the room. He goes into the bathroom and leaves the door open. There's a mural covering one wall of the room, a huge tropical beach scene more idyllic than the one outdoors.

I listen to the water running, picturing him in it. Andrew standing a little slumped, exposing the back of his neck. Water making rivulets everywhere.

When he emerges, towel wrapped, I ask, "What song were you singing?"

"What are you talking about?"

"You were singing a song on the balcony."

"I don't remember." He opens the suitcase and plucks out a T-shirt.

From the bed I can't see anything but gray sky outside. I say, "I just want to know what song you were singing out there."

"You're just feeling strange because you haven't gotten any sleep," he says. He perches on the bed and pats my foot. "Take a nap for a while, then take a shower."

When I close my eyes, I can feel him glancing in the mirror, hear him putting on his shoes. When he kisses me, he catches strands of my hair, pulling his fingers down to the ends.

At a café on the beach we sit beneath an enormous red-and-blue striped umbrella and order shrimp. Andrew talks about how he can't tell if time seems slower or faster here. He says, "The cities overload transformers because they can't afford to buy bigger ones. That's why there are so many electricity outs during the day. They do it on purpose, taking turns with different districts." He has learned this from reading all the English newspapers.

"The making-do with what you have," he says. "The ingenuity is amazing. Why are you so quiet?" He shakes his head at me, part contemplation, part disgust.

The waiter arrives with enormous tiger shrimp steamed in their shells, a plate of sautéed green beans, a pot of rice, and dishes of lime-pepper sauce.

Andrew keeps shaking his head until I clear my throat and say, "Sorry, I'm still waking up."

We begin gingerly cracking open the shells.

"Is there something wrong? Do you have a problem? Why do I always have to be responsible for keeping up the conversation?"

I say, "This could be like a honeymoon, this place."

"Yeah? Do you think there's a notary public in the hotel?"

"A notary public doesn't—"

"I know, I know."

He reaches for the green beans.

He says, "This must be what is called the prosaic life."

I can't answer.

He says, "I think we're spending too much time together."

I look away. Not far off an older couple is sitting side by side in woven beach chairs. Both wear sun visors. They hold hands in the small space between them. The image is too present to mention.

"I don't want to argue with you, Andrew."

It is the perfect moment for him to reach across the table and take my hand, the way people do when they want to make up.

"Let's just be happy together," he says.

Later I watch him swim. His skin seems golden. Iridescent. Like the pearly inside curve of a seashell. His body glides quickly. He seems irreducible. Uncontainable. I stand in the shade of a mango tree and watch him. All around me there are bougainvillea and hibiscus, paper flowers and bamboo.

■

HE WAKES me up, rubbing my left shoulder, the one with the vaccination scar. I have been talking in my sleep again, probably saying something inappropriate, something like *it's all fucked off*. He believes these are nightmares. I keep my eyes closed, pretend not to feel his hands nudging my body as if pushing me forward, up out of something. I listen to him tell me to go back to sleep, that things are okay, and finally, *shhh*. He shushes me until he falls back asleep.

■

ONE NIGHT I dream of the river. *Sông* is the word for *river*, though the ô is more oblong, hard, the intonation as close to sweet as the language can muster. *Câu* is the word for bridge, a harder sound. Meaning also *to wish, to pray*. I dream of tributaries in backyards, a moss of rubble and rubbish on the banks. The river appears bridged, the water expanding into separate deltas on either side, one cutting through the middle of the new downtown of high-rise hotels and upscale bistros, the other flooding out into the rice plains. I dream a drawbridge, the two halves pulling upward into a sharp angle.

How do we ever know we are loved?

I dreamed he married a woman with red hair, and that this woman walked into my living room, her bridal veil trailing behind her. I never dreamed he didn't love me. I never imagined he didn't love me. I dreamed he left me.

Greed shouldn't surprise anyone. Greed for flowers, for tubs of orchids. Some preferred roses; they preferred their men that way. But a real greed, a real impatience, may show itself in orchids. The tenuous, seeming fragility hiding a mercilessness. The extravagance of passion in the thousands of varieties. Ruthless, the orchids. Ruthless, the greed. Who will guarantee that the grief of love will last?

■

IN NHA TRANG we walk along the dirty sidewalks, along the waterside. When we look up, we see the big Marriott sticking out. In the morning and afternoon we go on long boat rides to visit some of the limestone caves jutting up from the water. There are thousands of them, a terrain of uninhabitable islands. The caves have been turned into tourist attractions, with ticket-selling booths built onto ledges of stone. The sign says FOREIGNERS: 30,000 DONG; VIET: 5,000 DONG.

At the Dau Go cave there is a poem carved in stone: "This poem cannot describe the wonderful cave. It is only a flower in a beautiful brocade." As we are leaving, I realize that the woman selling the tickets also lives in the little hut. She has a pet hawk that cannot fly. She caresses it, kneeling down to feed it from her hands. As the boat retreats from the cave, I see the woman standing on the steps leading up to the entrance. The hawk is at her side. I wonder how many times she has read that poem. I wonder what she does at night when she knows no one will come again for hours, when she knows she has nowhere else she can go.

I know that Andrew is watching her, too, but neither of us says anything. It makes me remember a day last summer when we were eating lunch at a diner and had gotten into some argument; he'd said, "You're being really crabby." He was anchoring the tip with his water glass and he said, "You'd better stop because I don't need to deal with it." I was still eating French fries. I said, "Oh, fuck you." He leaned in close and said, "Don't make a scene, please." He got up and walked away, toward the bathroom. I sat there for fifteen minutes until I realized he'd left by the back exit. Outside I saw him across the street at the Comerica building, standing next to the ATM.

He walked ahead of me. His car didn't have power locks. Sometimes he opened the door for me, sometimes he didn't. Once I accused him of using this way to show his passive-aggressive nature toward me. He said, "I just forget, okay?"

Sometimes when we drove I wished we could stay there forever, the two of us trapped in such space, in transition, never having to leave or face each other. We were unreachable in the car, our bodies in stasis. I hadn't before felt the wonder and security in sitting still. Let's be together like this, I wanted to say. The minute before one of us emerged from an airplane, the other in perpetual satisfying wait, in imminence.

I could love most things in this way. The trees tending toward the leafless, holding themselves up. I knew what he would say if I said this: you have to stop taking the world so personally. They're trees. Stop personifying. I had this urge to say, I don't want to love you any longer than necessary.

He might not be there in the hotel room, waiting for me to return from visiting my grandmother. He might be standing next to me, witnessing something awful or beautiful, but he might not tell me, as I might not tell him. Might never know what to say. He might not show up on time, or take my hand across the table. I would be left standing outside the car, watching him settle into a moment without me, waiting for him to lean over and unlock the door.

■

THE LAST wedding I went to was in Wyoming, Michigan. Red and gold Christmas garlands festooned the gutters of the bride's box house. Neighbors watched from their front porches. The groom's male relatives stood around in black suits, sweltering, bearing the weight of platters wrapped in red cellophane. In slow procession they followed each other into the house, forming a circle around the couple in the living room. A monk stood before the tall altar to Buddha. The bride's pale face seemed stiller than ceremony. Stalks of gladiolus dimmed her. Her *ao dai* was red silk woven through with gold, his a bright damask blue. Both wore headbands of heavy gold cloth.

At the wedding reception at the Imperial Seafood Restaurant my father danced with a friend's wife. They were both drunk, laughing through a long rumba sequence. Her violet dress blended into her dyed hair. I was sure she could not resemble my mother, but I saw how easy it was to see an idea of them. Had they begun that way, a courtship in dancing, turning hand to shoulder, facing, triumphant?

Last year when Andrew's parents returned from a two-week tour of China, they gave me delicate cloisonné chopsticks. I could not eat with them. Andrew said I should use them to hold my hair up in a knot. I said no. He seemed only to understand his own fascination. There was a slumbering shame, I wanted to say so many times, but he always fell asleep before I could begin. I tried to tell him that the morning light—our bodies rumbling in and out of dreams, bridging into morning—and the act of language created a breach, one against the other, against all the generalizations—*I love you, you are everything, you, us*—we made and staked upon each other, wishing to go on.

■

TELL ME again why you brought me here.

It doesn't feel like I did.

What does it feel like?

I like the flame trees. I like that we'll be gone before they fade.

■

HUNDREDS of years ago Vietnam was a matriarchal society. Women were creation figures (the important ones); they deposed rulers and took charge of harvest methods. I do not really know my grandmother, but I think she is like an opposite of rain; she is bright dust on the other side of the river—harbinger, past and future presence, my mother's mother. She is a visit, a return. Hundreds of years ago, were the seasons of rain and heat truly any different from now?

The day Andrew and I get back to Saigon it is raining hard, the rain blurring all objects. Andrew pulls the hood of my raincoat over my head and guides me out of the hotel against my protests. He waves for a taxi. As soon as we are inside and the door is shut he turns to me, slicks my hair back with his two wide hands, and kisses me on the mouth. When I draw away, he does it again, keeps his hands in my wet hair. The driver says nothing, but I can't help meeting his eyes in the rearview mirror when I pull away again. Andrew says, "Let's just drive. Drive in the rain. Drive anywhere, all over the town. Like Madame Bovary and her lover."

And this is what we do. We drive in the rain. We ignore the driver's eyes, the cigarette smoke, the techno music in the tape player. We have never seen more strange sights pass us—men transporting impossibly long metal poles on precarious tin bicycles, abrupt statues sitting calmly in the middle of jammed intersections of cars, bicycles, and mopeds. This is how we spend our last evening. Forty U.S. dollars of driving. We hardly speak. We huddle against each other. He is more beautiful like this, his face shaded in rain shapes.

This is not a rain with which to make a song. This rain hurts. It is a rain equal to heat. Intense as heat. Begins and ends with heat. I do not understand anything—I am a tourist with a boyfriend, looking for nice French bistros. The rain makes me afraid of drowning. It makes me look for the other girl I am, the girl I could have been, my theoretical double, the one who stayed in Saigon and grew up here, and, on this day, regards the rain. Does she love the rain or is she its opposite? Is *she* happy? Who imagines the other's life better?

When the rain falls meekly and begins to cease at twilight, I know it is getting later and later for me to say the thing that will matter, that will let the kissing of hair, of hands, solve us.

Andrew is looking out the window, his whole body turned away from me.

"Andrew." He shakes his head.

I have been afraid of his body walking into the known world, entering bookstores and other people's houses, driving the expressways. I know the way the slope of his back looks, moving. I know the plane will bring us safely back to Boston, back to the ground. His parents will meet us at the gate. We will sleep separately, as we always do at his parents' house, and we will tell the stories of the gifts we have brought. Stories of lacquer and jade and silk that will sound quite romantic, quite—though the word may not be said—*exotic*. People will ask for months afterward what it was like in Vietnam. It will be as cold in New York as it is in Michigan, and I know when we speak of Vietnam, we will each speak mostly of the intense, unending heat, the kind that withers all things, even those in motion. Even rain.

Saher Alam

Boston University

AMREEKI

A̲t the back of the *munzil,* the
women sat in the dark under the ceiling fan and waited. The
electricity had gone out again. On a table in the center of their
circle there were four cups in which the tea leaves had settled to
the bottom, four saucers, and Samina's empty bottle of Campa-
Cola. When it seemed, midway through dinner, as if the lights
would not return for several hours, the women didn't complain.
Instead, Samina's aunt Razia lit a path of candles from the dining room through the hallway to the back of the house. When
they had finished their meal, the women came out onto the
verandah hoping the night air would offer some relief. They
worked by candlelight and moonlight but kept all the switches
flipped on in expectation.

Samina held the fan above her grandmother's head and
twirled her wrist as steadily as she could. Sometimes when the
bijli goes, Samina had heard, there is some concern about
thieves—especially in the older parts of the city where a darkened house can become particularly vulnerable to raids or inva-
sions. Ever since Samina's uncle had died five years ago, friends
of the family had been advising her grandmother to hire a

watchman or buy a generator. But her grandmother dismissed these precautions. A house full of women, she was known to have said, has nothing to lose.

Samina watched her mother rub jasmine oil into her cousin Irram's hands and feet. Irram, who was getting married in two days, was lying propped up on her elbows while Samina's mother was sitting on the edge of the cot, almost kneeling, with her *rupatta* tucked behind her ears. Next to them, putting the final touches on her daughter's wedding suit, was Samina's aunt. She had just finished explaining to Samina that the oil was massaged in to preserve the *mehendi* but also to keep the skin soft to the touch.

"It is back?" Samina's grandmother asked.

"No," Samina said, and spun the fan a little faster. Usually her grandmother stayed inside and slept through the blackouts, but tonight was so hot she had been moved outdoors. Sitting beside her, Samina, who was in charge of keeping the heat away from the old woman, felt like a giant.

"No good can come of this," her grandmother muttered. Though she was bent over, her scarf slipped back onto her shoulders, exposing her hair. It was gray and oiled and combed stiff. It barely moved under the breeze, and her scalp showed through its steely rows. On her forehead, the skin was soft and as poreless as paper. Except for her temper, there seemed to be no sign, Samina decided, that she suffered from or even felt the heat. "I don't understand, Razia," she continued. "Last month the bill was the highest ever. Why are we paying it?"

Nobody said anything.

"What purpose is it serving?"

Without looking up from her sewing, Samina's aunt said in a loud voice, "I'm trying to take care of it."

The little figure nodded. Her hearing had been failing for years, along with her eyesight. Now she couldn't see anything that wasn't held under her nose, and she couldn't hear anything that wasn't shouted. She seemed satisfied, though, and began counting her prayer beads again.

Samina wondered how long it had been since her grandmother had left the house. Every time the rest of them went into town, the curtains on the Ambassador's windows were drawn as soon as the car pulled out of the gate. This morning, Samina, her mother, and Irram had left early for the salon, a tiny air-conditioned room tucked in the back of an alley, and spent almost the entire day getting the bride-to-be's waxing and *mehendi* done. On the way in, from the car to the salon's front door, Irram had pulled her *rupatta* out to cover her hair. Half an hour later, however, she lounged in little more than a chemise while a different person attended to each of her limbs. Samina, who had gone in wearing jeans and a T-shirt and refusing to cover her head, had been surprised by how easily the layers were shed once the doors were closed. She was even more surprised by how, on the way out, she herself would have given anything for a scarf.

Samina stared at Irram's hair. Its shiny black length hung straight down the center of her back. When she twisted her neck or moved her head, it swung from side to side like a tail. Samina's own hair was not as silky or straight, but until this morning, it had been long enough so that she could pull it to one side of her head. At the salon Samina asked her mother to tell the attendant to cut her hair into layers so that the curls would fall into place. Every time her mother said "layers," the woman looked confused for a second, but then nodded as if she understood. "Yes, okay," she replied, "steps." Before the woman started cutting, Samina asked her mother to stand behind and watch. When Irram called for Samina's mother, however, she drifted off; and by the time she returned, Samina's shoulder-length hair was gone. In its place were short puffy curls and bangs barely long enough to cover the expression on Samina's face.

Afterward Samina found out that while her hair was being cut too short, her mother—the woman who had not allowed her daughter to wear nail polish unless she wore it only on her left hand—had let Irram talk her into getting a manicure. Back home her mother had agreed to the left hand only after Samina had promised her that she would not use it to eat or to serve food. But now in this country, her mother had gotten the nails of both her own hands done without even noticing that "layers" did not translate well into "steps."

From where she was sitting, Samina could see, even in the candlelight, the orange stain darken to a deep red in the places where her mother pushed the oil into Irram's skin. Just hours ago an attendant had squeezed the paste onto Irram's hands from a cone as if she were icing a cake. The woman worked fast to form the lacy, dark green gloves which extended from Irram's fingertips to the insides of her wrists. Then she put a similar pattern on Irram's feet from the soles all the way up to the ankles. As the stenciled *mehendi* dried, it left a bright red stain on the skin. When Samina asked why all the way up to the ankle, her mother explained that all of the bride's skin needed to be covered one way or another. The lady who owned the salon said that skin was something to be covered at all costs; then she laughed and added, winking at Samina's mother, until it was uncovered at all costs. After the older women left the room, the attendant pulled Samina aside and explained that one of the ways a bride was made to get accustomed to her new husband's touch was through the washing of her feet. And so, she said, even ankles need to be as pretty as possible. Samina nodded though it didn't seem to make much sense. Nothing in India did. She wondered why they didn't just let the bride and groom get to know each other the normal way.

Samina's hand ached. Everybody at the salon had said Irram looked like a doll. Samina supposed it was true. Irram had the kind of skin that could get away with anything—shell pink blushes, ruby red lipstick, shimmery green eye shadow. The ladies who were there also getting ready for the wedding kept remarking on how much the twenty-two-year-old Irram looked more like a younger version of Samina's mother than her own. But even now with the candlelight casting the same shadows on their faces, Samina didn't think the resemblance between them was particularly strong. Her mother had Warm Peaches and Cream skin, but Irram's was Cool Ivory. Samina knew this because before they had left for India, she and her mother had spent hours at the drugstore matching Irram's requests with Revlon's cosmetic line. Her mother never let her wear any makeup, so Samina didn't know what kind of skin she had. She just knew that it was the kind that didn't let her get away with much at all.

Samina switched the fan from her right hand to her left. She had also gotten some *mehendi* put on. It was not as elaborate as Irram's, though, because she hadn't let the attendant leave it on long enough. The simple pattern on her own hands was already fading to a color that barely showed up against the brown of her skin. As they were leaving the salon, her mother bought a packet of dry *mehendi* and suggested that they could start a new fashion in America. Samina, who'd been trying to keep herself from crying every time she looked in the mirror, didn't say anything. She didn't agree or disagree with her mother, hoping her silence would announce that the haircut was bad enough and that she didn't want that green, sour, swampy smell following her home. But it didn't work. The salon owner stepped in, said it was a great idea, and persuaded Samina's mother to buy two more packets.

Samina sighed. This was their third week in Lucknow. She and her mother had come for the wedding and would be leaving a few days after so that Samina could return in time to start the tenth grade. By then, Samina thought, Irram *Apa* will be on her honeymoon, and the *mehendi* will have worn off. Or maybe it will have been washed off. Either way, there were still two weeks left.

"What purpose?" Samina's grandmother suddenly asked, as if there hadn't been a reply to her question. "Everybody's sleep is disturbed," she continued. "That one over there is getting married soon. This poor thing is melting. Now she'll never come back to visit."

"I'm fine," Samina said. She spoke in Urdu only to her grandmother. With everybody else, she could get away with answering in English. When the little figure cocked her head, Samina repeated herself in a louder voice.

Her grandmother nodded. "We want to make sure that you come back in a few years for your own wedding. Isn't that so, Sultana?" She called out to her daughter, "When are you going to get this one married?"

"Ask her, *Ammi*," Samina's mother answered, almost shouting.

"I'm not getting married," Samina said.

"What?" her grandmother asked.

"I'm not getting married here," she said in a raised voice.

"Why not?" the old woman asked with a chuckle.

"Because it seems that's all you do in this country—get married."

Everybody laughed—especially her grandmother, who also started coughing. "Now I understand," she said in a thin voice. "I know what you're doing. I understand everything now. *Amreeki* comes here—comes here to take the electricity back in buckets so that she doesn't have to return."

Now Samina laughed. "What would I do with it? We have enough."

"And why do you think that is?" her grandmother asked. "Because we don't. You make sure we stay in the dark." As if she suddenly remembered what she had been praying for, the old woman then reached for her beads and resumed counting.

The moonlight fell on the columns of the verandah and seemed to polish the stone into silver. Samina stared past the pillars, across the wide steps that led down to a cobblestone portico, beyond the long green lawn and its darker green shadows, at the wall that bordered the backyard. On the other side there was an intersection; and across the street, behind a row of small shops, was the neighborhood *masjid*. Its tower rose above the alley below. Five times a day the sound of a person tapping on a microphone signaled to the believers within hearing distance that the *azaan* was about to be sung. Wherever they were in the house, whatever they were doing, Samina's aunt and mother would stop to pull their *rupatta*s over their heads. When the call to prayer finished, the two would perform their ablutions and retreat to the back room to do their *namaaz*. Samina's grandmother spent the days sitting on a divan with her beads. She could no longer hear the muezzin's call, yet she somehow always knew when to do her recitation. Everybody in the house supposed that over time the old woman's body had just gotten used to taking her through the motions. But after observing her for a few days, Samina began to suspect that her grandmother used the pattern of the sun moving across the carpet to tell the prayer hour.

Samina watched a light hobble along the top of the back wall toward the intersection. Probably the *paan-wallah,* she thought, remembering that the vendor kept a kerosene lamp swinging from his cart. Her other cousin, Faizan, Irram's younger brother, had taken her to the stand a couple of times. Faizan had explained that there were better places to get *paan,* but he usually bought a few here once a week to oblige his longtime neighbor. The light turned the corner and slowly made its way to the left side of the house. It stopped just outside the entrance. Samina stared past the gate. She thought she heard music coming from across the street.

"*Maami,*" Samina asked her aunt, "why does the other side of the road have light?"

"Generator," Razia said with a shrug. "It's a temple, but they use it as a hall for weddings." She looked up in the direction of the music and reconsidered. "Maybe," she said, putting the portion of the *gharara* she was sewing aside, "something is wrong with the line to the house." She stood up and walked over to the edge of the verandah. "Or maybe just the connection to this side of the street. When Faizan gets home, he should check with them."

"I hope the hall we rented has a generator," Irram said, and sat up, looking concerned.

"Of course it does," Samina's aunt reassured her. "It has to. It's much bigger than this one." She stared at the sound of the festivities a little longer, then turned around. "Where is Faizan?" she asked, picking up her sewing.

"He went out," Irram said.

"Where?" Razia asked. Faizan was the only male left in the family. Samina's mother had told her that sometimes Razia *Maami* forgot that he was still a child and sometimes she forgot that he wasn't.

"I don't know—somewhere," Irram said, pulling one of her palms close to her face to examine it. "With Roshan, I think," she added quietly.

Samina's aunt grimaced. "Somewhere," she said, and settled down in her chair. "Somewhere," she repeated, frowning. "This close to the wedding—it doesn't look good. He should be here. He has to take care of these things. I can't—"

"He'll do it tomorrow," said Irram.

"It's the age, *Bhabi*," Samina's mother added. "At seventeen, eighteen—they're impatient. Besides, it's difficult to be the man of the house when you're not the head of the household."

"I do it," Razia said, glancing in the grandmother's direction. She picked up a spool and began to rethread the needle. "I don't understand why he has to be somewhere else at this hour." She pulled the thread through and bit off the other end. "Especially with—" She frowned again.

Irram's mouth tightened. "There's nothing wrong with him, *Ammi*." She leaned back onto her elbows.

"Nothing right either," Razia said, taking up the fabric in her lap.

First the lights came on, and then the ceiling fan shuddered awake. The current seemed to course through the inhabitants as well as the house. Hair flew in all directions and scarves fluttered.

Samina set her fan aside. "There it is," she said.

Her grandmother gathered her beads and called for her maid. "Where is Zeinab?" she asked. "Wake her up. Send her in. I want to go to my room."

A few minutes later the screen door opened, and Zeinab came in pushing a wheelchair and looking sleepy. She helped Samina's grandmother into the seat. Just as Zeinab was about to wheel the old woman across the threshold into the long yellow hallway that bisected the house, Samina motioned for her to stop. Annoyed, her grandmother snapped at the maid, "What are you doing?"

"See," Samina said, leaning in close to her ear, "I didn't take it."

Her grandmother smiled. Her teeth were stained red-brown from *paan*. "We'll see," she said. "We'll see. Who knows what you'll do tomorrow."

As soon as Samina's grandmother was inside, her aunt reached into the sewing bag. She took out a cigarette and lifted a candle to light its tip. She inhaled deeply, then blew a cloud and tossed the pack to Samina's mother. "If you want one," she said. Samina watched her mother dry her fingers on a towel before taking a cigarette. In India her mother seemed to have become a woman who couldn't say no—not to the people who put a little tobacco in her *paan* to give it a kick, nor to the salon lady who complimented her nails only after they had been manicured, nor to the vendors who charged her too much. Last week when they were walking out of a fabric boutique, Samina's aunt had asked her mother in exasperation if she'd forgotten how to live here.

Irram sat up and shook her head. "Sultana *Phoopu,* could you do this?" Samina's mother put her cigarette between her lips and swept Irram's hair back into a ponytail.

"So hot," Irram said.

"Yes." Samina's mother sighed. "I know. Summer is not the best time for a wedding, but with Samina's school, there was no other way we could—"

Irram nodded. "I know. I—" She stopped suddenly. "*Allah,* what if all my anniversaries are this humid?"

Samina's mother and aunt looked at each other and smiled. Samina looked up at the sky. The night couldn't be any clearer. The stars seemed low and bright. There was Pegasus, and Cassiopeia, and Perseus. In her backyard at home, she could never figure out who was who. The apartment buildings in the complex were staggered so that her family's yard was in an alley between two neighbors. There, her piece of the sky was very narrow. She saw only bits of constellations: Pegasus's tail or Orion's sword. But here it was different. The open sky was all around. Even without trying, she could connect the dots.

Samina stood up. "Can I go now?"

Her mother nodded, squinting through an exhale.

"Where are you going?" Irram turned to ask.

"Upstairs," Samina said. She tried to catch her mother's eye.

"Why?" Irram asked.

"*Ammi,*" Samina said, hoping her mother would remember that she had said Samina could go up when the *bijli* came back, "where did you put it?"

"Sammo's going to hide," Irram said with a smile, wiggling her fingers and toes in the air.

"No, I'm not," she said, pushing a few strands out of her eyes.

"It doesn't look that bad," Irram said.

"I know," she said. She moved behind the door, out of sight. "*Ammi,* where is it?"

"What?" Irram asked, her voice ringing out.

"My telescope," Samina said. "*Ammi—*"

"I moved it into the brown suitcase," her mother said. "Be careful. There are lots of things on top of it."

As Samina stepped into the hallway, Irram called after her. "It won't grow back any faster in the dark."

Her feet slid on the mosaic tile of the hall. Samina slowed down, then turned the corner into the study. The floor in there was even smoother. Glass cabinets lined the walls, but the dust was so thick that Samina could barely see the titles of the books inside them. Her uncle had been a barrister, as his father was before him, and as generations of men in the family had been before him. The large desk that had belonged to all these forefathers had been pushed aside to set up cots for Samina and her mother. Over the years the family had become so small that the second floor, where most of the sleeping quarters used to be, was no longer used. When visitors came, Samina's aunt had explained, it was easier to set up beds for them in the study than to air out the apartments upstairs.

Samina saw the suitcases in the corner behind the desk. As soon as their luggage had been emptied of the gifts they had brought for everyone, her mother had started filling it with the items she couldn't get back home. Although the trip was only half done, her mother had already packed and locked three of the suitcases. Now the last one was starting to bulge. Samina remembered her father warning her mother about coming back from India with more things than she was taking there. I'd rather have you back in one piece, he had said to her mother, than with a million pieces. He would definitely not like the look of the brown Samsonite. It lay on its side with a scarf hanging out like a tongue. Samina pushed open its mouth and started digging.

Under packets of Burma biscuits, tins of *paan-masala,* three *shalwaar* suits, and several cushion covers, she found what she'd insisted on bringing along. She moved everything out of the way, then pulled out the Tasco telescope. Samina made sure that the long red lens and the tripod were intact. Her mother had said it would take up too much space. Besides, she told Samina, there are so many things to see, why do you want to look up in the air? But Samina was equally adamant. If it's not going, she said, I'm not going. Why don't you just talk to people instead? her mother asked. Eventually, it was Samina's father who convinced her mother to make some room. Sultana, Samina heard him say, let her have her own fun. Samina closed the suitcase. Her father understood, but she could never explain it to her mother—not the reason why she wanted to see the same sky, the same stars from another place, nor why, for her, the best thing about India was that it was on the other side of the planet.

On the day they arrived, Samina had followed her mother and her aunt around for a tour of the *munzil*. This was my old bedroom, her mother said, pointing to a pair of shuttered doors on the second floor. Her aunt had brought a key for the padlock. When they stepped inside, the dust that had settled into the room over the years rose to greet them. The women brought their *rupatta*s across their faces, Samina borrowing a corner from her mother. The room was small and bare, but it didn't look any smaller than Samina's room back home. She didn't understand why her mother kept saying that she couldn't believe how tiny it was. I don't remember it being this way, her mother said. That was probably, Samina thought, because every room here is connected to another one. You could walk around the entire second floor without ever stepping out of the apartments. Samina herself was more interested in the outside, where there was a large courtyard surrounded by walls that would shield the view from city lights. Now she would confirm what she had suspected ever since she first saw the upstairs—that it was a perfect place to gaze at the stars.

Samina walked back through the hall and turned into the dining room. Along the way she blew out the candles. The extinguished wicks drooped in their translucent white mountains. She walked past the long dining table and the kitchen and into the dark stairwell behind it. She flipped the light switch.

The stairwell became a little less dark. Somewhere at the top of the stairs a bare bulb was casting a muddy brown light. The stone steps were large and worn. Samina had to lift her knees high to make her way up the spiral. She kept one hand on the walls, but lightly, because they were damp and cold. She didn't like the way they felt soft to the touch; still, she climbed.

After the stairwell, the night air seemed stuffy. Samina stood in the entryway. Behind her the spiral continued another flight up to a third floor, which was actually not a floor at all, just a square balcony overlooking the courtyard that was in front of her. At each corner of the balcony, a spire marked a small room. Samina's cousin Faizan had said he would show her the top floor and its four rooms someday after he'd had the servants air them out. He wasn't sure what was up there—birds, mice, maybe even bats. With a shiver, Samina stepped forward.

The moon lit the square in quarters. The corner directly across from her was the brightest; the adjacent ones were slightly darker; and despite the bulb in the stairwell, the one Samina was standing in felt the darkest of them all. She walked to the low wooden table in the center of the courtyard. Her steps clicked on the stone ground and seemed to echo against the walls. The sounds of the street were muted, but Samina could still make out the music from the temple and even the jingling of a *ricksha-wallah*'s bicycle. She set the telescope down on the *takht* and looked up. The house rose above and around her on all sides. At first, all she could see above its rim was the *masjid* tower's twinkling light. Samina waited for her eyes to adjust. The stars began emerging from the black sky as if they were being sifted. Slowly the Milky Way became brighter and brighter. When Samina could finally distinguish the band from its random neighbors, she knew she was looking right through the galaxy from one end all the way to the other. She tilted her head and stared straight up and felt as if she was standing at the bottom of the universe.

Samina pulled out the Styrofoam and began putting the telescope together. Once the tripod was screwed into place and set up on the *takht*, she took the cap off the lens. She pressed her face against the eyepiece. Her lashes trembled like spider legs.

She tried to stop herself from blinking. Close to the spire of the *masjid* tower she found Mars. At first she thought she was imagining the reddish light, but then she saw its roundness and knew it was a planet. The *takht* wobbled under her. Samina got off and knelt on the ground. She heard the engine of a scooter putter and then go quiet. She wondered whether it belonged to her cousin Faizan or somebody on the street. She found the North Star and tried to use it to locate Orion, but her eye fell on something blue green. Venus. She wished she hadn't left her pocket guide downstairs. She could see much more here than anywhere back home.

Samina didn't lift her head when she heard sounds coming from the stairwell. "Drop it, *yaar.* You did not."

Her cousin Faizan's voice identified itself by bouncing loudly off the walls, but Samina could barely make out the other one: "Still, she could have waited a little longer."

"What I don't understand," she heard Faizan say, "is why you don't tell me who it is."

"Because it doesn't matter" came the reply.

"I don't want to hear about this anymore. It's too complicated."

"When you grow up, I'll have someone explain all these things to—"

"Shut up," Faizan said. "If you can't tell me anything about her, why should I listen to everything else about her? Here, give me another one. Besides, if she said that to you, it's obvious that she never had any real interest in you at all."

Their steps were getting closer.

"Fantasize all you want or find another mystery woman—" Her cousin stopped. "Who's there?"

"It's me, Faizan Bhai," Samina said, standing up into the moonlight.

"Samina?" he asked, and then, quickly switching to English, he continued, "What are you doing up here? It's so dark. Isn't everybody on the verandah? Why aren't you down there with the rest of them?"

"I like it here," she said.

Light from the bulb above Faizan's head outlined him in silver. She could make out his stocky form. When he had first seen her at the airport, Faizan had pretended to be greatly offended by her height. *Phoopu*, he had asked Samina's mother with distress, what haven't you been feeding her?

He continued without hearing her. "Why don't you turn on the light?"

Near Faizan but behind him in the shadows stood a dark figure. The tip of a cigarette ashed and glowed near his mouth.

"I didn't know where it was," Samina said. "Besides, I'm—"

"What is that?" a deep voice asked in Urdu.

Samina turned away from the light. Her hair was short in the back but long enough in the front to get into her eyes. She let more of it fall forward.

"Looks like," Faizan said, pausing, "a telescope?"

"Yes," said Samina.

Faizan lit a match and brought it close to his face. "Where did you get that?"

"I brought it with me," she said, pulling the Styrofoam out of the box.

"All the way from the States?" Faizan asked with a smile. He shook the match out, and then he pointed with his cigarette. "Watch out for this one," he said to the figure. "She's going to be a doctor—or an engineer."

Samina could barely make out the other person's face, but his eyes looked large and white.

"Samina," Faizan said, "this is my friend Roshan." She saw the cigarette dip as if Roshan were nodding in her direction. "Roshan, Samina—my *phoopi*'s daughter. She lives in the States."

"So this is the one," Roshan said to Faizan in Urdu.

Her cousin continued, "Where was it? Detroit?"

"Troy," Samina said.

"Yes, Detroit, Michigan."

The cigarette dropped to the ground. "Does she understand Urdu?" Roshan asked Faizan, who was already headed toward the apartments. Faizan didn't hear him, but Samina did.

"Very well," she said in English.

Roshan smiled. His teeth looked as bright as his eyes. She watched him walk over and bend down to look through the lens. His hair was cut close to the scalp. "Can you see anything?"

Before Samina could answer, light from above a doorway fell into the courtyard. Most of it fell upon her.

"There," Faizan said, looking over his shoulder as he came back outside, "now we can see something." He set the fan he was carrying down and tugged on the cord. Then he picked it up again, pulled it as close as he could, and switched it on. "And now," he said, taking the cigarette out of his mouth, "we can breathe." Huffing a little from the exertion, Faizan walked around Samina and sat down on the *takht* in the line of the breeze. He looked up. "*Arre*," he exclaimed, "Sammo's looking damn cute."

She tried to smile. "We went to the salon today."

He lay back onto the table, smiling. "Damn cute."

"It's almost all gone."

"At least now we can see your face."

She looked down at the cover of the box and began gathering the parts of the telescope. She could feel Roshan's eyes on her cheeks.

"Sit." Faizan motioned to his friend. He pulled a hand across his forehead. "This heat. Why do you all always come in summer? Next time you should see the winters. October, November, until even February—everything is pleasant. Night feels like night, not just a darker part of the day. I don't know how you can stand it. The salon was air-conditioned, right?"

"The main room was," Samina said. She put the cap on the lens.

"Good," Faizan said. "Spend most of the day indoors." He lifted his arms and put his hands underneath his head. "*Yaar*, you know, you can see a lot of things up here." Faizan stopped and shook his head. "Anyway, that's what you should do, what we all should do. Sit in air-conditioning all day. Of course it's impossible to put it in anywhere in this house—"

"Are you finished here?" Roshan asked, looking up at Samina. His skin gleamed against the night, as if it had been pulled tight across his face.

"No, I—" she said. "It's hard to see anything with all this light."

"—ceilings are too high," Faizan continued, "every room has two doors, no closed spaces. How can you keep the heat out if you can't close the doors? Plus there's no privacy anywhere—"

"So," Roshan said, "what is *Amreeka* like?"

Samina didn't know what to say. She started to unscrew the tripod from the lens.

"Everybody is big and blond," Faizan interrupted himself to answer.

"Does everything you know come from a movie?" Roshan said to Faizan, then turned back to Samina. "No, really."

"Different," she said with a shrug.

"Why do you want to know?" Faizan switched to Urdu to ask Roshan.

"*Yaar,* that's the place to be," he said.

Faizan laughed. "For you?"

"You want to stay in Lucknow all your life and live in Muhammad *Munzil,* where there's no air-conditioning, no—"

"And what would you do in *Amreeka*?" Faizan asked.

"Make lots of money, buy anything I want—"

"The way her mother shops," Faizan said, winking at Samina, "you'd think you couldn't get anything in the States." Samina barely heard him, but she laughed anyway.

"—put an AC in every room of the house," Roshan continued. Samina could feel him staring at her. "—find myself an American girl to marry—"

"Listen to him." Faizan sat up. "You wouldn't know what to do with a girl—let alone an American girl—if one was standing in front of you."

Samina looked up. Roshan caught her eye. "I'd know," he said, and then, smiling, turned to Faizan, "more than you."

Faizan laughed again. Samina folded the legs of the tripod.

"Why don't you set it up on the rooftop?" Roshan asked. "You can see everything from there."

"Faizan *Bhai* said we shouldn't go up there. Things need to be cleared, and there are rats."

"He just says that because he's scared himself," Roshan said. "It's fine."

"I don't think that's a good idea," Faizan said.

"I'll take her up there. She'll get a good view of the city, too."

"No," Faizan said, frowning.

"You don't want to come, then why don't you go get us some *chai?*" Roshan said. "*Yaar,* you should be ashamed of yourself. I've been in your house for twenty minutes and you haven't offered me anything."

"No, I'll come," Faizan said.

"Samina might want some *chai.*"

"She doesn't drink *chai.*"

"Then a cold drink, maybe."

"I'll have someone bring something up later, after," Faizan said. "I'm coming."

"Are you sure?" Roshan said.

"The door might be locked."

"It never is."

"How do you know?" Faizan asked.

Roshan ignored him. "Don't want you screaming like a girl up there."

"Shut up, *yaar.* Let's go."

They climbed the steps slowly. Faizan was in front, behind him Samina with the accessories, and behind her Roshan with the lens. The door opened easily. Samina smiled when Roshan said something about how Faizan didn't really need to apply his shoulder. Faizan stepped into the entryway. "Wait," he said. Samina's foot slipped. She felt Roshan's hand on her back, steadying her.

Faizan searched along the wall with his arm. Samina heard Roshan click his tongue and sigh. He came up the steps, brushed past her and Faizan, and walked along the length of the balcony to the other corner. "Here," Samina and Faizan heard him call out after a light came on.

When they joined him, Faizan started to ask, "How did you know—"

Roshan shrugged. "You showed me all this—years ago. You just don't remember." He took the tripod from Samina and began setting up the telescope on the outside wall of the balcony. "I think this is the highest spot," he said.

Samina walked up to the wall and looked over its edge at the street below. She could see the whole neighborhood from here.

To the right was the *masjid*. But now she was looking down on its tower. Directly in front of them was the hall where all the music had been coming from. The Ambassadors parked along both sides of the road shone like big round beetles. The *paan-wallah* had rolled his cart even closer to the activity. Men were lined up around his stall. From here Samina could see into the entrance of the temple. Red, white, and green lights were strung together in the shape of tents. People were gathering along the inside of the gate. Behind a row of men there were women holding candles in the palms of their hands.

Samina heard cars honking. Faizan pointed down the street in the direction of the *masjid*. A parade was making its way toward the temple. At the center of the procession there was a person seated on a horse. Both the horse and the figure were draped in a curtain of roses. Roshan came to stand on the other side of her. He lifted his arms onto the wall and rested his chin on his hands.

"Bet you don't see this kind of thing in Det-troit," he said.

Samina shook her head. As soon as the procession turned the corner, the music from across the wall became louder. The people below began scrambling around. She heard women cheering. Men started throwing ropes into the air. The women poured out of the gate, their tiny flames agitating. The beaded tent started flashing, and then even more lights began turning on and off in time to the music. Roshan's nails were bone white against his skin. His fingers were long, and Samina noticed that the inside of his hand was pink.

"Did you see that?" Faizan yelped. Roshan glanced back over his shoulder toward Faizan, but his eyes fell on Samina. And then the dark fell upon all of them. "Fucking whore's son," she heard Faizan swear. She looked at him for a second, then turned back to Roshan.

"Look at that," Faizan said. The light was gone again. Samina could barely find the outlines of Roshan's face, but she knew he was watching her. "Shameless," Faizan continued. "Right under my own nose. I don't believe this."

"What?" Roshan asked, looking up at Faizan. "What the hell is the matter with you?"

"I knew that bastard didn't install a generator. Let me see that." Faizan grabbed the telescope and bent his head to look through it. "They're pulling it from our wires. *Sala* keeps stealing from our line. Just look. That cable there—it has a hook on one end. A hook. You see that? He gets it from us."

Faizan leaned over the edge and shouted, "You think I don't know what you're doing, you filthy fucking bastards? Get away from there."

The men below looked up, startled. Two of them dropped their cables. The rest left theirs dangling from the wire. Even people in the parade, which had started moving through the gate, stopped to look up.

"I'm coming," Faizan called down again. "I know who you are. I'm coming. I'm going to have your hides." He stepped away from the wall and began muttering, "All along, all this time, they've been telling us that something must be wrong with the wiring on our side of the street. Of course something's wrong with our lines—it's them. They even told Ammi they had bought a generator, had to take precautions because they're a business." He started walking back toward the stairwell, then turned. "Roshan, are you coming?"

Roshan looked from Faizan to Samina, then back to Faizan.

"Never mind," Faizan said. He pulled up his sleeves, exposing his thick arms. "I'll be right back."

They heard his steps slow down and then fade into the dark entryway.

"No wonder," Roshan said at last.

"What?"

"The *bijli* kept going today. They're having the *Mehendi*."

"So?" Samina asked.

"It's the most festive day of a wedding. The girl's side waits for the boy's side—that was the husband-to-be on the horse—to come in a *baraat*—like the one you just saw—to take the bride away. Then the two sides battle it out—or at least they pretend to, you know, for the bride. So there's a lot of fanfare to make up for the sad occasion. It's okay." He leaned across Samina. "I'll get it." He picked up the telescope, folded it, then set it next to its box. "You'll see soon enough," he added.

"When they come to take Irram *Apa*?"

"Yes," he said. Lights from the hall kept flashing across his face.

"She's so—"

"Beautiful," he said, and for a moment he looked angry.

"Yes." She stared at the floor.

"You look like her."

"People say I look like my father," she said.

"Maybe." He shrugged. "But you have the same eyes."

"I do?"

He nodded. "Same mouth."

He took a packet out of his shirt pocket. She watched as he swiped the match across the stone and lit a little brown cigarette. He pulled the smoke in without looking away from her. The tip cast a reddish glow around his lips.

"What's in those things?" Samina asked.

"Garbage."

He smiled when she said, "No, really."

"I'm not kidding. A little bit of tobacco, the rest is—God knows what."

She stepped so that her back was against the wall. She reached up to lift her hair off her neck, forgetting that it was no longer there. She pulled at the neckline of her shirt.

Roshan came and stood beside her. "Is that what girls wear on the streets in *Amreeka*?"

"I guess."

"But sometimes less?" he asked.

"Sometimes," Samina said and turned back to face the wall. She leaned a little bit over the edge. She finally felt as if she knew why the rest of the women kept *rupatta*s across their chests. "Some girls," she added.

"Here," he said. He turned the *bidi* in his hand so that the tip burned inside his palm. The skin there was pink and yellow. "Just don't tell him."

Samina took the tiny stick from him. The leaf was damp where his lips had been, and it tasted like mud. She drew a breath. For some reason, maybe because of the smell, which was something like saffron, she had thought the *bidi* would be sweet.

But it wasn't. The smoke burned her nose and throat. She coughed.

Before she felt his lips on the back of her neck, she felt his breath. "Slowly," he said. It was warm and soft against her ear. His lips left a cool, wet trail from her hairline to the corner of her jaw. She saw his hands on both sides of her, palms flat against the wall. She felt the stone press roughly against her stomach. She heard Faizan's voice rise from the street below. She looked down. Half the parade had stopped in the middle of the road. Her cousin was arguing with the men from the hall. She watched him point to the pole and draw the men's attention up its length, across the wire, along the line to the house, and then to the connection on the third floor—just a few angles away from where she was standing. She felt Roshan lick the back of her ear. She shivered. Faizan reached for one of the cables that still swung from the wire. The men surrounded him. He tried to walk past them, shouting. They closed in upon him. One hit Faizan from behind. His body crumpled. The cable he was holding on to fell to the ground.

She heard someone scream, "Stop." But it was too late. The light above her flashed on, bright and intense. It blinded her for a second. Then she saw the men begin kicking. There were shouts and more screams, but the loudest sound was the buzzing of the bulb above Samina's head. Suddenly a man poised to kick Faizan in the face was pulled off, and the crowd began to draw back. Samina caught a brief glimpse of the body lying in the road before three figures, their *rupatta*s sliding off their heads, down their shoulders and onto the ground, flew from the house and formed a circle over Faizan's body. People scattered in all directions, and soon the street was deserted.

Only the women, hunched over, cradling Faizan's head, remained. She saw them lift Faizan onto his feet. Irram pulled her brother's arm onto her shoulders, struggling to support his weight. Samina heard her order the driver to start the car and Zeinab to bring the wheelchair. They walked a few paces toward the house; then Irram stopped and began looking around. Samina watched the other girl's eyes search one end of the street then the other, stare at the side entrance of the house, then finally travel all the way up to the top floor. Samina's neck tight-ened. She felt nothing—behind her. The empty space came rushing in and surrounded her until she knew she was like a star in the sky, incompletely alone. She longed for the return of the hair that used to cover her neck, or the lips, or even that swampy green smell. Something, anything, that would make her want to be either here or there.

Christie Hodgen
Indiana University

THREE PARTING SHOTS AND A FORECAST

John Wilkes Booth

His Picture:

A three-quarter shot, Booth leering just left of center, casual, as if turning toward someone who has called his name. No doubt a beautiful heiress, an adoring fan. He has a devil's ear, angled tight and sharp against his head, and his hair is brushed into nonchalant curls. Dark-eyed with eggshell skin, he wears a black mustache combed into a frown. At the time of the picture Booth is one of the most celebrated young actors in Washington City, and he dresses the part. He models a loose jacket, cut in the latest fashion, its collar and breast pocket trimmed with silk thread. The top button is fastened, and the rest of the jacket falls open in a triangle like a tepee. The pocket sprouts a starched handkerchief. His right hand, fat and smooth as a baby's, props a delicate bamboo walking stick. A small brass key dangles from his vest's middle button. (A remembrance? A safe-deposit box? The door to his room? No one is sure.) A gold ring wraps the little finger of his left hand, which grips the handle of something resembling a whip. He is a gentleman, a gentleman.

It is a good time for actors. The president himself attends the theater with some frequency. Theater-going is a pleasant diversion, and Lincoln's only opportunity to nap in peace. The president's box hovers twelve feet over stage left, and is about the size and shape of Lincoln's childhood log home. It seats four comfortably, five in a pinch. The president lounges in a distinctive rocking chair. It is one of Lincoln's favorite places, cozy and warm as a cradle.

Imagine one particular evening Lincoln has trouble dozing off. A loony Hamlet trots underfoot. The actor's interpretation requires a certain amount of gymnastics. It is a promenade of leaping and screeching. TO BE! Booth booms, looks skyward, drops to one knee, rolls onto his back. OR NOT TO BE! He clutches the open neck of his shirt and howls. Booth turns a cartwheel and decides on the question. The crowd loves him. Perhaps they find his aerobics refreshing in such solemn times. What's a play these days anyway but a moment's distraction? Who wants to look death too plainly in the face?

The president decides to sleep out the rest of the performance, chin slumped on his chest. Just then, Booth steals a glance at the shadowed figure. Asleep! In the middle of his soliloquy! He stops for a moment, stumbles on the verse. Lincoln's legs are outstretched—propped on the banister—and the giant, scuffed soles of his shoes face the stage like twin hecklers. Imagine living under the reign of such an unmannered buffoon. Booth decides, then and there, to take some kind of action. Curiously, as the play wears on, Booth's performance improves. The audience remarks how distressed and convincing he is, as if he were really and truly at odds with an unrightful king.

Lincoln wakes, rested, as the lights come up. It is his best sleep in weeks.

There is little rest for Booth after his plan begins to materialize. During the first months of 1865, Booth dreams—nightly—his own set of tragedies. They take different forms. The worst of the lot occurs onstage. Just as he has the crowd in his grip, just as he works Hamlet or Romeo or King Lear into the most innovative and tortured interpretation of the century, the crowd howls with laughter. The gaslights jet up, flickering blue and then white. He sees people twisting in their chairs, the men clutching their stomachs, the women covering their faces with gloved hands. Booth checks to see that his fly is buttoned. "What!" he demands, stomping a foot. "Blast!" Booth likes to curse in the manner of all true southern gentlemen—forcefully, but with restraint. The audience can't seem to get ahold of itself. Booth storms toward the curtain, bats at it to split the seam so he can slip offstage. But the curtain is stitched together at its center and only sways from the rafters like a bemused spirit. The theater takes on the look of a large carnivorous mouth, its domed ceiling like a palate. The wooden seats like false teeth, the audience rolling and flapping like a crazy tongue. They will swallow him. There is nothing to do but submit. Booth drops to one knee and makes the motions of a prayer—an act, but isn't everything?

Suddenly the audience calms. Booth hears his name announced from overhead, a high-pitched and familiar voice, not quite human. "Booth," he hears again, and looks skyward. Lincoln stands in his elaborate box, tall as Goliath. He extends an arm toward the stage and turns his mouth into a wry smile.

Young man, you remind me of a story, starts Lincoln. Another one of his roguish yarns. A bawdy type of chatter, a rail-splitting, chain-gang story, a perverse parable. Lincoln continues: *One afternoon a fellow stopped by the office asking to be appointed minister abroad. Sensing my hesitation, the gentleman came down to a more modest proposal.* The audience snickers. Lincoln adjusts his atrocious hat. *After much of the same to and fro, the man asked to be appointed a tide-waiter.* The crowd crackles to life, even before the punch line. The old bag of wind is like a re-oiled machine. There's color in his cheeks, a twinkle in his eye. He strokes his beard and draws out the ending. *Now, let me see.* He smiles, rocks back on his heels. *Where was I?*

"The waiter, the waiter!" yells the crowd.

Oh, yes. When the man discovered he could not have that, he asked me for an old pair of trousers. There's hooting and roaring from all corners of the room. Booth sits on the stage in a droopy pile, playing with his fingers. *My boy,* says Lincoln, *it is best to be humble. Especially when one is illegitimate.*

Booth flushes red. His worst secret revealed by his worst enemy. It is true. Booth is a bastard, the spawn of an unholy entanglement. By rank he is less noble than the bumpkin Lincoln, born in wedlock. Worse, Booth is not really a southerner, as he so often claims. Hailing from Maryland—the gutless, wavering Maryland. Booth feels as if his very face were a fiction, a cloth mask stretched over borrowed bones. He tugs at his hair to make sure it is fixed to his scalp, and it plucks out in lovely curls. He gasps. He goes to scream but his teeth fall out of their sockets, long and narrow with ghastly pointed roots. He wakes with a furious heart.

Lincoln

Lincoln's story is perhaps best told by others, the ones left behind. Those things and people in Lincoln's employment during his final days. What remains is a curious testimony. Loosely stitched, and of course, unfinished.

His Picture:

Of the hundreds of images of Lincoln, one photograph is without question the most striking. One of a group of formal shots, taken the morning after Lee's surrender. He is seated in an ornate chair, its four legs formed from a series of polished wooden bulges that in threes resemble the curves of a woman's body. His legs extend forward toward the camera, long and crooked like the branches of a thin tree. His polished dress shoes could hold a half gallon of milk apiece and a little more. He rests his arms uncomfortably in his lap, thumb and forefinger of each hand pinched as if he were measuring salt or conducting music. He wears a wrinkled silk-collared jacket, a white dress shirt that is loose in the chest, and a lopsided bow tie. His hair, reasonably smoothed, is recently thinned. His beard—grown as a disguise while he took the railroad to Washington for his first inauguration—has, in four years' time, grown thick and then thin again, patchy in the cheek. Perhaps Lincoln loses his hair from sheer exhaustion. The follicles quit their grip on the strands.

Lincoln eats a bird's diet and rarely sleeps. At times it seems impossible that he is alive. Lines mark his face cruelly—long and deep. His flesh is loose on the bone, and his eyes have ceased to hold color. They are now like the skin settled over warm milk. Translucent, tenuously draped over a weak surface, barely holding shape. On this day of victory he looks like someone who is disappointed with death. He looks like someone who has been kept waiting a long while.

His Doorman:

The doorman is one of four guards hired to protect the president during the last months of his life. The guards are chosen more for their size than know-how. There is no reason to trust any of them to act well in a bad situation.

On a spring evening well past midnight one of the doormen hears a close-by double-barrel gunshot. He wrings his hands under the dim light of the White House's front entrance. Who else but the president would draw fire in the darkest hour of morning? The doorman looks up and down the avenue, searching for light in the shuttered windows of neighboring hotels. All is dark. There is no moon. Soon the doorman perceives the gathering crooked rumble of hooves over cobblestone. He peers down the avenue and recognizes the president, dwarfing his full-grown horse. Lincoln is bareheaded and without a jacket. His white shirt flags in the wind. He struggles with the reins, half-standing in the saddle and tugging back at the horse's long neck. Lincoln jolts to a halt and dismounts, breathing heavy.

"Riding alone again, sir?" asks the doorman.

"I can't seem to get to sleep." Lincoln hands over the reins and smoothes the horse's mane.

"What happened to your hat?" The president is never outdoors without his trademark stovepipe.

Lincoln touches his hair absently. "I must have lost it." He nods good night and shuffles inside, stooped. He is small and weary looking, his hair blustered into haphazard curls.

The doorman ties the horse at the front gate and leaves his post. He is not one for standing still, even under orders. He treks up the road, heels clicking on the stone. He walks in the middle of the street, head down. The square stones are wet with spring, caked with mud, swelled and upturned in places where they've burst with cold. On instinct the doorman turns down a narrow alley between two boardinghouses. The muddy pass is lined with garbage. A loose rooster pokes around in the dirt, clucking idly, pecking at various smelly heaps. It is not uncommon for fowl to roam the streets, feeding themselves from discarded scraps. What is peculiar about this rooster is its shape, its walk. The doorman watches its silhouette for some time. The rooster seems to struggle under the weight of its own gobbler, tipping forward and losing its footing. The doorman inches closer. In better light he sees that the rooster beaks the president's hat, which dangles and dips in the mud. He stalks forward, crouching, hands outstretched. The rooster squawks and flaps its wings, attempts flight. But the stovepipe is too much to bear. The doorman stomps his feet and manages a low growl. The bird releases the hat with what appears to be a certain amount of grief, as if it were abandoning the body of a favorite child. The doorman scoops the collapsed hat and examines it in the dark. It is mud covered, the black silk patched with stains, the brim trampled and bent. The top is tilted like a crumbling chimney.

Then he confirms his worst fear: the crown of the hat is pierced with a fat hole, the wound of serious ammunition. This marks the third known attempt on Lincoln's life, the closest shot yet. A bullet whisked through the hat's narrow cylinder, less than a foot from Lincoln's head.

Still, until the very night of his death, Lincoln continues to ride alone at night, Paul Revere-ing around, announcing his sorrow at every door.

After Lincoln's death, the doorman cannot help himself. He tells the story to anyone who will listen. Each time it is different. Each time his own role improves. Sometimes there is no rooster, and the doorman finds the hat in a driveway. Sometimes the doorman is shot at by rebels trying to finish the job. It is always the same with the hat, though. Pierced through the crown. A miss so narrow and terrifying it defies explanation, no matter how many times he tries, no matter how fantastic the circumstances.

The doorman never forgives himself. He rubs his fingers together absently, obsessively, for the rest of his life, imagining the silk hat against his skin, its thin, crumpled frame, its black band of mourning. He recalls the fabric torn in a rough circle, how the bullet left a star-shaped scar.

His Chair:

Lincoln is shot in a rocking chair. John Ford, the owner of the theater, brings the chair from his own residence when the president plans to be in attendance. Surely the president esteems the chair's construction, the ease it allows his legs. Or maybe he simply admires its beauty. It is a sleigh built for one. Cushioned in a rich red fabric, puckered with covered buttons, swollen at the neck with extra padding. The slender arms are carved from a dark wood. They run straight for the length of an average arm, then dip toward the floor and curl under themselves. The four legs are short and fat, perched on long, thin rockers. Today the chair would be placed in a nursery. It is small and delicate enough to raise suspicion. How could a man of any size—and a president at that—favor such a dainty throne? The top of the chair is marked with a biscuit-sized stain, seeped into the upholstery, thought by some to be Lincoln's blood. In fact it is the mark of a popular gentleman's hair pomade. In terms of evidence, indications of the president's brief and tragic patronage, the chair offers nothing. No print, no stain.

From Booth's vantage, the chair poses a particular problem. High backed, it obscures most of Lincoln's head, leaving a narrow, crescent-shaped target. Booth slows his breathing and pulls a brass-handled gun from his vest. He aims deliberately, both arms extended, head cocked. Onstage the play continues with its comic twists. Booth's shot is not heard over the crowd's laughter. When a frenzied man leaps to the stage waving his pistol, the crowd believes it is part of the script. Some clap and chuckle, drowning out Booth's dramatic parting soliloquy, borrowed from Brutus: *Sic semper tyrannis!*

Meanwhile the rocking chair thrusts forward and washes back, allowing Lincoln's body to ease into the blow. Perhaps it spares him a certain amount of pain. Doctors stretch him across the floor, find the wound, and work a clot from the back of his head, three inches above the left ear. Someone provides brandy. Someone parts his lips and lets in the fluid. False blood, false hope. Someone holds his hand the nine hours it takes him to die.

Later someone washes the blood from his hair, loosens the dried stain with water, sets it running again. Later someone places silver coins over his swollen eyes to weigh down the lids. And later the chair retires to an ill-frequented museum. It creaks and sighs whenever it is cleaned.

Boston Corbett

His Picture:

Not an unattractive man. His long hair is parted down the center and pulled together at the nape of the neck. He wears ill-fitted Union blues, a fat stripe running along the vertical seam of his loose trousers. He sits at a round table reading an enormous Bible. He is clean-shaven. His boots are knee-high, made of black leather, and have probably trampled across acres of blood-soaked ground.

Before Boston Corbett shot John Wilkes Booth at close range with a Colt revolver, he was a sergeant in the Union army, and before that, a hatter in Boston, Massachusetts. One of twenty-six men hired to pursue Lincoln's killers, Corbett did not shoot Booth under orders, in self-defense, or any other set of condoned circumstances save this: God told him to. The mandate from Secretary of War Stanton was to round up Booth alive and squealing. What good was a public hanging of the conspirators without their gallant leader, the most famous actor in Washington City? At the very least, Booth would provide an afternoon's entertainment, his final speech choked out as his trim legs kicked uselessly over the platform. Instead Stanton has to settle for a dead fugitive, shot in the neck by a mad hatter. As secretary of war, one learns to take what one can get.

It seems that Corbett was always waiting for this to happen—that he had spent his life in preparation for this one act, this favor to God. Even as he shaped hats in a small town he was practicing the gestures of precision, studying the relationship between his methodical labor and its eventual divine purpose.

Just as Jesus spent a certain amount of time learning carpentry, Corbett apprenticed himself in a tidy shop, fixing practical hats to warm his neighbors' heads.

Hats are made by hand then, meticulously. It is rare for a gentleman to walk the streets with an uncovered head. Every respectable man owns at least two, one for dress and a second for weather. It is considered good form to touch the brim of one's hat upon passing an acquaintance, to remove the hat completely when bowing to a lady. In Washington City the fancy top hat is in style. A black collapsible wool-felt blend with gros-grain ribbon trim. The streets are teeming with them. A taller-than-average person can watch the hats from above, clogging the streets with black and brown and gray, bobbing to and fro like shifting silt, like fish bellying around on a lake's surface. Corbett is familiar with the president's unusual choice in head wear. The lonely, poor-selling stovepipe. Why an overly tall man wishes to accentuate the problem is his own business. Corbett makes three hats on the chance that locals will want to imitate the presidential fashion. He sells one to a traveling merchant, and the other two sit on a shelf for most of Lincoln's adminis-tration.

In this part of the country the practical fur hat is still in style. Corbett works late in the shop washing the bloodied pelts of beavers and muskrats. He wets the fur in a basin of water, then soaps vigorously. The fur makes a munching noise against itself. Corbett runs the soap up his own arm, his hairless skin pink with foamed blood. When the pelt dries he applies mercury to separate the skin and fur. He rubs it into the roots with his fin-gers, and the poison seeps through his skin. He takes a moment to admire the cool liquid, how it skates across his palm and divides into an arrangement of spheres, like planets and their moons, a whole universe in silver reflecting the warm pink of his palm. He thinks of God's hand and his place in it. A small mirror.

The hair pulls from the skin and Corbett steams it onto sec-tions of felt. His fingers are silver-tipped. When he licks them after a meal, he sucks on the poisonous traces. It tastes like suf-fering. There are flecks of mercury in his blood, running slick through the veins like silver bullets, up to the brain. The mercury chimes in his head, God's voice. Corbett's hats become something of a legend in town. So precisely detailed, so finely stitched, so comforting and necessary. Tucked in the store window, such small and attractive wonders.

One summer Corbett works for a few weeks without hearing from God. His hats turn out mediocre, and he begins to worry that he has sinned in some way. He examines himself with unflinching scrutiny before settling on a minor transgression. Lately his thoughts wander. He has begun making ladies' hats, harmless enough. But in the process he has on occasion imagined himself unfastening a lady's bonnet, soaping a woman's hair right there in the shop, in his basin. He has even looked wantingly at the prostitutes across the street in their feathered caps.

Corbett crosses the dark room to examine an unfinished bonnet, sprawled across a workbench like a spider. The bonnet is light in his hands, made of a fine off-white muslin, lace-edged with mother-of-pearl buttons under the chin. He strokes the fabric with his fat red thumb. He circles the chin's button with a finger. "Women and their articles," he thinks, and rips the button loose. It pops on the floor like a weak gunshot. The room seems to shrivel. Its blue walls slant inward and the floor pushes up. It is always this way when Corbett thinks of women—their stifling and irresistible bodies. His breath comes quick, and suddenly the fumes clog his breathing. There is only one solution.

Corbett castrates himself with a pair of scissors to avoid the temptation of women. Only one of the sacrifices a true man of God must be willing to make. For it is better for a man not to marry, lest he be distracted from the Lord's work. Corbett sharpens the blades on a rod to make the music of a ritual. Afterward he wraps himself in the same manner used to diaper Jesus on the cross.

Corbett then eats a generous dinner and makes conversation at the table. He uses the right fork at the right time and remembers his prayers. He retires casually and takes a short stroll around the neighborhood before deciding to visit the hospital.

He is now a passionless man, unsuited for war. And he joins

the Union army and reenlists several times to preserve the sanctity of the whole. And now to ensure the final peace, he is sent after Booth to end it all. In his own estimation, Corbett serves as the final blow in the Civil War.

On April 26, 1865, Corbett and his company track Booth to a tobacco farm in northern Virginia. They have been twelve days on the hunt. The Virginia spring is cold, the pale grass still scattered loose over the frozen earth, crunching under their boots. It is a lot like war. The men keep low as they file through rows of planted greens and circle a large barn, weapons poised.

The barn is a limp wooden structure, warped in places and leaning to one side. Inside Booth and his toady, David Herold, make assessments. A dozen blues at least, maybe two. Closing in on them. The commander orders an immediate surrender and Herold, tired from days of scavenging, knows it is over. He steps from the barn, arms raised. Booth remains, waiting for the soldiers to approach. He picks up an old scythe from the corner of the barn and leaps around, slicing through the air. He holds it like a woman and takes a final spin around the barn. So little room for Booth's beloved gymnastics. The barn is crowded with strips of tobacco, hanging to dry. One of Booth's favorite smells, warm and genteel. The fumes engulf him. The soldiers have lit the barn on fire, and the flames jump from the ground high and fat, smoking furiously. The tobacco curls under the heat, mulching the floor. There is a crackled roaring, and the air goes soft, rising in waves. Booth decides to make a run for it, and he stands for a moment, gets into character.

Outside Corbett inches closer to the barn, crouching under the heat. Squinting, struggling for breath. It is something of a miracle that a man in this situation gets off a fatal round. Through a crack in the barn, two warped boards separated with a six-inch gap. Corbett raises the revolver. He aims through the traces of his own breath.

The bullet lodges in Booth's neck, severing the spinal cord. While the shot still sounds in the air, while the powder from Corbett's revolver lingers over the earth, several men race into the barn and drag Booth from the flames. One of the men swipes Booth's hat with a mind to sell it to the highest bidder.

The other men take turns guarding the body. Booth remains conscious for a few hours but says little. It is not until his final moments that Booth asks the soldiers to hold up his paralyzed hands before his face, so he can admire them. The soldiers take turns puppeteering. Booth stares into his palms and utters the word "useless" on his next to last breath. These faces peering over him. He flutters his eyelids and practices his most disdainful expression. An act? It is hard even for Booth to say.

Forecast

Boston Corbett is excused of all criminal charges in the shooting of John Wilkes Booth. He moves to Kansas, where he is less of a celebrity, and takes a job as doorman for the state House of Representatives in Concordia. He tips his hat to the representatives on their way in and out of session. He stands with his hands clasped behind his back and guards the door while men of good faith discuss earthly situations. Corbett imagines God's house to look a little like this, a single room where one must answer to his sins, where one is considered for approval or disapproval. Where one is discussed in a reasonable manner and occasionally fought over, good against evil until someone wins out. Corbett keeps his post without incident until one afternoon when he overhears two representatives mocking the ceremonial opening prayer. He pulls a derringer from his pocket and waves it around the room. He is seized and institutionalized before getting a shot off. Upon his release he tells a friend that he is headed for Mexico and is never heard from again. Possibly he makes it all the way south, where he is recognized by no one. Where the hats are fat and wide and simple, made of cheerful straw. Possibly he dies happy.

Perhaps Booth suffers the worst fate of all. He simply dies. He leaves a legacy of a name and little more. The occasional footnote, the odd wax statue in roadside museums. Historically, Booth is cast as the rogue and Lincoln the gentleman. If anything, Booth only heightens Lincoln's fame.

Lincoln is the first president to be depicted on American currency. A bill and a coin, both in threat of extinction. Given the popularity of the one and the ten, who needs a five? Pennies are kept in children's banks, out of circulation. There is talk of abandoning the cent, rounding everything to the nearest nickel. But no one can bring himself to do it. The whole system breaks down, falls apart in the absence of its smallest denomination.

The money artists are flattering. Lincoln's features are softened on the currency, his hair brushed in place. The penny's face shows Lincoln in profile with a regular nose and a dainty ear. We have our way with him. His image becomes something else, someone else, minted a thousand times over, practically worthless.

Lincoln's truest image is the least known. Look closely at the tail side of a new penny. Between the two middle columns of the Lincoln Memorial you can make out a miniature seated figure. It is barely perceptible when new, nothing more than a scratch, and the first thing to rub away with time. Scraped against the cashier's drawer and moistened with sweaty fingers. He is always sitting at a distance, waiting to escape, to slip between our fingers, to ride off unaccompanied and catch his death. Now it is hardly worth the trouble to fetch a penny off the ground.

Erin Dovichin

University of Alaska, Anchorage

COMMUNION

I am not a religious woman, though I was raised as a Catholic. And like the students here at the motherhouse, I attended Catholic grade school. I have not been to church in some time, and when I took this job, I thought it made little difference that my patients would be nuns. Lately though, I watch them with their beads and crosses, and I feel like I've lost something. I feel like I can't communicate with them, that they know things I am missing out on. And today, when I washed Sister Ann between the legs, water running down my arms and into the sleeve of my shirt as I wrung the sponge, sister making small quiet moans as I cleaned her, I became suddenly afraid. Both of us now women with bodies past their reproductive use, we seemed the same—despite my husband, despite my children and grandchildren—only she was happier. I wondered then if she had ever been touched by a man, and if not, what ecstasy she has known instead. How the hand of God has worked her body and brought her a pleasure I do not know, as she does not know mine.

I have tried not to think about the nuns like this. I have worked here in the motherhouse infirmary for several months and have kept all but a physical distance from these women—they are dying, after all, and as a rule, it can be hard if you get too close to them. Until now I have acted as if they are some declining species, and I am here to track their progress. I am here simply to help them die.

Since I found the girl from the sixth grade, though, things have begun to change. I look at my hands, my body, the lines deepening in my skin, and I realize I am not so far from these nuns. It is just a matter of time for me, too. And I see this girl, who is so young, just beginning, her body new and growing still, and I feel even older than my fifty-two years.

When I discovered her, she was curled against the statue of the Virgin Mother on the main floor—her slight body like some delicate and dying bird, so that when I first saw her, I thought of the times as a child when I wanted to gather small wounded creatures—baby robins, raccoons, squirrels—in my hands. Don't touch them, my mother would say.

I knelt down beside her and she opened her eyes.

Hello, I said.

I expected her to start up with surprise, but she didn't move.

What's your name? I asked.

Alison, she said.

Are you all right? I asked.

Who are you? she asked.

I hesitated then.

I'm a nurse from upstairs, I said.

She sighed, drew her knees up to her chest, a movement of hers I have since become accustomed to, and rested her cheek on the feet of the statue, her eyes watching me carefully.

I've had a bad day, she said.

Two weeks have passed since then, and each day I intend to call the principal, Sister Margaret, and tell her about finding the girl, despite the girl's request for me not to. Each day I think it is the right thing to do, but I am afraid if I do the girl will stop coming to the infirmary—as she has now almost every weekday since I first found her. I have grown to like her visits and I believe the nuns have, too. Why she was by the statue that day, I still do not clearly understand. She stole a picture of Mary from her art teacher, maybe, or committed some other offense, and was sent to the principal's office. But how that got her to the motherhouse proper, I don't know. I know she was very upset, because her face was streaked from dried tears, and her curly hair was matted on the side that pressed against the statue while she slept. I am surprised that a trip to the principal's office would upset her so—I've come to know her as a formidable little girl, not easily shaken, despite her fragile appearance, and there is something just beneath her skin, a sense of defiance, an energy, a vitality that is almost unsettling in someone her age.

It was that energy, I think, that compelled me to say yes when she sat up from the statue's feet and asked to see Sister Virginia. All of the grade school students have been assigned an elderly nun, either one from the infirmary or one from the living quarters on the second floor, to make cards for on holidays. Sister Virginia, Alison's assignment, lives in the infirmary.

When Alison arrived in the infirmary, however, she asked to be introduced to all nine of the sisters in the community room. I warned her that many of them are too weak to talk much, that they seldom talk even with each other. But their infirmity did not bother her—not their meagerness of response nor even their slack-jaw, vegetable mouths and sudden cries of pain. I was surprised. When I was her age, old women like these terrified me. I couldn't stand to be around them. I remember how my great-aunt would hold me as she recited a rosary, how I fought to get out of her embrace; I remember her shriveled face and the smell of her like damp dark places.

But Alison was unafraid, smiling as she learned the name of each of the nuns, meeting Sister Virginia last.

Sister, I said, this is one of the students who sends you cards. Her name is Alison.

The woman nodded, and Alison sat down in the chair next to her and told her about a card she'd sent sister, how she had tried to copy it from a picture she liked of Mary, a picture by a painter named Bellini. Sister smiled and nodded again, her blue eyes brightening in what seemed like recognition, and Alison smiled widely, her face relaxing for the first time that afternoon.

Since then Alison shows up each day after school has let out, when the children have already flooded the courtyard and disappeared again. She comes late because she cleans the cafeteria after school for work-study. Most of the students here come from wealthy families. You can see them outside with their trim stylish haircuts and their bright ski jackets with their winter ski passes attached like the badges of some fraternity. Alison is odd compared with them: her uniform blouse a gray white from much washing, her oversized navy peacoat unbuttoned and hanging awkwardly on her slim frame, and her wild intractable hair, which she tries futilely to slick back with wet fingertips. When she comes up the dark hall, I am uncertain she is real. In the dimness human beings possess a faint glow and, she in particular, an ethereal quality. Not until she steps into the fluorescent light of our nurses' station am I convinced she is human.

Each time she arrives she says a quick hello to me and asks to see the nuns. Then she goes from room to room, leaning in doorways and watching them. Finally she enters the community room and visits with Sister Virginia. There she pulls her drawing pad and bundles of crayons and markers and colored pencils from her bag and begins to draw pictures for the nuns. She chatters endlessly with them, regardless of whether they respond, explaining the flower she is drawing or relaying a story about her dog, the sound of her young voice rising over their coughs and prayers and muted cries. Then she returns to the desk and I ask her how she is. She spends little time with me. After several minutes she leaves to catch the city bus home.

I don't know what it is that brings her up here. I don't know what it is that attracts her to these dying old women, with their stale, sour-smelling bodies, or how it is that she communicates with them. I don't see what she sees standing in their doorways, watching them.

Today Father Jeffrey has come to give the nuns communion. I watch him as he moves from chair to chair in the community room, whispering quietly, Body of Christ, Body of Christ, as he places the wafers in their cupped hands. When he finishes his rounds, he tells them something a kindergartner said about God, and he laughs and the nuns' eyes widen and the creases in their faces crowd their mouths in toothless smiles.

He nods at me as he moves down the hall to the rooms of the bedridden sisters. I've watched him there too, how he lifts their heads gently and slips the wafer into their mouths so they too may receive the life-giving bread, and I've wondered how it tastes to them—the Styrofoam texture of wafer, the salty tips of his fingers. It could be the last thing they taste, I think; soon he'll be here delivering their last rites, and his voice will be a whisper then too—a trail of sound running gently into the beyond.

After they've passed, Jeannine, the undertaker, will come and prepare their bodies. She'll dress them in the traditional habit and wrap their rosary beads in their hands and lay them out in the parlor on the first floor for viewing. Then father will lead the funeral party through the winding dark halls of the motherhouse offices and into the grade school, down its long hall to the chapel entrance, the incense fogging the halls and filling our nostrils. Together we'll walk: the young nuns in their tasteful lay clothes, low heels, and understated accessories; the older ones in various versions of the habit; family and friends and myself in my white nurse's outfit, aware that we are one death closer to the end of a way of life, the whole of us moving like a single organism of grief and departure.

How close are we to that end? I wonder as I turn my head from where Father Jeffrey has disappeared into one of the rooms. I put down the charts I've been filing and walk into the community room to see if any of the nuns are still holding their wafers. Sometimes they do not remember to eat them, Sister Virginia in particular. Today I find her staring at the wafer in her hand.

What have you got there? I ask.

She smiles up at me, her eyes suddenly beaming.

Looks like your own little piece of God, I say. Better eat it.

I pick it up then and slip it into her mouth and I feel her tasting my fingertips.

That's good, I say as I watch her gum it, the wafer slowly dissolving in her mouth. I glance at the clock and realize the girl will be here any time now.

Your little friend will be here soon, I say to Sister Virginia. Perhaps she'll draw you a nice picture.

The woman nods and smiles blankly.

Today Alison stops and talks to me before she goes to the nuns. I am surprised and pleased. At first we talk about Sister Virginia and then she tells me she's in trouble again.

What happened? I ask.

Sister Marie went to the bathroom on the art room floor, she says as she picks at the scuff marks on her shoes.

What? I say.

She went number two.

On the floor?

She pulls her foot up to her waist so she can examine her shoe.

Yes, she said. We all saw her do it. But Sister Margaret says it is a mean lie I've spread and now none of the sixth-graders are allowed to talk during morning break. She won't let us. Everyone blames me. We can't talk at all. So I draw.

I'll see if I can do something about that, I say.

She smells too, Alison says, her gaze catching on the movement of one of the nuns as the woman peeks out from behind the crack in her bedroom door.

Who does? I ask.

Sister Marie. The whole room smells.

She licks her fingers and smoothes back her hair.

And I would like to use yellow in my pictures sometimes, she says.

She has told me that the color yellow is forbidden in art class because sister feels that a person can't see yellow from a distance. More vexing to Alison, however, is the rule about the sun. Once they pass third grade, the students are no longer allowed to draw the sun, because according to sister's logic, the sun is God's creation. At first I thought maybe sister and her students had somehow confused "sun" and "son," but it is for drawing a sun, as well as her report on Sister Marie, that Alison has been punished today. Sister Marie is rapidly becoming a concern of mine. She is eighty-six years old and growing senile—so much so that she should not, obviously, be teaching. And beyond her hygiene problems and her inscrutable logic, she is violent with her students, still using the old-school punishments the nuns used when I was a girl. I know how she was rough with Alison, shaking her harshly by the arms, because I remember, and because already I see the bruises flowering on Alison's tricep muscles, disappearing where the starched sleeve of her white Peter Pan blouse makes a stiff line across her skin.

I'm going to talk to Sister Margaret about her, I say. Sister Marie needs our care.

Don't tell her about me, she says, as she stands to leave. Please.

I nod. I don't understand how she can want to come visit these nuns after her experience with Sister Marie. Or even Sister Margaret. What Sister Margaret has against her, I can only guess. Sister is a very organized person; she likes things to be clean and orderly and well run. What attracts me to Alison repulses her—the girl's difference, her hints of unruliness, her refusal to fit in—the things that make me want to take her under my wing and protect her. The things also that unnerve me about her, that make me think she knows things that I don't.

This morning, before my shift, I find myself in the mother-house chapel. I stand for a few minutes in the doorway, watching, listening. The chapel is quiet and empty, the candles glowing in their deep red cylinders. Listening to this silence, I know I cannot not believe, but what it is I believe I'm unsure. Most of my adult life, I've looked down on all of this—the weekly Sunday rituals, the masses of people reciting their rote prayers, these preprogrammed missals I see tucked in the backs of the pews. My life was full without this. I had a home to make for my husband and children, and I've spent twenty-nine years doing that happily. But now I feel gutted. My children grown and gone. My uterus a hollow dead place. I can feel it there. Housing nothing, collapsing. All this time I lived for them, and now there's just me and my husband. And sometimes it's like he's a stranger there, across the table from me, putting the marmalade on his toast, sipping his coffee. I come to work and leave work, I sleep next to him and wake next to him, and always now there's this emptiness growing inside of me.

A nun appears and passes by me on her way to light a candle. I choose a pew and sit in it, running my hand on the rounded mahogany top of the pew in front.

Where's my piece of God? I think.

Above me the angels sing and to the left Christ struggles on his way to the mount. Down the hall, I think, Alison is in a classroom listening eagerly to her teacher and smoothing back her wiry brown hair, and on the third floor Sister Virginia sits with her hand cupped around the host as if it were a pearl.

In the afternoon the girl arrives with a rose for Sister Virginia. It appears homegrown, wrapped in wet paper towels and aluminum foil. I listen to her explain to Sister Virginia that the rose is a surprise, a late bloom in November. Sister does not answer her; her health has grown worse in recent days and she seldom talks now except to pray. I walk up to them, and I take the rose from Alison's hand.

She's giving you a flower, sister, I say, and I take the rosary beads from sister's hands and press the rose into her palm, but she will not close her hand on it.

Such a pretty rose, sister, I say. Don't you want it?

She doesn't want to hold it, Alison says. She wants to hold those.

The girl points to where I've set sister's rosary beads on the table.

Oh, I say. Both girl and nun stare at me as if to say they were doing fine without me, and I feel my face growing hot. I'll find a vase, I say.

When I return, the girl is kneeling at sister's chair, examining each of the beads as sister says her Hail Marys. I unwrap the rose and put it in the glass of water I've brought and set it near sister.

The girl gets up and follows me to the nurses' station.

She always holds those beads, she says.

Yes, I say, picking up a clipboard, acting as if I'm busy. Alison studies me momentarily before speaking.

You know what happened today? she says. An eighth-grader tried to kill himself.

I put down my work.

Robbie Fuller. He's that big boy. He's not supposed to be in eighth grade—he's too old, but he keeps flunking.

What happened? I ask.

The ambulance came to get him. He ate a bottle of Tylenol and Jason found him in the boys' bathroom. They were going to pump his stomach, my friend told me.

That's terrible, I say.

She nods. Have you heard of Medjugorje? she asks, stumbling over the word's foreign syllables.

Still reeling from her first news, I am surprised again by this sudden change in subject, and I shake my head.

It's in Croatia. Mary came to some little children there, she continues. They call her Gospa. Lots of people go to see her there. My teacher told me about it.

I nod.

I wouldn't want Mary to come to me. Or God either, she says. Sometimes I pray to God, please God, please don't come to me, because I can't handle it.

She licks her fingers and smoothes her hair back again, and suddenly she seems to me all eyes—her eyes grown large with excitement and fear and uncertainty. And I feel it, too, this excitement and fear, and I realize how much she scares me. This eleven-year-old girl who believes God might come to her. Who converses easily with ninety-year-old sisters. Who knows how to pray with them.

She examines my face and something in her senses I am unsettled by her.

I have to catch my bus, she says.

And suddenly she is disappearing into the dimness of the far hall. The gentle tap of her shoes grows faint and ghostly.

These past days it is as if my life is only here in these dark corridors. I find myself eagerly waiting for this child to come down the hall, as she did yesterday, carrying the rose for sister. And last night, even at home, I thought about her. I imagined the girl brought roses for me, a bouquet of white ones, their buds perfectly closed and waiting. Only my thoughts turned dark, and I became trapped in the locked community room with the nuns dying around me one by one, staring at me, as if each were about to say something just as her eyes brightened and stilled. Out in the hall stood Alison with her roses, calling my name.

And today, for some reason, she did not come, and I'm missing her. And this feeling of loss is as sharp as when my youngest left home for good. I stand in the community room and watch Sister Virginia, watch her hand open and close over the rosary beads, her lips fluttering as if she is being kissed lightly. As I come near her, I hear the gentle drone of her voice.

Hail Mary, full of grace, the Lord is with thee.

I kneel beside her and place my chin on the arm of the chair.

Blessed art thou among women and blessed is the fruit of thy womb, Jesus.

I reach out to touch the beads and sister places her cold hand partly over mine. I grasp the beads—they are smooth and warm.

Holy Mary, mother of God, pray for us sinners now and at the hour of our death. Amen.

Amen, I say. But when I look up I feel myself fill with anger. How can this be so easy for you? I want to say. How? I stand up and wait for her to respond to me. But she does not stop; her fingers move to the next bead. And she begins again.

Alison has returned today with the sixth-graders' cards for the nuns.

Missed you yesterday, I say.

I was sick, she says. She enters the community room and distributes the cards. When she is done, she comes to my station.

Where is Sister Virginia? she asks.

I believe she's in her room, I say.

The phone rings and I answer it. It's Lisa, the pharmacist. She says there's a problem with a prescription for one of the nuns. The day has been full of these things, one problem after the next, and I have hardly had a chance to leave the desk. After a few minutes, Alison appears in front of me, waiting for my conversation to end.

I cover my end of the receiver. What is it? I ask.

Sister is dead, she says, and she turns before I can respond and walks back to Sister Virginia's room.

I tell Lisa I'll call back, hang up, and hurry to sister's room. When I arrive, Alison has already crossed the nun's arms over her chest and placed her carved wooden rosary beads in the woman's hands. On Sister Virginia's eyes lie pennies.

That's what they did to Abraham Lincoln when he died, she says. They put pennies on his eyes to close them and now he's on the penny.

I stare at her.

Like what happened with the cloth Veronica wiped Jesus' face with, she says. His face got on it.

We stare at each other. She looks so strong there on the other side of the dead nun. Sister Virginia between us, holding her rosary, her face peaceful around the pennies.

We should wait, I say, until Father Jeffrey decides about the last rites.

I lean over and take the pennies and sister's eyelids spring open again, her blue eyes staring directly into mine, and I stumble backward.

Don't be afraid, I say, my heart in my throat.

Of what? Alison asks.

Sister Mary George, the mother superior, closes the door to Sister Virginia's room. Everything is under control here, she says, why don't you go out and check on the girl? I'll call Sister Margaret and let her know what's happened.

I grab my coat and take the elevator down to the front door. I go outside where Alison is sitting on the steps, her knees drawn up to her chest, her uniform skirt gathered against her legs.

Your mother should be here any moment, I say.

She nods. He kissed me, she says.

Who did?

That big boy. The one who took the pills. He came into the cafeteria after school the day before he did that and he said, I want to show you something that feels good and he held my arms and he kissed me. She hesitates. With his tongue, she says.

I am silent. I realize that Sister Marie may not be the only one responsible for Alison's bruised arms.

It felt good, she says. Very soft.

She licks her fingers and touches her hair and stares at me.

Do you think he'll live? she asks.

I have heard nothing about the boy, but I nod. I think so, I say.

She gazes up at the third floor, and I look at her and she is ancient like the nuns listening for death at the edge of their prayers. She is young like their questioning eyes and innocent like their bodies. But she will feel no need to change the touch of flesh for the love of God. She will taste both again and again.

I think of sister's eyes, that wide, seeing blue, and wonder if the imprint of what she sees could be on the pennies, like the girl says, and I search for the two coins in my pocket, moving them through my fingers like sister would her beads. I know I am supposed to say something. I know I am supposed to say, Did he touch you anywhere else? Did he hurt you? I have rehearsed these questions for my own children's children. They are the right questions.

But instead I want to tell her something else. I want to tell her that this is the beginning. The beginning of love and pleasure. The beginning of loss. Because it is all so much harder than those questions. Harder than having husbands and making children. Harder than beads and prayers. But I imagine she knows it somehow. Or she will know it. When she looks back and counts the bruises. She will begin here. She will begin with the bruise on her left arm—one for the nun. And she will begin with the bruise on her right—one for the boy. And she will see the beginning—she will cry for it and she will laugh for it, too. And they will be here, their eyes bright for the coming darkness. And I will be here, too, my arms ushering them to the other side.

Dika Lam

New York University

JUDAS KISS

The woman would never forget the taste of his tongue, sharp and acidic and seasoned with lies, the push of her incisors as the pad of flesh gave way, her chomp traveling the sandwich of his taste buds, vessels, nerves.

It was over so quickly, cleaver-swift, that he hardly had time to struggle. Her lover's attempts were futile—the ineffectual hands barreling into her shoulders, the fingers that had come up to caress her cheek now clawing at her head.

Her jaws were the strongest vise in the world now, the blood too calm as the tip of his tongue tore off, as she savored the fragment, a treasure under the teeth. Aware of medical advances, the woman swallowed the flesh to prevent the likelihood of an emergency reattachment. It quivered a quick passage down her throat—a flapping, severed triangle that tasted of ham.

The whole process reminded her of childhood, like swapping gum, cherryraspberrystrawberry, like adolescent lipfumbling. As a little girl, she'd swallowed her gum by accident, she'd been about to speak and the tiny wad, creased like a brainbit, slid to the back of her mouth. The myth followed her into adulthood even though she knew it was untrue, the chants of her seven-year-old classmates ringing in her ears: *You know, gum doesn't dissolve, it stays in your stomach forever and ever.*

She'd swallowed her gum on the first day of convent school in England—a lofty, alien place, rows of identical children with wailing pink mouths. She'd clenched her fingers around her father's pant leg, eyes reddening as he deposited her with a teddy bear and a pack of Doublemint.

"You can come home on holidays," he reassured her, strong hands peeling her fingers from his leg. "Maybe you'll even have a nice new accent by Christmas."

In the dormitory she balled herself into the bunk bed to make herself smaller, limbs curling like broken ferns, jaws working furiously.

She hadn't intended to do her lover harm. At first.

"I can't wait to see you." The woman had cooed into the phone, one hand locked around a ball of paper. Blinking, she looked out her hotel window at the curve of the Mediterranean, the sparkle of the bay in the hot light, the slow pastel ripple of the roofs. She imagined the roughsoft symmetry of her lover's lips and breathed slowly, as if timing herself.

"Meet me in the usual place." Even then, it still gave her a jolt to utter the old clichés. She opened and closed her fingers, working over the already mangled note on peach-colored paper: *I know who you are. Stay away from my husband.* It had been waiting for her when she checked into the hotel.

Just minutes before, she had sat on the bedspread in her hotel room and prepared to cry large salty tears. She realized that the idea of weeping was repugnant to her, the tears blanching long soggy trails all the way down to the chin. It seemed absurd at her age. She permitted herself the luxury of a few dry hitches before calming her body with a deep breath and picking up the phone.

For years, she had come to the south of France for *rendezvous*, the word so unremarkable that she should have recognized the commonness of her situation. Her French was terrible, but she liked the environs of Nice because they appreciated all kinds of

bodies here, no use wearing slim-fitting black pants to camou-
flage her assets. On the beach she wore string bikinis, allowing
her hips and buttocks to assert themselves in the burning sun. It
was here, on the promenade, that she met him, and it was here,
by the side of the water, that she muted him.

It began two years ago. At a café he'd overheard her talking
to a friend over a bowl of fish soup. He said it was the sound of
her words that had lured him in the first place: the woman's
voice possessed a hybrid grace, as changeable as an actor's.
They shared similar backgrounds: he'd been a *dip kid,* son of a
diplomat, at home everywhere and nowhere.

But then it had become more complicated. The woman
came to crave the swirl of his unplaceable laughter, his expan-
sive gestures. She liked to watch him order his rare beef, his lob-
ster platters. She loved the red stretch of his smile.

She found herself wanting to live a little longer in his world.

When the woman reached the bar in Villefranche, he was
already there, surrounded by a circle of new friends. Arms waving, he was leading an old French drinking song. "*Chevaliers de
la table ronde . . .*"

"*Salut,* girl!" Her lover gathered her close, one hand offering
a long-stemmed rose. He was unintentionally tan, his face as
familiar as a brown paper bag, eyes cutsharp.

"How are you," she said.

"All's well here. All's well." He gestured to the bar, to the
happy patrons with their gleaming forks.

He was balding, but still solid in the midriff, where she
placed her hands. Against the white of his shirt, her fingernails
bright burgundy, as if lacquered in blood. His own hands were
fat and ringless, no trace of a tan line on the most important finger of all.

"Let's go for a walk on the beach," she said. She took the rose
and held it just under the crimson head, her fingers pinching
the stem.

At her second boarding school, the woman had memorized
facts about the faculty of taste: the tip of the tongue is reserved

for sweetness. Bitter substances are tasted at the back, sour at the side. The whole surface is democratically designed for the scattering of salt. Whenever she ate her favorite foods, she mulled over the partnership of flavors, the division of labor as the tongue worked its perceptive magic.

As her teeth slammed down that day, elation rang through her. She realized gleefully that she was taking her lover's capacity for sweetsense away from him. She was sure he would still be able to know bitterness, sourness. He would still dive into the Mediterranean and come up sputtering a mouthful of salt water. But he would no longer taste the pleasures of chocolate and honey, toffee and cake. His sweet tooth would ask for what it needed and he would answer it with numbness.

Later, in the hospital, her lover would scribble notes to the police on pieces of paper. He would try to convey his message in French before discovering he was no longer able. Attempts in his other languages—Spanish, Italian, Russian—failed him, and it was only in a fading English that he was able to write, "That was a real Judas kiss."

When the woman disappeared, her absence was absolute. The hotel had no record of her (she'd paid in cash). As for her wounded lover, he knew only that she traveled often, that it was always she who had left him billets-doux in his post office box. He realized he knew nothing about her.

When the local news corps interviewed the police, they said there were no leads. No women of her description had been seen in the area, no missing tongue had been found.

"Are you sure she swallowed it?" they asked the lover. "How do you know she didn't just pretend to swallow it? Maybe she threw it into the sea. Perhaps it will wash up with the tide."

The man shook his head, his mouth molten and crusted with blood.

"Aren't you glad she didn't bite off another part of your anatomy?" snickered the doctors.

The man's wife came to see him. Her anger was translated into the many zippers of her clothing—the closed teeth of her red skirt and jacket, the serrated slash of her pockets. She folded herself into the image of a vigilant wife, poised by his bedside, reading magazines.

The wife did not speak. She sat in a chair in the corner of the room, and her silence was the most deafening thing in the world.

On the airplane the woman's stomach flipped and flopped. She decided to forgo dinner, watching out of the corner of her eye as her seatmate stabbed at the dry pieces of his in-flight meal, arranged in four chambers like a porcelain heart. "Airsick?" he asked, smiling at her pale face before settling down with his magazine.

"All's well," she said, her lover's voice echoing in her head. She gave a start. The seat belt felt too snug all of a sudden, a boa constrictor around her belly. She unfastened it.

The woman was sure she could feel the tongue somersaulting inside, a freshly caught fish. It was not altogether unpleasant. The trapped wedge tickled her interior, reminding the woman of that species of stomach butterfly endemic to first dates. In the back of the plane, she found herself waiting in line for the restrooms, one hand clutching the head rest of an empty seat. She felt strangely pregnant, not that the woman had ever been pregnant in her life, just that one worrisome time in Rio when she had suspected and feared . . . but then *I have just swallowed a tongue,* she said to herself, calling to mind the beef tongue that her father's maid had prepared on holidays, the pimpled surface of that gray and filmy meat on the serving plate.

The door to the rest room opened and a middle-aged woman emerged, dressed in a crumpled linen suit and orange sandals. It occurred to her that she and the woman wore the same clothes, that they resembled each other in more ways than one, the veined and jeweled hands, the busy haze of russet hair. They looked affluently tired together, feet swollen with altitude, eyes dark and hard.

Airplanes were strange places—compressed societies where it was okay to reach out to strangers. She briefly considered saying something funny and comforting (*Hey, I like your suit?*) but the words died in her throat. On second thought, she was at thirty thousand feet in a closed tube—the loneliest place in the world.

As they crossed paths, both pretended not to notice their similar tastes in fashion. Perhaps this was her doppelganger, thought the woman. She'd heard of the dangerous double in literature and movies, but had always found the idea of a second self to be comforting.

In the tiny lavatory she splashed water on her face, dampened her hair, and opened her mouth in front of the mirror. Her teeth were as straight and inflexible as an army—peering at their whiteness, she did not know what she expected to see there. The woman thought of her ex-lover and his stunted tongue, like a red carpet gnawed raw. A laugh bubbled up from her, but instead of her usual high-staggered sound, she emitted a wet chuckle. The sound of her ex-lover's laugh. She gasped. The tongue danced in the hollows of her body. She draped one arm over her waist as if trying to hold herself in.

Back in her seat, the woman found herself ordering a martini. It was an odd decision—her drink of choice was usually a white wine spritzer. The cup, however, was cool and clean, the martini a silvery pleasure in the gullet. She pulled the olive off the stick and it rolled blithely onto her tongue, a green-tasting nub with a slash of pimiento. It was sour and heady.

After swallowing, the woman remembered that she hated olives.

She drank coffee on the Boulevard St Michel, savoring the bitterness of the liquid as it trickled down her throat. She had always been more familiar with the smell than the taste, recalling the steaming brew on the room service trays in Villefranche, remembering the vim and vigor flooding her lover's body with each addictive sip. Now she too felt the brightening. The drink drummed through the cloud of her fatigue.

After landing in Paris, she had decided to lie low for a time—purchasing dark clothes, investing in a headscarf, even coloring her hair black (dyeing it blond might have made her more noticeable). She did not dare to go home, where they might be looking for her. On the computers stringing the continents together, there would be a description of her, probably a photograph of a creased face hidden by a sun hat, a large pair of sunglasses, the mouth busy around a frozen yogurt or some such impediment to identification. She comforted herself with the likelihood that her lover owned very few pictures of her.

Thinking of lemon sorbet, the woman finished her drink and walked east along the quai. Strolling down the Rue St-Louis-en-L'Ile, she paused outside Berthillon, the famous ice-cream shop, and watched the tourists in line, their mouths heavy with melting flavors, fingers curled around rich cones.

She was surprised to feel nothing. The craving had left her. As she passed, one of the Berthillon workers winked and called out to her in French, don't you want any ice cream, and the words slipped from her lips, a torrent: *Non, ça va, monsieur, je ne fais que regarder.* There were other phrases that rose easily now, at the hotel, in the cafés and bars, in the Métro, whole conversations with attractive men in the Pyramide du Louvre. Twice now, she had led a few bars in her rendition of an old French drinking song. *Quand je meurs, je veux qu'on m'enterre dans une cave où il y a du bon vin! Mes pieds contre la muraille et ma tête sous le robinet!*

There was no doubt in her mind that the swallowing had been a blessing, a catalyst. With the ingestion of her lover's tongue, she had also eaten his lexicon, the chatter of worlds in the width of a single pink slice. With her daily dose of coffee, her increasing fluency, she felt a burgeoning power. Whenever she spoke, she could feel the tongue jigging and jogging in time to the foreign cadences.

She had been terrified at first by her newfound ability. Even the sound of her old voice had become as unreal to her as a manufactured fog. Instead of aching for a place to feel at home, she now itched to try her lingual abilities in Madrid, in Rome, in St. Petersburg.

Every morning she woke to see the sun painting the roofs of marble buildings, the glimmering necklaces of bridges. The outside world held the promise of pastries and the scent of baguettes. In the spring air, she even allowed herself to relax the requirements of her disguise. She removed her sunglasses to converse with young men. Her headscarf blew into the Seine while she was walking along the Pont Alexandre III, but instead of panicking, she took the time to admire the gilded figures at the top of the bridge.

She imagined her lover and his wife and wondered what he could possibly have to say to her now. She wondered if his wife was French, or perhaps South American. Women of a certain class looked the same all over the world, herself included, with a few variations in the degree of brassiness in the coiffure, in the frequency of designer logos dotting the body. Many of them were conversant in several languages.

As for the woman, she had always been stubbornly unilingual. Even in the international boarding schools of Switzerland and Germany, she had failed to acquire any new language.

The woman emptied her third glass of wine and set it on the table, the ruby residue contrasting with the white tablecloth underneath. Before her were the remains of a lavish dinner—crumbs of goat cheese, a pool of rare juice from her filet mignon, a few fries trailing coats of salt, a fork with tart crust clinging to its tines. The waiter was taking his time removing the evidence of her gluttony.

The tongue had affected her in other ways. Back in California, she had eaten all variations of spa food: steamed asparagus, wild rice, poached chicken breasts, with their skin stripped away to reduce the fat. Now, instead of seeking fish and quinoa grains, she wandered the boulevards looking for *steak frites*. She scooped up melted Brie with crackers and apple slices. She quaffed so much cabernet that her tongue was stained red.

By now the woman had grown accustomed to the urgings of the gem inside her belly—in moments of severe craving, it made her whole body shake like a jellied slab. At other times, it gently waltzed.

From across the room, she caught the gaze of a young man also dining alone—he looked like he was in his twenties, with pliable brown eyes and a chin-length sway of chestnut hair. A warm smile slid over her face and he was suddenly there, at her table.

Tu as faim? she asked, knowing that he had just ordered, that he'd been gnawing ravenously on a piece of bread. Normally, she would never ask a stranger, a mere boy, if he were hungry.

Tu parles bien français, he said, daring to use the familiar address, his breath redolent of ashtrays and lemon tea.

In his apartment, a student dwelling near Jussieu, they lay on the wood planks and shared a Gauloise. This was her first cigarette, an earthy plume in the throttle, somehow familiar and unfamiliar at the same time, the sensation sanctioned by the arbiter of taste in her gut. An image came to her—the uniformed girls of secondary school, bonding over the shared transgressions of tobacco and candy. She had never felt welcome to join them.

The woman smoked long and hard, remembering the sight of her old lover's fingers around a cigarette. Back then she'd noticed how it seemed like a live thing, a ghostly cylinder, one end glowing like a booster rocket. She studied the flaws in the ceiling.

Painfully aware of her age all of a sudden, she asked, *Je suis une femme d'un certain âge, ça ne te dérange pas?* It did not bother him, he replied, not at all. She curled her fingers around his smooth face and kissed him then, the first kiss since that fateful meeting of lips back in Villefranche, but just as she was savoring the Merlot-nicotine seasoning of his mouth, the tongue in her gut gave a violent snap.

She sat up. The tongue kicked her from within.

The student asked what was the matter, was it the issue of age, had he offended her in some way?

But it was the pain that concerned her now, the invader cutting out parts of her belly as if it were the beak of a caged bird. Doubled over, she placed her hand over her stomach and ran to the bathroom. She almost didn't recognize the face in the mirror—ashen, framed by a lightless mess of hair. The tongue fell quiet.

It doesn't approve, she murmured to herself, leaning on the sink for support. She felt the heat of the student's body as he came up behind her, his arms creeping around her waist.

Arrête, she said, pushing him away. Not too long ago, she would have welcomed any kind of embrace. The touch of strangers, especially, had always seemed the most familiar.

*   *   *

Before leaving for New York, the woman was so sure she would be stopped by the authorities that she took pains to secure a false passport—a French one, no less. At JFK, her mouth as dry as Styrofoam, she watched as the officer stamped her papers and waved her through. From there, a flight to L.A. Since the kiss with the Jussieu student, she had stayed away from men, careful to please the tongue inside. She indulged it with fatty foods, with pâté and puff pastry and exorbitant lunches. Its movements were a gauge of its mood—if it danced, it was happy, if it stung her, it was displeased. In an attempt to defy its taste, she had gone back to Berthillon and ordered two large sorbets. But when she lifted the first scoop up to her mouth, she vomited all over the sidewalk. For one hopeful moment, she thought she had rid herself of the tongue forever, but with the sense of her belly crinkling like a ball of foil, she realized it was still present. On the plane ride home, she fought the disconcerting urge to smoke a cigar. At the back of the in-flight magazine, her horoscope read: *Gemini, you are not alone.*

Home. The house where she was born, the father no longer alive, the maid long since replaced by an immigrant from Mexico who attended her from time to time. When she unlocked the door, all was quiet, everything a pale and peaceful space of open stairs and vistas of the ocean filling the plate-glass windows. When she set down her suitcase, it made a resounding thunk on the tile. Everything was sparkling and new to her—she wandered around the house touching sculptures and light fixtures and crying softly in the clean darkness.

Ready for sleep, she heard the Pacific lapping against the pillars under the house, the wash and pull of the tide as it slid over the sand. She had been away for less than two months, but the bed felt cramped and unfamiliar, giving off a smell of baby powder. She got out of bed and walked to the bathroom like a blind toddler, banging into walls before finding the light switch. Again the mirror. Again the stranger's face, older, more weathered (she made a note to dye her hair back to its natural coppery shade in the morning).

She stepped onto the bathroom scale and the needle swung to the right like a slap: an extra twenty pounds.

Naturally, she thought, all those unhealthy Gallic foods were responsible for that significant weight gain. How could she ever have worn string bikinis on the beach? Even her arms seemed to have gained the heft of small trees. She slept little, and more than once during the night, she found herself in the kitchen drinking hot cocoa and slamming Oreos into her mouth.

Over the next few days, the weight gain continued. She called to make an appointment with her hair colorist in Beverly Hills but was stunned by the babble in her ear. "Hello?" they repeated. "Is anyone there?" They could have been communicating in Morse code, their voices a series of clicks and burbles. She turned on the news to see if the police might be looking for her, but the experience was akin to watching a foreign newscast. She paced the house, enraged by the meaningless parade of magazines that turned up in the mailbox, uninterested in the books in the bookshelves, even the bookshelves themselves. The tongue had decided that the furniture did not speak to its likes, that the entire dwelling was too contemporary. She threw a vase across the room and it thudded onto the carpet, unbroken.

When the maid came to dust and vacuum, she seemed startled by the woman's presence.

"You're back!" said the maid, her inflection rising as if she were waiting to be proven wrong. Arms folded like a mother's, she stood smiling in the doorway, as comforting as sunlight in her pale yellow uniform.

The woman tore at her arm like a child. "Rosa, you must make me an appointment with the colorist. You must." The plea came out in a rain of Spanish, a bellowing growl that sank the woman's voice by a couple of octaves. Her hands flew up to cover her mouth, eyes widening. She made a small choking noise.

The maid's eyebrows lifted in surprise, her hand hovering over the woman's unfamiliar hair as if gauging a force field. Rosa took her employer by the elbow and led her to her room, where the woman dropped into a silken heap on the bed. It was already two P.M., and she was still in her bathrobe. Twisting and sobbing, she clutched at her abdomen. Next to her lay a paper bag from the drugstore.

"*Necesita un médico?*" asked the maid. "A doctor?" Rosa's face was cracked with worry, she smoothed back the woman's hair, tested her forehead for fever.

"No!" said the woman. "No doctors." She turned her face into the pillow as the maid leaned over, very slowly, and kissed her on the forehead. For a minute, the woman imagined herself back at the convent school in England, where one of the nuns was trying to comfort her.

Closing the door to the bedroom, Rosa sighed and picked up the phone in the hallway.

From a long way away came the sound of a calliope, the carousel at the Tuileries gardens back in Paris. A smile dragged across the woman's lips as she lay on the bathroom floor, the chilled tile edging into her back. Looking up at the ceiling, she craved a French kiss, a cigarette. As she lit one, she watched the smoke snake upward in time to the rhythm. The steamy wheeze of the pipes was receding now, replaced by the music of sirens. She knew they were coming for her, they would probably have a shrink and a couple of officers along, her demi-tongued lover in tow, maybe even his wife. It occurred to her that she was in no way ready to receive guests.

Lying on the floor was the bag from the drugstore, the crinkled paper retaining the shape of its former contents. Next to it, the shreds of a small box. In the middle of the tile, like a hopscotch stone, lay a small plastic wand.

Back in the old days, the rabbit would have died, thought the woman.

After a few minutes, she picked up the wand and stared at the accusatory cross in its telltale window, blinking a few times to see if it would change. It remained the same, a stubborn plus sign, no hint of metamorphosis. She sighed.

Under the humming of the fluorescent light, next to the gurgle and slush of the toilet, the woman heard the distant slamming of car doors, an arrangement of feet on gravel, then a trail of footfalls up to the second floor. Murmurs and mumbled orders. They knocked on the bathroom door, a quiet tap at first, then a vivid thumping as if they were beginning to remodel the house.

"Miss Price, this is the police. Are you all right in there? We would like you to come out so we can talk."

"Miss Price, may I call you Candice? This is Dr. Janice Boston. Rosa is here with us and she is very, very worried about you."

The words made absolutely no sense to her. She felt like she was listening to dolphintalk, to a rare recording of whalesong. At the same time, she liked the way their voices closed the spaces, stuffing the corners of the house, mixing with the sound of many shoes. She had never had many visitors as a child.

Rosa calling to her in Spanish, *I know you took the knife from the kitchen,* she was saying, *please I don't want you to hurt yourself.*

Oh yes, the knife, the woman remembered. Its flat blade lay coldly across her stomach where she had pulled up her nightgown. Like an obstetrician, she stared clinically, diagnostically, at her own belly.

Listening to the invisible gang outside the door, she thought of her lover's voice before realizing she could no longer remember his timbre, that Rosa's exhortations were the only ones that made sense—echoing the clear treason of her whisper when the maid had asked her if she needed a doctor, the maternal memory of her mouth as she'd planted a kiss on the woman's forehead.

She just wanted to be left alone, to deal with the problem by herself. This was no time for a child.

That was a real Judas kiss, thought the woman. She grappled with the knife, her fingers slowly darkening around the handle.

Laura E. Miller

University of New Hampshire

LOWELL'S CLASS

Once a week Paul Melczyk drives down from New Hampshire to Boston to teach a poetry workshop at the Cambridge Center for Adult Education. Despite his three books, his stints as poet-in-residence, his collection of small grants and prizes, he needs the meager check. But Paul finds the retirees in the Cambridge class refreshing. The course is about creativity, he tells them, and he brings musical tapes and postcards to the tiny overheated classroom.

Hurrying to the Cambridge Center from his overpriced parking space, he sometimes glimpses one or another young man rushing past in the other direction with papers spilling from a notebook, take-out coffee sloshing from a paper cup. These eager, scattered kids remind Paul of himself at twenty-two and twenty-three, when he still lived in Boston, when everything in his life felt like a train he was about to miss. He was a hayseed from the Midwest, a milk-fed Polish boy. In those days, in Boston, such things mattered.

After teaching Paul eats lunch at the Wursthaus, which has managed to survive the invasion of ferny salad bars throughout Harvard Square. There he eats the kinds of meals he rarely eats anymore—mixed grills, fried eggs with a side of sausage. This was where he used to eat, what he used to eat, on his salesman's salary. At the table he marks his students' manuscripts. He believes in offering encouragement where he can, and he's able to find something to admire in all his students' work. He has never believed that his job is to stand guard at poetry's gate.

Once, years ago, when Paul was leaving the Wursthaus, he passed his former teacher walking with a hive of students toward a Spanish restaurant on Brattle Street. Paul immediately recognized Lowell's loping walk, his wiry hair, and the eyeglasses that often seemed askew on his face. Lowell's boozy lunches have become legendary, with their countless pitchers of sangria and unchecked gossip about who ranks where in poetry's pantheon. Paul knows of these lunches mostly from others' published recollections. He himself was never in the group of privileged students. The day he saw Lowell, Paul ducked into a coffeeshop until everyone had passed. But at his apartment later, he tried to describe the moment in a poem: he imagined himself standing gloveless on a dark platform, while a train that carried Lowell and the others raced past him, belching smoke and blowing his hat onto the tracks. After dozens of false starts, Paul gave up. It would be years before he could write that poem.

From the Wursthaus, Paul usually goes on to the Grolier Poetry Book Shop on Plympton Street. When he was younger, he'd spent hours browsing in the Grolier, somewhat wistfully and a little lustfully, the way he used to look at the weight lifters' bodies in the back of Archie comics when he was a boy. His heart pounding, Paul would skim the latest issues of the *Partisan Review* and the *New Criterion,* trying to understand what his rivals possessed that he didn't—what got them into print and left him behind. Now whenever Paul goes into the Grolier, he can't help doing a little rearranging, shifting his latest collection so the cover faces out.

"You always seem angry after you go to Boston," his lover, Victor, said recently. "Like you have a score to settle."

"That's ridiculous," Paul snapped.

It isn't anger, but he can't say exactly what it is.

*   *   *

One day in the Grolier, a woman rushes over. She has wild gray curls and an open toothy smile. Paul knows he has seen her before—at a retreat, perhaps at a colony. While he's trying to place her, the woman exclaims, "Lowell's class! That's where I know you from. I'd know your face anywhere. But I'm afraid you'll have to help me with your name." Her stack of bangles clinks when she moves her arm.

"I'm Paul. Paul Melczyk."

"Of course. You've been making out like a bandit lately. I remember you perfectly. . . . You don't have the faintest idea who I am. That's okay. I'm Elaine Gruper."

Yes, he remembers her now. They were classmates in Robert Lowell's poetry workshop at Boston University. Suffering as he did from alternate bouts of thrall and terror in Lowell's class, he managed to learn only a few of his classmates' names.

They decide to head up Massachusetts Avenue to a Moroccan café on Brattle Street, one more holdout from the old days. Across the table from him, Elaine takes off her glasses and studies him. Her face is quite wrinkled now, but her smile is friendly. Her body is youthful in jeans and a dark sweater. He wonders how he seems to her. The creases in his own face always surprise him when he sees them in a mirror.

They talk about the small grants they've managed to receive, musing about how the fellowships always manage to come through just when they're feeling all washed up, when they're contemplating taking up a new trade. Elaine mentions her husband, so Paul mentions Victor, and she nods and smiles, as if he just answered a question she has had for years. Elaine's a good person, Paul thinks. We could have been friends. Once she had cornered him in a hallway and complained about Lowell's caste system. He is not proud of himself, but he rebuffed her then. Her naked hurt repelled him. She seemed dangerous. His female double.

"Well, amazingly, though he tried hard, Lowell did not crush my spirit badly enough to make me stop writing. After he died, my poetry took off. I started publishing here and there. I even received an award last year. The state gives a prize every year to an older poet whose work hasn't been sufficiently recognized. That's me all over. Older and not sufficiently lauded. I give readings, I visit schools. I see my grandchildren. It's fine."

"That was quite a class." Paul shakes his head.

"It was like boot camp."

"We're both still writing, anyway."

"We're both still alive," Elaine adds.

Paul thinks of Sylvia Plath in her schoolgirl cardigan and her muted rage. Anne Sexton, square-bodied and sexy in a bright chiffon dress, defiantly smoking forbidden cigarettes. People called Anne gay, before the word came to be used about men like him.

Sylvia Plath, dead. Anne Sexton, dead. And, of course, Lowell himself has been dead for more than twenty years.

Paul and Elaine sit quietly at the table. They listen to the North African music, a pulsing, intricate braid of flute, drum, and string. He used to come to this café and order mint tea, because that was all he could afford. Once he ended up following one of the waiters back to a shabby walk-up in Central Square.

"What was it that people always said in Lowell's class?" Elaine asks. "There's no 'you' in the poem. That meant you weren't writing about your psychoanalysis or how much you hated your family."

How could Paul possibly put himself in his work, with Lowell's stream of jokes about queers? One day, speaking of Auden, Lowell winked at the class. "You could call him precious. After all, he is a bit light in his loafers." Everyone looked down at the table, and one student let out an embarrassed guffaw that seemed to speak for all of them.

Of course, no one ever questioned him. It was the 1950s. It was Lowell's class.

In 1957 Paul took a bus from Cleveland to Boston. He arrived with two goals: to become a poet and to overcome his attraction to men. He was twenty-one and had graduated magna cum laude from Cleveland State. In his early years of college, he earned trophies as a varsity wrestler; his baby face belied his ferocity on the mat. His trophies sat home on his bedroom shelf. The larger of his two suitcases was filled with books.

He found a place on the back side of Beacon Hill. In 1957 one could live on the back of the Hill affordably. That was how wellborn Bostonians said it, referring to "the Hill" and using the impersonal "one." The year before Paul arrived, a girl was murdered in a building one block away from his apartment.

Paul got a job as a salesman at Jordan Marsh selling suits to men who held managerial positions in the financial district. He learned the difference between pinstripe and chalk stripe, between herringbone and Harris tweed. He learned when to recommend single-breasted and when to suggest double. When business was slow, Paul wrote lines of poetry on discarded shirt cardboard. He envisioned the men as gladiators, suiting up to do battle in buildings of steel and glass.

So many men. Many of them were young, with bodies made muscular from tennis or rowing. When these men stood in front of the three-way mirror for their fittings, Paul marked their shoulders and the tapering of their waists in chalk on the fabric. When his hand brushed powerful leg muscles under gabardine, he often dropped the chalk.

Nights he sat at an ink-stained desk that he had bought secondhand and tapped out poetry on a Royal portable. Writing, he became Osiris! He was Thor! He threw bolts of lightning. He flew over the earth with wings on his heels. When he did leave his room, he went to readings in libraries and in university lecture halls. He made himself stay for the sherry hour afterward and introduce himself to the featured poet. Three parts terror and one part hope, he left carbon copies of his recent poems with Allen Tate and William Carlos Williams. *Who do you think you are?* A voice, possibly his father's, challenged inside him.

Without poetry, he knew he wasn't much: a second-rate suit salesman with pansy tendencies.

Paul had been living in Boston for over a year when the call came. The city had revealed itself to be a cold place, unwelcoming to strangers, as he'd been warned back in Cleveland. Usually, it was his mother calling, to give him the phone number of a girl she knew of in Boston, the daughter of a neighbor back home. Or she called to ask if he needed money, whether he was still thinking of law school. Paul's only response to her tentative kindness was anger, and often he snapped at her. But that night it was one of the poets calling. Paul had left his manuscript with him some weeks earlier.

Sometimes Paul imagined that his work had been deemed so promising it was submitted for a prize without his even knowing. In his fantasy, he found acceptance letters waiting for him on the radiator where his landlady left his mail. At other times, Paul swung into despair; he imagined the latest poet having a good laugh over his manuscript with friends at a bar. *Who do you think you are?*

As it happened, the poet was calling to recommend a workshop at Boston University, taught by his good friend Robert Lowell.

"Robert *Lowell*?" Paul repeated.

Years later Paul would describe that poet's phone call as his invitation to *a country of crevasses and granite fathers. He lacked the necessary gear.*

"I can write a note of introduction for you," the poet said to him on the phone. "Send him your work, but fix the typos first. Cal, of course, cannot spell himself, but I do advise you to put your best forward."

Lowell's friends called him Cal, short for Caliban from *The Tempest*. Others said it was short for Caligula. To Paul he remained simply Lowell. A monument.

On the first day of Lowell's class, Paul slipped into a seat close to the door. Under his jacket his shirt clung to his damp back; it had been no small feat talking his boss into letting him rearrange his schedule in Men's Suits. On his way over to the university, he'd gulped down a hot dog from a vendor, and now he burped silently, retasting the relish. A dark-haired woman across the table let out a smoke-scarred laugh as he arranged his books.

"Smart kid. Always sit near the exit." She lit a cigarette.

Paul soon learned that her name was Anne Sexton and that

she was publishing everywhere. She cavalierly defied the university's no-smoking rule.

Lowell swept into class a few minutes after two. His hair was wild, his jacket bunched up under the pile of books he carried. His eyes, magnified behind glasses, surveyed the silent group. Then he opened his Oxford collection and began to read. Lowell's voice was surprisingly indistinct and passionless, a hybrid of broad Boston vowels and southern drawl. With his fullback's body and straight-on stare, Lowell filled the classroom. The other students sat with their pens laid out beside their notebooks like surgeons' tools.

" 'Felix Randal the farrier, O is he dead then? my duty all ended / Who have watched his mould of man, big-boned and hardy-handsome / Pining, pining till time when reason rambled in it and some / Fatal four disorders, fleshed there, all contended?' Of course, the poet is. . . ." Lowell lit a cigarette and gestured impatiently with it.

"Swinburne?" someone offered.

"Tennyson?"

Each class session would open like this. No one said hello or good-bye. Poetry was a perpetual motion machine. Lowell stabbed the page in the book with his finger and asked: What is Hopkins doing here? What sort of sonnet is it? Why an Italian rhyme scheme? No one answered. They were dumbstruck by the volley of questions. Paul scribbled in his notebook. He had never heard of a farrier.

What do we know of Felix Randal from the poem? Yes, but what do we *know*? Why choose one word over another? Questions piled on questions. Lowell turned toward the window, squinting out at New England's legendary fall leaves and the dull brown ribbon that was the Charles River after a dry summer. Then he turned and rested his hands on the table, leaning into the group. He held forth about the fierceness of Hopkins's religious belief and how Felix Randal's magnificent, monstrous power was broken only by his subjugation to God's will. Lowell spoke of Randal's physical suffering as his pathway to grace.

"I think we've mangled Mr. Hopkins enough for now." Lowell suddenly closed the book and lit another cigarette.

* * *

In New York and San Francisco, Paul knew, poetry was turning itself inside out. Rhyme and meter were passé. Allen Ginsberg and Gregory Corso were writing jazzy, nervy manifestos that upended Paul's understanding of what poetry was. In the face of these developments, Lowell talked about Mr. Hopkins or Mr. Stevens as if they were headmasters at a prep school. In class he could puzzle for an hour over the placement of a single word. The students sat in stunned silence, except for a tall woman named Sylvia Plath. She'd recently joined the class and was married to a famous English poet, and she knew everything. Still she kept up a nervous habit of flaking the paint off her pencil with her thumbnail when she spoke. Paul scrawled lines, citations, references to other poets in his notebook. He didn't believe he would ever catch up.

In class Lowell read student work aloud as well. Each week he riffled through the pile of manuscripts in his hand, with a tired, almost bored expression. Paul could hardly swallow: Please not me. Please let it be me. Let it be good. When Lowell liked something, he lingered on it; his voice caressed it.

"This has a bit of Baudelaire in it," he might muse.

"Here. This line," he might whisper. "Keep that. It has a certain odd music."

"Where are you in this piece?" Anne Sexton often asked in discussions of Paul's work.

"A long time ago, I had a workshop so tough, I swallowed a bottle of Maalox each week before class met," Paul always tells his students on the first day of his workshop. They nod at him, afraid to laugh.

"All of us sweated blood for the teacher, and he'd shuffle through the pages to see who was going to come up for critique. So casual. He was like those girls on TV who pick the winning lottery numbers."

Paul goes for levity. He means to reassure his students that in his class they have nothing to fear from him.

After class one day, a skinny woman with frizzy hair and tense, peering eyes grabbed Paul's sleeve and began walking with him down the hall. "I came here to write poetry, and what do I get? Rush Week."

Paul glanced at her in bewilderment. He had forgotten the woman's name.

"You know what I mean. There are two kinds of students in this class. The chosen and us. He encourages *them*. He tells them where to send their work out. You and I are just as good as the others. He just worships Sylvia Plath's Seven Sisters background. But I'll tell you something: she isn't any better than the rest of us. Her poetry is bloodless."

Paul had nothing to say to this woman, who, in her desperate eagerness reminded him of the garment wholesalers who called on his boss in Men's Suits and showed off the fabric by rubbing it between their stubby thumbs and fingers. Paul could not let himself sink with this woman into the cesspool of unchosen poets. He said, "I'm only here to write."

"So am I. So are we all. I paid my tuition like everyone else, so I don't appreciate it when there are lunch parties and office hours and I'm not told about them." She leaned into him. "Can I ask you something? Where did you go to college?"

Paul and the student—Elaine Gruper, he finally remembered—paused at the building's exit. Outside, rush-hour traffic streamed past.

"I went to Cleveland State," he replied.

"Aha! My theory is right! It's a matter of pedigree. I went to Brooklyn College myself. I had immigrant parents. I don't have a Peck & Peck wardrobe. But I work hard. So do you. Sylvia Plath doesn't fart perfume, okay?"

"Look," Paul cut her off. He was afraid of the revelations to which this conversation might lead. He could not afford them. "I don't care who went where or what pedigree anyone has. I'm only here to write."

In February one of the other salesmen from Jordan Marsh invited Paul to double-date with him and his girlfriend at Mount Ida's Valentine's Day dance. "Hey, maybe you'll get lucky," Mort, the salesman, ribbed him. "You sure look like you could use it."

The dance had gone fine. Paul had stepped on Patty's foot only twice. He remembered to bring her a glass of punch and a couple of cookies from the refreshment table, which had been littered with hundreds of small paper hearts. He remembered not to prattle on about poetry and to ask her about her interests, as "Dear Abby" always recommended. After the dance, Mort drove the four of them down to Cape Cod, where his family had a summer place. In the car, they passed around a bottle of whiskey.

Paul slouched next to Patty on the sofa in Mort's family's cottage. Mort and his girlfriend, Lynette, had disappeared into a bedroom with a pile of blankets and a rusty electric heater. Patty sat hunched in her wool overcoat, while on the radio Ethel Merman belted out "Everything's Coming Up Roses." She had the dreamy gaze, Paul thought, of girls too self-conscious for glasses. Things could now go only in one direction. Earlier when he'd been dancing close with her, he had started to get aroused. He reached over to the end table and turned off the lamp. Maybe he would, after all, get lucky.

Paul knew what to do, or the mechanics of it. His brother, Eddie, had filled him in on the particulars of tits and pussies. Paul had kissed some girls after high school dances, after group dates to the movies. He had slid his hand under their sweaters, surprised to feel the bare skin jumping at his touch. Now he reached under Patty's overcoat and eased the zipper down through the taffeta of her powder blue dress. He began to slip the coat from her thin shoulders.

"Jeepers, your hand's freezing!" She shuddered.

"I'll warm you up soon."

Paul pressed his mouth hard against hers, hoping that the pressure would light his lust, the way a match set off a poof of flame on a gas stove.

"Whoa. Easy does it," she said. She pulled away and then began kissing him more lightly. The match lit, small but warming. He slipped his hand down her back, opening the zipper a little more. He eased her into a reclining position on the couch.

When he kissed her, a warm somnolence spread over him, but he didn't feel the sharpness and urgency that he felt when he thought about the lean, muscular bodies of men. Kissing Patty, Paul was distracted by the roughness of her wool coat against his arm. He wondered how much longer he could bear selling suits, when he would finally write the poem that would spring him from mediocrity. He tried to keep his mind on Patty. She was a perfectly nice girl with pretty red hair. He wondered, why not her?

Patty sat up and pulled her coat back over her shoulders. "I'm sorry," she said. Her elaborate hair arrangement, done up for the dance, had slipped.

"What for?"

"We don't have to keep doing this if you don't want to."

"Don't be silly." Paul brushed her hair off her forehead. In truth, it was a relief just to sit.

"It's okay." Patty reached up and wiped her eyes with the back of her hand. "I know Lynette's a lot prettier than me."

"Hey. No. That's not true." Paul folded his arms around her. Patty continued to wipe her eyes. Paul didn't know what to say, so he just held her. They sat through "Wake Up Little Susie," and then through a song by the Shirelles.

Driving back to Boston, Mort steered the car with one hand and kept his other arm draped around Lynette. "Love me tender," Elvis Presley implored on the car radio. In the backseat, Patty sat far from him and stared out the window. Paul knew he should reassure her, take her hand, do the kind of things people did on dates, but he didn't touch her. He doubted now that anything—even a red-haired college girl—would cure him.

Later, back in his room, Paul made himself a cup of instant coffee and began writing a sonnet about Patty. He transformed her into a goddess who levitated above the mundane paper hearts of the Mount Ida dance like Botticelli's Venus on her clam shell—Patty, who had avoided his kiss when he walked her to her door.

The disappointments of the evening faded as he wrote. Patty's light blue gown became nothing less than a cerulean swatch of sky from a distant part of the world, a magical place where it never got dark. He gave Patty Venus's baleful face, a face which seemed to apprehend but also to forgive man's folly. He worked on the sonnet through the night. The next day at work, his head was cottony from sleeplessness, and he failed to hear his customers' questions.

"Looks like Patty came through for you after all, my man," Mort remarked when they were both in the storeroom. "You going to call her or move on to greener pastures?"

Nights Paul sat up with the poem. He named it "For Patty, Who Believes She Lacks Beauty." Each night he worked like a jeweler, selecting each word, laboring over its placement, and then polishing, polishing. He'd read more soppy, breathless love poems than he cared to count. Paul swore he would never himself produce such bathetic rubbish. He believed he had glimpsed and captured Patty's goodness and her human frailty. He had honored her with a piece of work that was generous of spirit and flawlessly made.

Paul brought the finished work in to Lowell's class. That day discussion of Yeats's "Easter 1916" dragged on for over an hour. How does Yeats create the furious motion? How come the repetitions of phrase work here, when they so often fall flat in lesser work? Lowell paced the room while he waited for answers, bumping the table once. He bounced his pen on the table as he scanned the lines until the pen slipped from his fingers and rolled away.

"Someone in class has written a similarly powerful work," Lowell said, closing his Oxford collection. "A whirlpool, I'd call it. It has such a fantastic energy. Yes, there are some slips here, some off rhythms, but listen to this, if you would."

Lowell frowned and riffled through the pages of student poetry in his hand. Paul felt his heart knocking against his ribs. Was it possible that "For Patty" would be his breakthrough poem, the one that would set him free? "Ah!" Lowell lifted a sheet from the rumpled pile. He began reading in a hoarse voice that contained the coiled rage of Anne Sexton's words. Paul put down his pen and listened.

In the poem Anne described her mind as a cracked mirror,

then as a fishbowl, swollen to nightmarish proportions. The shattered glass and funhouse distortions in the early lines gave rise to images of stars and then, finally, to a vision of healing and renewal.

After Lowell finished reading, Sylvia's shoulders sagged. Her lips disappeared into a hard smile.

"It's brilliant," said the man with a thin face and shadows under his eyes. Paul knew that he was an editor at Houghton Mifflin: a fugitive from his job, as Paul was from Men's Suits. "I can't say I've heard anything like it."

"I agree. I'd say this is quite new, very much itself," Lowell replied. "Whereas some of you are still persisting with writing pretty words that say nothing."

Again Lowell shuffled through the pile of poems. Paul's mouth went dry. Carefully made did not necessarily mean empty, he told himself. He had labored over this sonnet. He had handpicked every word. When Lowell began to read, Paul heard the lines of his poem, but now the rhymes, with which he had wrestled long into the night, sounded obvious and singsong. Lowell was ruining it on purpose, Paul thought, the way he read it in his droning voice. Lowell was making him sound like an idiot. As Lowell read on, Paul saw that his pileup of adjectives—*seraph-sewn, moon-kissed, star-blessed*—was mannered and overdone. There was no subtlety, no courage in the writing. Worst of all, Patty wasn't present at all; she was bits of silk and porcelain. His poem was lifeless. A sterile museum piece.

"What can we say about this?" Lowell asked.

A long silence followed.

"It's very nineteenth-century," the man with the goatee ventured.

Sylvia Plath spoke through a clenched jaw. "I detect the spirit of Empson. In a line or two."

"It feels distant, though. It's all description and no feeling."

Paul rested his palms flat on the table so that no one could see how his hands shook.

"It's all sensibility. And manufactured sensibility at that," Lowell agreed.

"No joke. He beat the poor words into submission."

"It's almost a parody of the genre," said the Houghton Mifflin editor.

"It's not a real woman he's writing about. He's making love to a china figurine!"

That was Elaine Gruper. She had had it in for him ever since she had cornered him several weeks earlier in the hallway.

So the verdict was in: his work was all sensibility. All decor. Adolescent claptrap.

"Paul!" Anne called out to him as the students were walking down the corridor after class. "Sylvia and I are going to the Ritz. You look like you could use a drink."

Paul crumpled his copy of "For Patty, Who Believes She Lacks Beauty." Across the top, Lowell had simply printed "NO." Before climbing into the backseat of Anne's car, he dropped the crumpled ball of paper onto the sidewalk.

Anne was a wild driver, swinging wide turns into narrow streets, passing everyone, leaning heavily into the horn. "Jesus!" Sylvia laughed. Her laugh, deep and ferocious, surprised Paul. In an alley behind the hotel—an illegal spot—Anne jammed on the brake.

Inside the hushed red-carpeted bar, Paul looked down at his scuffed shoes. He looked up again and ordered a martini, his first.

"Here you are, sir." The young waiter was eager and obsequious, the way Paul often felt while working in Men's Suits.

He stirred his martini, suave as Cary Grant. His first sips recalled the taste of cod-liver oil, but then the warmth coursed down to his feet. Piano music rippled over from across the room.

"What on earth are you drinking now?" Sylvia peered at Anne's tall glass.

"A Sea Breeze. In honor of Paul's joining us." Anne glanced at her watch. "Two hours before my date with Dr. Orne. Paul, you don't see a shrink, do you?"

Paul shook his head. Witches, twelve-fingered, cackling women haunted Anne's work. She had written of being strapped down for shock therapy. And in the poem that Lowell had read in class earlier, she dared to show herself as bloated, cracked, freakish. When Paul was growing up, there had been the gamut of straitjacket jokes among the kids on his block, the finger twirled around the ear. If someone's relative was truly crazy, no one spoke of it at all.

Anne said, "So, Sylvia, what's the verdict on our professor?"

"He has been very nervous lately." Sylvia looked up from her martini glass.

"I don't think he's written anything at all this year."

"A *year.* My God."

"I wonder when it's going to happen this time."

"When what's going to happen?" Paul had finished his drink. He felt looser. Beside him, Anne tilted her head back and took the last swallow of her Sea Breeze.

"When he snaps." Anne held up her empty glass and tapped it for the waiter.

"Snaps?" Paul asked.

"Don't you know? Lowell's mad as a March hare. He has a lifetime membership at McLean Hospital."

Paul looked searchingly at Sylvia.

"He has been quite jumpy." She chewed her olive.

"So you can't hold him responsible for the way he is in class. Not completely. Where the hell is that waiter?" Anne craned her head toward the bar.

"He likes *you,*" Paul said.

"I'm crazy, he's crazy. Together, we're a corporation of crazies, right, Sylvia?"

The two women threw back their heads and laughed. Sylvia broke her martini stirrer in two.

Paul sipped his new drink and sat back and listened to Anne and Sylvia discuss other poets whose work Paul had read in magazines, comparing his own meager talent with what lay in print before him. Anne lit what was probably her thirtieth cigarette. A dirty old man, she decreed as one name or another came up. A suck up. She blew out her match and flicked it in the teeming ashtray.

When the waiter came by with the third round, Paul pulled out his wallet and checked his bills. He still had groceries to buy, his rent to pay. Anne rested her hand on his. "Put that away.

Think of it as keeping company with two loony poetesses."
Sylvia smiled. After several martinis, her smile seemed wider
and more genuine.

Anne and Sylvia discussed their classmates. Sylvia called
Elaine Gruper "a rather ferretlike person." She and Anne had
such unassailable faith in their own talent! Such breezy disdain
for others!

"Don't mind us. We're terrible gossips." She rested her hand
on Paul's thigh. "Listen. Don't be discouraged." Anne tapped
Paul's wrist with her manicured hand. "Jesus, that line in your
poem today. When you look into that girl's eyes and see the
man you'll one day be. That was a lovely moment."

Years later, after Anne had gassed herself in her car, Paul
would always remember this kindness that she extended to him.
Outside the Ritz, she gave him a sloppy, vodka-scented hug. To
his surprise, Sylvia also hugged him, though stiffly; their bodies
hardly touched.

On the street Paul nearly walked into a woman who was loaded
down with shopping bags. When he signed the lease, his landlady had warned him that she didn't want any trouble, and now
he could barely walk in a straight line. When he passed under a
movie marquee, he decided to sober up inside.

He entered during the opening credits for a Busby Berkeley
musical. It was the dinner hour, so the theater was almost
empty. The air was stale with old cigarettes. His thoughts about
the afternoon drifted like clouds, floating away before he could
get hold of them. Was the world of poetry really one of petty
rivalries and lecherous madmen, as Anne and Sylvia had suggested? Was madness a prerequisite for success?

The chorus girls in the film opened and closed their legs,
forming grotesque flowers. Paul could not grasp the flimsy
excuse for a plot. Time passed, and he felt himself starting to
doze. Jerking awake, he was now aware that someone had
slipped into his row and taken the seat beside him. It was a man,
and he sat with his legs open, claiming his space without apol-
ogy. The man sat with his knee mere inches from Paul's. Paul
did not bother to move his leg.

The man inhaled, and his shoulders seemed to expand sideways so that they, too, nearly grazed Paul's own.

On the screen, chorus girls in thick plumage careened down a slide, one after another. They blew kisses to the audience with giant darkly painted lips.

Suddenly the man's knee pressed against Paul's. Paul felt his heart jump in alarm, but he did not move his leg. The heat from the man's touch spread over Paul's entire body. He knew the martinis had slowed him down. He was also recalling Anne's breezy touches back at the Ritz. And maybe, at that moment, he just knew. Paul and the man beside him inhaled, then exhaled in unison.

Paul leaned forward to whisper that he would be waiting in the bathroom, but the man held out his arm and pushed Paul gently back in the seat.

There were only a few scattered individuals in the rows in front of them, all men. Smoke rose from their cigarettes in dusty rings. No one turned around, not even when Paul gasped with excitement and terror. No, he breathed. Then yes. Paul never thought it would go like this, with no words exchanged, no names. The man found Paul's zipper and opened it with one deft stroke. He kept his left arm draped on the empty seat beside him, as if embracing a phantom girl.

All Paul knew of the man at the movie theater were his broad thighs in khaki and the odor of his breath. He knew that if he saw him on the street he would never recognize him. After he got home, he tossed his stained trousers in the garbage. Sissy. Fruit. Queer. Fairy. Faggot. Those were the words the boys on his old street had for men like him, miming limp wrists and mincing walks. He knew that men like him got beaten senseless and left for dead in alleys.

Work was unbearable. Mort had been throwing him funny looks lately. Paul suspected that Patty had talked to Lynette. And twice in one week his boss yelled at him for mistakes he'd made in writing up receipts. Nights Paul sat up and could not write a word. He read through each poem he had written for Lowell's class. He had written about patina-covered statues of war heroes, about battles in the *Iliad*. He'd tried some sonnets about World War I. Knockoffs of Wilfred Owen. "Derivative," Lowell had dismissed in his blocky print. "Tone deaf." Paul knew his work was not worth using to line a birdcage.

Lowell, Paul fumed. He had scrimped for months to come up with the tuition. He'd had to do some fast talking to get the time off from Men's Suits, and his boss had agreed only after Paul promised to work every Saturday in exchange. Paul had signed up for Lowell's class in good faith. Not for name-dropping. Not for the interminable free-associating. Elaine Gruper had been right all along, only she glared at him in class now like he was Senator Joseph McCarthy himself.

One day, on the day that Lowell was rumored to keep office hours, Paul decided to call in sick at work and walk over to the university. He'd demand that Lowell tell him what he was missing, what it would take for him to become a poet. After all, that's what he'd paid for. Storming over to Boston University, he nearly knocked into an old man with a cane, who was out for a stroll in the Public Garden. By the time Paul arrived on campus, he had worked himself into a keenly focused rage. He rapped on the opaque glass of the office door.

When Paul entered, Lowell's face looked rumpled, as if he'd been sleeping, as if he'd forgotten exactly who Paul was.

"Yes?" Then, "Paul. Sit down."

Paul remained standing, with his arms crossed over his chest. If he sat, he might not be able to say what he had come to say. He blurted out, "Professor Lowell. I . . . I am confused. I'm trying my best, but . . . could you tell me, what am I doing wrong?"

"Sit down, Paul. Please." Lowell took off his glasses and rubbed his eyes. They looked sunken, the way Paul's father's eyes looked when his asthma was acting up. "Writing a good poem is much more than meter and rhyme. The poet is putting them at the service of something that is best described as alchemy. I hardly understand it myself. Why do you want to take up with such a difficult thing?"

Paul sat down in the wing chair that faced Lowell's desk. On the desk was a pile of worn books and an ashtray filled with mashed-out cigarette butts. "I don't know." Paul's words came out a whisper. He cleared his throat and tried to speak again. "I've always loved words."

"Yes. Good. That's a start."

Lowell sighed. Paul noticed that flecks of spittle had dried in the corner of his mouth.

A girl in a sweater set burst into the office. Paul had seen her before, among the group that went places with Lowell.

"Just a minute," Lowell said sharply to her. Paul realized he had lost him; his gaze had traveled over to the girl. Instead of leaving, she leaned her hip against the door frame and announced, "Everyone's waiting downstairs. Ciardi's here."

Lowell turned back to Paul and put on his glasses. "My apologies. We can talk another time. I wish I could invite you along, but, you see, we already have too many people."

Go out and play. Get out of here with your goddamn questions.

It was early April but freakishly hot. Lowell had just finished reading Auden's "Musée des Beaux Arts," and the class sat silently, stunned by the heat. Paul shifted in his chair, and Elaine Gruper looked up from her book and glared at him.

"What do you make of this?" Lowell asked. He, too, seemed undone by the false summer. His hair hung limp and greasy over his forehead, yet his eyes blazed, enormous behind his glasses.

Anne slipped off her spectator pump and tapped her cigarette ash into it.

Paul stared at the last stanza of the Auden poem, where the clipper ship sails on toward the fortunes that await its passengers. Icarus's white legs disappear into the sea. The forsaken cry goes unheard.

"It's almost childish, the 'doggy life' in the first stanza. Why is it so effective here?" Lowell waited. His cigarette remained unlit in his mouth.

The class ventured suggestions about the juxtaposition of the mundane and the miraculous. Humble daily activities versus an otherworldly event. Lowell frowned. Nothing anyone offered was the answer he was looking for.

"What about our view of Icarus's fall? Why show the aftermath and not the fall itself? Paul, any ideas? After all, you came to me last week wondering how to write a poem."

Paul rubbed his head. He was still not sleeping well.

"What does it mean? What do you see? A simple question, is it not? Of course, you are familiar with the Breughel work?" Lowell circled over and stood beside him.

Paul rested his pen on his open notebook. He had seen a reproduction in an art history textbook. "I've seen it."

"So what is it about then? Tell me, what exactly did they teach you back in Cleveland, anyway?"

Paul's voice was calm in his ears, though his hands trembled beneath the tabletop. "What one sees is a pair of legs vanishing into the water. Just like Auden says. People are working. Having picnics while he disappears."

"More." Lowell leaned in so that his face confronted Paul's. "Come on. Auden may be an old queer, but we aren't splitting the atom here."

Something snapped inside Paul. Lowell's voice faded beneath the roaring in his ears. The furies dove into his body like bats, dark and insensible as Achilles' wrath. He felt his wild double leap up. "What do you want from me, anyway? For Christ's sake, tell me! Every week, it's one question after another. What does it mean? You tell me!"

He could feel his Oxford collection fly out of his hand, could hear it smack the wall.

In truth, Paul only got up from his seat and left, quietly closing the door behind him. In the corridor he punched the wall again and again. His fist made no sound at all when it struck the polished brick. Several hours later, a large blue bruise would bloom over his knuckles. Paul walked out the building, down Commonwealth Avenue, leaving his Oxford collection on the table in Lowell's classroom.

Years later when Paul was in San Francisco watching an Italian film, he found himself suddenly overcome with emotion. In the movie a stonecutter carved an angel for a child's grave. At night the angel came to life and flew up like a dove, free from the stone foundation that kept it tethered to the earth. Paul began to weep in the dark theater.

It had been like that when he began to write again. After

Lowell's class, he had nearly ten silent years. During that time, words had no special weight or color or sheen for him. They were merely functional, uniform as boxcars, like the men he met occasionally in the bathroom of the Boston Public Library, with no names exchanged. When he finally sat down to try to write again, the words he used were simple: street games, the names of different weaves of wool. After many rusty months, his lines took off at last, lighter than air. He had broken free from the formalism, all the contemplation of Lowell's class. Yet sometimes he could hear Lowell's voice guiding him, helping him find the music and strip the lead. The Lowell who queried him was exacting but gentle, the teacher that Paul had needed so fiercely and who the real Robert Lowell—Cal, Caliban, Caligula—could not be.

Paul published *Night Scull.* Several poems in the collection lingered on the grace of men's bodies: rowers on the Charles, a vendor in Mexico City who broke coconuts with a machete. He wrote, finally, about being jerked off in the dark of a movie theater. He wrote about being yanked from bed on winter mornings to fill the living-room heater with kerosene. He wrote about the heaviness he'd felt in his legs as a boy, when he crossed the train tracks behind St. John Avenue. Lie down, lie down, the train's approaching whistle lured him: a deadly siren song.

It was 1975. Both Anne and Sylvia were dead. One day his publisher forwarded a letter from a New York address.

"Dear Paul Melczyk," he read. "I was quite pleased recently to come across your book. I am glad to see that you have retained your fine formal control and have added a courageous candor. When one of my students finds his voice as a poet, it fills me with a humble sense of gratitude that I was able to shape his development, no matter how small my influence might have been."

"It's from Robert Lowell," Paul said aloud.

Paul's lover asked, "The crazy guy who made you not write for ten years?"

"Dear Professor Lowell," Paul wrote. "You taught me everything I know about the craft of poetry. I only regret that I could not appreciate it at the time."

Unctuous, he decided, a slobber job. He began again.

"Dear Mr. Lowell. In class, you wanted more of me, more *confession*. Who I was, who I am, is queer. How could I write about that when, week after week, all you showed was your disdain for homosexuals with your constant cracks and innuendos?"

"Dear Professor Lowell," he tried again, "I realize I needed things from you that were perhaps unreasonable for a student to expect from his teacher. I had no idea that you were suffering and that you were ill."

Paul had heard: Lowell collapsed in class several weeks after Paul had dropped out. Over the years he kept getting better and slipping under again; they all did. The last time Paul heard Anne Sexton read, her rich voice had been ruined by drink, or medication, or some lethal combination of the two. She could not remember who he was when he came up to see her afterward.

"Dear Mr. Lowell. Please answer this question: Is spreading pain, rather than offering guidance, or a loving touch, a necessary teacher?"

Months passed. Paul heard through the poetry grapevine: Lowell was deteriorating. During a PEN luncheon, he had been seen with his hand halfway down a woman's blouse. Lowell died one day in a New York City taxi before Paul could figure out what it was he wanted to say.

"I don't know what I would've done if I'd received a letter from him. Of course, I reached fame and fortune after his death." Across the table from him in the café, Elaine flashes a rueful smile. She creases her napkin.

"I wish you and I had known each other," Paul says. "You tried to reach out once, and I behaved like a first-rate jackass."

"I know a thing or two about teaching. If he had been a different kind of instructor, it would have been easier. He didn't encourage us to act decently to one another." Elaine grabs the bill from his hand. "Paul, no. Coffee's on me!"

They leave the café and wander down Brattle Street, peering into window displays of minimalist and unimaginably expensive housewares. They pass the Spanish restaurant, which Paul had seen Lowell approach with his chosen students forty years ago. He and Elaine walk on in silence, exhausted from talking but not yet ready to part. The street musicians have claimed their places on the sidewalk. African drumming gives a jazzy backbeat to the plaintive notes from Andean panpipes.

"I wrote some truly awful stuff in Lowell's class." Paul laughs. "I shouldn't say that. I always tell my students that work isn't bad or good. It's just a warm-up for the next thing."

"I like what I wrote. It just took everyone else some time to catch up."

At the corner he and Elaine exchange phone numbers. They promise to stay in touch and then they kiss before walking in separate directions. When a kid whizzes past him on skates, Paul doesn't even bother to yell at him to get off the sidewalk. Cambridge is a marvelous circus at this time of day. Paul slows down his pace. He doesn't want to miss any of it. In front of a juice bar, a white boy with wild dreadlocks attempts to juggle three plastic pins while pedestrians hurry by, turning their heads away from his artlessness. Paul hears the boy curse softly each time one of the pins falls from his hand. He takes the boy for a refugee from suburban predictability. Despite the hair and all the piercings, the boy's clothes are clean; he looks well fed. Nonetheless, Paul drops a five-dollar bill into the kid's empty baseball cap, upturned on the sidewalk for coins.

"Keep practicing," Paul tells him, and then he starts walking toward his car.

Robert Barclay

University of Hawaii

GOOD FRIDAY 1981

Sunrise Friday on the Marshallese island of Ebeye: Jebro Keju and his brother, Nuke, left their home for the pier and a fifteen-foot aluminum boat they would take across the lagoon. Jebro carried a military duffel bag. His brother carried a small, one-strapped backpack. Each held a gallon jug of water. Around them ruddy morning light caught lingering smoke from the dump, and where there were no shadows everything seemed charmed with a magic, bloody pastel glow. Hinges squeaked. Water splashed. Bodies coughed and spit. Calico cats moved low and quick past helter-skelter cemeteries where sleeping mongrel dogs lay by concrete crosses that bore, in English, the names and dates of the dead. From near and then nearer the long wail of a child seemed to announce, like a rooster's crowing, the rising of the sun.

The brothers walked unhurriedly, two among dozens spilling from a chaos of slum shacks and blockhouses along nameless puddled alleys, passing on their way the Reimers store, Hideo's boat shop, the Seventh-Day Adventists' missionary school, one-room plywood bars, the one-room concrete jail, the Islander Disco, and the silent power plant's tin shack that stank of oil and a damp dead fire. They met up with the others, mostly workers going to ride the ferryboat two islands up the chain to Kwajalein Island. That was where the American missile range was, and where three thousand American civilians and fifty army officers lived in country club comfort, and where about six hundred of the eight thousand Marshallese people living on Ebeye were permitted to work. Because of falling missile debris and warheads launched into the lagoon from submarines and from California, most of the ninety-three islands of the atoll were off-limits, leaving Kwajalein—at twelve times the size of flat, mile-long Ebeye—and Ebeye itself as two of the few places to live. The Marshallese were not allowed to live on the outer islands that had once been their homes, and they were not allowed to live with the Americans on Kwajalein, but a few American men had married Marshallese women and lived in the slum on Ebeye. Other islands were off-limits because of the ground-based missiles there, the *kill vehicles* used to shoot at the incoming warheads.

Jebro and Nuke cut between a wall and a concrete cistern and turned right onto Pier Street. Rusted taxis and pickup trucks, some of the cabs and beds reconstructed with plywood and two-by-fours, grumbled and rattled over the coral gravel road in low gear. A wave of the hand slowed vehicles enough to hop inside. Those walking talked or listened between hits on cigarettes or sips from paper cups of coffee—some listening on transistor radios to Jim Denny's morning show broadcast from Kwajalein. From not too far away came the deep diesel drone of the ferryboat, the *Tarlang*, sounding like the chanting of Buddhist monks. Jebro smiled at his yawning twelve-year-old brother and handed him a slice of dried fish. "*Mungai.* Eat, Nuke," he said. "You must be strong today."

Jebro had been back in Ebeye only a week. For almost two years he had been helping the family of his dead uncle on Ailinglapalap, an island in an atoll of the same name lying two hundred miles to the south. Jebro helped them build a store on the side of their house, and it was he who suggested they buy and repair the broken freezer offered for sale by a trader on the

Micro Pilot supply ship. Car parts from the dump made for a free but less-than-perfect fix of the freezer's guts, and the cut-to-fit hull of a beach-washed dinghy was an ugly but insulating replacement for the rusted-through lid. Although the freezer made it the noisiest store on Ailinglapalap, it was successful for its size because it sold the cheapest fish—fish caught by Jebro and his young nieces and nephews, and their friends too. Jebro's plan worked because people liked a good deal on fish— they liked Jebro for being good that way—and when they came they would buy other things such as corned beef or menthol cigarettes.

Jebro had returned to Ebeye because his father, who worked at the Kwajalein sewage plant, had talked his boss into giving Jebro the recently vacated, entry-level position of Waste Worker III. The job was forty-eight hours a week, paying two-fifty an hour to start, and he would start on Monday. Like his father and all Marshallese who worked there, Jebro would have to catch the *Tarlang* to Kwajalein in the morning and then back again before six in the evening (unless given a pass for overtime) or be fined for trespassing, a fine more than twice his daily pay. He would not be allowed inside the American stores (prices were three times higher on Ebeye), and he would be searched at a checkpoint before leaving. Not even a can of Pepsi would be allowed back to Ebeye. Jebro had wondered, when he went for his orientation on Wednesday, if a sign he had seen outside of one of the American clubs, written in Marshallese but not in English, was a joke, a mistake, or a serious warning. It read: NO MARSHALLESE ALLOWED ON THESE PREMISES. ANYBODY CAUGHT WILL FACE IMPRISONMENT AND WILL BE RUINED.

The sign had made Jebro angry, and so he had softly whistled, a Dr. Hook tune, which is what he did when he was angry and did not want it to show. He knew a guaranteed check every two weeks was better than any other opportunity around.

During his week back on Ebeye, Jebro had been repairing his father's boat, a fifteen-foot aluminum skiff with a twenty-five-horsepower outboard. The hull had a few holes but the seams were tight—some epoxy putty made it sound. The engine was frozen, but only from disuse. A little taking apart and putting back together, new oil and a new plug, and it was running well enough, although it still smoked more than it should have. It was loud too, but Jebro could tell, having a feel for things, that the engine would not fail him. On Thursday he put the boat in the water and moored it near the pier. He would take his brother turtle fishing, something Nuke had never done, and spend the weekend with him before starting work on Monday.

Ebeye pier, where Jebro and Nuke now zigzagged to avoid milky puddles, was a fractured concrete remnant of Japanese occupation during the Second World War. In large spots on the top and on the sides it had broken open, exposing twisted rusting rebar and coral rubble that the Japanese had used as fill. It listed a little to the left, toward Kwajalein, as if within it there were a spirit longing to break free of Ebeye. Moored to plastic balls in shallow murky water to the right of the pier were aluminum skiffs and about a dozen plywood powerboats with brightly painted hoods on their outboards. A broken strand of sulfur-colored sand, the beach, stretched in littered patches from the pier to the dump at the end of the island. Gray slum shacks on stilts hung over the water, and the mass of shacks tight behind them seemed to be swelling in the strange red morning light.

The *Tarlang,* a military LCM given two welded upper decks to accommodate its hundreds of passengers, had throttled down and bumped lightly against the pier, causing a small tremor. Men and women crowded toward the boarding platform. Jebro dropped his duffel bag and water jug, then elbowed out of his shirt and pushed it into Nuke's chest. He whistled and waved his arms to clear a path to the water and, as a joke, he shouted that he was *crazy in love* and pretended to chase two young girls in floral dresses. They screamed, laughing, and ran away, one pulling the other. Jebro flexed his muscles in an exaggerated pose for Nuke's admiration, then ran and dove off the pier.

He broke the water fingers first and swam quickly, porpoise style, just above the dead coral bottom, and then with one strong movement he shot out of the water and pulled himself into the stern of his father's boat. A silver spray flew from the water as startled stickfish moved from their hiding place in the shadow of the bow.

Nuke hauled the gear to the bottom of some narrow concrete steps and waited, talking to children above him while Jebro started the engine and brought the boat toward the pier. The children jumped banzai bombing style off the pier and over the boat when it bumped sidelong to a stop.

Nuke handed over the gear.

"Sit to the left up front," Jebro ordered, pulling on his shirt. He checked to make sure that everything was in its place, that the boat was balanced, that no children were near the path of the prop. When Nuke sat down, they pushed off from the pier and cut a clean wake across the lagoon.

The sun was low over the Pacific Ocean in the east, a blur sometimes revealing a bright point of light behind a wide dark bank of clouds. Above the clear sky showed its first signs of blue, and to the west, across the flat gray surface of the lagoon, a few stars still shone brightly.

The boat sped west-northwest, its hull slapping fast through the calm water, its engine droning, almost whining, leaving a bubbling wake to gently roll toward small jungled islands dimly visible to starboard. Black terns flew low and fast, some alone and others in tight groups. A flying fish leapt from the water and crossed the bow.

Jebro whistled to get Nuke's attention. "We'll get rain today," he said.

Nuke nodded, looking east at the approaching storm. "Should we still try for Torrutj Island?"

"I don't think the rain will bring big waves. Why, are you scared?"

"*Errorr!*" Nuke shouted, rolling his *r*'s to make the Marshallese exclamation of disgust. "Nothing scares me."

"I am proud to have such a brave little brother." Jebro smiled and tossed Nuke a warm Pepsi. "Bravery is half of what you will need in life."

Nuke, grinning, studied Jebro's face for a moment. "What is the other half?" he asked.

"A fear of your older brother." Jebro ducked as Nuke sprayed him with Pepsi. "*Errorr!*" he shouted, and turned the boat sharply so that Nuke had to grab the side.

"What about the helicopters?" Nuke asked. "What if they see us there?"

"Torrutj is where I was born," Jebro said, trying not to smile, "so we must defend it. If the Americans try to make us leave, we must dig bunkers and attack them and shoot down their helicopters with our slingshots until they accept defeat."

Nuke laughed. "They have guns and missiles."

"We know kung fu." Jebro raised a death claw and high-kicked his leg at Nuke. "*Owaaa!*"

It took three hours to cross the lagoon, and in that time the wide dark bank of clouds had moved in from the east and split the sky into two even hemispheres of blue and gray. Half a mile in front of the boat lay a string of lush green islands, each on its own fine white carpet of sand. Their turquoise shallows seemed stained black in spots where coral groves disrupted the sandy bottom.

"Do you know which one is Torrutj?" Jebro asked his sleepy brother.

"The big one?"

"Yes, can you see the rocks that come out a bit and curve toward the pass? That formation was built long ago before the Americans came, before the Japanese, before the Germans— even before Marshallese. Do you want to hear the story?"

Nuke hunched forward over a cigarette and lit it with a match. "Tell me."

"Tell me first why you smoke."

"Everybody smokes, even girls now."

"I don't."

"Maybe you're scared."

"Okay, give me one then."

"You don't smoke."

"I don't want my little brother to think I'm a coward. Besides, I haven't seen you in two years—we should do everything together while we have the chance." Jebro idled the engine and held out his hand. Nuke gave him a cigarette. "Am I supposed to wait for lightning to light this?"

Nuke handed him the matches. "Do you know how to smoke?" he asked, then took a drag.

"I'll watch you and learn." Jebro lit his cigarette and gunned the throttle. He put the matches in his pocket.

"So tell me the story of the rocks," Nuke said.

"Wait now, I want to enjoy my smoke with you." Jebro leaned back, a look of mock euphoria on his face.

Nuke giggled. "*Kwe bwebwe.* You're crazy. Are you sure you know how to catch turtle?"

Jebro exhaled a stream of smoke and flicked his cigarette into the water. He thumped his bare chest and said, "I am the best."

A light windblown rain fell as Jebro guided the bow of the boat onto the beach at Torrutj. The island was uninhabited, a little more than half a mile long, and boomerang-shaped with tall palms that leaned over the water. Farther inland the biggest palms grew in rows, survivors of the copra plantation the brothers' family had once farmed. A scalloped white beach strewn with coconuts and lines of flotsam stretched around to the ocean side of the island.

Jebro killed the engine and tilted it out of the water. "You pull and I'll push," he said and jumped out of the stern. They got the boat high on the beach, and at Jebro's insistence covered it with vines and dead brown palm fronds. "The helicopters will never see it. Let's have a Pepsi and then we'll get started."

"So do we cover ourselves with palm fronds too?"

"Yes, tie some around your waist and on your legs." Jebro held out a frond but Nuke, laughing, slapped it away.

The brothers sat in the sand without speaking, sharing the soda as the warm rain came down a little harder and silenced the cricket noises coming from the jungle. Sand crabs poked their long eyes out of holes on the beach.

"*Bejik.* Shit," Nuke said, wiping the water from his face.

"No, rain is good—better for catching turtle." Jebro stood and slapped the sand from his pants. "*Itok.* Come," he said, taking his duffel bag from the boat, "let me show you how."

Nuke crushed the empty Pepsi can and threw it into the jungle. He walked with Jebro to the rock formation they had seen earlier. Jebro took a foot-long piece of two-by-four out of the duffel bag. Four-hundred-pound-test braided nylon rope was wrapped around the wood, and a length of thick monofilament with a 7/o hook at the end was tied to the rope.

"This is my secret turtle catching technique," Jebro said. "I give it to you, but don't ever tell anybody how it's done." He looked into Nuke's eyes.

"I promise."

"*Emon.* Good, now watch close." Jebro took a green papaya out of the bag, cut it into quarters, and scooped out the black mass of seeds. He threw the seeds and pulp into the water and jabbed the hook into the yellow meat of one of the quarters, then threaded it through the narrow top so that the barb poked out. Where the nylon rope was knotted to the monofilament, Jebro tied a fist-sized rock. "Here," he said, handing the rig to Nuke, "hold this while I play out the rope." Jebro coiled the rope in large loops and hung them over his palm. "Now, follow me out to the end of the rocks."

The massive black rocks, curving in a line some thirty yards into the lagoon, looked as if they had once been level and fitted tightly together. Now gaps let water flow freely between them. With a few treacherous leaps, however, it was still possible to walk from one end of the formation to the other. Jebro jumped onto the first rock. "Watch your step." He looked back at Nuke. "These rocks are slippery."

They walked out to where the rocks started curving to the left, then stopped. Jebro took the baited papaya and the rock from Nuke. He handed Nuke the line's end and told him to kneel; then, gripping the knot where the nylon met the monofilament, he swung the rig three times around his head and let it fly. It splashed twenty yards from the rocks and sank to a sandy area fifteen feet deep. Maybe fifty yards of slack line remained. "Now we go back and wait," Jebro said.

The sky turned a thick uniform gray, but the rain, momentarily, had slackened to mist. Jebro sat on the beach and handed Nuke the rope. "You hold the rope and I'll tell you what to do." Nuke wrapped the rope tightly around his hand and stood ready, his eyes focused on the water where the bait had gone down. Jebro laughed. "Relax, little brother, it takes time. Sit." Nuke sat next to Jebro, the rope still taut going into the water. Jebro took it from him. "Hold it like this," he said, letting the rope go slack. "If you wrap it around your hand, you might lose your fingers, and if you keep it tight, then you won't hook the turtle."

Nuke took hold of the rope and fumbled to remove a pack of cigarettes from of his pocket. "You have my matches." Jebro reached into his pocket and handed them to Nuke. He struck one, then another. "The matches won't light."

"I think they're wet."

"*Errorr,* you should have put them in the bag."

"Sorry, just let them dry. You can smoke again tomorrow."

"I can't do that."

"I have some other matches in the bag—waterproof ones."

"Good, give them to me."

"I have only three, and we need them to make a fire tonight. Wait till then."

"I can't do that."

"I'll give you one match—just one." Jebro took a film container out of the bag and pinched a wooden match from it. He struck it on the zipper of his shorts and cupped it in his hand. Nuke leaned over and lit his cigarette. Jebro stuck the match in the sand. "Keep your cigarette away from the rope."

"Of course—do you think I'm stupid?"

"No, but I lost a fish once that way. Do you want to hear the story of the rocks now?"

"Yes, tell me."

Jebro leaned back on his elbows and shook rainwater from his hair. "*Ettimonmon anin.* This island is haunted, especially this spot by the stones."

"Who are the ghosts?"

"Just listen. Long ago, before Marshallese found these islands, a race of dwarfs lived here on Torrutj. They were great fishermen and lived a good life. One day a sorcerer flew in on a canoe—"

"Wait—how can a canoe fly?"

"I said he was a sorcerer. He used magic. So he flew in on his canoe and he told the dwarfs he would help them build a great city. They told the sorcerer—"

"What was the sorcerer's name?"

"His name was Nuke—now be quiet and let me finish the story. The dwarfs said they were too busy fishing and making canoes to build a city. So the sorcerer used his magic and made fish jump onto the beach. He said he would provide for the dwarfs, give them fish, make breadfruit and coconut fall from the sky already cooked. He did that and the dwarfs had no excuse for not building the city." Jebro pointed to the large black rocks. "The sorcerer flew these rocks in on his canoe and dropped them on the beach. Have you ever seen rocks like these anywhere else, on any other island?"

"No."

"So you see this story is true. The rocks are from magic. The sorcerer instructed the dwarfs to pile the rocks in the lagoon, to build the city up out of the water and—"

"Wait—why didn't the sorcerer just use his magic to build the city?"

"Because he was evil. He wanted slaves. He made the dwarfs work very hard, and they did so for many generations. They forgot how to fish, and forgot their customs and their religion. When the city was finished, the sorcerer told the dwarfs that they would not be allowed to live inside. Only he could live there and the dwarfs would have to serve him and pray to him if they wanted food. The dwarfs grew very mad at the sorcerer. *Raar maijek leo im mane.* They ganged up on him and killed him."

"What happened to the city?"

"These rocks are all that's left. The rest is buried under the sand."

"*Eban!* I don't believe it!"

"*Engai!* It's true!"

Nuke looked at the short, smoldering end of his cigarette. "What am I going to do when I want another cigarette?"

"Wait until tonight."

"I can't do that."

"If you were a fish, I'd know what to use for bait."

"Just let me keep one more match, for later."

"No, we need them for the fire. There is only one thing you can do. How many cigarettes do you have?"

"Almost two packs."

"Okay, light another cigarette from the one in your hand. I'll help you *baibtonton,* chain-smoke."

"That's a waste."

"What else can we do?"

"Build a fire now."

"The helicopters will see the smoke."

"*Errorr.*" Nuke lit another cigarette, and stubbed out the other in the sand.

"Pass it to me, I'll help you." They shared the cigarette without speaking, and then lit another one.

Nuke pointed to the line of rocks. "So what happened to the dwarfs?"

"They all died. They had forgotten how to catch fish and how to open a coconut. The sorcerer had provided for them too much, and after they killed him, they all starved to death. Their ghosts still haunt the island. Do you believe it?"

"Where did you hear that story?"

"Mother's father told me when I was your age, not long before he died. He brought me here one day to catch turtle, but he fished a different way. We walked out there to the end and put rocks inside a breadfruit so that it would sink. While we waited, he told me the story."

"How did he fish for turtle?"

"When a turtle came for the breadfruit, he dove in and tried to flip it over so that he could push it to shore. But he was too old. The turtle cut him with its claw. You should have seen him splashing around out there, cussing at the turtle. I couldn't stop laughing."

"That's a story I can believe."

"You better light another cigarette—that one is almost out."

"Okay. So why don't you use breadfruit and fish like Grandfather?"

"I could. I know many ways to fish. Today I want to fish with rope." Jebro nibbled at one of the papaya quarters. "I use this instead of breadfruit because turtle can't resist it. They smell it and go crazy. They have to eat it no matter what—can't stop, and then they get hooked. Can you think of anything that works like that on a man?"

"*Biiibi.* Pooosy." They fell over laughing.

"That's not what I was thinking." Jebro slapped Nuke on the back, causing him to cough. "Hey, what do you know about *bibi* anyway?"

Nuke cleared his throat. "I know plenty."

"Oh yes, I saw you talking to Emily the other day."

"*Errorr! Errubrub ledik en.* Ugh! That girl farts all the time. I don't know why she likes me."

"Because you look like me, very handsome."

"*Errorr.*" Nuke looked out at the water. "If your papaya is such great bait, why don't I see any turtles going crazy out there?"

"I also learned from Grandfather to be patient. We waited all morning before a turtle came. But don't worry—my papaya will bring one soon." Jebro took a drag from the cigarette and passed it to Nuke. "Quick, light another one."

"This is stupid. I'm going to run out."

"What else can we do?"

"You should have kept my matches dry."

"You should have brought more."

The rain fell harder. Out in the lagoon, at brief intervals, a circle of terns dove now and then at schools of mackerel boiling the surface of the water. From not far away came the muffled whump of a helicopter, becoming louder. Jebro took a gray tarp out of the bag and used driftwood to make a small lean-to. They huddled under it, smoking as they stared out at the water. The helicopter passed somewhere behind them. Jebro passed Nuke the cigarette. "Here, you're on your own now. I can't smoke anymore."

"Good, you were just wasting my smoke."

"Do you want to hear another story?"

"More ghosts?"

"No, about something that happened when you were younger."

"Tell me."

"There was a boy who hanged himself one day—"

"Lots of boys hang themselves."

"This is different. Listen. He hanged himself inside a shack behind the beer bar that used to be by the dump—"

"He was drunk."

"I don't know, maybe, but he—"

"They're always drunk when they hang themselves."

"Yes, I think so, but listen. Some other boys found him, four of them, and they saw he had a pack of cigarettes in his shirt pocket—"

"It's a cigarette pocket, that's what it's for."

Jebro gave Nuke a push. "Who's telling this story? Listen, this is weird. The boys took the cigarettes and ran away. By a month later, all those boys had hanged themselves too."

"It happens all the time. I don't think the cigarettes had anything to do with it. Where did you hear this?"

"I knew one of the boys, the last one to die. He was my friend. I saw him one day on the pier and he told me the story. I remember him saying, 'I'm afraid I must be next.' A week later he was hanging from the roof of his house. Can you believe it?"

Nuke nodded and flicked sand with the slack rope. "I'll tell you a story now." He looked Jebro in the eyes.

"Go on, I'm listening."

"About three months ago, a boy in the house behind ours tried to hang himself. Did you ever know Rujen?"

"No, I don't think so—maybe. I know the family there—they have many children. What do you mean he *tried?*"

"Yes, he tied his rope to a beam inside the house, but when he jumped off a table, the beam broke. Termites had made it weak. He wasn't hurt, but the roof had a big hole after that and then a storm came. The house got all wet and the father was so mad that he made Rujen go live somewhere else." Nuke paused to take a drag.

"That's the story?"

"No, Rujen died, that's how it ends. At low tide he walked the reef over to Ebijierikku and climbed a coconut tree. Then he jumped."

"Look!" Jebro pointed toward the water.

"What?"

"I saw a turtle come up for air. He was far, but headed this way." Nuke stood and held the rope with both hands, a short cigarette clenched between his teeth. Jebro tugged him back down. "Relax, it will be a while yet. When you see it taking air near the bait, then get ready."

Nuke lit another cigarette and leaned his head on Jebro's shoulder. He took a light drag and held the cigarette so the smoke would blow out of the lean-to. Jebro put his arm around Nuke and said, "It's funny how turtle live in the water and have to breathe air. They lay their eggs on land too. Have you ever seen a turtle lay eggs?"

"No."

"They come at night and crawl way up the beach. By morning they are so tired they almost die trying to get back in the water. Most of the babies die when they're born—they run down the beach and birds get them, and fish get them too because their shells are still very soft. It's like they can't decide which world they want to live in, so they try and live in both. I think it would be very hard to live as a turtle."

Nuke let the cigarette fall from his hand. He watched it go out in the sand. "I can't smoke anymore."

"That's okay, you tried."

"I feel sick."

"It will pass. Just relax and think about something else. Tell me, why do you think so many Marshallese boys hang themselves?"

Nuke made a drinking motion with his hand. "Too much Budweiser."

"That's all?"

"Maybe they want to die like *Jijej Kuraij*. The missionaries say that *Jijej* sacrificed his life to save the world."

"That's interesting. I never though of it that way."

"I still think it's too much Budweiser."

"I'm sure that has something to do with it, but I think there is more." Jebro looked at the water, and then he looked at the rope. "Many Marshallese boys' lives are full of boredom, full of nothing but nothing. They have no reason to keep living, nothing to look forward to." Jebro threw a chunk of papaya in the water. "We have lost too much knowledge of how to be Marshallese and we can never have the life Americans have. Marshallese boys are stuck between two worlds, and the rope is an easy way out."

"Do you know of another way out?"

"When I lived at Ailinglapalap, I went to one of the outer islands, Wotja. Old people there try to live according to the old ways, but so much has been forgotten, and they cannot support themselves without canned food and bags of rice. They must sell copra to stay alive, and the work is very hard on them. I lived there for a couple months, but it's no good unless everybody does it. A village needs children, beautiful women, strong fishermen with good boats—not just elders husking coconuts. I left because I was bored, more bored than living on Ailinglapalap or Ebeye."

Jebro drew circles in the sand with a stick. "So that's not a good way anymore. Marshallese can never live like it was before. But this is how I see it: I am a fisherman, maybe not as good as Marshallese in the past, but I know a lot. I'm going to take that job on Kwajalein, doing the Americans' dirty work, but I will not be a worker who fishes sometimes. I will be a fisherman who does other jobs. I have my own identity, not one the Americans give me. To them I am just a slave, nobody. I take the job because money is a necessity these days—that's how it has to be—and I can't make enough by fishing. Someday I will build a good boat and do nothing but fish all day, teach others how to fish too. That is my way between the two worlds. How about you, Nuke, what will you do?"

"I never thought about it."

"Tell me when you think of something. Until then, anytime I go fishing you can come with me if you want. I will teach you, and we can learn new things together."

"I know where we can steal some wood to build a boat."

"We don't need to steal," Jebro said, looking into Nuke's eyes. "That's what an American would do. But yes, we should start thinking about a boat. Wouldn't that be something: the Keju Brothers' Fishing Company?"

Nuke laughed. "We better not fish for turtle because we will make very little money!"

"*Errorr,* have patience. I saw a turtle very close only a minute ago."

"You have good eyes. I haven't seen anything." Nuke leaned forward as he scanned the water. "Jebro, tell me something. Did you ever try to *kilaba,* kill yourself?"

Jebro smiled as he reached over and mussed Nuke's curly wet hair. "One time I was going to, but when I was tying the noose, I discovered a great fishing knot."

Nuke knocked away Jebro's hand and laughed. "Is that the same knot you used at the end of this rope?"

"Of course."

The rain plunked steadily on the tarp, and Nuke leaned his head on Jebro's shoulder as he looked out at the water with half-closed eyes. Jebro ate the rest of the papaya and threw the rind into the lagoon. Rivulets of water ran down from the jungle and through the sand on their way into the shallow surf. One, then two helicopters droned by.

Nuke jumped. "*Won!* Turtle!" he yelled. "Right over the bait!"

"Yes, I saw it. Get ready. This is what's going to happen: it already smelled the papaya, and now it cannot help but try and eat it even though it can see the hook. Keep the line slack. The turtle will not go for the papaya with its mouth—it will try and knock it free from the hook with its fin. The rope will get tangled on its fin—I don't know why, but it always happens that way. When the turtle tries to swim away, the rope will run the hook right into its fin. Just keep the line slack and give it more when it starts going out. I'll tell you when to pull back. Can you—"

"Quiet, you'll spook the turtle. I understand." Nuke stood ready, and after a minute the rope started to go out, slowly at first then faster. He looked to Jebro.

"Not yet, not yet—NOW!" Nuke jerked back on the rope. "Hold it! Don't let it get a running start!"

Nuke knocked over the lean-to as he stumbled sideways. The rope stretched tight and the turtle broke to the surface with a large flapping splash. The rope ran fast out of Nuke's hands. "*Aiii!*" He dropped it and pressed his burnt hands against his wet shirt.

Jebro dove for the rope, dug his heels into the sand, and kept the turtle from gaining any farther distance. He got up in a crouch and began to haul it in. "Here, you do it."

"I can't, my hands hurt."

"I'll fix your hands later. Here." He held out the rope for Nuke and he took it. "Lean back. Good, good, pull like this: side to side with your elbows out. Now you're doing it." Nuke's knees trembled as hand over hand he hauled in the turtle. His face expressed pain, but his lips were smiling.

Jebro ran into the shallow water. "Pull it right in front of me. Good, you're doing good, just a few more feet."

Jebro grabbed the turtle by one of its front fins. He hauled it up the beach and flipped it upside down. It flapped madly for a moment then lay still, breathing loudly, snorting. Nuke ran over. "We got it! We got it!"

"Yes, you did a good job. It's not as big as I wanted—maybe ninety pounds, a young one—but there is plenty of meat."

"How young?"

"I don't know, maybe your age. Let's go have a Pepsi and relax."

The brothers sat on the beach in front of the turtle and shared another Pepsi. Jebro cut strips from the bottom of his shirt to cover the rope burns on Nuke's hands.

The turtle was hooked in a soft spot where its fin met its shell. A narrow stream of blood ran into the sand. A film of mucous covered its eyes and fell in drops like thick sticky tears.

Nuke touched the turtle's fin with his bare toe. "It's crying."

"No, I don't think so. That's just what happens when it comes out of the water. Its eyes need the salt."

"Shouldn't we take out the hook?"

"I think you are feeling sorry for the turtle."

"No, but . . . this is my first turtle. I learned with this one, and I can catch turtle anytime now. Maybe it learned too . . . maybe it has learned how to avoid the hook and the rope. I think it deserves to live for helping me learn to catch it. Is that . . . do I . . . can we put it back?"

"Are you sure?"

"You won't be mad?"

"No, if that's what you want. There are many turtles out there, but I have only one brother. Go ahead, put it in the water and say good-bye. We'll take the boat into the ocean and catch tuna. They bite very well in the rain."

Nuke carefully removed the hook and dragged the turtle into the shallow surf. He flipped it over and the turtle shot away, leaving a cloud of stirred-up sand. "*Yokwe*. Good-bye," he said. "You don't have to sacrifice your life for me."

Lani Wolf

University of Virginia

HELIUM BALLOON

"Jack ripped all my clothes off the hangers and strewed them across the lawn. Then he turned on the sprinklers. Of course, he was high again. It was all because he was high—" Mrs. Hebener pauses, but Doctor Bruster does not let the silence last long. *We know it was all because he was high again, Mrs. Hebener. That is why we are all here today* is what the look of impatience on Doctor Bruster's face says. The pen in his hand is burning to record her words in his own secret code language. The pad of paper balanced on his knee is screaming out for ink. *Cover me with symbols.* The words slanting out of his mouth say, "Carry on, Mrs. Hebener. You're doing just fine."

On Wednesday nights Doctor Bruster likes to say, "Talk to me." He likes to say, "Tell everything." He likes to say, "Start with 'This is a true story' and go from there." And especially he likes to say, "I see" when he doesn't see and "Hush now, it's okay," when it's not okay. When it's better just to scream.

"Well, Jack let the sprinklers run until there was a muddy lake in our front yard. I remember my blouses and skirts actually floating. I have nothing to wear to the office now. Everything's just so filthy."

A good detergent can loosen dirt, grass stains, grease, even blood, Mrs. Hebener, I want to say. Molecules of soap do battle with molecules of, say, blood, pry them loose from threads of white, break their fierce, red grip. Clean-dirty, dirty-clean, Mrs. Hebener. They're reversible. Think of that. Clothes will be white again.

"Come now, no tears," Doctor Bruster says. " *'Everything's just so filthy.'* "

"Yes, everything's just so filthy, but the worst part was how he climbed up in the attic with a big knife and cut my wedding dress out of the vacuum box where I'd had it preserved and hung it from the branch of a tree in our front yard."

Doctor Bruster eats his words: Mrs. Hebener is doing better than fine. She's doing great. Outstanding. Spectacular. She should get a gold star. Because this is just the kind of thing he wants to hear. He is on the edge of his seat, guarding his notepad jealously, shielding it with fluttering hands in case any of us get too near. Because the page is no longer empty.

"And now I keep having this dream where it's my dead body inside the dress hanging from the tree. In the dream I am a sad white ghost dressed in a filthy wedding gown."

When he is writing, Doctor Bruster looks so beautiful. His skin and hair turn to fire. His lips want to move with the hieroglyphics he etches out on his notepad. Then we can see his white teeth flash. He writes out our stories in a language none of us can understand.

"And in real life that's what I am, too—a sad white ghost in a filthy wedding gown. That's all I am to Jack. That's all I am in the world. Dear God, I don't even know what I am anymore. . . ."

*   *   *

Why doesn't Doctor Bruster go to her and make everything better? Why doesn't he say, *That's why we have laundry rooms, Mrs. Hebener. Add soap, add water, and presto!—clothes are white again. None of this has to mean violence. Detergent, Mrs. Hebener, detergent. Tide, Wisk, Gain, All—it's your choice.*

But the dreams are too good. Doctor Bruster remains in his seat writing everything down. He couldn't stop if he wanted to. He is furious. Burning. The sight of his hieroglyphics flowing from the tip of his pen excites him like nothing in the world. The look on his face says *Yes, this is precisely why I chose the field of psychiatry. Keep going, Mrs. Hebener. Don't even think about stopping.*

Sometimes we refuse to talk. We sit in our circle and grunt like cavemen, chase after the story we are to tell with spears and darts. When we catch it, we tear it to bits with our bare hands, swallow the pieces whole. Afterward we want to write it down. We want to record it and remember it always, this taste of blood on our lips. But we have no language. Words refuse to come.

"A white wedding gown, a brown wedding gown, a pink wedding gown," Doctor Bruster sings, catching our eyes in his and rocking in perfect time with the rhythm of his own voice. "A white wedding gown, a brown wedding gown, a pink wedding gown. Come. Everyone picks her color. Around the circle." "A yellow wedding gown," "a blue wedding gown," "a green wedding gown," we go (we've really got it down), "a purple wedding gown," "a red wedding gown," "an orange wedding gown" (Doctor Bruster cannot write fast enough), and before I know it, my turn is upon me, and I say, "a gray wedding gown," Silvia "a cream wedding gown," Tammy "a silver wedding gown," and Doris "a black wedding gown." A black wedding gown. Now that's a funny one! Ha! Imagine. White, brown, pink, yellow, blue, green, purple, red, orange, gray, cream, silver, BLACK! But now it seems we've run out of colors, and around us settles a stillness, a silence that makes Doctor Bruster squirm, until someone says, "A polka-dot wedding gown," then "a striped wedding gown," then "a silver wedding gown." Wait! Someone already did that one! You can't say the same color twice. That's the rule. "Fine. A gold wedding gown then. Is that okay?" "A white wedding gown, a brown wedding gown, a pink wedding gown," we croon, until Doctor Bruster clears his throat, raises his hand, and says, "Question: Who dreams in color and who in black and white?"

When the words stick in our throats, we make pictures of our kill. We draw with charcoal and soot on stone walls. We put our pictures in the deepest recesses of the cave. Never near the mouth. Sometimes we have to crawl on our hands and knees through dark and dripping tunnels to reach these places.

"The story has to be told," Doctor Bruster says. He yanks the words from our mouths like rotten teeth.

"I'm tired of sleeping—or trying to—in the car in the parking lot of K-Marts. I'm tired of Katie and me having to wrap towels around our heads to block out the floodlights. I'm tired of taking turns staying up so we can watch for Louie's truck. I'm tired of buying McDonald's the next morning with whatever change we can scrape together from the bottom of my purse. Goddamnit—I'm tired of peeing in Styrofoam cups and dumping the contents out on the pavement."

Doctor Bruster stops writing. U——. The corners of his mouth turn down. Ur——. Uri——. Doctor Bruster doesn't much like this story. I don't think it's so bad.

"Cannibal sandwiches. Raw beef. Cold out of the package. Not cooked at all. That's the way Bruce likes it. And it has to be Pomperdale's whole-seed rye bread with the crusts cut off. Just a spot of horseradish, but lots of mustard. A dill pickle wedge on the side."

You and I are Stone Age men. We write in pictures. We speak in grunts. Our music is knocking bones. Our clothes are fur. We drag our knuckles across the bare earth and pass our time sharpening sticks. We hunt and kill and eat and then draw on cave walls. Our pictures are as close to life as we can make them with our crude and gnarled hands. Mammoth faces full of agony. Antelope muscles pulsing on raw stone. Our beasts die full of power and marvelous strength. They were not easy to kill. They run in great profusion over the stone ceiling and walls, one on top of the other on top of the other, us pursuing with spears and darts, our mouths open. Black, soundless hollows. This is what we paint in the underground darkness. We do not distinguish between image and reality.

Doctor Bruster belongs to a different age of men entirely, a future race. His are men possessing words and pens and paper, men who walk upright with measured steps, men who wear woven cotton, and whose music is harps. To us, Doctor Bruster is a magic man. We do not know whether to one day become him or to kill him. Thousands of years separate us.

"But the main thing is, Bruce likes for me to spear the slices of rye bread with a little plastic sword. He won't eat it any other way. It has to have that little plastic sword. The exact type of meat doesn't matter much, so long as it's red meat."

"But Miss Scott," Doctor Bruster says. "We were talking about what *you* want. Forget about Bruce. Bruce doesn't exist. Only *you* exist. Come, let's begin again. Repeat after me: 'If I were trapped on a desert island, and I had only one choice of food, and I had to eat it for the rest of my life, and I wasn't allowed anything else, it would be—'" His mouth stretches into a ventriloquist's smile. Invisible words ease past his pale lips. *Why oh why have you ceased concentrating?*

"Raw meat. The bloodier the better," Miss Scott says.

Where oh where has our story gone? Tell, tell, tell, tell. There is no such thing as a secret.

When we eat, we tear and grab and choke and smear. We are unconcerned with dirt on our bodies and blood on our faces.

We need meat to live. We are willing to fight over the biggest pieces. Doctor Bruster eats only words. He plucks them from the air like tiny birds, claws them and chews them and spits them out, and when he does, they are changed. At our feet, we see mangled feathers and crushed bones. Tiny beaks stuffed with mud and silence.

"One day I didn't have Pomperdale's whole-seed rye bread and the market was closed and all the 7-Eleven had was white. I even checked two more places—one was out of bread, and at the other it was moldy around the edges—and I had to end up getting the white. I didn't *want* to get the white, but I didn't have a choice. I cut the crusts off and fixed it just the way he liked with the little spear and everything, but it wasn't rye bread. Bruce took one look at the sandwich and dumped the plate over on the floor. 'You don't give a flying fuck,' he said. Then he threw the plate against the wall and stormed out of the room, turning over chairs as he left. He refused to sleep in our bed that night. He dragged some blankets into his den and slept there instead. I tried to get in a couple times, but he had locked me out. I needed for him to know how sorry I was. I needed it so bad. So I put my lips up to the door crack and told him. 'Bruce, I love you, and I'm sorry,' I said. He wouldn't answer. He just ignored me. Then I got out a pen and paper and made these little notes explaining our whole lives. I kept shoving them under the door. I couldn't stop myself. You want to know why? Because the whole time I imagined him like a tiny little boy. Curled up in the blanket on the floor with his fingers in his ears. That was the exact image I had. No matter how hard I tried I couldn't get it out of my head. Oh, God. Bruce must really hate me. He must just absolutely despise me. And the awful thing is he's probably better off without me. I wish I were dead."

Doctor Bruster caps his pen and slides it into the neat blue pocket of his shirt. He looks at us with narrowed eyes. What a bunch of loonies we are! Plum crazy. Off the rocker. Playing without a full deck. Three bricks shy of a load. One sandwich short of a picnic. Just plain ape-shit. We can read the words in his lizard eyes.

* * *

I hope Doris Fitzsimmons comes next week and tells us something funny about Ted. Her story is always the best. She gets a laugh every time.

"Get this. The first thing Ted does on his first night out of rehab is call up 'the gang.' I say 'Don't even think about it, Ted,' but he's already out the door. I follow him into the driveway and watch him get into the front seat of his Cutlass. He starts the engine and rolls down the windows. Guns it a couple times. *Vrrooom! Vrrooom!* Real badass motherfucker. But the cruddy old shit-heap needs to warm up, and he can't go anywhere. Ha!

"I say, 'Where you going, Ted?'

"He says, 'Doris, can it.'

"I say, 'Ted, how long you planning to be gone?'

"He says, 'Doris, about an hour.'

"I say, 'One hour my ass, Ted.'

"I'm shouting and Ted's throwing empty beer bottles out the window at me, but the neighbors don't even bother to call the police. They're used to this.

"Well, I don't see him again until the next morning. He's bleary-eyed, sniffling, and sweating like a pig when he walks through the door. I don't even have to ask. It's written all over his face. And then he starts talking about green people in the trees. Give me a break. He's got a gun in his hand and the dog on a leash. *'Don't let me catch you snooping in my business, Doris,'* he keeps saying. The man sounds like a broken record player. I tell him that, too. I say, 'Ted, you sound like a broken record player, you paranoid son of a bitch.'

"And then he takes himself out into the backyard and plunks himself down on the ground in front of the back fence. He's just sitting there staring at the knot holes and the splinters and crap. Then he gets up, fishes his camera out of some old box in the garage, and starts shooting photos of that damn back fence. He must have gone through eight or nine rolls of film at least. That's like two hundred fifty separate photographs.

"And as long as we're on the topic, I guess you all may as well know he installed an extra set of locks on all the windows and a third—or is it fourth now?—dead bolt on the front door. I can't keep track of all the keys. I swear it takes me at least a half hour to get out of the house. And if you want to know the truth, sometimes I can't get out at all. That's why I've been missing sessions."

Doctor Bruster has heard all of this before. *Ho-hum.* He sits cross-legged and immobile. *This is getting old, Doris.* Stony-faced and bloodless, he does not write a word.

Most days I keep quiet, but today I have a story to tell. I call it "Silver Bullet on Scar."

Once upon a time there lived a man with two depressions in his skull from where a bullet entered and then exited. The man made the mother and daughter put their fingers in the pair of holes. The entry spot. The exit. Right temple. Left. He made them sink their fingers down and feel the grizzled hair, greasy skin, scar tissue. Neither the mother nor the daughter could get away without admiring the smart silver tattoo, bullet entering on one side, explosion out the other. The man held their wrists.

To the daughter the man liked to say, "Listen up, I survived a 44-caliber slug in the brain." To the mother he liked to say, "I need you like I need a hole in the head." That was all. Clothes: off. Bed board: humming.

Sometimes this man would get in bad moods and play dirty tricks on the mother and daughter. Once he dressed up as the pool man and filled the bed of his truck with buckets of chemicals and nets and vacuums and sweeping brushes—all stolen— and in this way got past the security guard. When the mother and daughter got home that day, he was sitting in the living room in what had once been his favorite chair, before they had moved to the house protected by the guard and the dogs and the concrete wall, before they had tried to escape him.

"I always did like this chair," he said to the mother and the daughter, neither one of whom could think of anything to say in response.

"What's the matter? Don't you recognize me?" the man asked, grinning.

Right then, the man reminded the daughter of the Big Bad Wolf. *Oh, grandmother, what nice teeth you have.* The daughter was very young then. Fairy tales played in her head. The Gingerbread House. The Evil Stepmother. The Poisoned Apple. And the savage songs of childhood that awoke her in the deepest part of night. *Cinderella dressed in yellow went upstairs to kiss a fellow. Peter Peter pumpkin-eater. One-two buckle my shoe!* She would pull the blanket over her head and squeeze her eyes shut and put her fingers in her ears. *Little Tom Tucker sings for his supper. Peter learned to read and spell. Three-four knock at the door!* She could not stop the sweat from breaking out on the top of her lip. *And then he loved her very well. What shall Tom eat? White bread and butter! How many doctors did it take? Five-six-* She could not keep the sounds from coming. *Pick up sticks!*

(But the story's getting longer now. The past is coming into play. "Silver Bullet on Scar" is supposed to be quick. Gripping. The way Doctor Bruster likes.)

Then the man stood up and held his arms open to the mother and daughter, as if in embrace. It was a nice thought, except that in one hand he was holding a gun—or was it a kitchen knife? A canister of Mace? Leather belt? Big stick? (These are the kind of details Doctor Bruster likes so much. The kind that slow otherwise good stories down. Make them tedious.)

"What you gonna do 'bout it?" the man laughed—oh, it was funny—his arms wide open. "Are you gonna scream?"

No response from mother or daughter.

"Go 'head," he says. "Scream." (Doctor Bruster applauds this detail. The very dramatic verb "scream," he says.)

"Top of the lungs." (And another winner!—"lungs"!)

"See who comes running." (Bravo! Standing ovation!)

Katie brings in a booklet of crayon pictures and finger paintings she made in school that day. "It is a book," she says. "This book has five pages. I can count them. One-two-three-four-five. I like my book." "It is a flower," she says. "This flower is pretty. I like my flower. It is for my mom." "It is a truck," she says. "This truck has wheels. It has two pink ones and two green ones. I like my truck. It is not Louie's truck." The blank expression on Doctor Bruster's face says *This is but a kindergarten girl. I have no expertise in child psychology, nor interest. No—I do not think I much like kindergarten girls.*

When Mom's turn comes, she cries. She puts a hand over her face. Her shoulders tremble. Tears seep through her fingers. Sometimes she makes choking and heaving sounds. When this happens, Doctor Bruster says, "Barbara, close your eyes. Do not open them until I say. Pretend that you're holding an empty balloon—a red balloon—in your hands. Stretch it once or twice. Stretch the red rubber. It is you against the balloon. Now concentrate hard. Think of all the scary and bad and mean things in your head. Focus. Think harder. Good. Good. Direct it—all the scary, all the bad, all the mean things—from the inside of your head down to the tip of your tongue. Taste it there, bitter like a copper penny balanced on the tip of your tongue. Now put your lips to the opening of the balloon, and blow. Blow the penny into the balloon. Deep, hard breaths. Empty your lungs. Empty your head. Now nothing is left on the tip of your tongue. The taste of metal is gone. The bad, the scary, the mean is gone. Tie a knot in the balloon. Trap everything inside. Hold the red balloon in your hands, feel its lightness, feel its weight. Decide to let that balloon go. Really want it gone. Open your hands. Look! It's helium! Watch the balloon float up, up, and away into the sky, into the deep clear blue, into the puffy white clouds. Watch the balloon until you can't see it anymore. There." Doctor Bruster claps his hands. "You can open your eyes now."

The first thing Mom sees is Doctor Bruster's mouth smiling at her, his perfect white teeth all in a row.

"Joseph and I met in college. One year of official dating, one year engagement. He got into med school. I got into law school. Our parents were ecstatic. Dad paid for a fifty-thousand-dollar wedding and sent us on a paradise honeymoon to Jamaica. I was Silvia McCallister Reed at last."

* * *

"Joseph—Reed, did you say?" Doctor Bruster says. "Spell that. Is it with an *a* or an *e*?"

Doctor Bruster licks his lips at this newcomer. *A wolf, a wolf, a wolf!* he says. *A wolf in sheep's clothing!* He will not stop scribbling in his unreadable language.

". . . The Jamaica part is the best. I'll admit it, we drank a lot of piña coladas and got too giddy, but mostly what we did was take long walks along the beach and just talk. One time he pointed out a man-o'-war for me to step over. Another time I found a small orange starfish washed up on shore. I held it in my hand, and we watched it for a long while. I remember wondering why it quivered and groped so, and then Joseph threw it back into the sea. He reminded me of a twelve-year-old boy skipping stones across the surface of a lake.

"But the most important time was the morning—Joseph was still asleep—I saw his sneakers lying on the floor next to the bed, one overturned, one upright. The amazing thing was the wind. It was blowing through the open window, scattering the two little piles of beach sand from when he had dumped them out the night before. Those shoes, the fragrant wind and scattering grains of sand, meant something to me. This little scene seemed important. I couldn't figure it out."

Doctor Bruster is fascinated by none of this. The expression on his face is bored and also annoyed. His time is being wasted. What he wants to hear is the part Silvia neglects to tell until much later.

"On that same honeymoon trip, Joseph took our rental car for a drive in the mountains. I thought we were just sight-seeing, but then Joseph purchased a one-ounce bag of marijuana for ten American dollars. He spent the next two days smoking as much of it as he could. I had to shove wet towels under the door of our hotel room to keep the smell from escaping. I didn't want the bellhops to catch on and throw us out. I couldn't stand the idea of Mom or Dad finding out. The third night I flung my diamond engagement ring from the balcony into the ocean. Joseph didn't even try to stop me."

Would it make any difference to her to imagine that the ring is probably still there, lying on the sandy bottom of the sea floor among sponges and stingrays? That it has taken on a life of its own? That now it has nothing whatever to do with the story as she told it.

Tammy is a funny lady. She shows us pictures of men from a little collection she keeps in a zippered compartment in her purse. She calls it her "Rogues' Gallery" and keeps it with her always in case she needs to identify one to the police. The men are different men every time, but they always have ugly faces. I know, because I see them close up. Tammy says all her boyfriends end the same: a blowout fight, he does something crazy like pop all four tires of her car with an ice pick, she kicks him out, he stalks her, and despite the restraining order, he ends up clinging to her window at night like a tree frog, batting the glass with a stiff hand and wanting in.

"Get it?" she says. "My Rogues' Gallery? Ha ha."

A fair number of us laugh, but never Doctor Bruster. His face says *Jokes get stale the second time around, Tammy.*

"Pool party gone bad," Doris says, holding up the arm in a sling with her good arm. "See, Ted gets this bright idea to throw a 'monster bash'—his words—in celebration of something, I'm still not sure what. Well, you-know-who shows up and trots out you-know-what. A noseful of that, and Ted starts climbing the palm trees and throwing the coconuts into the pool, me as the target."

"You-know-who? You-know-what? Doris, be specific," Doctor Bruster says. "Tell. Tell. Tell. Tell. There is no such thing as a secret." Doctor Bruster has been far too unhappy far too long. Doctor Bruster is presently glaring. Women who think they can make a tragedy into a joke!

*   *   *

One day I tell a true story that I hope will please Doctor Bruster to no end. I would really like him to sink his teeth into this one.

Dad and I sit in our corner booth at Denny's and order from Louise. This is our routine. The first Tuesday of every month from seven to eight P.M. we do this thing. I order a Junior Grand Slam breakfast and a large Coke, and Dad orders a reuben sandwich and an iced tea. Louise, who has got night-shift non-smoking, is our waitress every time. She knows our orders by heart, but she's a good sport and makes a show of writing everything out on her check pad. Sometimes she tries to flirt with Dad, but it never looks to me like he flirts back.

I like Louise. I can tell the kind of person she is from the different colored neckerchiefs she wears to spice up her Denny's uniform, her jewelry when holidays come around: heart-shaped pendants on Valentine's Day, American flag earrings on the Fourth, rhinestone Noel pins during Christmas. The other waitresses look ugly in their shapeless brown smocks, but not Louise. Louise doesn't ever look ugly.

Dad and I don't have much to say, sitting across from each other in the Naugahyde booth, a lamp hanging low over our heads and lighting the contours of our faces too bright. I can think of nothing exciting in my life or worthwhile of telling. We already covered what I learned in school that day and the fact that everything's about the same at the office during the car ride over here. Our immediate environment—the menu selections, the decor, the cleanliness or dirtiness of the rest rooms— offers nothing either. Dad and I have been here so many times now.

We are thankful when dinner comes. Our two bodies do a lot of pushing around of food on the plate. Some time passes, Louise drops the twelve dollar and seventy-two cent check on the table—a last-ditch coy smile—and Dad pays with a ten and five, which he tucks under the napkin holder. The same tip for Louise: $2.28 always. Then we walk out across the parking lot and get back into the car. There is a silence lasting about ten minutes during which we listen to Phil Collins and Kenny G on Lite 101.5 FM, a stifling tension in the empty space of air between us, until Dad says, "Well, here we are." Neither of us ever mentions it, but we both know why he drops me off in front of the Spanish-style stucco house exactly two doors down from Mom's instead of right in front. Then he does a three-point turn in the driveway, one back tire sinking into the lawn, and speeds away. I watch the red taillights disappear.

The people who live in the stucco house don't seem to understand that any of this goes on: Louise, the Junior Grand Slam breakfast, Kenny G on the radio, red fading lights. My idea every first Tuesday of the month is the same. To walk past the mailbox, up the driveway, and to the front door. To knock on the front door—I don't even know their names—and when someone answers say, "Look. Look what happened. See the ripped place in the grass?"

I wish I had a funny Ted story like Doris Fitzsimmons. None of my stories are very funny. The father story is a failure. Nothing happens. The language is often clunky. Too many adjectives. Not enough verbs. I could tell the whole thing in two sentences. And the character of the father remains vague. You have no idea who he is by the end of the story, not even simple facts like his profession. On top of that, you are kept out of private jokes, secrets, between the father and the daughter. Now why is it that neither of them mentions it, but they both know why he drops her off in front of the Spanish-style stucco house exactly two doors down from the mother's house instead of right in front?

Next week I might tell Doctor Bruster I'm never talking again. I will keep all my stories to myself. One I'll call "Funny Ted Story." It will have lots of colorful pictures. They will be stick figures in crayon and finger paints, but they will be beautiful. They will do the work of the words and save me from talking. All I will have to do is turn pages and point.

. . . Ted showed up at our doorstep with a grimy duffel bag and a red-haired mutt on a leash. He had a big mustache and was dressed in flip-flops and a pair of cut-offs. He wore no shirt, but he was wearing sunglasses. He looked like Tom Selleck in *Mag-*

num, P.I. I remember thinking it was a good sign that he rang the doorbell before entering. He didn't just barge in.

"I'm Ted," he said, "and this is Chuck. I've got a couple more pets out in the van."

I looked at Ted's van parked at the curbside. It was a fancy brown-and-orange conversion model with radial tires, TV antenna, tinted windows, and *BachlrPad* license plates. Suddenly: two big paws on the roof, and a shaggy brown head. Lolling tongue. Wow—Ted had a sunroof, too.

"Introducing Jo-Jo," Ted said. This dog barked twice. Chuck, who had started wagging his tail and turning circles, barked back. Ted yanked the leash. "Shut up, Chuck," he said. Chuck shut right up.

"What a dog," Ted said. I must admit I too was impressed. . . .

I like my Ted story so far. I think it's pretty funny. I'll tell more.

. . . I was impressed, and also hopeful. Not as hopeful as Mom, perhaps, but I was willing to give the guy a chance. *Innocent until proven guilty,* as they say. And I had to admit Mom was right: he was making an effort.

Ted would take us out for steaks, for instance, and entertain us with stories of how he had befriended the hoboes. So what if he paid with penny rolls? It was still money, and more important than that, it was *his* money.

And he would buy Mom stuff. On one occasion, a lavender wraparound dress with silver sandals to match, which Mom modeled for us in the living room. "Fashion show," she said, twirling around on her tiptoes to show off the fullness of the skirt.

Ted looked at me, raised his eyebrows. "Rummage sale," he said. "Five bucks, the whole set."

"What a deal," I said. "You're quite a shopper, Ted."

"Yeah, well. Give the credit to your mom. Put her in a paper bag and she could pull it off." Ted looked at me. "Isn't she a pretty lady, Erin?"

"Yes," I said. "She is."

"Not every kid's got a mom as good-lookin' as yours."

Mom would go to him then. Their kisses were deep and long. . . .

I can see already that "Funny Ted Story" is headed for some real trouble. In all good stories something goes wrong. I know that much. I know also that Doctor Bruster, were I to tell this story so he could hear, would be shifting in his seat, squeamish at "kisses deep and long," grimacing like a child being fed a spoonful of castor oil. Doctor Bruster doesn't like stories that end with "And off they walked into the sunset" or "They lived happily ever after." He despises the tale of the frog prince. *Come come come come,* he would say. *Let's be realistic. A frog is a frog. An Amphibian.*

. . . But it wasn't roses all the time. There were fights that would begin with Ted saying, "No interrupting—that's the rule," or "Okay, maybe I'm not some hotshot lawyer or doctor, but I'm a damn nice guy," or "Look: we're supposed to be a husband-wife team here," or "If you can't accept me for who I am, we've got a major problem."

I'll admit it. Once there was a car chase. Mom and I were driving home one day, I-95, rush-hour traffic, fifty-five miles per hour—and suddenly, above the rumbles of the engines, the screech of wheels, the honking of horns, I heard the words "I love you, Barbara!" I turned my head, and what I saw flash by was sunglasses and mustache. It was Ted in his van the next lane over, leaning out the window, his hair whipping around his face.

"Exit on Sunrise," he called, his hand cupped around his mustachioed mouth. "Pull into the Chevron. I just want to talk to you. I'm sorry for all . . ."—but the wind sucked his words away.

"Erin," Mom said, "roll up your window and put on your seat belt."

After a time of dangerous lane changing and checking the rearview mirror and getting flipped off by perturbed motorists, we did exit on Sunrise Boulevard. But instead of pulling into the Chevron, we pulled into City of Sunrise Police Headquarters. We parked next to a squad car and just sat there. I watched Ted's van, which had remained close behind us, cruise on by. Ted knew Mom meant business. He wasn't going to monkey with that.

"Mom, maybe we should go indoors and file a report," I said.

"Damn right," Mom said. "Let's get that guy behind bars.". . .

(The mother in my story would never cry. She would not hide in the backs of closets or under beds when she got upset. She would not tell the daughter she was going to slit her own wrists. Nor would she be afraid to use bad language or to carry a knife. She might carry a gun in a thigh holster. If need be, this mother would not hesitate to lift her skirt and shoot.)

. . . But when we finally got to the end of the line, the officer told us, "Sorry, ma'am, we can't help you. The incident began in Palm Beach County. This is Broward, ma'am. Now, the best thing to do would be to get back in your vehicle." . . .

(*Yes,* Doctor Bruster would say. *And when the clock struck twelve and Prince Charming turned out to be a snake, she would shrug her shoulders, wave good-bye to her yellow gown, her glass slippers, and with the help of her fairy godmother simply poof in a swirling cloud of stardust back into the pumpkin patch.* "Oh well, I knew it was just a fairy tale from the start, and not a true story at all," this mother would say, brushing the dirt off her brown rags, smoothing her fallen hair, and letting the bright silver light of the full moon bathe her.)

This is how my funny Ted story would end.

. . . One morning Ted announced that he had made up his mind for good: he wasn't going to be sticking around. It was time to hit the road.

"It's nothing personal, Barbara," he had said. "I just gotta keep movin'. Gotta keep those wheels turnin'." Mom didn't seem to have much of a problem with that. She even paid for one last tank of gas to expedite the process.

"Groovy," said Ted, "but the only thing is, can I store my stuff in the garage for a while? The van's packed full. I can't fit anything else. Chuck and Jo-Jo—those guys need space to romp."

The conversation went like this:

"How long, Ted?"

"Two weeks."

"No. One. You've got exactly one week to clear out your stuff."

"Don't worry. I'll be back."

"That's it, Ted. Seven days. I'm not responsible after that."

"Barbara. There's something you gotta understand about me—"

"The less I understand about you the better, Ted."

"—I *always* come back."

Mom spent the next seven days watching clocks: the oak grandfather clock in the living room, the little digital one on the microwave, her wristwatch, the one with the lighted red dial on the dashboard of her car, the *Return of the Jedi* clock next to my bed. I went about my business as usual.

When the first second of the first hour of the eighth day hit—it was a Tuesday, 5:00 P.M. on the nose, still no sign of Ted—Mom took me out into the backyard and gave me a shovel, a brand-new one with the price sticker still on the handle. She had a shovel of her own, just as new. Well, what happened was we dug a hole, me and Mom, and into this hole we put Ted's stuff. Just buried it: R.I.P. We didn't even bother to box it first. We just threw it in: shirts, shoes, papers of one sort or another, a few unopened cans of dog food, an empty pickle jar full of pennies, an electric razor, a tire-pressure gauge, two or three containers of flea powder, the lavender wraparound with matching silver sandals, and then on top of all that, a Styrofoam cup that had once contained urine, a gun–kitchen knife–canister of Mace–leather belt–big stick, a collection of ugly photographs, some empty beer bottles, a vacuum-packed wedding dress, a shot-up garbage can, many rolls of film, a plank from a wooden fence, a diamond engagement ring—it didn't matter. It all went flying. When we finished, Mom brushed the dirt off the knees of her jeans, looked at her wristwatch, smiled at me, and said, "There. That's done: 5:47 P.M. No more junk. Right, Erin?"

Every six months or so, we get a postcard in the mail from some off-the-beaten-track kind of place, for instance, Hot Cross, Texas. Usually the postcards are corny and risqué at the same time:

Hot Cross: We got the Best Buns in Texas.

They always end with the promise of his return: *Am planning to swing back your way pretty soon now. Will pick up my stuff then.*

So far Ted hasn't showed back up. I'm pretty sure everything's still where we buried it.

I think I would like that ending better if I added the words "Mom cut every postcard in two with scissors" and "We never laid eyes on Ted again." Doctor Bruster, I know, would prefer a dramatic return and then bloodshed.

But I have another story to tell, one that happened many years later. It is the most important one. I had no way of knowing about it on any one of those Wednesday nights with Doctor Bruster. I couldn't have told it if I'd wanted to.

What happened was I had been trying to pry out the car cigarette lighter with a pen. It was rusty and jammed a lot, and I'd developed a system.

I wasn't watching the road. I must have been doing seventy-five at least. I needed to light my joint.

But that wasn't the problem. The problem was that a deer ran out in front of the car. The impact did two things. One: sent the car flying. Two: unstuck the lighter. I remember it landing on the passenger seat and burning a little hole in the paper McDonald's bag lying there, and then the little hole becoming a bigger hole, and then the paper bag igniting, and then the seat going up in flames.

When I next opened my eyes in what I would later understand to have been the IC unit of the hospital, Mom was looking at me. Her hair hung down around her face. I spoke through the press of her hands. I told her it was a Merit Ultra

Light I had been trying to light—those were my exact words, *It was a Merit Ultra Light, Mom.* I was cutting back. Eventually, I wanted to quit altogether. I didn't know how much sense I was making.

Suddenly, Dad was there too. His face came into the picture. Eyes. Ears. Nose. Mouth. Chin. At first it was hard to put it all together. Then his mouth started moving, and I saw lips and teeth. Words came out. I could see them flying from his throat like tiny birds with featherless and beaten wings. I watched them hovering in the air, waiting there, singing to me. One by one the words took on meaning. Feathers grew long and lush; flesh covered bone, and I began to understand the thing he had been trying to tell me all these years, through all the silence.

Mom and Dad were in the same frame of vision. They were looking down at me lying in the plastic hospital bed, a tube in my nose and needles in both my arms. After I spoke, they looked at each other. I never remembered them so close to each other. I never even remembered them in the same room. Even when they were married and lived in the same house, they'd always been in different rooms.

But now their eyes met. Their kisses were deep and long.

This is the best story. We cave people pounce with spears and darts, tear it to bits with our bare hands, swallow the pieces whole. Afterward we want to record it and remember it always, this taste of blood on our lips. But we have no language. Words refuse to come. So we draw with charcoal and soot on stone walls. Pictures. No words. Only grunts and moans that echo deep in the recesses of the cave. Sometimes we have to crawl on our hands and knees through dark and dripping tunnels to reach these places.

This is a language Doctor Bruster cannot understand. Each sound is a mystery to him. His Sumerian plate remains blank. It screams out madly to be covered.

Our blood-smeared faces tell Doctor Bruster he can write again of the helium balloon, if he likes. We have no interest in stopping him there.

Lisa Stolley

University of Illinois at Chicago

YOUR OWN
PERSONAL PROJECT

In the spring, in Buffalo, it's cold and stays that way until it turns suddenly hot and deadly humid overnight. This particular spring, in 1976, Olivia's friend, Bebe, comes up to visit her at school. It is Olivia's second semester and she is sitting, wrapped in a sweater, at her desk in her dorm room trying to finish her anthropology project. It involves a survey of all the girls from Long Island in the dormitory. Olivia has handed out questionnaires that ask: What do you want to do when you get out of college? Almost all of the girls have responded *get married* and those who haven't, said *work for a while, then get married.* Next question: What kind of man do you want to marry? There are three possible answers here: *lawyer, doctor, accountant.* There are other questions too, like which parent are you closer to? *Mother.* How long will you wait to have a baby after you're married? *One to two years.* "God," said her teacher, a teaching assistant actually, a younger man with bad acne, when Olivia showed him her partial results. "Haven't any of these girls heard of Betty Friedan?" Olivia, embarrassed— though she's heard of Betty Friedan, she's never bothered to read that book, whatever it's called—laughed as if she knew what he was talking about. The TA didn't have much else to say about her project besides agreeing with her that, based on the similar answers she's received, she could draw some conclusions about girls from Long Island. It's a stupid thing but it's all she could come up with.

Olivia can hear the commotion Bebe's causing in the dorm. There's Bebe's voice echoing in the corridor, the loud click of heels, the sudden ending of conversation, the doors closing—probably all the girls who have curlers in their hair and don't want to be seen. There is also a male voice that belongs to a dark-haired guy with a beautiful mouth who steps in front of Bebe when they get to Olivia's room and sticks out his hand. "You look a little like Bebe," he says and Olivia tries not to smile with plea-sure, although she doesn't really believe him and it is probably just a come-on. Bebe is beautiful and big, with blond hair and brown eyes, almost six feet tall, and she is a model in New York. Olivia is shorter, maybe up to Bebe's shoulder, with brown hair and, yes, her eyes are brown too, but they're too big and so is her mouth; it's always a bit swollen looking and by the time that becomes popular, she'll already be in her thirties and what she looks like then won't matter much anymore, because she'll have learned that it really is true: looks can only get you so far.

Bebe and Olivia didn't become friends until their senior year; it was as if Bebe adopted her, swept her away from the hordes of stuck-up ponytailed Scarsdale girls and made her a best friend. Even after Olivia left for college, Bebe continued to call her from New York. Olivia is a good listener, that's probably why Bebe calls her so much, because she has a lot to say and Olivia doesn't. And now here she is with this guy who is a little older, maybe twenty-five or so, who is staring at her while Bebe paces the perimeters of the room. "Elliot," he says. Olivia takes his hand, shakes it, stares at his lips, feels a sudden and momen-tary jolt of relief; finally there's something to make her heart beat a little faster.

Bebe sits carefully on Olivia's bed, folding her legs under-neath her, patting the space beside her. "Come sit down," she says. "Not you, Elliot, you. God, could this room be any smaller? Where's your roommate?"

Olivia sits down beside her. The roommate is gone, off to another room with her best friend from Garden City the first week of school. So Olivia pushed the beds together, covered them with a big Indian spread and it looks like she has a king-size bed, although the beds separate with the least movement. "I don't have one," she tells Bebe. "She ditched me. You know, guys aren't allowed in the dorms."

"Oh, what bullshit," Bebe says. "So what do you do here?" she asks. She leans over and grabs a book from the desk. "Abnormal psychology."

"Don't read that," Olivia says. "I did and I have all the symptoms of a schizophrenic. Maybe catatonia too."

"What's that?"

Elliot laughs. "Never mind, Bebe, you don't want to know. Too close to home." He looks at Olivia in a way that is supposed to make her complicit in his joke.

"Screw you," Bebe says. She stands up and shakes out her white Mexican skirt. "Let's go. This place is claustrophobic." She gives her coat to Elliot, who puts it on her. He helps Olivia on with hers too. "We're staying at the Hilton," Bebe says as they walk out. Olivia nods. She's used to Bebe not being like other girls. No one Olivia knows stays in hotels but Bebe does all that: flies to places for weekends, rents cars, orders breakfast from room service. She called Olivia once from the Hyatt on Sunset Strip. "I'm having a bowl of strawberries and a mimosa," she said. "Don't you wish you were here?"

Up and down the hall, girls are peeking out their doors. All those girls who are vaguely nice, who ask her the same questions over and over again because they're not interested enough to remember the answers, who probably secretly think she's a drug addict and maybe a slut because she goes out with different boys and smokes pot in her room. "Bye," she says loudly, but no one answers.

Outside they get into a rental car. "There's nothing really to do here," Olivia says from the backseat. "I told you that. I should have come down to the city." Though there is no way she could go to New York. That would mean she'd have to go home, and she isn't going to do that. Her parents are in the middle of their divorce and she can't stand either of them. When she does go home, her mother follows her around saying things like: "He's going to realize that this is the worst mistake he's ever made," and "I feel sorry for you girls, this has got to be so hard on you," and the worst, "I know he calls you all the time at school, what does he say?" Olivia doesn't feel sorry for herself. She's a little worried about her sister, Melly, but not enough to go home, and besides, Melly is so into gymnastics she'll probably just parallel-bar herself into oblivion. When her father does call, which isn't all the time, more like once every couple of weeks, it's just with a guilty question or two: "How's school? Do you need anything?" *Dad?* Olivia wants to say. *Is it the biggest mistake you've ever made? Because if it isn't, will you please tell your wife to shut up?* It isn't that Olivia doesn't feel sorry for her mother, she does, but her mother is just so pathetic right now, she's got no pride, she's a meltdown, all high tremulous voice and wet eyes. Snap out of it, Olivia wants to tell her. Just stop. Get some backbone.

"There's an Alice Cooper concert," Elliot is saying. "The band is staying at the hotel. They're playing at, what do you call it, the Dome."

"I met the road manager," Bebe says. "He says there're tickets left."

"Guess who Bebe has a crush on," Elliot says.

Olivia sits up straighter. She thought Elliot and Bebe were together. She leans forward and taps Bebe on the arm. Bebe turns around and Olivia raises her eyebrows. Bebe shakes her head. "For you," she whispers.

"What?" Elliot says. "Are you talking about me?"

"Mind your own business," Bebe says. "Drive the car. You know, Olivia, Elliot went to college too. You two can talk about the boring things you learn there."

Elliot laughs again. Olivia likes the way he laughs. He's mellow. She would like to tell him about the Greek myths she's learning about in her mythology class, the only class she really likes. There's Echo, the nymph who wouldn't shut up, so Juno sentenced her to a life of echoing others: her own voice was gone, just like that. The way myths work irritates and pleases

Olivia. It's so easy. You screw up, make the gods mad, and that's it. Basically, you're fucked. She pulls out a joint from one of the pockets of her painter's pants, which are so not-all-right for an Alice Cooper concert; she wishes she'd worn something different. "Here," she says, handing the joint to Bebe. "Light this." To Elliot, she says, "So what do you do?" A boring question. Stupid. Bebe brings her a gift and look what she does.

"Nothing," Bebe says. "He's a free spirit."

"My father wants me to be a lawyer," Elliot says. He looks at Olivia in the rearview mirror. "I don't want to be a lawyer, but I'll probably do it anyway."

"Otherwise he won't get his inheritance," Bebe says. "And then he won't be able to pay me back."

"You wouldn't know what to do without me," Elliot says. "You'd be lost without me. I'm the perfect escort."

"It's true," Bebe says. "He's perfect. If I liked nice lawyer boys, I'd go out with him."

"If I liked big model girls, I'd go out with her," Elliot says.

"But he likes little college girls," Bebe says. She turns around and winks at Olivia.

"All the girls in my dorm want to marry lawyers," Olivia says. "Except me."

"Oh, shit," Elliot says. "I'm going to have to come up with another career."

■

BEBE'S room at the Hilton is a mess. Clothes are flung everywhere and there is mascara all over the mirror in the bathroom. "You should seriously consider him," she says, taking off her skirt. "He's a really nice guy. I think he'd be good for you."

"What about you? Why aren't you with him?"

"He's not my type."

"Well, maybe he's not mine either." Olivia isn't sure she likes being Elliot's type. What's so different about her and Bebe?

"No, I think he is. You both have that Tastee-Freez softie thing going. But if you two get together, you're going to have to come to New York." She lies down on the bed and begins to pull on a pair of Fiorucci jeans, wiggling them over her hips.

Olivia stands in front of the full-length mirror on the bathroom door. "I can't go to a concert like this. I shouldn't go. I need to finish my anthropology project."

Bebe, her jeans successfully zipped, comes to stand behind Olivia. "You could model," she says, lifting Olivia's hair up and piling it on top of her head. "Look at that face. A perfect junior."

"Please," Olivia says. "I couldn't be a model." Her eyes are too big for one; she always looks startled, a deer caught in the headlights. Now they're all red from the pot. She is very stoned. Everything is a bit hazy and she wants to see Alice Cooper. She wants to hear songs about dead babies and nightmares. She's in the mood for that.

"Yes, you could," Bebe says. "Elliot's right, you do sort of look like me. A miniature version. Except your hair is darker. You could get it blonded." She goes over to her suitcase. "Here," she says. "It's my Norma Kamali, but you can wear it."

It is a layered dress, gauzy, in black and pink. On Olivia it comes down to her ankles, but it's better than painter's pants. "Wow," she says.

"Come to New York," Bebe says. "Come be a model."

"My father would kill me," Olivia says. "He's paying a lot of money to keep me here."

"So?" Bebe says. "What's going to happen when you get out?"

"I don't know," Olivia says. When she wakes up every morning and joins all the other girls in their flip-flops and terry-cloth bathrobes in the steamy bathroom, she'd like to be anywhere but there, but instead she's brushing her teeth next to the girl who's her lab partner in science, who wears matching knits and lives for class breaks so she can throw herself into her khaki-trousered boyfriend's arms. The little noises she makes when she hugs him make Olivia sick. This girl, her name is Tina, or maybe Gina, filled out one of the anthropology questionnaires. Olivia wonders what this girl's boyfriend would think if he knew that she expects him to become a doctor, even though he's a liberal arts major, and that she cries when he doesn't call her, puts her head on her pillow and weeps until her girlfriends pat her back, saying, It's all right, he'll call, don't worry, he's crazy about you, he's going to marry you, you'll see. Olivia has seen this with her own eyes.

If she drops out of college her father will kill her. So will her mother, but it is her father who'll give her that hurt look, that surprised eyebrow-raised, what-happened-to-my-little-girl look. You'd think at this point he'd stop getting disappointed. He knows she's had too many boyfriends and an abortion, and that she's done a ton of drugs. But he doesn't see what's in front of him.

"Let me do your makeup," Bebe says.

"Not too dark," Olivia says and tilts her face up, gives herself up to Bebe who does things with dark pencils and colored powders so that when Olivia finally looks at herself, she is a different person—fit to go to an Alice Cooper concert.

"Gorgeous," Bebe says, and quickly brushes on her own makeup; she's a pro, she can make herself look like a magazine cover in a minute. But she's not what Olivia imagines models would be like: she's not a Charlie girl, all sassy and soft at the same time, she's not Cheryl Tiegs with that little face and cat eyes. She's got big lips and eyes and boobs. She doesn't cry; she's hard. She gets everything she wants and she never has to beg for it. Men fall all over her. She stays in hotels by herself and pays for them with her own money—with only a little help from her father, who owns a bank in Scarsdale just up the street from where Olivia's parents' house is.

They stand by the mirror side by side. The only thing that doesn't quite work are the shoes Olivia's wearing—they're Bebe's with some toilet paper stuck in the toes. They make her feet look like canoes. But the dress is long enough that you don't really notice them. "Look at us," Bebe says. "We're beautiful." She is a good friend. Olivia loves her.

"The road manager's going to love you," Olivia says. "He's going to want to marry you."

"Fuck marriage," Bebe says. "I have no interest in getting married."

"Oh," Olivia says. "Well, he'll want you to be his lady love."

"First I have to see if I want to be his lady love."

They look at each other in the mirror and laugh and it will be years before Olivia discovers that Bebe wants exactly what all those dorm girls want, she's just going about it in a different way.

Elliot is waiting for them in the lobby and he takes Olivia's arm, guiding her out to the car, which is waiting in front of the building. He doesn't say anything, just hands her into the front seat and then opens the back door for Bebe. "Sorry, sweetheart," he tells her. "But she's queen tonight."

"Didn't I do a good job?" Bebe says.

"Well, you started with good material," Elliot says.

"Good line," Bebe says.

"Excuse me," Olivia says. "I am breathing here. I'm not deaf and dumb." She spreads the dress out over her knees. She puts her hand on Elliot's knee when he starts the car and they drive like that to the concert. Before they get out of the car, Elliot takes a little white envelope out of his pocket and opens it. There is white powder, which at first Olivia thinks is cocaine—which she's done a couple of times before and which she loves—but it's not and Elliot won't let her have any. "You don't want this," he says, lifting a pile up with the end of a matchbook. "It's only for weirdos like me."

"Don't do any," Bebe says. "I did once and I thought I was dying." She hands Olivia a Seconal, which Olivia swallows dry, and then they go in.

Alice Cooper is just getting onstage when they get to their seats, which are near the front—all Bebe had to do was say the road manager's name and the ticket guy sold them these seats. They don't sit down because everyone is standing up and yelling and passing joints and bottles of wine. Alice Cooper starts playing with his snake before the music starts. "Its name is Katrina," Bebe says. She isn't dancing or carrying on. She just stands there, smoking a cigarette slowly, squinting at the band through the smoke. "There's Mark," she says, pointing to a long-haired man who runs onstage to do something to the bass player's microphone. Then the band starts playing with a surge of noise that makes Olivia move closer to Elliot, whose mouth is open a little; he's looking around and when his eyes stop on her, he smiles and holds out his arms and there's no reason not to go right into them. "You're different," he yells over the music.

"There's something about you. I bet you would like me, I'm a good boyfriend for a girl like you."

"You said you're weird," Olivia yells back.

"Yeah, but I'm really, really nice. That's why Bebe set us up. She thinks you need a nice boy like me." He kisses her wildly, pressing his mouth on hers, his hands moving through her hair. "I am so stoned," he says into her ear. He drops his hands and moves away. Then he leans forward again. "I want to feed you a club sandwich," he says. "We can get one at the hotel in my room. I can feed it to you bite by bite."

The music stops for a minute. Bebe's road manager comes out and starts doing something with the speakers at the front of the stage. "Mark," Bebe says, not even that loudly, but the guy somehow hears her and signs at her to come to a black door at the side of the stage and just like that she's gone, without a word to Olivia or Elliot.

"Good," Elliot says. "Let's go. I hate this group anyway."

"Wait," Olivia says. "I want to listen to another song." Also she wants to make sure Bebe is gone for good, because how awful if she came back from behind that black door and no one was there, but then she realizes that Bebe isn't thinking about anything but the road manager. After the song is over, Olivia follows Elliot out to the car and they go back to the hotel. Elliot peers at street signs along the way, asking, "Is that light green, can I go?" They get to the hotel and Elliot gives the car to the valet and leads her by the hand to the elevator. Olivia starts to get that kind of dead feeling she gets when she's about to go to bed with a guy, unless it's someone she really likes, and even then it's never what they say, fireworks and all that bullshit; she hasn't figured out how to make it feel good for herself and the guys don't know either. It's just exercise and sometimes it hurts because she gets dry and mostly she could live without it. The Seconal is wearing off and things are getting too straight. "Maybe I should go back to the dorm," she says. "I have to finish my project."

"I'm your project tonight," Elliot says. "Your own personal project." He puts her hand to his mouth and licks her palm. "Don't worry, I can't get it up anyway. Dust does that to you."

"I'm not worried," Olivia says. She feels suddenly better, like she's back in control, like maybe she could have some fun with this guy. She thinks about what Bebe would do, what she's learned from watching Bebe. Elliot is a present from Bebe. She can't forget that. She takes her hand away. "Okay," she says. "If you're my project, then you have to do what I say."

"Oh, I like that," Elliot says.

The elevator doors open and they get on. There is a mirror at the back and Elliot says, "I look so much like my father I want to kill myself."

"You're really hung up on your father, aren't you?" Olivia asks.

"What makes you say that?" Elliot says and makes a face at himself.

Elliot's room is neater than Bebe's. There's nothing but a hairbrush on the bureau and a joint, which Olivia lights up as if it's hers. Elliot does more of his white powder but won't let Olivia have any. "No," he says. "This stuff is just for people like me. It might do bad things to you and that would make me sad." His voice is getting dreamy sounding and he lies back on the bed. "Order a club sandwich, please," he says. "And some French fries. And some wine." He closes his eyes. "Then tell me what I should do to you. I'll do anything."

Olivia stares at him. This will become familiar, this staring at him as he lies on beds, off in some angel dusty world where she can't and doesn't want to go. She doesn't like drugs that take you that far away. Enhance what's there. Make it better than it will ever be. Elliot's zoning out will become old and stale, though right now she feels protected by it, sheltered by his closed eyes. He's the most devoted man she will ever know. She'll end up leaving him on a doorstep. "I want a back rub," she says and takes off the dress and the too-long shoes. She stretches out next to him in just her underwear and he straddles her and gives her the best back rub she's ever had. He hums while he does it and when the food comes, he signs the bill, saying, "Is that the line where I sign? Is this a pen?" He feeds her French fries and bites of the club sandwich. It's the best thing she's ever tasted. Elliot rubs her back some more after they eat and drink the wine; he rubs her back until she's tired of that.

He massages her feet and then tickles the inside of her arm, something her father used to do when she was a child to help her fall asleep. "Why do you hate your father so much?" Olivia asks. It seems somehow important that she know this before she falls asleep on the good hard hotel bed.

"Because he won't leave me alone," he says. "He thinks I should be like his sorry ass. He doesn't understand that I like being like this." He puts his head next to hers and stares at her with cloudy eyes. "Your father thinks you're the bee's knees, doesn't he."

"Yes," Olivia says because she doesn't know what else to say, because she has no idea what her father thinks of her. "What do you want to do if you don't want to be a lawyer?"

"I don't want to think about it," Elliot says. "I don't want to have to make any big decisions." He smoothes his thumb over her eyebrows. "Do you want me to do anything else?"

Olivia looks at his mouth. "Kiss me," she says. "No, let me kiss you." And she does, and he just lets her and she can't remember enjoying kissing so much. When she's finished, she makes him tickle the inside of her arm until she falls asleep.

■

SHE WAKES up because there's something at the foot of the bed, warm and soft beneath her feet. She lifts up the covers and there's Elliot, curled up like a fetus, smaller than she would have imagined he could make himself. He's as curled up as a sleeping dog and there are little doggy snores coming from him. Olivia decides she should just let him sleep and so gets up carefully, putting back on Bebe's dress and shoes, taking a few dollars from the wallet in the first drawer of the bureau for cab fare. She stops at Bebe's door, a floor below Elliot's, and presses her ear to it, but she can't hear anything. It's still pretty early, not yet eleven. She imagines Bebe in bed with her road manager, all tangled up with him, exhausted from all that sex, and she's embarrassed that she and Elliot didn't have sex, didn't do anything except kiss. But no one has to know. She likes Elliot a lot. She could imagine having sex with him and telling him what to do to make her feel good. Thinking this makes her shiver. She wishes she had a joint. She goes downstairs to get a taxi back to the dorm.

Her hallway smells like Cheetos and perfume. A couple of girls stare at her as she walks to her room but no one says anything. It's possible that she could be caught for having spent the night out—you can get suspended for that, but there's no note on her door, nothing to indicate that she's in trouble. There's a phone message on her desk: *Call your mother.* At the bottom of the message is scrawled a note: *Why didn't you interview me for your project? I'm in room 110. Constance.* Olivia has no idea who she is but it's another body for her project, so she goes down to 110 with a questionnaire. She can hear girls talking in the room and she stops outside the door. "If he doesn't ask me out, I'm going to slit my wrists," a girl says and another—Olivia thinks it's Gina or Tina—says, "Well, don't let him know that." The first girl says, "I'm not even sure Craig knows my name." Gina/Tina laughs in a grim way. "If I didn't remind Dave every day, he'd probably forget mine."

Olivia knocks and lets herself in, holding the questionnaire in front of her like an offering. The two girls are on one of the beds, leaning against the wall, with a box of Mallomar cookies between them. "Here," she says and gives it to the girl who is not Gina/Tina. "You're Constance, right?"

The girl, who is Constance and is still in her nightgown, nods. She looks over the questionnaire. "I can answer these in a minute." She reads a question and says, "Tina, what did you say about when you want to have a baby?"

"A couple of years after marriage," Tina says. She is wearing matching velour pants and top and her hair is up on her head with a few deliberate messy strands around her face. She looks like a kitten.

"Good," Constance says. She reaches for a pen on her desk and, propping the questionnaire on her knees, begins to neatly print answers.

Olivia stands there. She is aware of herself in her too-long dress and shoes, her makeup-smeared eyes. Tina is taking tiny bites out of a Mallomar and looking at her. "So," she says, "what's your major?"

"I don't know yet," Olivia says. "What's yours?"

"Lit," Tina says. "With a psych minor. My father wants me to major in pysch because he's a shrink but there's no way I'm going to a bazillion years of school so I can listen to crazy people. The psych minor is a compromise."

"Oh," Olivia says.

"Nice dress," Tina says. "Unusual."

Constance finishes the questionnaire and hands it back to Olivia. "That was easy." She smiles. "Thank you, Olivia. I was feeling left out. It seemed like everyone but me got to fill one out."

"No problem," Olivia says. She backs out of the room. She is a freak in this room and as soon as she closes the door behind her, Tina and Constance will talk about her in whispers, widening their eyes and laughing a little. Olivia doesn't care. She stalks to her room, swishing her dress around her, trying not to lurch too much in the big shoes. In her underwear drawer is a bag of change for laundry and she grabs a handful of quarters and goes to the phone at the end of the hall. There's a line of girls waiting, most of them questionnaire girls, except for two who are known as the local nerds because all they do is study and read and they're fat and wear glasses. Olivia wonders why all the smart girls look so bad. It must be deliberate. Maybe they'll bloom once they get done with school. Maybe they're ugly ducklings and they'll be swans when all the questionnaire girls are on their first face-lifts. But right now, they're huddled together, talking quietly, protecting each other from the bright prettiness around them.

When her mother answers, Olivia hangs up. She tries her father's office in the city. He's been spending a lot of time there since the divorce proceedings started. When Olivia was home for Christmas, he came home, but he slept in the den. They all pretended everything was fine. Her mother's lips were pale and pinched but she cooked the holiday turkey just as she did every year. Melly brought a book to the table and no one said anything, and Olivia, who'd smoked as much pot as she could before dinner, ate everything in sight. Her father sat at the head of the table, ruddy from martinis and wine, and talked about the newest books coming out at the publishing company he runs. Olivia told her mother later that she'd never do that again, sit at a table with parents who were getting divorced. Don't be silly, her mother said, it's nice that we can still be friends.

After ten rings, her father picks up. "It's me," Olivia says. "Olivia."

"Olivia, honey, how are you?" Her father's voice is rich and loving. He sounds like he's in a good mood. "How's school?"

"That's what I'm calling about," Olivia says. She waits a beat. "I want to take a year off." That sounds better than dropping out. She can persuade him, she knows. It's just a matter of finding the right words. "I think it'll be good for me. I need some life experience."

"That's what college is supposed to prepare you for," her father says.

"Well, it's not. It's only an extended version of high school, as far as I can tell," Olivia says. "I'm not learning jack about life."

"Have you told your mother about this?"

"No, I wanted to talk to you first."

Her father sighs. "I don't think it's a good idea," he says. "What will you do instead? Work at Woolworth's?"

"You could give me a job at your company," Olivia says, just to be mean, because he's never offered her a job, because of course she can't do anything. There are lots of fathers who give their daughters jobs even if they can't do anything though. "I want to be a model," she says.

"Wait, hold on," her father says.

Olivia can hear a woman's voice in the background, a woman in her father's office on a Sunday: it must be a new girlfriend. Olivia tries to picture the woman, a face for the low voice. She doesn't usually care about her father's girlfriends, stopped caring a long time ago when she found out he had them, but this one is getting in her way. "Hey," she says. "Dad."

"Okay, I'm here," her father says. "All right, now what do you want to do?"

"Be a model. Bebe will help me."

"Who's Bebe?" He puts his hand over the receiver and Olivia can hear him talking to the woman. Then he comes back: "Nell says modeling is an extremely hard career to try to get into. Not that I don't think you could do it, but are you sure it's what you want?"

"Who's Nell?" Olivia asks. A girl behind her waiting for the phone sighs loudly and jingles coins in her hand.

"She's a friend of mine. You'll like her a lot. Honey, can we talk about this later? I'm not trying to put you off, but I have lunch reservations. Can I call you tonight? I promise I will and we'll talk about this some more. If you really think you want to leave college, I'm not going to force you to stay, but I think you're making a mistake."

"Okay, Dad," Olivia says.

"Bye, honey," her father says and then, "really, I'll call you later, or first thing tomorrow morning, and we'll talk about this." Before he hangs up, Olivia can hear the woman's low murmur and Olivia wants to tell her to shut up while people are on the phone.

She goes back to her room and takes off Bebe's dress and shoes and lies down on the bed. She's going to quit college and move in with Bebe and have a life. If she can't model, she'll find something else to do. But first she has to finish her project, so she gets up and puts on jeans and a sweatshirt and sits at her desk. She reads the last questionnaire. Constance answered everything right. She's perfect for the results. These girls are like road maps. They know exactly where they are going. They are as planned out as a grid. *Thus,* Olivia concludes, *there are obvious similarities between the girls who live in this dormitory. It can be suggested that these similarities are based on upbringing. All of their families have a working father and a mother who stays at home. All of these girls feel closer to their mothers than their fathers. This may be the reason they all want to be like their mothers and be married and stay home and do nothing with their shallow little lives except breed and hope that their stupid husbands won't fuck around.* She crosses out the last sentence. She doesn't give a shit why these girls do what they do. She wants to get out of this Cheeto-smelling dorm before she goes out of her mind. According to her psych book, she's suffering from feelings of displacement and alienation. She's experiencing low self-esteem and irrational anger. When she hears Bebe's unmistakable footsteps, she feels unreasonable exhilaration. She rushes into the hallway. "Hi," she says, leading Bebe and Elliot back into her room. Elliot kisses her and Bebe says, "Oh, isn't that sweet," and Elliot says, "You're just jealous."

Olivia tells them she's moving to New York. She tells them that she'll finish the semester and then she'll be coming down and she'll need Elliot to help her move her stuff into Bebe's place. She doesn't give either of them a chance to say anything and they nod their heads and Elliot smiles.

"I did a good job," Bebe says when Olivia stops talking. "The road manager was a bust, but I like the way this worked out."

"We're supposed to say, 'Thank you, Bebe,'" Elliot tells Olivia.

"Thank you," Olivia says. "But something would have happened anyway."

"Ha," Elliot says. "Olivia gets in a last word. Good girl."

Then they say good-bye and leave because there's a plane to catch back to the city. Olivia waits until she can't hear their voices or footsteps anymore and then she digs out some more quarters and goes back to the pay phone. She's going to call her father and tell him that it's for sure that she's taking a year off. She's going to make it clear, there's no arguing, there's no dissuading her. Maybe she'll pretend to talk to Elliot while she's on the phone with him. Who's that talking? her father will ask. Oh, no one, she'll say. Just a friend. You don't know him, she'll say. He thinks I should take a year off, too. She'll hang up, having firmly established that she's not going back to college after this semester. Then she'll go back to her room and finish the project.

Clark E. Knowles

University of New Hampshire

LITTLE GEORGE

November 26

Here's what we know:

Her parents work in the local school district. Mom is an administrator. Dad teaches Earth Science. They moved here ten years ago from Maine to start a family. They fell in love with our town, made friends, joined the neighborhood watch, went to neighborhood meetings. They own a small brick house near the bend in a long U-shaped street of brick houses. Their yard has trees and flowers and looks out over a nice-sized duck pond.

His name is Chester, but he goes by Chet. His hair is pitch-black, like fresh tar. He wears vests and will sometimes drink too much and laugh too loud at jokes that aren't quite funny. Her name is Michelle. Her hair is red but not too red. She wishes she were thinner but doesn't obsess. Her favorite song is "You Light Up My Life" by Debby Boone.

They were blessed with a healthy baby boy, George, and a year later with a healthy baby girl, Sissy. Sissy was born with bright red hair, as if her head were on fire. George is small and sandy haired. He likes frogs. To the world, he seems very brave.

The cameras find George particularly appealing.

Sissy was wearing a light blue dress. In front of the cameras, it is all Chet or Michelle can remember: the light blue dress.

She was walking down the block, they say.

God help us. Where is our baby?

She was going to visit a friend.

I was George's age when a North Vietnamese soldier shot my brother. The first bullet struck his spinal cord two inches above his waist, bringing him to his knees. I imagine the scene: screaming men, smoke, explosions, my brother paralyzed but conscious, wondering why he is there. The second bullet hits his shoulder only seconds after the first, knocking him face-down into a stream. The wounds might not be fatal, only crippling. In the blur of battle, no one notices a drowning man. He dies holding his breath, before his buddies can pull him clear.

My hair is blond. I live next door.

There are things we don't know. I imagine this: yesterday morning, their last as a family. Sissy and George eating soggy, sugary cereal, Michelle and Chet a little harried, trying to get everything in order before leaving the house, a television in the background broadcasting the weather forecast, the morning anchors discussing a cold Thanksgiving holiday weekend.

Chet kisses his children. Michelle kisses Chet and straightens her daughter's jacket collar, pulling it out of her dress.

How'd you get your collar stuffed down inside your dress? she says.

It just happened that way.

Silly girl.

I am not. I'm not silly.

Okay then, goofball.

I am not a goofball.

I know, I know. Let's go.

Sissy's red hair bounces as she walks to the car, Mom's hand on her back. Chet unlocks the doors and the kids climb in. Michelle sits on the passenger side. Chet checks the mirrors and very carefully puts his car into reverse and backs out of the driveway.

There are things a camera cannot see.

Police have detained a man named Randall Sawyer. Witnesses reported sounds of a struggle in his van. He is being questioned. A plane has crashed somewhere in Switzerland. Beer tastes great. The gulf stream is pushing warm air our way. Cold air is coming from Canada. There will be a clash of temperatures.

November 30

The van is in a field behind the Wal-Mart. Camera crews are on the scene.

Traces of blood are found in the van.

Police officially deny everything, meticulously avoiding a wrong move.

We are moving, they say, as fast as we can. In a case like this everyone has to be patient.

Action News tells all. They have sources. They are camped out in the street, our street, my street, waiting for Sissy.

I am patient until two o'clock in the morning. I am inside watching the cameras outside. There is constant movement with no apparent purpose. More trucks arrive. Vans leave. I walk outside to wait, to watch with everyone else. The midnight sky rests just out of reach. The grass crunches under my feet. The world is cold.

Randall Sawyer is officially charged with abduction.

December 2

Police Chief Charlie Jenkins pulls his mustache and explains that sources close to the suspect have given new leads to the investigation.

Sources say Randall, an expert hunter and trapper, knows his way around a knife. They say he is quiet and has never been trouble.

Cut to the anchorwoman. Her hair is perfect. She has dimples. She introduces Marv Trimble, who is reporting live from Randall Sawyer's house. Marv is an inexperienced shaver. His chin has several small nicks. He wears a silver wedding ring.

Randall Sawyer lives with his mother. She is crying. I expect her to say it couldn't be her son. There's no way. He's too kind.

He was always disturbed, she says. Her voice, oddly enough, is squeaky.

Finally, I think, someone is being honest. The camera presses close, too close, to Mrs. Sawyer's face. She looks aggravated.

Disturbed? says Marv Trimble. His face is serious and composed, his eyes the deepest blue.

Mrs. Sawyer closes her eyes, sniffs the air. The camera highlights a dark patch of skin the size of a nickel to the left of her lip. It looks serious.

He was on medication, she says, but I don't know what. He pulled the legs off spiders.

The camera catches her eyes, old and blank. She blows her nose. Behind her, police move in and out of her house. They are finding things and categorizing.

He was always disturbed, Mrs. Sawyer says again.

Marv straightens himself, squares his body to the camera, reports by the book.

There you have it, Kathleen, he says, Randall Sawyer's mother indicating a disturbed mental state in her son. Sources now tell us a video camera has been found in Sawyer's room. No word yet if a videotape is in the camera or what that tape might reveal.

Dramatic pause. The wind blows Marv's hair. Clouds move quickly across the screen; a fluffy, ominous backdrop.

He lowers his voice a notch, calls up an authoritative baritone. Reporting live for WTTW Action News, this is Marv Trimble.

Back to the anchor.

Traffic set new records over the Thanksgiving holiday weekend, but there were fewer driving fatalities than ever before. State highway officials are pleased so many motorists drove with caution and consideration. Coming up next, more on the approaching cold spell and Jerry Canon's Week at the Movies.

*   *   *

I see myself in George. I waited for my brother. The blurry pictures of Vietnam mixed with the sharp images of flag-draped coffins off-loaded from flat, squat military planes. The cameras swooped down onto battlefields to film tired soldiers fighting an invisible enemy, swooped down onto families standing at the fresh graves of dead sons.

Every flag-draped coffin was my brother. Every dead Vietnamese soldier was my brother's killer. I didn't understand protesters. I wanted more bombs and more guns. When my brother finally came home, my family traveled to San Francisco to meet his coffin. The cameras were watching. I have seen footage of myself standing stoic at the airport with other families. My face went out across the nation.

Little George is on television. If I angle my television, I can see him outside my window, on the other side of my hedge, as well as on the screen. I turn down the sound and listen hard but hear only the wind and soft hum of my furnace.

I turn the volume up too loud. This is news, after all. Little George is one hundred feet from me and yet so close. He is screaming from my speakers.

Why did he do this? he says. Why did he take my sister? I just want my sister.

His boy face is scrunched up beneath the glare of the television lights. His shirt is rumpled. He is holding a doll with yellow yarn hair. His eyes carry the seriousness of someone who deserves an answer.

Little George, I think, you will own tape of this night. You will buy a VCR and play this tape. You will wonder why he took your sister. You will ask yourself why you were not crying.

Even the reporters call him "little." Little George Young. He is the focal point now. Sissy is just missing. Everyone wants to see George. I stand up and walk to my window. The cameras are pointing at my house, at the low spot of the hedge where Randall Sawyer reportedly stood with his video camera. Police combed my property earlier today and asked if I had seen anything.

No, I said, I haven't.

Nothing suspicious?

No sir. I was in my office. I have an office here in the house. I'm an accountant.

He was on your property. Right there. On your property. We think he stood next to your hedge.

I don't really look out much. My office is downstairs.

We'll have to investigate your property.

Of course.

The cameras saw the police talking to me and rushed over, as if I were the missing link.

What can you tell us?

What is your name?

Did you know the victim?

Had you seen the suspect before?

They are showing the tape of me. I appear taller than I am. My hair is mussed. I haven't shaved in two or three days.

No, I say, I haven't seen him before. No, I don't know who he is. I heard his mother say he was disturbed. That's all I know. I only know what you people tell me. I mean, only what I've seen. Just like everyone else. I really can't say.

My shirt is untucked. My cheek twitches. I want to tell them something important, to compose my face.

It is all too sad, I say. My eyes droop.

So sad, I say again.

I talk to my ex-wife several times a year. She moved to New Mexico, where things are warm. She was tired of a cold house. Sissy was one when Mary and I divorced. After Mary left, the Youngs brought me a casserole.

We know how hard things like this can be, Michelle said.

I was married once before, Chet said. Even if it is the best thing, I know how hard it is.

I thanked them. Later that summer I invited them to a backyard barbecue and we laughed and drank beer. We watched the sunset glisten on the pond and listened to the crickets.

Mary called tonight after watching the nightly news with Dan Rather. Our town is national business. The country is taken with Little George. He is the newest darling. Everyone thinks he is so sad and brave.

He is so sad, Mary said.

Yes, and brave, I said. I have been watching the whole thing.

Watching? she said.

Yes, well, yes.

You're right there.

I have work to do.

I should let you go.

They say most Americans will get to be on television at least once.

Who says?

Someone, I guess. I heard it somewhere.

I never heard that.

I did. It must be true. This is twice for me.

That's right. I forgot.

Here I am again. Right where the news is happening.

You must be lucky.

Yes, maybe that's it.

December 3

Terry McManus, a friend of Randall Sawyer's, has been arrested. He is charged as an accomplice. Action News reports that Terry helped Randall abduct and kill Sissy Young. There has been, apparently, a confession.

He admits he helped. I do not want to believe him.

Police have him handcuffed and covered with a coat. People are screaming as he is pushed through a crowd toward a brown state police cruiser. A bony wrinkled hand grabs the arm of the coat covering his head and pulls it off. He is a normal-looking man with dark brown hair and a large nose. He looks scared, and I don't want to believe that he helped kill poor Sissy Young.

Cut to the Young house. A candlelight vigil. Chet has come outside, a brave man, a sad man, to thank the crowd. The cameras are close. They seem to be on top of him. Microphones touch his lips.

Thank you, everyone, he says.

He tries not to cry, a grown man. He starts shaking and cannot stop. The camera watches. The microphone is close. He tries to talk but breaks down again. Michelle is next to him. Her eyes are dark and red. Her voice is whisper-hoarse.

Find my baby, she says. I want to see my baby.

Chet holds her and they cry together. I tell myself to stand up and turn off the television. The candles outside my windows are brilliant, holy.

The camera pulls away to Marv Trimble, tired and gaunt and older after a long week on the scene.

Police, he says, will begin dredging the pond behind these houses early tomorrow morning. Terry McManus has told police that Sissy Young was put into a plastic sack and dumped into the pond. Reports say the bag was wrapped tight with duct tape and weighted down with broken pieces of cinder block.

Marv's voice catches, as if he can't believe what he is saying. He looks at his note cards and then back at the camera.

The people here at this vigil, he says, are already calling for the death penalty. It looks as if he might cry as well. It looks as if everyone might start crying. The crowd listens to Marv speak.

Again, he says, police believe Sissy Young's body to be somewhere in the pond behind her own home.

The wind gusts. Marv puts his hand to his ear, covering his earpiece. And then he does something most unprofessional. He shrugs, admitting to a speechlessness. He is surrounded by people, old and young, holding candles in mittened hands. He remains silent. The camera is now hungry for him. This is drama unparalleled.

This, he finally says, will be a long night for all involved. A long night especially for Sissy's family. His hand remains at his ear, waiting, it seems, for direction.

People start singing. A hymn. Something inspirational. And then they are chanting, praying, calling for the death penalty. Marv Trimble is gone. During a commercial, I go to the window.

I felt the same things so long ago. The hate builds inside me like a geyser.

My breath is short. My heart pounds.

Kill them, I whisper. Kill them both.

I pray for a camera. Just one camera to show my anger this time.

Kill them! I shout. Kill them!

The sound rings in my ears. My face is hot. I press my face against the window, welcome its cold hardness. There is frost on the ground. The weatherman predicts an early snow.

Kill them! I scream, my face pressed against the glass. My voice, loud at first, catches in my throat and I slide to my knees. I watch the outside and listen to the television.

I once went to the Vietnam Memorial in Washington and found my brother's name. It is a very long wall of names. There was a small booth set up away from the wall. The path to the booth was muddy and the grass brown. Several Vietnam vets sat, talking among themselves. They wore faded fatigues and were drinking coffee from Styrofoam cups. I asked if any of them had known my brother but none had. A long-haired vet with no left hand helped me find my brother's name. He walked and talked with me for at least an hour. I told him about the cameras, how I was a national news figure. He nodded and asked me if I missed my brother.

It was a long time ago, I said.

When his coffin was coming off the plane, we could feel his soul passing before us. It was a silly thing to feel but we all felt it. My mother, my father, and me. The temperature dropped slightly for no apparent reason. We looked at each other. The wind was warm and yet we all had chills. I was hate-filled even then, with my brother's soul so close.

At his grave site I prayed whoever killed my brother would die a horrible death. I imagined hacking off a faceless man's arms and legs with a hatchet. The small hatchet I used in Cub Scouts.

I stood next to my brother's coffin and watched it sink slowly into the ground. I told myself I loved my brother and would miss him. He was everything. He was going to teach me how to drive.

Sometimes, on late night television, on the History Channel, or on various news stations, they show footage of coffins coming off the airplanes. Two or three times now I have seen the footage of me and my family. My eyes are drawn to my own face.

I think the next time I see that footage, I will look up and see my parents' faces. I promise I will not watch me, but will look instead at my parents. I tell myself, if anyone has the right to hate, it is the parents. But I never look. I am fascinated with my own face. I am fascinated with my hard, thin lips, with the wind pulling at my shirtsleeves, with the dark corners of my eyes looking for someone to blame.

December 4

My property runs straight to the water. In the summer I go to the edge and catch fish and feed the ducks. I set a chair up at the edge and read the paper on Saturdays and Sundays.

Now near winter, the water is cold. Most mornings there is a thin layer of ice. Police trucks full of special equipment drive through my yard to get to the pond. Men unload boats and diving gear and chains and hooks. The crowd is enormous. People line the streets, but the police won't let anyone near my house. Tire tracks cover my lawn. I go outside several times. It is my house. I can go almost anywhere I want.

From my patio I can see men in the water. Chet and Michelle are standing on their deck. Little George holds his sister's favorite doll. Instinctively, I raise my hand to wave, the good neighbor, but catch myself, put my hand in my pocket and look again at the men and the boats.

I imagine it like this: Michelle and Chet pick up their children at school and strap them into the backseat.

Randall is already waiting. He already has a plan.

Chet and Michelle drive home slowly, singing a song. *I love you, you love me.* Something silly.

Chet jokes with Sissy.

Knock, knock.

Who's there?

Orange.

Orange who?

Orange you glad I didn't say banana again?

And Michelle says, I can't hear you, there's a banana in my ear.

Everyone laughs. George shows everyone the picture he has drawn in art class. It is something happy and colorful, a picture of their home. Mom, Dad, sister.

Chet and Michelle pull carefully into the driveway. They are looking forward to the upcoming weekend. Michelle plans a nontraditional Thanksgiving. She wants to make a Mexican feast. Enchiladas. Burritos. Homemade salsa. She plans in her head the time it will take to cook everything. Sissy is excited. She has never had enchiladas.

I've never had enchiladas, Sissy says.

You will soon enough, Michelle tells her.

They are the last words mother and daughter share. They hug and Sissy runs down the driveway.

Be careful, Chet says, take it easy.

Sissy slows down. Okay, Daddy, she says.

It is the last time anyone sees Sissy.

Except for Randall Sawyer and Terry McManus.

How they take Sissy, how they coax her into the van, how they force her away from her life, how they change everything, I cannot imagine.

I try to picture how they did what they did. I cannot.

My legs are weak.

I lean against a cast-iron patio chair and stare at the water.

A man breaks the surface.

Cameras capture me standing at the edge of the pond. The divers have found Sissy. I sense the urgency. Three men in a rowboat look intently at one diver in the water. They all point.

Several policemen yell at me. My breath comes in spurts. The men in the boat look over toward me. They are not too far from shore. One man wears a uniform. His face is red and he is smoking a cigarette. The other men look as if they don't want this any more than I do.

Is it her? I scream. My voice is scratchy.

Hey, someone shouts at me, what are you doing? Get back.

What am I doing? I say.

Back away from the water.

I sit here and feed the ducks, I say. This is where I live.

The wind catches my shirtsleeves. I look over my shoulder, up into my yard and see a camera watching me, my face. I am shivering.

Can you feel her soul? I shout to them. I can feel her soul!

And, as if on cue, a diver lifts something from the water. The men lean down and pull Sissy over the side of the boat. My heart jumps in my chest. Chet and Michelle are hysterical, screaming. Cameras catch their tears, then pan to Little George, who holds Sissy's doll, pulls it to his chin, waiting.

Nicholas Montemarano

University of Massachusetts, Amherst

SLUMMING

1. *Means so much less than nothing* (1993)

Hanging at the park with Ricki Sanchez and his friends on a
school night, Ricki toasted again. Alma making out with Ricki,
his tongue as cold as a beer can. Then: Ricki fired up, breaking
Bud and Colt bottles, talking trash, Dr. Jekyll and Mr. Hyde act
in full effect. *Get me more fuckin' beer* one minute, *love you love
you Angel* the next. Better if he was just Hyde, maybe then she
wouldn't give a shit, but she needs Jekyll. Needs Hyde too,
can't be in love with one without the other. By the end of the
night it's all Hyde. She takes it and hopes for something different tomorrow, takes it all and hopes when she sees him in the
hallway at school it will be Jekyll passing her by, Jekyll smiling
at her, touching her hair, never mentioning Hyde, who's gone
for the moment but always lurking.

*I was stupid crazy last night, girl, talkin' a whole buncha shit, we
had a good time though, right, me and you, girl.*

Yeah, had a great time in the stupid park with his stupid
friends. Didn't need to fall asleep to have a nightmare, had a
big one right in the middle of the park.

Yo, check it out, bro, watch this shit, check this shit out. His friends crowd around him as he turns to the group of girls smoking in a circle ten yards away. *Come over here, girl, I need you for somethin'.*

Alma starts to walk over, dumbass dumb dumb dumbass, stupid smile on her face like she can claim any part of him. Sticks his finger in her ass yet there's no part of him she would dare call her own.

Not you. Points at Alma, scowl on his face, can barely keep from laughing.

She stops like she's been shot in the head.

You, pretty thing. Points to another girl, yes she's a pretty thing, prettier than Alma, stupid Alma. (Can't cry, won't won't do it, keep that lip steady, smile like it means nothing.)

Come on over here, gimme what I need. Pretty thing walks over, takes the gum from her mouth, tosses it to the ground, and kisses Ricki Hyde Ricki on the mouth, her turn to taste his beer tongue; he's so drunk he falls over and takes her down with him.

(Smile when you look at them, means nothing at all.)

They stop making out. *You still love me, girl?* Looking at Alma now, already knows the answer. Still on the ground with pretty thing.

'Course I do, Ricki. (Laugh like a good girlfriend, Alma.)

What about now? Kisses pretty thing again.

Yeah. (Keep lip steady.)

And now? More kisses, grabs pretty thing's tits this time.

Yeah. Gotta give Hyde his satisfaction, gotta feed the monster. Besides, it means nothing, means so much less than nothing.

2. *Alma, you're a necessity* (1995)

Alma Reyes: Nineteen-year-old Puerto Rican girl (she doesn't feel comfortable calling herself a woman); attractive enough to get stares and comments in the subway (a cop once told her he could spot her big green eyes all the way from the Bronx); receptionist at a Manhattan law firm; Brooklyn in her clothes (run in her stocking, button missing on her white blouse, pizza stain near the elbow of her blazer); in her style (large gold earrings her mother described as gaudy, patchy red fingernail polish she forgot to touch up the night before); in her walk (booty goes boom-boom, boom-boom, the neighborhood boys had told her); in her talk (*why don't ya shut up, whattaya want from me, howya like that*); described by her family as intelligent (in the way that people who don't do well in school are described as intelligent, as in: she could have been more than she is, done better than she did, amounted to much more than an attractive Puerto Rican receptionist from Brooklyn).

A necessity.

That's what Jayson told her she was, although he didn't say why she was needed or for what or by whom. He didn't call her a necessity after she handed him his lunch or poured him a cup of coffee, not when she saved him from embarrassment by reminding him of an important appointment; if he had said it then, his meaning would have been clear. But he told her while on his way to the men's room: *Alma, you're a necessity.* And from that moment she could no longer think of herself as anything else; she was, and would be, whatever he told her she was, regardless of whether she was high in the air above Fifth Avenue, or sleeping in Bushwick, twenty yards away from the El.

She was starting to remember, again, the meaning of the word love—not the unconditional love a mother might have for her children, nor the sappy first love she had known when she was thirteen—but the make-your-toes-curl kind of love she, Alma Reyes, had been feeling when she was around Jayson. Alma craved and feared this love, the kind that distracts one from the here and now and forces one's attention on the future. For what good was the present—any present—without the prospect of a happy future? And what was happiness if not love?

Jayson had been telling her this, and many other things, for the past several weeks. He told her when they were alone in elevators—how being in love was better than winning an important case, better than anything he could think of, how he would trade his career for just one day with his soul mate, who, he felt, could be anyone in the world, maybe even her. He told her these things when no one else was around. Sometimes when other attorneys stood near him, or when another receptionist sat next to her, he slipped her a wink or a smile. He left her short notes, never addressed to her or signed by him, not even his initials. He wrote phrases Alma was sure she had seen in Hallmark cards or fortune cookies . . . *Love can overcome all differences* . . . *Love means experiencing each other's worlds together* . . . *Love is nothing to be ashamed of* . . . yet she didn't let her suspicions about his sincerity distract her from the attention she was getting. For it was this attention, if nothing else, that separated her from the rest of the people she saw each day; this attention, she told herself, had nothing to do with loneliness or shame, and had everything to do with tomorrow and the next day.

Alma and the other receptionists usually bought lunch at a deli on Sixth Avenue—she couldn't afford Manhattan lunch prices, but she would rather spend three dollars on a tiny portion of salad than bring something from home in a brown bag. Jayson ate at a different restaurant each day, usually with clients. Occasionally he had food delivered from the same deli Alma went to, but his orders cost nine or ten dollars (plus a three-dollar tip). Alma knew this because she called for him. Crabmeat on a hard roll, tomatoes and lettuce, sautéed mushrooms on the side, a bottle of mineral water. Or smoked turkey breast and Swiss, coleslaw and Russian dressing on the sandwich, always the sautéed mushrooms on the side and the bottle of mineral water. Every few weeks Alma tried to save enough money to buy these lunches for herself, and when she had only a few dollars to spare she ordered just the mushrooms. This was her way of speaking to him; she couldn't leave notes for him (she was afraid someone would find one and think she was foolish), and she didn't know how to wink (both eyes closed whenever she tried, or if she was able to keep one eye open the wink looked awkward and forced, which was really no wink at all).

The first time they kissed was an expensive moment for Alma.

They were in a small bar on the Upper West Side. Not too many people there. A few men wearing suits, three guys wearing baseball hats and sweatshirts, an old drunk trying to show one of the bartenders how to play pool. The place smelled like a subway station. She and Jayson got a few stares when they walked in, and after they sat at the bar Jayson removed his jacket and tie.

Jayson touched Alma's shoulder. "What do you want to drink?"

Alma clenched her toes, trying to think of something sophisticated she could order. "Bud, I guess."

"Why don't you get a good beer?" Jayson took a twenty from his wallet.

"Bud's a good beer."

"Of course it is, but you should try something different. An imported beer."

"What are you having?"

"I had this great beer when I was in Prague last summer. I forget what it was called. Radegast, I think, or something like that. Maybe they have it here."

"I guess I'll have one of those."

The only imported beers the bar carried were Beck's and Corona. Jayson ordered one of each. "We'll share," he said.

Alma hadn't had time to look in the mirror before she left the office. She wondered if her bangs were falling the way she wanted them to, just above her eyebrows, or if her lipstick was even, or if her breath smelled of the mushrooms she'd had for lunch. "Where did you go last summer?" she asked.

"Prague."

"Where's that?"

"In Europe."

"Near Russia?"

"Not really, it's in the Czech Republic."

Alma looked blankly at Jayson. The bartender placed the Corona in front of her. She took the lime from the top of the bottle, and sucked it for a few seconds before trying the beer.

"It's near Poland," Jayson said. "You know, where the pope's from."

"The pope's from Rome, right?"

Jayson laughed. "Right, you're absolutely right."

This was when he moved closer to her, touched her cheek with his right hand, and kissed her briefly on the lips. He lingered near her face for a moment, smelling her skin and her hair. "God, I love it when a girl smells like you do," he said. He kissed her again, longer this time, and as he slowly pulled away he put the tip of his finger in her mouth. She brushed her tongue against it before he took it out.

She was embarrassed now, yet she had never blushed when Ricki Sanchez called her late at night and talked dirty to her (her mother and brother sitting a few feet away from her) . . . *Gonna come on your face, gonna fuck you blind, baby . . . love you, love you . . . love to fuck you silly, angel* . . . never blushed when Ricki asked if he could stick his finger in her ass, when he asked if she could get him off with her feet.

The next day Alma spent forty-three dollars on anything she could find that would make her smell the way Jayson wanted her to smell: lipstick, shampoo, conditioner, soap, shower gel, body lotion, perfume, mousse, hair spray. But even as she removed these items from the shelves, even as she gave her money to the cashier, she told herself: *Told me I smell good. Means nothing, means nothing, nothing, nothing. Means I smell good.*

3. *Krazy Glue Alma* (1994)

Her brother Manny told her not to do it, said Ricki was bad news, *lucky if he becomes a pimp some day, only things he's qualified to do are get drunk and treat women like animals.* Told her he was embarrassed that his sister was going with a guy like that. But she was holding on, no way she was letting go, and if that meant moving upstate with Ricki she was willing to do it. Ricki's mother kicked him out of the house when he refused to stop drinking, and now he wanted to get as far away from everyone as possible. He had no job prospects, no family anywhere else but Brooklyn and Queens, but he said they could stay with a few of his friends in Binghamton (they were gonna let him in on "some of their action").

They slept in the bus station the first night, then Ricki parted with a few dollars for a room in a cheap motel. Hardly talked to her for two days, he was so pissed about spending the lousy forty dollars on the room. Threw her on the bed or the floor when he wanted sex. Asked her questions when he needed something.

Where the fuck is the toilet paper? I know you got a big ass, but there ain't no way you used the whole roll.

Better to hear him speak, even if he ranted and raved, much better than quiet Hyde in front of the TV, no telling when he would explode, or worse, no Hyde at all, gone from the room, gone away from her, five or six hours without Hyde or Ricki.

You bring any money with you? I didn't think so, now shut up and bend over.

Her brother told her she had Krazy Glue on her fingers. That was the last thing he said to her before she left home: *You got sticky fingers, Alma. If that shit dries while you're clingin' to him, you'll never get away.*

They left the motel after five days, still no plans. Ricki rented a car using his older brother's license and credit card. Drove around for ten hours, up to Elmira, over to Albany, into Massachusetts, back into New York, west to Syracuse, back down to Binghamton, into Pennsylvania—Scranton and Wilkes-Barre— and finally, back to the same motel in Binghamton. Ricki was agitated, breathing heavy, pacing the room, walking outside, smoking cigarettes. Had a crazy look on his face. Alma tried to sleep, but whenever she closed her eyes Ricki made a loud noise—turned up the volume on the TV, punched a wall, opened the window and screamed into the night, jumped on the bed. Told Alma she was going to stay awake, said no one was sleeping if he couldn't sleep, especially not her since it was her fault in the first place, her fault they were in this mess, anything that would ever happen would be her fault. Two days and nights without sleep . . . *If you close your eyes you might not open them again* . . . her body ready to give up but her hands still wet with Krazy Glue.

Sometimes she closed her eyes or wised off just to make sure Hyde was still there, if all his parts were working: his fist for her nose, his head for her head, his elbow for her lip, his cock for her mouth, his boot for her ribs. Needed contact with Ricki, even if that contact had to come from Hyde.

Too many kicks to the ribs, too much trouble breathing, too much time (almost three days) with no sign of Ricki. Too much Hyde, never thought there could be too much. No longer scared of losing Ricki, just scared. She could not afford another kick. She told him she was leaving—she hoped he would try to stop her, hoped the glue would dry and she would no longer have a choice—but he showed her where the door was. She went to the bathroom before she left, stole fifty dollars from his pants hanging on the shower door—and again she hoped he would catch her—but he told her to hurry the fuck up and get going.

She waited in the bus station for four hours, almost went back and showed him the money she had taken, almost wanted another boot in her ribs, but it was getting harder to breathe, and when she cried it felt like her side was going to rip open and scream, felt like Ricki was in there tapping on her cracked ribs.

4. *Kisses* (1995)

They had been seeing each other for almost three weeks, and Jayson had done little more than kiss her face softly. Everywhere on her face—cheeks, chin, forehead, tip of her nose, corners of her lips, eyelids, the space between chin and mouth. His hands holding her head, positioning it as if only he knew where it needed to be. To the side: kissed her cheek (free of rouge and foundation), her earlobes (dangling pearls, no more gaudy cowbell earrings), the side of her neck (where she dabbed the perfume he had given her a week before). Straight ahead, nose to nose: kissed her forehead (fatherly), her lips (the almost clear lipstick Jayson liked, rather than her usual deep red), her chin (she made sure to pluck any stray hairs), her eyelids (less mascara on her lashes), her lips again (she carried a toothbrush and a small bottle of Listerine to work each day, brushed after lunch and during breaks, used the mouthwash before she left the office).

5. *A little piece of Ricki Sanchez* (1995)

—He's slummin' with you, girl. Don't you know that much, don't you have that much sense in your head, haven't you been through enough to see the truth once in a while? Muthafucka's probably married and shit, don't believe a word he says, I'm tellin' you right now and it's the last time I'll say it.

—You said it, now shut up.

—I said it three hundred times but you don't hear a word, you just stay in your little fantasy world, dreamin' and sighin' and shit, and then he'll show his true colors, okay, and then what, huh, then what happens, he goes on with whatever it is he does and you sit here for weeks feelin' sorry for yourself when you should really feel good about gettin' rid of a guy who's only slummin' in the first place.

—Enough with the slumming shit, Jesus Christ already.

—You tell your white-bread friend enough with the slummin', you ask him and we'll see if his face turns red. Probably talks about you, Alma, tells his white friends about the piece of ass he scored from one of the other boroughs, probably brags about gettin' a girl who lives ten fuckin' feet away from the El.

—Enough, I said.

—You got it this time, Alma? You got the story down straight this time? No good, get out now, simple as that.

Her brother could not forget about Ricki Sanchez, talked about it once a week: *Heard Sanchez is in jail again doin' time for assault and drug possession. Good thing you got outa that. I could still break his ass for what he did. Better never see you with the likes of him again, I'll put an end to that shit real quick. Saw this lady yesterday on the corner of Myrtle and her man was pullin' her around and shit, just grabbed a handful of hair and started yankin' like he was draggin' a sack or somethin'. She fought at first but then it was like she gave in and let this asshole drag her around the street callin' her two-timin' bitch and smelly cunt, and soon people are lookin' but they don't seem to care, and the guy looks proud of what he's doin' and she's laughin' because there's nothin' else she can do, and then he kicks her in her ass and I'm just thinkin' how this guy needs to have his balls ripped out just like Sanchez. But little Ricki's getting his now I bet, no more shit from him.*

Whenever her brother talked like this, Alma felt an urge to protect Ricki. Even now, over a year after she had left him in Binghamton. Still kicked herself in the ass for not telling her brother how she and Ricki met. How he saved her life, and how, from that moment on, she felt like she would never be safe without him. No matter how much he hit her or how many names he called her, she told herself it was more dangerous to be alone. Two older men wouldn't leave her alone that night at the Myrtle Avenue station. Told her she shouldn't be so selfish, keeping such a nice piece of ass all to herself. Said it would be a shame if she fell off the platform and her sexy little body broke against the street below. A hand on her ass, another under her shirt, and somehow she could not scream. And then a hand was on her leg, another grabbed her hair, and soon there were too many hands and still no voice to scream. And then there was Ricki, yelling and kicking and smashing bottles over their heads, and then grabbing Alma and dragging her down to the street where he found one of his friends to drive her home.

But her brother didn't know this, and even if he had, Alma told herself, it would not make a difference. Everyone was Ricki to her brother, and no one could be trusted, especially not Jayson. And who knew, maybe he couldn't be trusted, but he was certainly no Ricki. Slumming or not, he was no Hyde. Worst part was this: Alma was starting to believe what her brother said, all the stuff about slumming and Jayson bragging to his friends, and maybe he was married and lying about that too, maybe some woman, some scorned wife, was after her, Alma, Puerto Rican receptionist from Brooklyn.

At the office, Jayson's notes had changed. No more love and smiling faces, no more *you look like an angel,* no more *necessity.* Your skirt's a little short, don't you think? When you bend over you're an open book. Dinner tonight at seven? Or: What happened to the necklace I gave you? Haven't worn it in three days. One you've been wearing doesn't seem to be you. Coffee after work? Or: Can't believe you hang out with Roxanne and Jean. Not a good idea. Rox cheats on her husband and she's only been married three months. Every other word out of Jean's mouth is fuck or shit, sounds like she's in a bar not an office. Why do you associate with them? Then, something to make her soft: Let's do something in your neighborhood for a change. We'll take a cab from work tomorrow night. Sound good?

Necklace around her neck every day. No more short skirts. No more movies and drinks with Rox and Jean after work. Small talk in the cafeteria, nothing more. Didn't want to hear about Rox's affairs, cringed when Jean opened her mouth.

When they called her at home, she would tell her brother to say she wasn't there.

—Who do you think you are, uptown girl? Too good for your friends? Guess you're slummin' when you spend time with your own family. So that's how it is, huh. How quickly we forget where we've been, Miss Upscale 1995.

—Look at you talking with your jeans hanging off your ass like the rest of them on the corner. Who are you trying to be?

—Just bein' who I am. Who are you? You don't even know, do you?

—And you're gonna tell me.

—You're Puerto Rican.

—Latina.

—You're a receptionist.

—Employee of Mayerowitz, Schmidt, and Bernstein.

—Receptionist.

—For now.

—You live in Brooklyn.

—New York City.

—You live in a shitty little section of Brooklyn near the El.

—New York City.

—You can feel the fuckin' train pass when you're sleepin' at night.

—I sleep just fine.

—You didn't go to college.

—I might start taking classes in the fall.

—Where?

—Hunter College.

—With what money?

—Jayson said he'll help me figure it out.

—Oh well, in that case it's okay, you two got it all worked out. Where you gonna find the time?

—I'll work part-time, maybe twenty-five hours a week.

—What about the bills?

—We'll use the money from your job. . . . Oh, that's right, I forgot, you don't have a job.

—I'm still in school, smartass.

—Since when is high school all day?

—Basketball practice for two hours at least, plus the gym.

—You won't sacrifice, why should I?

—Who's gonna be talkin' about sacrifice when I get a college scholarship to play ball?

—Then I suppose you'll make it to the NBA.

—Maybe.

—Yeah, and I'll be a partner in the law firm next week.

—Sleep with enough of the lawyers, you never know.

—You're just jealous.

—Don't matter how pretty he is, I wouldn't want to sleep with him.

—You can't stand someone from the neighborhood doing well.

—Jesus, you can be so stupid sometimes. You want to forget where you're from.

—And you won't let me.

—That's right.

—Wanna shove Ricki Sanchez in my face every chance you get. Wanna brand my ass with his name.

—He probably already did that with a cigarette.

—See what I mean. It's like you're gonna hold that over me for the rest of the century and shit. Like you're happy he did what he did to me.

—There's no way that's happening again. We can't afford for you to sit in some shrink's office twice a week and figure it out, so all we got is you lookin' out for you and me lookin' out for you.

—So you gotta bust my ass about every little thing I do.

—No, only every little person you do.

—He's nothing like Ricki.

—Sounds more like Ricki than you think.

—He'd never hurt me.

—May never hit you, but he'd hurt you.

—What do you know?

—Bring him around, I'll give him a chance.

—I'm gonna bring him here?

—If there's nothin' wrong with it, there should be nothin' to hide.

—Why am I even listening to you? Why do I let you do this to me?

—Because I know how to recognize.

—Recognize what?

—Recognize when somebody's got a little piece of Ricki Sanchez sittin' inside waitin' to pop out.

—Better look in the mirror. You got a little piece yourself.

6. *Dinner at Romario's* (1995)

They took a cab from the office to her street, where they decided on a restaurant. Jayson said the M train went through too many bad neighborhoods. Alma didn't mind the train. Gave her a chance to clear her head. The metal shaking and twisting, the conductor's voice like a scratched record, doors sliding left to right and back again, sneakers and clunky boots scrambling for seats, newspaper open on someone's lap, an exhausted man's chin resting on his chest, lipstick stains on white coffee cups. Alma liked to look into the windows of apartments, felt a bond with those who slept under the El, wondered if strangers looked into her bedroom when they passed the Wyckoff station.

A yellow cab in Bushwick might as well be a wedding procession, cans tied to the rear bumper. People want to see who's splurging for the wheels, who got a night off from the El. Didn't help that Jayson was still wearing a suit, leather briefcase under his arm rather than hanging at his side.

Jayson looked like he didn't know which side of the street to choose. There were five kids by the subway station—hats on backward, jeans falling off their hips, cigarettes behind their ears. They sat in front of the twenty-four-hour store and browsed through the porno magazines. They shoved some down their pants. When Alma and Jayson walked past the kids, they blew kisses to her, showed her pictures from the porno mags. *What you doin' with dat white boy, sweet thing? You might get lipstick on his clean white dick, you know what I'm sayin', sweetie.* Jayson tried to act nonchalant, smiled as they taunted him, slowed down as he passed them. Didn't fool Alma, she saw him clutching his briefcase.

Seeing him scared, though, was better than seeing the look of pity on his face when they passed the shit stores on Myrtle Avenue on their way to Romario's. Filled with white people's leftovers, clothes Jayson could have worn five or ten years ago. Even the names of the stores embarrassed Alma, though she had never given them a second thought before: Amigo Fashion, best place to buy acid-washed jeans, pink button-down shirts, aqua and tan Members Only jackets, ten-dollar green-and-red sneakers that fell apart in a month; Sav-On Furniture, home of scratched coffee tables, brown leather sofas, polka-dotted recliners; Wild & Sexy Fashions, lingerie with too many holes and rips; Pay Less Furniture Discount; Alfshin's 99 Cents Plus Store; Bottom Line Prices; 99 Cents Taco; Carl's Army & Navy; King Arthur Discounts; Glitter Jewelry; Sleek Look; Street Gang Haircutting.

Alma had been to Romario's dozens of times. She went there with Manny and her mother on the night her father left for good. That was the first night she had seen Manny act like a jerk, and she knew what did it to him, knew it was the fact that their father had left. Manny always stood up for him when their mother was giving him hell for wasting money on the horses.

What's a few trips to the OTB? Manny would say.

Your father's a nice man, their mother would answer, *but he never grew up and it's killing us every day.*

Manny thought he could take care of everything after that night. Barely thirteen and he thought he could run the family. Grouchy son of a bitch ever since. Family watchdog, had to make sure everybody kept their noses clean. Started acting like an old man. Mean tongue on her brother. Used to call him Junior, can't even do that anymore.

Inside the restaurant, Romario and his two sons, Sandy and Carmine, were watching soccer on the local Spanish station.

Romario fawned over Alma, as he usually did when her mother wasn't there to be the center of his attention. He kissed her on the forehead and gave her a long hug as if he hadn't seen her last week at the shoe store two blocks away. A bottle of wine was waiting for them on the table when they were seated. Romario poured them each a glass.

Jayson looked at his glass and then at Alma. "Is there a wine list?"

"This wine is no good?" Romario said.

"I'm sure it's fine," Jayson said, "but we may be in the mood for something else."

Romario looked at Alma and shrugged his shoulders.

"This wine is fine," Jayson said, flustered. "Don't go to any trouble."

Romario walked away shaking his head.

While they were eating their salad, a group of kids came in to watch the second half of the game. Louder than Sandy and Carmine. *Fuck dat guy, he can't play for shit. . . . You wanna bet yer ass on dis game, I'm givin' you a two goal lead. Two fuckin' goals, Sandy. . . . Yo Carmine, crack me out some a dat shit you were eatin' yestuhday, you know, the stuff with the cheese on the inside.* Jayson slammed his fork every minute or so, as if that was going to convince them to shut up.

"I think I should ask for the check," Jayson said.

"I don't understand," Alma said. "What's wrong?"

Jayson motioned with his eyes to the kids watching the game.

Romario was bringing over their dinner. "Please don't," Alma said. "He's a friend of my mother's. It would embarrass him."

Romario set down the plates. "That sounds like some game," Jayson said. "You guys really get into your soccer around here, I guess."

"Only when we're in *the mood.*" Romario winked at Alma and walked away.

"It's obvious he doesn't like me for some reason." Jayson wiped his mouth and stood up. "I'll go ask for the check."

Alma closed her eyes and rubbed her hand over her face.

If Manny could have seen her now, he would have said: *See, what did I tell you? What did I say about Sanchez bein' everywhere?*

Sandy turned up the volume on the TV, and one of the kids told him to get the fuck out of the way. Jayson shook his head at

Alma, as if it were her fault that kids used the word fuck in this neighborhood. "As soon as I looked in, I knew this wasn't a good place to eat," he said.

"Well, the food's here, can't we just eat it?"

"I'd rather not," he said. "And I didn't want to tell you this because I thought it would embarrass you, but I found two hairs in my salad."

"How do you know they weren't yours?"

"I just know," Jayson said. "I hate to say it, but when you're in a certain place you can just tell."

Alma looked outside and saw a bus pull to the curb. The door to the restaurant was closed and the bus was silent, she could hear nothing from the world outside; it was as if she were wrapped in a bubble, and she could hear nothing but what was inside it—Jayson saying he was sorry, it was okay, these people were no reflection on her. The bus pulled away.

Jayson walked over to Romario and gave him his credit card. He said he had to leave for an emergency and asked if he could call a cab.

"So you're in *the mood* to leave now," Romario said.

"You givin' Romario a problem?" one kid said. He wore a leather vest and a bandanna over his head.

"Who's givin' my man a problem?" another one said. Soon all of them were watching Jayson instead of the TV.

Jayson looked helpless, like a boy being picked on by his schoolmates. He returned to the table a few minutes later and told Alma they would have to walk for now, until they found a pay phone.

She told herself she would let him go—she would stay at Romario's and finish her eggplant parmigiana—but a voice popped into her head, one she recognized: Krazy Glue Alma telling her they would find someplace else to eat, telling her the date the night the whole damned thing wasn't over. Keep the night going, it's still early, wait until tomorrow to think about what happened.

"Don't worry, I paid for the whole meal." Jayson dropped a twenty-dollar bill in the middle of the table. "That's what you have to do with these people. Leave them a fat tip just so they know who you are." He stood next to the table and held out his hand, and everything was very quiet.

And then Alma remembered something her brother had told her. Or was it something she told herself? *You were the one slummin' when you were with that Sanchez asshole. Same thing with this lawyer guy. He thinks he's slummin', but it's you. You're slummin' again, and you gotta stop it.*

She left with Jayson and walked with him along Myrtle Avenue, but as he looked into one of the restaurant windows she noticed something coming down the street, something big and blue, and she could hear it. When Jayson wasn't looking she hurried to the street and watched the bus get closer, and only as it pulled to the curb did she start to wonder if she had enough change. But even if her purse was empty, she told herself, she would manage to get on the bus somehow. It was one thing she had always been good at.

Samrat Upadhyay

University of Hawaii

DEEPAK MISRA'S SECRETARY

The trouble began for Deepak Misra when he ended up kissing his unappealing secretary in the office one day.

But later he figured that the trouble had actually started some time before that. It started when his wife, Jill, who had left him a couple of years before, came back into his life. One mid-morning an acquaintance called Deepak Misra to tell him that his wife was back in the city after nearly two years. Deepak didn't know what to think.

"Where?" Deepak asked, his voice strange.

"She's staying at the Annapurna Hotel. She said she's looking for an apartment."

"An apartment?"

"Looks like she's here to stay, Deepak."

After he hung up, Deepak called his secretary, Bandana-ji, to bring a file into his room. He asked her to wait while he scrutinized the documents in the file. "My wife is back in Kathmandu," he said shortly. When she didn't respond, he looked up.

"Is there something wrong with the account?" she asked, pointing to the file.

"Just checking," he said, and he handed the file back to her. She went back to her desk outside his room.

Deepak Misra had been a successful businessman for seven years. When his wife, Jill, left him two years earlier, everyone had thought the business would collapse, but Deepak showed remarkable strength. Three days after his wife disappeared without even a note, he was back at the office, making phone calls, sending faxes, and tinkering with numbers on his new computer. His secretary, Bandana-ji, an extremely thin woman who constantly cleared her throat, said, "It seems unnatural." She had been with him a little more than a year and was undiplomatic in her dealing with people. She was strange, but he liked her because she was the best secretary he'd had. She possessed a quick mind and a no-nonsense manner that softened his clients.

The secretary before Bandana-ji had been a young woman, Anju, who was preoccupied with her hair. She sat at her desk and combed her shimmering, shining, waist-long hair so that it seemed to breathe. The floor beneath her desk and chair was always littered with strands of hair, and the cleaner who came in every morning complained. When Anju started oiling her hair in the office, Deepak discovered smudges on important documents. Even though most of the time all she did was comb her hair and look at herself in a small, portable mirror, Deepak didn't have the heart to fire her because her brother was a friend of his. Also, and Deepak admitted this to himself reluctantly, he found her pleasant to look at. When she lifted her mirror and scrutinized her face or put *kazal* on her eyes, he became entranced, not in a lecherous way, but as an observer who could never fully comprehend what he was seeing. But after receiving numerous complaints from his clients about important documents that had never reached them or about wrong calculations in their yearly assessments, Deepak finally decided to let her go. He called her brother and apologized, but the brother only said, "I'm surprised you kept her so long."

When he first hired Bandana-ji on the recommendation of a Marwari businessman, he was skeptical. She looked like she was used to foraging through people's garbage for glass and metal to sell at the recycling plant. Her thin hair was combed back with an awful-smelling oil, and she wore a purple sari that had been repaired in a few places. On the right side of her face she had a skin disfigurement, a pink-purplish colored map that started at her temple and curved down toward her chin. Later Deepak decided the stain looked like a pregnant woman whose protruding belly pointed toward Bandana-ji's nose. She came into his office clearing her throat, at one instance so vigorously that it startled Deepak. But her bio-data was impeccable. She had worked for some of the top businessmen in the city, and all of them had written her lavish recommendations. She even knew how to use computers, a skill her previous employer claimed she had learned on the job in a single day! When Deepak expressed interest in hiring her, she asked in her coarse voice, "How much are you going to pay me?" When he told her, she smiled, scrunching the pregnant woman's belly on her cheek. She picked up her dilapidated folder and walked out. He sat there, stunned, then ran after her. She had disappeared into the hustle-bustle of New Road outside his office. Two days later he called her former employer and got her number. She answered the phone, and he quoted a price he thought she would accept. "Won't do," she said. Afraid that she'd hang up, he asked her what was on her mind. "Eight thousand rupees," she said, which was followed by a vigorous clearing of her throat. He promptly agreed. After he put the phone down, he wondered why he had agreed to her exorbitant demand. She would be the highest-paid secretary in the entire city. He could easily have acquired another secretary, perhaps equally competent, for half that price.

She was waiting outside the office door when he reached it the next morning. "I need a key," she said, and he rushed to the key shop down the street and had a duplicate made. From then on when he reached his office at nine, she was already there, and from the amount of work accomplished, he knew she had been there a good hour. The second day he made an extra cup of tea in his room and took it to her. "I don't drink tea," she said, her eyes glued to the computer. "Soft drink?" he asked. "I don't drink soft drinks," she said. He stood there, helpless, holding the cup of tea, watching the hair on the back of her neck. She never drank anything, nor ate in the office, and she was there all day! A few days later he told her that she should feel free to take an hour off for lunch. If she brought her meal from the house, she could put it in the refrigerator. If not, he suggested some restaurants down the street. The Punjabi Restaurant has the best tandoori chicken in the city, he said, laughing. "All right," she said and went back to her desk. The next day when he came out of his room around lunchtime to go for a walk (he always took at least one walk around the block every day to clear his mind of the numbers), she hadn't left her desk. "When you go out for lunch, make sure you lock the door," he said pointedly. She was still there when he came back.

When he finished work, Deepak went to the Annapurna Hotel. The receptionist checked the computer and said, "Yes, Jill Misra, room 223." He went upstairs and knocked on the door. There was no answer, so he came down and waited in the lobby. He ordered a beer and let the cold seep into his stomach. He finished his beer and got up, and just then she came in with a man. He was about to call her name when something stopped him. She had put on some weight, and there was a glow to her face. The man with her was a Nepali, probably of Newar caste, and he sported a mustache that ran all the way down to his chin. They walked past him and got into the elevator.

That night Deepak drank half a bottle of whiskey and listened to some ghazals he and Jill had been fond of during their three years of marriage. She likened the wordings of the ghazals, especially the surprise endings, to strokes of her paintbrush. She was an artist, and her paintings had been exhibited in Kathmandu and Singapore. Before she left him, she had been trying to get exhibitions in New Delhi and Bombay, cities that had strong artist communities.

Deepak became so drunk the room started to spin. He thought he should eat something, and went to the kitchen to make an omelette. But it was too much of an effort. An egg dropped from his hand and cracked on the floor, the yolk spilling out, still intact, forming an eye. Deepak wished he had not let go of his servant boy a few days earlier, but the boy stole money and had become lazy. Deepak staggered out of the house and without thinking, got into his car. It was nearly ten o'clock. The streets were abandoned. The car was weaving, but he didn't care. He was driving quite fast until he nearly hit a bicycle at the corner in front of the palace.

At the Annapurna Hotel, he tipped the doorman an exorbitant hundred rupees and walked into the Chinese restaurant. There were no other customers. He sat in a corner and ate a ginger chicken, which nauseated him after a few bites. He wondered if the mustached man was with Jill in her room upstairs, or perhaps they had gone out. She liked to dance, so he asked the waiter if there was a dance club in the hotel. Deepak went to the bathroom, washed his face, combed his hair, then stepped into the dance club with its rotating lights and darkish atmosphere. A deejay was about to change the music, and he was droning about the "rhythm" of the forthcoming piece. Once Deepak's eyes adjusted to the light, he spotted her. She was at the edge of the dance floor, tapping her feet, a drink in her hand, talking to the man with the ridiculous mustache.

"Welcome to Kathmandu," he said stupidly in English when he reached them.

She looked at him not in surprise but with amusement. "I had a feeling," she said in stilted Nepali. Her Nepali had been more or less fluent when she left him. She introduced the mustached man as Birendra, and Deepak offered his hand.

"Well," she said.

Deepak went to the bar and got a drink, though he hardly took a sip after he went back to them. She was telling Birendra about an incident in Cleveland—where she had grown up and gone to college—that involved a man and his dog. A thousand questions leapt up to Deepak's throat. When she finished her story and Birendra laughed, Deepak grabbed hold of her arm and said, "Just a moment." He took her to another corner of the dance floor, the revolving lights on the ceiling making her figure jerky, and he stood there, not knowing what to say. She asked him how he was, and he nodded, waved a hand in the air.

"You want an explanation," she said.

"Well, it is—"

"I have none," she said. She looked around the dance floor. "It just got too much. I had to get away. I guess we should file papers for divorce."

He gazed at her. She was wearing a *phuli* on her nose, its diamond glittering, and her beauty pained him as it had when they first met at an exhibition of her paintings. He recalled how his parents, who had died soon after he married Jill, had advised him not to marry a foreigner. "You'll suffer later, son," his old mother had warned him.

"We could file papers, I suppose," he told Jill now. He gulped his drink in one shot and said, "What makes a woman leave her husband just like that? What had I done? No letter, no postcard. Nothing."

She stood there, holding her drink in her hand. "You knew I wasn't happy," she said.

He nodded. The anger left him, as suddenly as it had appeared. He glanced at Birendra, who was staring in their direction. "Your friend," Deepak said.

"He's nothing," she said and asked Deepak whether he would take her for a ride to the Swayambhunath temple, which was a few miles away. She left with him without saying good-bye to Birendra.

In the car she started on a lengthy explanation about why she had left him, but he found that he wasn't listening, even though the question had burned his mind in her absence. They climbed the steep steps to the temple, and he kissed her at the top. She didn't resist, although her hands pushed his shoulders back. Then in his drunkenness he started to cry, and she held him, as one holds a teenager who has become overly emotional. In a burst of excitement he told her he was willing to forget what she had done to him, although he knew it was the alcohol that was making him say that.

He wanted to take her home, but in the car she said she wanted to "go at it slowly," and he accepted this, his mind envisioning a near future where she would come back into the house and everything would be like it was before.

* * *

"We should probably make today a holiday," he declared to Bandana-ji as he walked in.

"I like work," Bandana-ji said. She didn't ask him why he wanted a holiday. She rarely looked at him when she spoke to him about things other than office matters. Deepak went to his room and dialed the hotel. The receptionist told him that Jill Misra was not in, and he left a message asking her to call him back. Although there was much work to be done, Deepak's mind wandered. Once he looked through the glass partition at Bandana-ji and saw her staring at the wall. He wondered if she wasn't feeling well. She hadn't missed a single day of work since she started. One Saturday afternoon a few months after she had joined him, he came to the office to fetch his address book and found her at her desk, working. "I don't want you to work on a holiday," he told her, although when the long-haired secretary had worked for him he had wished she would come in on weekends and finish her tasks.

"Will you please just let me do my job?" Bandana-ji said sternly.

"But you work—"

"I don't like people interfering in my work," Bandana-ji said, as if he were an outsider.

He picked up his address book and walked out. She was a strange creature, all right. She never wore a sari other than the one she had on when she first came to him. The next Saturday he had called the office just to check, and her coarse voice answered, "Deepak Financial." He put the phone down.

Now after watching Bandana-ji staring into space, Deepak called her inside and asked her if she was sick. "I feel fine," she said.

"I saw you thinking—"

"You want me to work like a slave?" She cleared her throat.

Deepak was startled, then amused. "No, I mean—"

"Did you see your wife? Is that why you are happy?"

He looked at her face closely. Her eyes were small behind the high-powered glasses she wore. He started to tell her about the previous night, but she interrupted him.

"What does she have to say?"

"Nothing," he said, now unsure whether he should talk to her about Jill.

"These foreign women," Bandana-ji said, her face angry.

"She is just . . ."

"They think they can play with other people's lives," she said and went back to her desk.

Deepak was touched by her concern for him. She had never given an indication that she thought about Deepak's life outside of office concerns. When he started working on the third day after Jill left, his secretary said only, "It seems unnatural." He thought she was referring to his coming back to work so soon, but now it occurred to him that perhaps she was referring to Jill's abrupt departure.

His mind on Jill, Deepak didn't say anything to Bandana-ji for the rest of the day. After work he drove over to the hotel, where the receptionist informed him that Jill had checked out an hour before. Deepak asked him if she had left a forwarding address, and the receptionist, an effeminate man in an over-sized suit, shook his head. "Did she get my message?" he asked. She must have, the receptionist said, because there was nothing in her box. For a few minutes Deepak hung around the lobby. He checked the restaurants, the dance club, the swimming pool, and so on.

He came out of the hotel and walked toward Ghantaghar and Ranipokhari, leaving his car in the hotel parking lot. Near the Ghantaghar clock tower, he saw students walk into Trichandra Campus for their evening classes, the girls holding their notebooks close to their chests. The clock tower chimed six as he walked beneath it. At Ranipokhari he stood near the railings that surrounded the pond and watched the greenish murky water that could no longer support life. Then he moved on to Asan, the bustling marketplace, wanting to get lost in the crowd so that he would become distracted from the incessant blabbering inside his head.

As he went past a sari shop, he saw in one of the large mirrors inside a reflection of Bandana-ji, who was looking at the colorful saris laid out on the counter by the shopkeeper. Deepak stood still. She scrutinized a sari and bantered with the shop-keeper. Then she looked up and their eyes met in the mirror. Deepak wanted to pretend he hadn't seen her, but she was star-ing at him, so he stepped in.

"Buying something?" he asked.

"I'm trying to," she said. "But he's asking for a high price."

The sari was a bright pink one, with a thin strip of velvet around its edge. It had a faint embroidery of flowers and hearts.

"How much?" he asked the shopkeeper, who, seeing a well-dressed man, became deferential. "Only three thousand rupees, sir," the shopkeeper said. "Discount price."

"Pack it up," Deepak said, and he reached into his pocket and gave the shopkeeper the money. He was expecting a strong protest from Bandana-ji, but she stood there, clearing her throat.

They exited the shop and moved toward Indrachowk, as if they had planned this encounter. She walked with short, brisk steps, holding the bag of sari in one hand, not looking at him, and he found himself matching her steps. He knew she lived in the opposite direction, toward Baghbazar. They were constantly separated by other pedestrians, and every time they rejoined, Deepak had nothing to say. The sun was about to set, and there was a pink glow to the buildings. The crowd lessened once they reached New Road, near his office, where Deepak felt com-pelled to ask, "Where are you going?"

"You?"

"Just walking around." He told her he had left his car at the Annapurna Hotel.

"It's a beautiful evening," she said. She was attempting to smile.

"Are you going to wear that sari to the office?"

"You want me to?"

He nodded.

"Then I will."

Together, they walked to the office. Now she walked close to him, her bag held at her chest, her shoulder occasionally touch-ing his. He opened the door to the office and thought, this is crazy. Inside they walked into his room. She looked at Jill's paintings on the wall, as if she had never noticed them before. He sat in his chair and watched her.

"She's not that good," Bandana-ji said.

"She's talented."

She came to him and sat on his lap, still holding the bag. He felt the bones of her buttocks against his thighs. "Deepak Misra," she whispered. Deepak put his hand on her back, feeling the protrusion of her shoulder blades against his palm. Her spine jutted out because there wasn't enough flesh between each vertebra. He laughed, shook his head, and pulled her face toward him. He kissed her on the lips, lightly, then with more strength. Her lips were surprisingly juicy, and he sucked on them while his hand went to her breasts, which were so small that he chuckled inside her mouth. She responded with vigor, darting her tongue against his teeth while her palms held his head. "Deepak Misra," she whispered again. When he found himself groping for the gap between her thighs, he became aware of the absurdity of the situation and pushed her aside. He opened a file and bent his head.

"You're thinking about her," she said accusingly.

"Who?" He brushed his hair with his fingers and sat up straight.

"Your American wife."

Deepak shook his head. "I'm going to leave now."

"She'll hurt you. You want that?"

"Bandana-ji," he said. "This is unbelievable. If you don't mind my saying, it is none of your concern."

She stood before him, her arms crossed over her scrawny chest. She started to clear her throat, but he said, "Don't," and she stopped.

"I always think of you, Deepak Misra," she said softly.

Deepak didn't know what to say to her, so he laughed.

"Don't laugh," she said. "I will give you much more than she will."

Deepak moved toward the door, but she was in the way.

"I thought she had gone back to her country," she said.

Deepak wasn't even sure whether Jill and Bandana-ji had ever met. Now Bandana-ji's small eyes behind her glasses were getting moist. He put his hand on her shoulder. "This shouldn't have happened," he said. "You are my secretary."

On the drive home Deepak was troubled by what he had done in the office with Bandana-ji. He hadn't tried that stuff even with Anju. And now Bandana-ji was acting like she was somehow competing with Jill.

Deepak took home some Chinese food and listened to the sarod playing of Amjad Ali Khan, another of Jill's favorites. She was crazy about Indian classical music. What he had liked about Jill was the tremendous enthusiasm she had for life. She was extremely energetic, and there was a glow to her personality that seemed to illuminate everything around her. She was a bit selfish, but who wasn't? The morning she left, he got up around six o'clock, just as the sun was coming up, and saw that the bed beside him was empty. He knew then, somehow, that she was gone, although for the rest of the day he pretended that she had just gone to visit some friends. What Deepak remembered most clearly about that morning was that the neighbor's cat, which always somehow managed to come into the house and cuddle up next to Jill in the mornings, now was sitting on the windowsill and staring at him, its green eyes eerie in the grayish light in the room. When he reached out to stroke the cat, it struck at Deepak's face, making four straight lines of blood on his left cheek.

"It's your wife," Bandana-ji said when she transferred the call.

"I need to talk to you," Jill said.

"Speak," Deepak said. "What can I do for you?"

She told him she was coming over.

When she appeared at the door, Bandana-ji didn't look in her direction. Jill was wearing a sari, and as she walked past Bandana-ji, she said, "You're still working for him." Bandana-ji quickly looked at the computer screen. She hadn't yet worn the sari that Deepak had bought for her.

"Is she still as strange?" Jill whispered as she sat in front of him.

Deepak nodded. "Why didn't you tell me you were checking

out of the hotel?" She was wearing the gold necklace he'd given her for their wedding. Her earlobes sagged with long earrings, and she had her hair pulled back so that the smooth skin on her cheeks shone under the office lights.

"Didn't have time," she said. "Birendra offered me a room in his apartment." She had lost money in the casino, she said, and now since she didn't want to stay with Birendra, she needed to borrow money from him.

"The house is still there," he said.

"I can't stay with you, Deepak."

Deepak opened the safe in the corner, extracted ten thousand rupees, and gave them to her.

"I'll return this soon," she said.

He waved a hand in the air, and became conscious that Bandana-ji was watching them. "Let's go for lunch," he told Jill.

They went to a rooftop restaurant nearby, and Jill told him that Birendra wanted to sleep with her. "The other night he just came into my bed and slipped next to me," she said. "Nepali men, you know. Either it's a mother, a sister, an aunt, or it's a whore."

Deepak laughed, and she, pleased to see him happy, laughed with him. Before they parted, he extracted a promise from her that she'd call him when she found an apartment. When he came back to the office, he found the door locked. Inside, on Bandana-ji's desk was a note, "I am not feeling well." Finally, Deepak thought.

The next morning Bandana-ji came to the office wearing the pink sari, with a matching pink blouse. "How different you look," he said. He wasn't sure a dark person like her should wear such a light, buoyant color. He also noted a trace of pink lipstick on her lips, and he was reminded of the story of the crow who wanted to become a swan.

Deepak and Bandana-ji ended up making love in the office that evening. He had asked her to stay after closing to finish some important documents that needed to be mailed the next day. She came into his office, and they were cross-checking some numbers together when he reached out and touched her lips. As the lipstick smudged his fingertips, he told her, "This color really suits you, Bandana-ji." She smiled, and the room became lighter. She bent her head toward him. "Deepak Misra," she whispered. "Every night in bed, you come and settle in my eyes." They kissed, and his hands roamed her bony body. He unbuttoned her blouse, pushed up her bra, and sucked her breasts, darting from one to the other. Her breasts were so small and delicious. He had never tasted anything like them before. She helped him undress, and as he sat ridiculously naked on the Tibetan carpet, his penis firm and standing like the tower of Dharahara, she carefully took off her sari and petticoat. She left her glasses on. She reminded him of a stork as she stood in front of him, her palms feebly covering her breasts. She smiled shyly, like a bride, and he felt a surge of happiness.

When he entered her, she kept repeating, "Oooohhhmmm," which sounded awfully like Om, the mantra for Lord Shiva, and it made him laugh. Bandana-ji also laughed. Deepak pounded away, his erection stronger by the minute. He was alive, as if the cells inside his body had come out of their sleep and were now ready to enjoy the pleasures of this earth.

They did it in the office once a week. Deepak became convinced that he had never experienced such pleasure in sex before. Although sex with Jill had been satisfactory, she liked to talk about her paintings while he was inside her, and that bothered him. It excited her to talk like that, she said. Bandana-ji gave him her complete attention, and a sweet feeling entered his heart and lasted for a couple of hours after they climaxed. They lay on the carpet and she fell asleep, her head tucked neatly on his chest. When the pleasant feeling had passed, Deepak got up abruptly so that she asked, "What happened?" He quietly dressed and walked out without uttering a word.

For a few days they became boss and secretary again, but her face became more and more beautiful to Deepak, and he couldn't resist. Even the disfigurement on her face appeared to him as a sort of a beauty mark, something that enhanced her appearance, not diminished it.

* * *

At Jill's housewarming party, Deepak sat on a chair with a glass of whiskey and watched Jill and Birendra whispering in a corner like lovers. There were roughly a dozen people in the room, most of them expatriates working as artists or journalists in Kathmandu. Earlier he had talked with some of them briefly, but he became bored by their incessant complaints about the Nepalese bureaucracy. When they went on like that he wondered why they bothered to live in a country with which they only found fault.

Birendra was laughing at something Jill had said, and as the whiskey warmed his neck, Deepak walked over to them. But they continued as if he weren't there.

"Excuse me," Deepak said. "Could I talk to my wife alone?" He sounded belligerent, but he didn't care.

"Wife?" Jill laughed.

"We're not divorced yet," Deepak said, smiling.

Birendra looked at him with a smirk. "Deepak-ji, you're quite a man."

Deepak took a sip and stared at Birendra, thinking of something to say.

"My Deepak," Jill said. "He's so sensitive. He should have been an artist instead of me." Today she was wearing a Punjabi *salwar-kameez* and had let her hair down.

"I need to talk to you," he said.

"Okay." She walked out to the balcony, and he followed her. The city lights were spread out before them.

"How long are you going to continue with him?" he asked.

"Why do you want to know, Deepak Misra-ji?"

"Can't we—"

"It's hopeless, Deepak. You're insisting on something that's not possible."

"Why?" he said, his voice higher.

"There was a reason I left. And it had nothing to do with you."

"Then why are you here?"

"You don't have a monopoly on this city," she said, throwing back her hair.

He felt ashamed, pleading with his wife to come back to him.

They stood in silence for a while. Then she put her hand on his arm and said gently, "Let's go back inside."

Deepak left the party shortly, and wandered through the streets. He shook his head a few times to drive away the feeling of depression that threatened to take over. His throat was parched from the alcohol. Then he thought of something and started walking toward Baghbazar. The address was somewhere in the back of his mind, and he found the house, which was located off the main street. He was standing in front of the three-storied building and wondering whether he should knock on the bottom door when he looked up and saw Bandana-ji in the second-floor window. Only her head and shoulders were visible to him, but he could tell that she wore the pink sari and the blouse. She glanced down from the window and spotted him. When their eyes met, she stood still. She smiled, and he hurried away, his heart throbbing.

Deepak decided he couldn't go to the office. Over the phone he gave instructions to Bandana-ji, who didn't mention anything about his standing outside her apartment. Mornings he stayed in bed till late, then got up and listened to music. In the evenings he drank whiskey and walked around the house, looking at photographs of him and Jill, or Jill by herself. On the afternoon of the fourth day he was listening to ghazals by Jagjit and Chitra Singh, the famous husband-wife singers, when the doorbell rang. Bandana-ji stood in front of him, clutching some files. "I need your signature," she said.

They sat on the living-room carpet, where he signed the papers. It occurred to him then that he hadn't heard Bandana-ji clear her throat since they started making love. As he sat there, his head bent over the papers, Bandana-ji started to sing to the voices of Jagjit and Chitra Singh. She had a beautiful voice, and he stopped his pen to look at her. She smiled as she sang:

> *If separated after meeting, we won't sleep at night.*
> *Thinking of each other, we'll cry at night.*

He reached over and turned the volume down so that he could listen to her more clearly. The words from her throat penetrated his heart, and he closed his eyes. He had never heard such a melodious voice. When her voice went higher, he felt a shaft of pleasure enter his ears and run down his body. With his eyes closed, Deepak imagined the voice belonging to a different body, someone with a long neck, large deerlike eyes, and an aquiline nose that was an artist's dream. Then he imagined it belonging to Jill, and he saw her pale face rapturous as her tongue played with the words, her eyes suggesting a million possibilities for love. Her hand reached out and caressed his face, then started unbuttoning his shirt. He opened his eyes and let Bandana-ji undress him. Then he undressed her, his throat dry with anticipation of sucking her breasts. She kept singing even as he entered her.

Deepak kept to his bed all day, sometimes reading, sometimes staring at the ceiling, often drifting into long, vacant sleeps. He got up in the evening, put ghazals on the stereo, and slowly drank himself to oblivion. Every few days Bandana-ji came to him for papers to sign. Now he even stopped asking questions about office matters: he brought out his pen and signed the papers. Then he waited for her to sing. When he heard her voice, each cell inside his body moved as in response to a deep, tender massage. A warmth spread from the bottom of his spine all the way up to the top of his head, and he arched his neck to hold on to the sensation.

The phone rang in the house all day. Later people started ringing the bell and knocking loudly on the door. Once he heard Jill's voice, "Deepak, what's the matter? Open it up." He only opened the door for Bandana-ji, and when she told him that some clients were becoming irritated with his absence, he said, "Tell them I've gone to Singapore for a conference." When he finished his stock of whiskey, he drove to a small shop nearby and bought two cases. Every hour without Bandana-ji became a long stretch of boredom, and he constantly thought of her minuscule breasts, the pregnant woman on her face, and the bones of her hips.

One afternoon with Bandana-ji humming on top of him on the carpet, Deepak saw someone move past the semitransparent curtains on the window toward the back of the house. Bandana-ji's eyes were closed. There was a creak, and he knew that someone had opened the back door, which he had forgotten to close the night before. He knew from the walk that it was Jill, even though she had come in softly. Deepak saw Jill's legs at the entrance of the living room, and he looked at Bandana-ji. Although Bandana-ji's eyes were still closed, somehow Deepak felt that she was aware of Jill's presence. What a sight, Deepak thought: the whole house smelling of alcohol and he on the carpet straddled by this unappealing creature. Deepak moaned, and their movement became quicker until they climaxed. As Bandana-ji's head came to rest on his chest, Deepak turned his head and saw the empty space where Jill had been a moment earlier.

Today the pleasure of sex was mixed with a strange feeling of satisfaction, as if he had won a battle he'd been fighting for days. But the feeling didn't last long. After Bandana-ji left, Deepak became filled with self-loathing. He drank so much whiskey that he found himself bumping into tables and lamps. In the living room he picked up a large photograph of Jill and after staring at it briefly, put it back facedown. He studied the other pictures of her alone or of him and her together. He felt Jill was laughing at him.

Despite all the whiskey he drank that night, Deepak couldn't sleep. He kept tossing and cried out a couple of times, shouting Jill's name. In the middle of the night he got up and took a cold shower. Then he made himself a cup of tea and sat in the living room, gazing out of the window into the darkness. He could hear the frogs outside, and their croaking somehow calmed his nerves. As the darkness gave way to a grayish light and the birds started chirping, his head became clearer, and he came to a decision, although the thought of letting her go pained him.

The next day he went to the office, his body tired but his mind fresh, and asked Bandana-ji to submit her resignation. She didn't protest. She went to her desk, typed on the computer, and came back into his office. He had a stack of money in front of him, much more than what he owed her, but she carefully counted the money and only took what was due. He wanted to tell her that he was sorry, but the only thing he could do was stare at the money left on his desk.

It took him less than a week to hire another secretary, an older woman short in height but with a loud voice. She wasn't as efficient as Bandana-ji but she caught on fast, and her phone manners were impeccable for someone with such a booming voice. For about a week Deepak felt his life had gone back to a semblance of normality. The pleasure he had experienced with Bandana-ji seemed unreal to him.

Then the restlessness started, and along with it the feeling of emptiness. Now his mind constantly compared his current state to the rapture he had experienced when Bandana-ji sang to him, or when his lips tasted her breasts. His everyday life appeared so lacking in color or tone that he thought something had happened to his brain. When he went to Jill's apartment for another party, this time in celebration of a solo exhibition in the city, she appeared unappealing to him. He wondered why he had become so desperate about wanting her back. It was evident that Jill and Birendra were lovers now, for they held hands throughout the party, their bodies close to each other.

A small boy delivered a package to Deepak at the office, and he opened it to discover the pink sari. He stared at it briefly, then picked it up and smelled it. It no longer smelled of her, so he deduced it must have been through the dry cleaner. After work he drove over to Baghbazar. With the package in his hand, he knocked on the bottom door. An old lady appeared and told him that Bandana-ji had moved out, and that there was an Indian family in her flat now. No, she didn't know where Bandana-ji had gone. The old lady shook her head, revealing toothless gums as she smiled. "She was a strange one," she said. "She didn't talk to anyone." She paused, and a wistful look came to her face. "But she sang beautifully. Oh, what a voice. It can only be God's blessing."

It was getting dark. Deepak decided to leave his car there and walk around the block. There were many sari shops in this area, and he peeked into each one as he went past, the package with the pink sari in his hand, in some absurd hope that she might be buying another sari. The street was semilit with lights from the shops, but there were no streetlamps above. Whenever he saw a thin woman, he peered to see if it was Bandana-ji. Once a woman cleared her throat, and Deepak was startled. He kept going until he didn't know where he was. His fingers were moist from clutching the package. Now many shops had closed their doors and turned off their lights. After about an hour he realized that he had walked all the way to Thapathali. He sat on the steps of a string of shops near a bus stop. Most of the shops were already closed. Then he heard some music around the corner and he approached it. The music was coming from a stereo shop, and Deepak recognized the voices of Jagjit Singh and Chitra Singh. A small dark man inside smiled at him. Deepak stood in front of the shop, listening.

> *This night I have to stay awake till dawn:*
> *My fate is etched like this.*
> *Sorrow has entered my heart.*
> *Stars, why don't you fall asleep?*

Deepak closed his eyes, and he heard Bandana-ji's voice, not those of the famous singers. And it was her face he saw, the face with the bloated woman. Arching his neck, Deepak waited for the overpowering sensation of bliss to enter his body.

Bret Anthony Johnston
Miami University

SMOKE

What I want to explain is how my father became scared, desperate really, and set fire to our house and cheated the insurance company out of its money. All of this happened in 1979. We lived on Whistler Road in Portland, Texas, a small town compared with Corpus Christi, but sizable when you included those living on the Naval Air Station, where my father worked. He left for his job hours before the morning paper came, so when he returned in the afternoons he read it while chewing a thin cigar. Over the years my mother has suggested that something he'd read triggered him, but I've never learned where all of our money went or what convinced my father we were in such poor shape. I was fifteen then, and our lives seemed normal to me.

Robert Jackson—my father—was a man who knew how to do many things. The year I turned ten he added a second story to our house and only twice asked Obie Meek, our closest neighbor, for help. A year later, after a woman repossessed our new Oldsmobile, he paid fifty dollars cash for a van with a foldout bed, then rebuilt its engine to drive our family twelve hours for a vacation in Louisiana, the state of his birth. Both he and my mother kept pictures from that trip at work, hers in a silver frame and his under a heavy sheet of glass on his desk. My father supervised the air-conditioning department at the base, and my mother worked as a secretary at a hardware company, where she sometimes stuffed new doorknobs and brass hinges into her purse. On weekends my father installed these and I knelt behind him, handing him tools.

The bad times started four years after he restored the van. It was early January and I worked barefoot and bare-chested clearing dead limbs under our mesquite tree—there are no winters that far south. My parents sat at the kitchen table, punching our debts into an old calculator. I'd been sitting there with them, but my mother asked me to water her garden after my father started cursing. Bad language was not uncommon around our house, so I didn't understand why my mother insisted that I leave, but I walked out the back door and toward her tomatoes and peppers. When I passed the kitchen window and peeked at my parents, I saw their elbows on the table, their hands in the air. The window was raised, and as my father pushed back his chair and removed his glasses, he said, "We have to do *something*."

I thought my father had suggested moonlighting to offset our bills, something he'd done in the past. Every couple of years he took jobs at a local garage, or a furniture refinisher, or a lumberyard, and twice he had worked as a janitor at my school. Some mornings during those periods I opened my locker and found it cleaned and organized. Other times notes that said "Always look out for number one" or "Keep control, keep ahead" turned up in my desk. The notes were written in my father's small, stiff print on yellow squares of paper, which I crumpled as soon as I had ransacked my locker. I told everyone the school had contracted him to do air-conditioning work. It took the same amount of time for my father to exhaust himself as it did for him to grow comfortable with our finances again, and eventually my mother always convinced him to quit.

On that January evening he marched into the yard and touched my shoulder. He told me to go inside and help my mother wash the dishes, then went into the garage. My mother closed the window when I stepped inside.

"We're in a scrape now, Darren," she said, her hands invisible in the gray water filling the sink. "Your father feels boxed in."

I stood beside her and toweled the dishes she handed me. "Is he going to find another job?"

"No." She blew a few strands of hair from her face. "I don't know what's going to happen."

"I bet we'll end up fine," I said and at that time I believed it. But my mother understood that we were living with a man who wanted another life for us, one he couldn't afford.

My mother scrubbed the remaining dishes and handed them to me in silence. Then she dried her hands. "People go crazy at times," she said. "They think in ways you can't understand." She was talking about my father, and when I saw him later that night I wondered what he'd done to make her say that. He was scanning the want ads and didn't look insane. I didn't disturb him, but went to the window and looked at the yard, perfectly trimmed.

I was earning fine grades. Aside from Chad Hollins, who'd promised to punish me for refusing to write a paper for him, school never troubled me, because I had a good memory and liked reading. My father tacked my report cards to a corkboard above his desk and told everyone I would go to medical school. Neither of my parents had finished high school, so they pampered me when it came to my studies. But I wanted something else. I wanted to listen to a car's engine and understand why it stalled. I wanted to know the difference between a catalytic converter and a drive shaft; I wanted the ability to distinguish a burned-out clutch from a shot transmission by their odors. These were my father's talents, things he mentioned in conversations like the names of relatives. But he denied them to me, deeming me too intelligent to clutter my mind with such information. "You'll have a different life than me," he'd said more than once. "When you need something fixed, you'll hire someone." These words came from beneath one of our vehicles, and in between them my father described what I should hand him. Every time I placed a tool into his greasy palm I memorized its name, hoping he would quiz me on it later.

I believed my father's refusal to teach me about his tools stemmed from something I'd done wrong at one time or another. Maybe I had answered a question in a way he didn't appreciate or maybe he never forgot that in grade school a girl had blackened my eye. Or maybe it hadn't happened yet. Maybe my father saw something in me, a potential for flaw in my character, that discouraged him. Maybe he knew that in a crunch, I would hesitate and flounder, or I would rush and cut the wrong wire.

"I'm sorry," I said when I cross-threaded a nut on my bicycle, when I busted his shovel, when I swallowed some gasoline while trying to learn to siphon, when I knocked a hole in a piece of Sheetrock.

"It's not your fault." His voice was calm, his mind already assessing the damage, plotting the repair. "It was my mistake."

"I'll do it right the next time."

"No, Darren." He always used my name when he tried to console me. My father was good at consoling people. "We're done with that now," he'd say and change the subject, and no matter how I tried to get the conversation back to what mattered, I failed. The blame was all his now, and it was out of my range. Even long after my father died, I would try to seize that quality of his which was lost on me, but my attempts were always anchored in inability, as if I still lacked the right tools, as if my small, clumsy hands were trying to grab smoke.

The previous Christmas my parents had decided not to exchange gifts. I'd overheard them agreeing on this, but I didn't believe it until the only presents they held were what my grandmother and I had given them. They unwrapped a wallet and set of stationery from me and sweatsuits from my grandmother—black for him, pink for her. But neither handed a gift to the other. It still seemed like a good time in our lives, and I hoped that in the future we would look back on it and smile. We were sitting on the floor and listening to my grandmother's holiday records when, as my mother pressed herself from the carpet, my father asked, "Is that a bird in the tree?"

It was absurd, yes, but we all turned toward the Christmas tree, and on his urging, my mother spread the limbs to look for the bird. "Stop teasing," she said, and though it sounded like she was going to say my father's name, her mouth opened too wide for words when her eyes lit on the thin gold chain hanging among the tinsel. She hesitated before taking it from the branches, and when she turned—eyes fixed on the necklace, tinsel tangled in her hair—she only shook her head. Nothing would've pleased her more than to have given my father one small gift, while nothing would've made him more sad; even then I knew that. Tears slipped down my mother's cheeks, and my father rose and held her to him. He smirked and accused her of scaring away the bird. Then he stood there embracing my mother and did not say anything for some time.

After the new year they both started working more overtime and spoke of selling my mother's car. I suggested that I could find a job—Portland was a town where a boy of fifteen could find dock work and get paid in cash—but my father insisted I concentrate on school. We canceled our newspaper delivery and my father pawned his rifle and some of my mother's rings. Every night my parents suggested ideas to each other, things they'd fretted over all day. Then they argued. Once I overheard my mother say she would not be a party to such a thing and if he tried to drag her son down with him, she and I would disappear. That fight ended like the others: my father withdrew into the garage while my mother walked around the block. And I closed myself in my room, as if hiding from a tornado, waiting for the roof to be torn off.

"The only irreplaceable thing is family," my father said as he and I drove across town to straighten my grandmother's garage. My mother was already there.

At first I let the words pass over me, then I wondered what had prompted them. In my mind I questioned whether he'd even said anything at all. I could only guess that he was laying the groundwork to confide that my grandmother was dying, which she was, but we never spoke of it.

"This van, our house, jewelry, money—they all come and go." He shifted gears and went silent.

"I know."

"I'm not a rich man and I'm not smart." These words

sounded heavier than the others. "But I'd do anything for my family. I would do anything for you."

"I think you're smart," I said, and it was true.

"I'm not. I've got good sense, but I'm not smart." He didn't look at me. "You're smart."

"I'd do anything for my family too. I'd do anything for you."

"Don't ever get sentimental, boy. Ever."

"I won't."

We pulled into the driveway leading to my grandmother's small house, gravel pelting the van's carriage. I thought we'd knock on her door and drink a glass of iced tea before beginning, but without telling anyone we'd arrived my father went straight to work, and I followed his lead. When the sun started to drop, my grandmother eased herself down the steps and into the garage. The smell of lilacs followed her and she patted my wrist when she stepped close to me. My mother stayed in the house, watching us from the doorway and looking tired. "Oh, yes," my grandmother said. "Plenty of room."

That night Obie came over and my father invited him to stay for dinner. He and my parents drank some beer after we ate, though by nine o'clock my mother had gone to bed, leaving the three of us watching television. My father got up and went into their room after a minute, and I thought he would kiss her good night and return, but he stayed in there for some time. Obie scanned the channels and said, "Your parents really love you."

I didn't know how to respond. "Thank you," I said.

"All day at work your old man raves about you." He crushed an empty pack of cigarettes and dropped it into his lap. Obie's wife had left him two years before and he told prison stories, though we knew he'd spent only two nights in the county jail for unpaid traffic tickets. "Did he tell you about that rattlesnake?"

"No," I said. "He didn't."

"Some old boy set one loose in another old boy's truck. Can you believe that?" Obie shook his bald head. Maybe because he was the one telling the story, I pictured a snake slithering inside the trashed Dodge Charger Obie kept on cinder blocks in his driveway.

"Yes. I believe that."

"Then that second old boy put a trash can full of rotten shrimp on the other's porch, and set it on fire." Obie scratched his pink scalp. "I'm sure your dad will tell you. Just act surprised."

My father stepped from the bedroom at that moment, and for some reason I thought my mother was still awake and thinking about us. His eyes were glazed and watery.

Soon Obie left and I considered asking my father about the snake, but I didn't. We stayed up most of the night, way past the hour when all the stations except PBS sign off. A program about a man missing one leg aired, and we learned that he'd been trapped under a rock while hiking in Yellowstone Park. The man—the program labeled him "Joseph Henson, Survivor"—freed himself except for his right ankle, which remained hopelessly lodged. He claimed to have heard wolves howling in the woods and to have seen bear tracks not fifty yards from where he lay helpless. But what drove him to rip off his sleeve, tourniquet it around his calf, and saw off his leg with a pocketknife was the cold. "No one was going to save me," Joseph Henson said. "I was either going to freeze to death or hack off my foot." He dragged himself to a ranger's station and lost everything from his knee down due to complications. The camera panned across his family and dropped to his plastic leg. He explained that when he detached the prosthesis he could still feel the ghost of his real limb and sometimes reached to scratch it.

"That's a smart son of a bitch," my father said and took a swallow of beer. "A smart son of a bitch."

On the last Sunday in January my parents again sat at the kitchen table, plugging at the calculator. I studied beside them. My homework lay scattered among their ledgers, receipts, bills, insurance papers.

"Done," my father said. He removed his glasses and rubbed his dark eyelids. "They're all paid."

I looked at him, less because of what he had said than the way he said it. His words sounded stiff, rehearsed.

"Why don't we just pay a couple a month?" My mother seemed to be thinking aloud. "If you want to know what I'd like, that's what it would be. Let's take our time about this."

"We're fine this way."

"How much is left?" she asked.

My father shook his head to mean he didn't want to answer her. "Jean."

"What about college?" She darted her eyes at me.

"Jean."

"We can't afford this." My mother touched her fingers to her lips and held them there for a few seconds.

"They're almost paid now. Is that better?" He rolled his shoulders. "We're in good shape."

"You have no idea what you're doing."

My mother wanted to say more. I heard that in the silence. But she only stared at my father, whose hands hid his eyes. They stayed like that for what seemed like a long time, then my mother grabbed her cigarettes and barged outside into the night. My father exhaled, loudly, then started double-checking his calculations. After every ten or twelve keystrokes he raised his eyes over his glasses to consult his figures. He appeared to know what he was doing. The only thing that made him look like a man who wasn't an accountant was the scar splitting his left eyebrow.

"How did you get your scar?" I knew the story, but at that moment I wanted to hear my father's voice.

He said a black man had hit him. My parents had stopped for gas in Baton Rouge and the man shouted nasty things at my mother as she walked to the rest room. As he spoke, my father didn't look at me, so I tried to see my mother outside, but I saw only the two of us reflected in the windows. My father had ignored the man in Baton Rouge until the man had run toward my mother. My father said he'd forgotten how he'd been hit, that he hadn't even noticed until they were back on the road, which seemed impossible to me.

"What about the man?"

"I clocked him with a tire iron and left him on the cement." My father looked at me for the first time. "Your mother had nightmares about him for a while, but she's forgotten him now. Every so often I wonder about him, but it doesn't matter. Maybe he died right there."

My father returned to his numbers then, and I imagined telling him I'd hit a boy named Chad Hollins with a tire iron. Chad muscled everyone around at my school. He took mostly shop classes and smoked while he worked. His shelves and footstools earned A's, while mine always wobbled and splintered. But I thought of hitting Chad because he knew that he terrified me, and I didn't want my father to know anything scared his son.

In the week after my father said he'd paid our bills, we ate at restaurants with cloth napkins and my mother received flowers at work. My parents went out alone on the first Friday in February and left me twenty dollars for pizza—though I stuffed the money into the jar under my bed, the one I'd always believed would please my father—and watched a baseball game until they returned. My mother came in first and huffed the word "unbelievable," then she dropped her purse onto the floor. The purse fell over, and I could hear her keys and compact spill onto the wood. A minute later my father entered, closed the door behind him, and gathered her things from the floor. Crouching there he said, "Get some sleep. Tomorrow we're painting the house."

We started before dawn, me stirring the paint and my father taping our windows and bunching tarps around the foundation. Even though I wanted to ask questions, we spoke very little. It was difficult to see my hands or what color paint I was mixing, and twice I tripped and fell to the hard black ground. Once we started painting, my father showed me how to brush in long vertical strokes, though eventually I botched a section that he would have to sand and repaint and he relegated me to cleaning our work area.

Around noon my mother stepped outside and loaded a box into her car. It occurred to me that she might be leaving and might take me with her, but when I asked my father what she was doing he said she was taking things to my grandmother's. When she appeared again, with another, smaller box, I asked her why she wasn't helping with the painting. I intended it as a joke.

"This is your father's project." She sounded irritated and shot a look at my father. He was rinsing his brush with gasoline.

"You'll like it when it's done," he said. They glared at each other.

"And now, Darren," my mother said. Then she ducked into the car, started it, and drove away.

Each afternoon when my father returned from the base we painted for two hours. I felt good helping him, so good that I thought about little else. My methods improved and mostly he'd stopped inspecting my work. When we began to paint the interior, we started sleeping at my grandmother's to escape the fumes. My father asked Obie to watch the house in the evenings and handed him a piece of paper with my grandmother's phone number on it. Obie commented on how fine the paint looked, but he didn't say anything about how long it was taking. A couple of times Obie invited my father to take a break and drink a beer with him, which my father did, and then he returned and worked as carefully as a thief.

When we had made some progress, my father suggested I invite some friends over to show off our work. I decided against this because it seemed like a strange thing to do, but a few of my parents' friends visited and offered compliments. Each day my father and I inched our ladders and buckets farther around our house. Inside my mother dusted and rearranged with the windows open. She would poke her head out and ask where my father had put their wedding album or where I kept my old scout uniform. She packed these things to store in my grandmother's garage while my father and I sanded small sections of our house, working until it grew too dark to see.

My grandmother's house was close to the beach and had two bedrooms. She slept in hers, my parents took the guest room, and I spent nights on the tweed couch that was much older than I was and made my skin itch. Soon I started sleeping in the van. No one noticed because I snuck out after they had retired for the night and shambled inside with the sunrise, well before my father started frying eggs for breakfast. Ever since we'd started sleeping there, my parents fought more. My mother didn't like my grandmother to hear them, so they argued behind the guest-room door and ignored each other at dinner, passing serving dishes without allowing their eyes to meet.

On the night that everything happened, my father stepped from his room wearing the black sweatsuit my grandmother had given him for Christmas, and this made her smile. It was the first time I'd seen him since the morning, because he'd worked on the house without me that afternoon. I'd come home ready to paint, but he'd left a note telling me to take the day off because I'd been doing such a good job. That evening he didn't say anything to me or my grandmother, but went outside to smoke. The smell of sweet cigar smoke crawled under the door. A few minutes later my mother stepped into the hallway and stood still, as if she were confused about where to go. Then she moped into the den and lay on the couch, resting her head in my grandmother's lap. Seeing her like that saddened me. We watched the late newscast but in the middle of it my mother raised herself from the couch and clicked it off. "I would like to hear happy stories sometimes," she said to no one and walked down the hall. "I would like to hear that things are improving." That night I decided against pulling out the bed, but just stretched out on the van's seat and thought about my mother. I fell asleep still in my clothes, trying to remember a positive news story for her, but I could think only of Joseph Henson's, which she didn't know.

I awoke shortly after the engine started. Outside the night was a dark, dark blue and I lay as still as I could, wondering what I should do, where my father was going. The van was cruising slowly; my father turned off the radio. In the driver's seat he mouthed something, and though I couldn't decipher his words I thought he was making a list. And just as I resigned myself to stay hidden and see what my father was doing, the van stopped and his eyes fixed me in the rearview mirror. They narrowed in a way that made me think of cold. He glared at me, but I turned to the window and realized we were parked near our house. We stayed quiet. He was quiet, I think, because he felt trapped and didn't know how to proceed, and I was quiet because I could think of nothing to say.

"I was asleep," I said.

He continued staring at me in an awful way, as if I'd accused him of having an affair, which was something that had crossed my mind. His eyes held me for several long seconds before he said to get out of the van and stay quiet. All I could think was that we were going to paint. My father eased the door closed behind me until it rested on its casing and the van's interior light had dimmed. We crept to the porch. Clouds covered the small moon and no porch lamps burned on Whistler Road. We moved in darkness, me behind my father. When I asked again what we were doing, he raised his hand for me to hush, so I did. I fell in behind him and in front of me he became invisible.

Inside we turned on no lights. My father hustled around the house picking up things and replacing them, as if he'd lost something. The air reeked of turpentine. He whispered that we wouldn't stay long and vanished into his bedroom. Because I could think of nothing else to do, I went into my room. My eyes had adjusted to the darkness, but I still couldn't see clearly and stretched my arms forward to stop from bumping into things. Drawers in other rooms squeaked open and closed, and then my father entered with a satchel over his shoulder. He handed it to me and my arm jerked with its weight; he told me to wait outside.

"Wait for what?"

"For me," he said, ferreting through the cupboards.

"I feel like we're robbing ourselves." I laughed a little and expected him to smile. But he only told me again to go outside. And though I never actually thought we were stealing what we already owned, I realized that whatever we were doing was something other fathers and sons did not do.

Once outside, acting normal escaped me. Sitting on the porch I felt vulnerable, while standing made my hands seem heavy and awkward. Painting equipment lay around the foundation of our house, strewn in a way that my father had punished me for in the past. Even in the moonlight I could see paint drying in the bristles of brushes and cans left open since that afternoon, two of them dumped over and bleeding onto the leaves of my mother's garden. I peeked inside to find my father, and when I didn't see him I moved to clean the mess, but before taking two steps I changed my mind and inched back to the porch. I glimpsed my father inside. He patted his pockets, and the tip of his cigar glowed like lava. Everything fell silent. I turned away and he came outside and locked the door behind him. We drove away without turning on our lights.

My grandmother answered the phone and screamed, screamed in a way you do not want to hear anyone close to you scream. We sped to our house still wearing pajamas. My grandmother sobbed and I kept asking what had happened, but my parents were too shocked to answer and soon I understood why. Though the sun was just starting to climb through the morning clouds, enough light filtered down to see the house was a complete loss. The fire was out, but its scent lingered. Flames smell different than smoke. My mother collapsed into my grandmother's arms the way I pictured our second story collapsing onto our first. Tears jiggled in Obie's eyes and he dawdled around, adjusting his glasses and trying to comfort everyone by squeezing their shoulders. Everything was black and saturated and reeking of sulfur. For some reason I feared causing more damage, cringing every time a piece of wood or glass cracked beneath my feet. I tiptoed to where my room once was and tried to identify things. Cold water seeped into my shoes and soaked my socks. I remembered that pioneers had burned old barns to save the nails and I wondered what anyone could salvage from our house. The firemen talked and gestured to my father, circling our foundation. Two-by-fours snapped beneath their feet and they kicked pieces of our walls and rummaged through the ashes of the attic. One of them asked my father if he had any enemies and he answered that he had no more than any man. Then they spoke of turpentine and electrical shorts.

I returned to my mother sifting through the remains of her garden. Charred paint cans cluttered the small space where she had planted her bulbs. She stood and placed her palms on my cheeks and looked into my eyes as though she wanted to apologize for all of it. Her hands bruised my face with soot, and I started crying. She pulled me to her and our bodies shook together. Over her shoulder I noticed the small plastic fence around her garden. Much of it had melted into nothing, but a few of the stakes had survived the blaze. They stood blackened and gnarled, bowed in on themselves, pointing at each other like fingers.

In the following weeks we continued sleeping at my grand-mother's. Fire investigators and insurance adjusters flocked to our old house and ruled that faulty wiring had caused the blaze. When my father relayed this news, it was the first time in two days that we'd heard his voice. During this period of our lives my parents didn't speak much—to each other or to me. And taking my cue from them, I held my tongue.

One night my mother did stalk into the living room as I was trying to fall asleep. She smelled of salt water and cigarette smoke; that combination still conjures images of my mother today. I didn't recognize her dress, maybe because very little light shafted through the blinds. I thought she was leaving, and it surprised me when she sat in my grandmother's chair.

"I went for a walk on the beach," she said, as if she were answering a question.

I adjusted my pillow, doubled it over so I could see her better.

She exhaled. The sound made me expect a ribbon of blue smoke to stream from her mouth, but it did not. "My father was a fisherman. Did you know that?"

"Yes."

"A shrimper," she said.

I remembered that my grandfather's skin felt like an old bas-ketball, one bounced only on concrete. I looked hard at my mother then, at her skin, and for the first time realized that she had once been beautiful.

"He told us stories." She pulled at the hem of her skirt, and then placed her hands in her lap, where they reminded me of baby birds. "I think I'm a poor mother because I can't remem-ber any stories for you."

I didn't think this was why she felt like a poor mother, though I didn't say that.

"But I thought of something tonight, something he used to say, and I want to tell it to you now."

"Okay," I said. A moment passed before she spoke.

"The ocean has no memory."

And although she stayed in the room with me, this was the last thing my mother said that night. Something outside, maybe a raft of clouds floating across the moon, eclipsed what light slanted inside and the room fell to blackness. My father rolled over in the next room. When my mother stood, I thought she would go to him or maybe leave through the front door, but she took off her shoes, one then the other, and lowered herself onto the couch beside me. She wiggled into the blanket and became still. I draped my arm over her and her back relaxed into my chest. Her eyes closed, but her body remained tense. Under my arm it felt like one strained muscle. Soon, though, the muscle released and lapsed into a set of quiet, desperate whimpers, then finally she began to cry hard. I doubted her thoughts were far from mine. Despite what we told everyone and each other, things were not going well and they wouldn't recover for some time, maybe never.

What followed over the next few months, I see now, accorded perfectly with my father's plan. A claims adjuster called my grandmother's house daily and visited almost as often. Now I think his frequent visits meant that our family was under some suspicion, but at the time I knew only that my father preferred to talk to him alone and eventually the man ruled that the fire had spread quickly because of the turpentine and scattered painting supplies. On his last visit he promised enough money for another house.

The next day we bought new clothes at a discount department store. I followed my father through the aisles, loitering first in the tool department and then in the automotive section. Finally my mother located us there and directed us to Men's Apparel. My father picked three flannel shirts and two pair of work pants and pitched them into our shopping cart. I found what I wanted and threw the clothes on top of my father's, with the same disinterest, but my mother stuffed them back into my arms and walked me to the fitting rooms. I stood still in that tight space and didn't try on anything. My parents were bickering outside the door, and in the mirror I seemed small.

We moved into our new house in the middle of summer. During the day, I stayed there alone while my parents worked. Furniture came slowly, due to a delay with the insurance, so we slept in sleeping bags and ate on the floor like campers. The house was smaller than our other one, yet it seemed bigger, emptier, and though my father had installed a window air-conditioner, the heat stifled me. The end of summer approached and we probably looked like any other family getting used to a new house, except ours smelled like someone else's home, a place we would visit but would not live. One night when we returned from buying groceries, my father's key broke off in the lock.

The last check cleared by the end of August and we finished arranging the house before I returned to school. My mother started lifting nicer hinges and light-switch casings to replace the cheap ones included with the house, while my father stained cabinets on weekends. The house was evolving into something resembling our old one, if only in stolen fixtures and the smell of varnish. My father still refused to let me help with repairs and renovation. We started eating homemade dinners, then retiring to the den and watching cable. With every new pillow or set of curtains, we grew more comfortable. Obie visited a few times, and my parents started laughing again.

The night before school started my father drove me to the bay. He told my mother we were meeting Obie. We went to the private piers where doctors and lawyers docked their sailboats. Security lights illuminated the area and a guard paced in front of the yachts. Gulls squawked above us, though they became visible only when they swooped into the light. We walked to the end of a pier and leaned against the guardrail, where my father opened his pocketknife and began shaving his fingernails. He cut toward his body, a method he'd cautioned me against, and let the edges of his nails spiral into the ocean. The waves walloped against the pylons and my hands stayed in my pockets. "Where's Obie?"

"I guess he got tied up." My father looked into the sky.

The security light caught the blade of his knife and I watched him slowly slice into his thumbnail.

"He thinks someone from the base torched our house, Obie does. I wonder, Darren, what you think."

I shrugged and leaned toward the ocean, trying to follow one of my father's nails to the water. I thought of the story Obie had told me about the rattler and how the men who worked under my father resented him. But in my heart I knew they weren't responsible. Of course I didn't say any of that, though I don't think it would've angered my father.

"Obie's a good man," he said and I looked at his face. My father bestowed this honor on very few, and I immediately admired anyone who received it. "He's smart."

"Sometimes I think Obie lies."

"He does. You're right." His voice sounded low because he was focusing on his hands.

"I try not to lie," I said. I paused, waiting for him to commend me, but he only studied his fingers. "I don't think you lie."

"I have lied. But I would never lie to you. Or to your mother."

"I've lied—"

"You can ask me anything in the world and I'll tell you the truth as I know it." My father continued to stare at his fingers, so I looked as well. His blade was taking dead skin with the nail. I thought hard for something to ask him, something to test his claim, but found nothing. He continued, "Sometimes there's a difference between telling the truth and telling everything."

My father looked at me then, harshly, and I remembered painting two and sometimes three coats over stubborn sections of our home. I also remembered he'd written me a note saying I'd done a good job, but that he still hadn't allowed me to work at the new house. I considered asking him about it, and asking too if he'd really paid all our bills that night at the kitchen table. But instead I said, "You can ask me anything too."

He brushed the tips of his fingers against his palm and knotted his brow. I supposed he was trying to find something to ask me.

"I don't need to," my father said after a moment. He clipped his knife closed. "I know I can trust you. You're my son and we're in this together." He placed his hand on my shoulder and squeezed chills into my neck. His touch seemed to say that soon no secrets would wedge between us, and we stood like that in silence for a few minutes, on the verge of truth and change, two liars staring down the darkness.

*   *   *

We never spoke of the fire again, despite what I thought, hoped. In the days after the night on the pier, the topic seemed to exist just beneath all of our words, our movements, so that soon it would burst through the thin barrier between us. But it did not. The days became weeks, and though I felt my father was only waiting for the right time to explain things to me, the chance of that happening was as slim then as it was a month later, when he died.

He was reshingling the roof. As the doctor explained it to my mother and me, sitting in a cramped room with only a sofa, an end table, and a small brass crucifix, his heart exploded. I knew he was dead, but I thought an exploding heart sounded nice, as if my father's kindness had killed him. My mother sat beside the doctor, her hands covering her eyes. A priest whose face looked like a canned ham knocked on the door, then entered. The room became very crowded. We listened as he said we could find comfort in my father's quick, painless passage to the eternal. But almost before he had finished the sentence, my mother wiped her eyes with the back of her hand and said, "I find no fucking comfort in my husband's death."

After my father's funeral, where a man in a suit handed me a flag folded into a triangle, I hated going home. The house felt too spacious and its emptiness constricted me. My mother took an extended leave from work to stay in her bedroom all day and sleep on the couch at night. I tore the posters off my walls and pushed my bed to the middle of my room. Even then I saw the pathetic nature of our attempts at recovery. One night I came home later than usual and found my mother asleep at the kitchen table. Her nightgown had fallen open and I could see the bottom of her neck where my father's wedding ring dangled from that thin gold chain. I couldn't help staring any more than I could make myself move to wake her. I watched her chest fall and rise, and when the phone rang I started. My mother came briefly to life and answered, spoke for a few minutes, then handed me the receiver without a word. In my grandmother's voice, I could hear the cancer that would kill her in less than a year.

When I returned to school, people touched me. Walking down the halls, hands fluttered to my shoulders and arms pulled me toward bodies I didn't remember knowing. Teachers, students, janitors—almost everyone missed my father and apologized for the tragedy. I thanked them and rushed to class to stop from crying.

In the middle of lunch period, as I dropped the food I hadn't eaten into the trash, a heavy hand pressed itself into the small of my back and a voice said, "I'm really sorry about your dad." When I turned, Chad Hollins squinted his eyes sympathetically.

I found myself afraid, unaware of what to say. "What?"

"Your father." He glanced over each of his shoulders. "I'm really sorry he passed away. I sold him some paint."

Just then, maybe because he seemed like the boy my father might've been, I punched Chad Hollins in the throat. He gasped and his eyes widened like a shot deer's as he tumbled into the stack of trays, knocking them down and filling the cafeteria with the loud, sharp sound of trouble. He held his neck as if he were strangling himself and scuttled backward across the floor, like a crab, small and awkward and afraid. Everyone glared at me. Someone went for the principal and as I waited for him I envisioned my fate: His office would feel cold and clean. He would look at my record and act friendly because of my grades and extenuating circumstances, and I would sit quietly when he said, "This is a tough time." I would not answer when he questioned my relationship with Chad. Did I know him outside of school? Had there been static between us before? Was there anything he should know? Only when he asked how I felt would I speak. I would say, "Fine."

Robyn Kirby Wright

George Mason University

WATERSHED

The home of my childhood sits alongside the Hudson River—a solitary cedar-planked house, watermarked and weather-beaten, hidden under a wild covering of trees. I am thirteen years old, sitting on my father's kayak, mindful that it is my father's kayak and if he should come down to the bank I had better hide before he sees me. The river is tumbling, pooling around my bucket of bait. I have no intention of fishing. The bait, a mixture of white bread, Cheerios, and sharp cheddar cheese, is my mother's attempt to clean out the pantry before her next trip to the grocery. It is a cloudless, blue day, like so many that pass unnoticed because of their similarity to the day before. The air smells of wood chips and citronella. The smells of summer winding down. My sister, Abby, is sunbathing in her black tank suit; a pale red buoy props her head in the sun. Her toenails are painted Malibu pink, the same color I have painted over my mosquito bites to keep them from itching. I lay down beside her, pressing my feet into the ground, staring up at the sky. Her right leg, not quite two inches shorter than her left, is propped on a beach bag. Her blond hair is piled on top of her head, a wide barrette clipping it in place, a few loose curls falling in her eyes—the usual organized mess that comes to her so effortlessly. She is working the sand with her fingers, drawing hearts, droopy flowers, and an occasional star. We are both singing the same song, the one that's been stuck in our heads ever since Duncan said it was his favorite. We make up our own words because we've only heard it once and neither of us can remember anything but the way he sang it into his fist, the windows of his truck rolled down and the air-conditioning blowing cool on our faces, making it hard to catch our breath.

We are best friends when school is out—me doing cartwheels down the hill, Abby lightening her hair with lemon juice, the two of us sitting in the shed smoking cigarette stubs and talking about Duncan. We will be best friends for twenty-seven more days, and then I won't see her again, at least not the way I see her now, sunburned and thirsty, with tiny new freckles on her nose. It is a hot day, the kind with mirages, only I don't see an oasis but a waterfall, and my mouth is open and it all just pours inside. I am wearing my soccer uniform—a red mesh jersey with the number five ironed on in black and cleats, an outfit I have in my head as looking good on me though I have not played soccer yet that season.

"It breathes," I say, pushing my fingers through the holes of the shirt.

"Sarah," Abby says. "It only looks authentic if you have grass stains on your shin guards."

"There is a reason why I'm wearing this."

"You've got a game in a month or so?"

"It was the cleanest thing in the hamper," I say. I don't tell her about the uniform looking good on me or how I want Duncan to know I'm registered for soccer in the fall. She wouldn't understand that.

She laughs. We laugh at stupid things. We laugh secretly at my dad, but not to his face, when he tells Abby she is not allowed to ride alone with Duncan. "He's out of school for God's sake. . . ." my father says. Duncan, known by my dad as the "polite boy with the putty-colored face," is our neighbor and my sister's true love. He is true in all the ways a first love should be. He brings her flowers from our garden for her hair. He carries her on his back and pulls splinters from her thumb. He writes her name with a felt-tip pen on the inside of his arm. He sings songs into her skin. My father doesn't know any of this. What he knows is: Duncan dropped out of high school at seventeen to start his own construction business. He has manners and a ridiculous haircut—ridiculous because it hangs below his shoulders and sometimes covers his eyes. He works long hours to pay off his father's loan on the family gas station on Brockton Highway. He builds decks, gazebos, and porches, two of which my father needs, and so despite his misgivings he employs Duncan. What I know about him is that he can't sit still unless he has something in his hands—broken things, scrap wood, spare parts, and pinecones. He likes all these things and he drives a Chevy truck. Sometimes, I think, he likes me.

Even though my sister gets motion sick, we go off-roading. We have done it a thousand times—plowed through mounds of cakey dirt, dust clouding our vision, wheels spinning out under us while my sister turns hard to the left in an attempt to steady the truck. In the rain we go for speed. Mud fills the tread of the thick tires, spraying the windshield until we are sightless, going on feel alone as the radio blares static between stations. We are a little out of control. It's my job to shift gears while they hold hands, and to run into the Stop and Go to buy lemonade and chips. Sometimes I imagine Duncan and I are alone in the truck, and it is me who passes him a soda when he's thirsty, finds his wallet from under the seat, puts my fingers in his thick hair. I allow myself to think this while I'm locked in the bathroom, after Abby has gone to sleep and can't read my mind anymore.

"Don't tell those weird stories today, Sarah," Abby says, stretching her arms over her head. "Act natural. And I don't want you hanging around after." She is still lounging in the sun, fanning herself with a bookmark.

Natural does not come easy. Act natural, she says, as if I am capable of acting any way at all around Duncan but stupid. She believes I can do this. She is generous that way. I never can act natural around him and if I do, I wonder if he knows I'm acting. Like the natural way I smile so my braces don't show, and how my eyebrows have a natural arch but sometimes look as if I am surprised, and my naturally curly hair that doesn't curl so well in the humidity. I never seem to get it right.

"He's here," Abby whispers. "Pass me my shoes. Pretend we're talking about something important."

He walks down the wooded path, arms extended, carrying a jug of water, running his hand along spiked plants. He is shirtless; his hair is the color of potato peels, a soft sun-bleached blond. I sit on the kayak, draping my legs over the overturned body, as if it were my very own piece of the river. I spread my towel across the ridge, patting the space beside me, and invite him to sit.

"Which one of you girls wants to drive?" he asks.

He smiles and I hardly notice his chipped front tooth. He is wearing a necklace made out of bones, something he dug up somewhere on vacation. It is the most exotic thing I've ever seen.

"All I know is"—Abby stands up to brush the sand off her suit—"I'm not riding on the hump."

"That's what Sarah's for," he says, smiling, touching me on the knee.

I try not to focus on his hand, but there it is, ready to move, and I'll do anything to make it stay for a few more seconds. Someone whispers, "I love you." I recognize my own voice and cover my mouth. No one hears but me. The river gurgles and spills shiny new stones onto the bank.

My mother once told me the river had a memory. If I whispered my secrets into the water, my words would mix with those of lost sailors and gypsies and pirates. And these words, some light with laughter, others weighty from heartache, would be carried downstream and thousands of years later, bathing children would swim in my story.

*   *   *

Duncan walks to the bank, squats and puts his hands in the water, letting the current pull at his fingers.

"Only thing you're going to catch with this," he says, lifting up the bucket of bait, "is a skinny preteen with blond hair."

"Very funny," I say, acting natural. "Now can we go for a ride?" My cleats sink into the dirt. I am short again. A stray branch, clean as a switch, brushes against my thigh. "Come on," I say.

Abby starts up the trail. Her step, a light hop, disappears into the uneven ground. It is her own distinctive walk, which I've tried to imitate, though my mother's told me I am the fortunate one not having to contend with all the difficulties Abby's had.

We are almost the same height. She wears special shoes, never runs, and has learned how to be so light that nobody notices the weightiness of mismatched legs. My legs are even, the knees line up perfectly. Sometimes I am proud of this; sometimes I wish one leg would quit growing. Abby waves to my mother, whose gloveless hands are elbow high in dirt, turning the soil with her fingers. She is planting more rosebushes, the old-fashioned kind that smell like sachets and drawer liners.

"Don't forget my tomatoes," she yells after Abby. "And take your sister."

"I can't," Abby says, smiling. "She's got a soccer game this afternoon."

"No, I don't," I snap. "I'm only wearing this because everything I own is in the laundry."

We drive Route 232, the sun bleaching the truck's dashboard, scorching the top of my thighs. I cover them with an old work towel. Abby is checking her teeth in the side mirror. They are perfect, straight, china-doll teeth, white as chalk.

"See there, Sarah?" she says pointing to the water tower. "You should climb that. I bet you could see forever from up there. I'll do it, too, someday."

Duncan believes she is afraid of heights. I don't say anything. It is not my place. We drive and drive until I don't recognize the road anymore, slowing down only when we pass through the heart of town. A tiny woman, light as a salt shaker, stands against a gas pump, stroking the fur of a fat gray cat. We pass the bait and tackle store; a young boy in overalls scoots across the front porch. The windows are down and the air is going but I can't even feel the cool.

"Go faster," Abby says, smoothing out the creases in her dress. "Faster."

My hair is blowing the wrong way, getting snarled, sticking to my cheek. Duncan is sweating. Tiny beads of wetness sit on his face and drip down his back. I catch myself staring.

"Let's go to the new market in Kernerville," he says. "They got a band that plays on weekends."

Abby and I nod, excited about being in his truck, being with him. We pass countless trees, I say countless because I count them, promising myself a prize if I can come up with a reasonable number. At first it's dinner out with shrimp cocktail and hush puppies—then it somehow becomes marriage, three boys, and an A-frame house right on the river with Duncan.

"Three hundred and forty-three trees in that stretch of land," I say, gesturing to the entire New York countryside. "I counted."

"Like we care, Sarah," Abby says. "It scares me when you say things like that. Besides, there were at least five hundred and twenty-two."

Duncan smiles. I am happy that indirectly I am the reason for his smile.

It is a long drive to Kernerville, but it goes fast. Fast like it always goes when your arm is touching the arm of someone you love. We stop at Fletcher's Market and rummage through baskets looking for one sturdy enough to carry our load. Duncan and Abby go under the tent to the watermelon tank. She is up on a footstool leaning over the side, trying to lift a melon from the cold water. I run my hands over plump strawberries, examining them for brown patches. I pick up a bunch of grapes and hold them to my ear. "Look at this," I yell across the tent to Duncan. "You like my earring?" I feel stupid as soon as I say that.

I arrange a perfect assortment of color in my basket, choosing summer squash instead of zucchini because there is too much green in my pile. I sneak a plum from the bottom of a tidy stack and bite into the thin skin, the sweet juice running down my chin.

"Caught you," a woman says, throwing a melon rind on the floor. "Who can resist?"

I rattle my change as if I'm going to pay for it. There is a man with a guitar sitting on an overturned whiskey barrel, one foot resting on a crate of oranges.

"Hey, little girl," he says. "How about a Patsy Cline tune?"

I am not sure he is talking to me, so I count ears of corn and watch him out of the corner of my eye.

"Hey, you," he says again. "Have any 'Sweet Dreams' lately?"

He doesn't wait for my answer but turns up his amp and starts to play. I am mesmerized by the sadness. I watch him pick the strings, his eyes closed, neck wet with perspiration, and I wonder why it feels so good to feel that bad.

The corn is five ears for a dollar. I pay for it in dimes. The tomatoes are fat— "Big Boys," the clerk says as I hold them to my nose and breathe in their ripe smell.

"Are you sure these are not vegetables?" I say. "Because they don't smell like fruit."

A cat scratches the dirt floor. My sister has her face toward an industrial-size fan; the blades, thick as oars, make a whirring sound. She is pulling on her damp sundress, airing it out in the breeze. She is smiling.

"Look at me," she says. "I am drenched."

Duncan is holding her around the waist and with one easy sweep, he picks her up. She is laughing, her head gone back, feet kicking. He is trying to weigh her on the gigantic scale, and she is covering the numbers with her hands. I think she has forgotten that her shoe could fall off and then he'd know the truth. She is happy. Happy like I've never seen her. Patsy Cline is still coming out of the cowboy, only I don't understand the words anymore. His voice is like the buzz of the fan, constant and dull. Duncan's foot is holding a watermelon in place on the platform. He is pointing at the numbers, holding on to the sash of Abby's dress. I run with my basket toward them, losing a lemon from my pile. My cleats puncture the ground. I run hard, zigzagging through the maze of fruit, ducking to miss the swinging vines of vinca growing down from the rafters. There is a stabbing pain in my chest. I am having a heart attack. Still I keep running. I am grateful for my cleats. I fall over myself, trying to get there, but I am too late. Before I can reach them, he has held her face in his hands, wiped the hair from her forehead, and kissed her on the lips.

On the floor of the river there is a boat named the *Sister Mary*. There were no survivors—nothing recovered except a metal spatula, a makeshift grill, and a rubber shoe. I have been told that the morning after the wreck, two oars floated downstream. They were crossed at the center, with the owner's name, Curtis B. Plumbstone, burned into the light oak wood. The oars washed ashore four miles away, so Plumbstone buried them there, side by side in the sand. He marked the graves, empty except for the oars, with a string of clam shells and a torn fishing net. Curtis B. Plumbstone was a superstitious man. I have been told this happened the summer it rained for six weeks straight and my parents put a tarp over their heads just to walk to the mailbox. I have been told the *Sister Mary* was named after a dead woman and that woman wasn't his sister.

"Where is she?" I ask Duncan.

Abby and Duncan are sitting on the shore, lighting matches, flicking them into the river. I am leaning against a tree, half hiding behind the kayak.

"Get back inside," Abby says. "You're not supposed to be here."

"Neither are you," I snap back. "I want to know where she is."

It is late. My parents are watching television in their room.

"The boat or the woman?" Duncan says.

"The woman," Abby says.

"The boat," I say.

"What happened to her? Nobody knows," Abby says.

"She was never found," Duncan says. "And the boat, she's almost rotted away. I'll take you there now if you want to go."

"I want to go," I say.

"Now?" Abby asks.

"Come on," he says. "I have snorkels in the flatbed and my dad's flashlight. It will be like daytime."

"Is it far?" Abby asks. "Because I don't want to go too deep."

"I'll watch over you," Duncan says. "It's not that deep."

We stand in water under a pale moon, our great shadows taking up half the river. There is no flatness, just ripples and tides rising in the darkness. Our arms are linked together in a daisy chain, each of us cautiously stepping forward, trying to contain our forms in the blackness. We walk until we reach a sandbar. Beyond this, I know there is more river than I can possibly swim, and for a moment, I want to go home. Duncan squeezes my elbow, pulling me forward. Abby plants her feet firmly in the riverbed.

"I'm not going," she says. "I don't like the water at night, and I don't want to see a dead woman's boat."

"It's not that far," Duncan says, nudging her.

She loosens her grip and waits for us to follow.

"Come on," she says, walking backward to the shore. She says this in her soft voice that sounds as if she is about to cry. "I got a bad feeling," she says.

I run my hand through the waves, the wake trailing green under my fingertips. I pretend I don't know that tone of voice. I pretend I don't hear. The river is crackling and spitting. It is alive with color. It is past midnight, the stars are low, and I am glad for their light.

"Come on," I whisper into Duncan's ear. I put one hand on his shoulder as he guides me under the light of his flashlight to deeper water. I can see for miles.

"Keep your eyes on the beam," he says.

I turn to look for Abby. She has gone back to shore, sitting now in her wet pajamas, cross-legged, drinking chocolate milk from a carton.

"Five minutes," I say, trying not to speak too loudly as my parents' window is open. "We just want to see the thing. Swim through a porthole or something."

"Hold on," Duncan says. "The current is strong."

I am scared but in a good way. "Do you hear that?" I whisper.

"What?"

"The noise the river makes."

"I don't hear it."

"Like someone's crying," I say. "I've heard it before."

"You're a crazy girl, Sarah," Duncan says, and he dives under the surface, sliding from my hands. I follow the line of bubbles until he is near again. We are paddling in place, trying to catch our breath. The moon, speckled like a duckling egg, is fat and low in the sky.

"You hear that?" he says.

"What?"

"Sounds like an old man snoring," he says with a smile.

"Oh that," I say. "That's only my father."

We swim until I have no more breath. It is cold in the river. My chest is heavy from the wetness, but I am buoyant, light as a cork.

"Come on," he says. "We're almost there. It's even with the flagpoles."

We dive down, the flashlight beam reflecting off the scales of silvery fish. I see the shape, the murky dark outline of the *Sister Mary*. She is a fishing boat. Not how I imagined her; the body split in two, her insides exposed. I am disappointed by her brokenness. There are no hidden crevices or holes to swim through; she is there, open for us to see. I break the surface only to gather another mouthful of air and I dive deep this time. I follow the beam of light to the steering wheel. Small creatures swim past me. Tiny bubbles bead on my skin. I strain to see Duncan. He is a large looming shadow behind me. My hands are numb to the cold. We swim arm in arm, locked at the elbows, touching the decaying wood. I follow the beam of light, running my fingers along the knobby protrusions, trying to break free a piece of the ship, a small token of our dive together, a piece of the *Sister Mary*. I go deeper inside, releasing Duncan's grip, mesmerized by the light. The planks of wood give easily with only a little pressure. I take a side panel from the boat and tuck it into my shorts. It is light, textured like the palm of my hand. Single-handedly, I can dismantle this ship and bring it piece by piece to shore. There I can rebuild it from inside out and paint its hull a deep shade of green like the pine trees that withstand even the coldest winters. I am thinking all these things: a dead woman, fresh paint, restore, the tips of Duncan's fingers grazing against the back of my neck. The river has a bottom.

Duncan pulls me up, guiding me toward the surface. His motions are frenetic, anxious, without understanding. We are even with the waterline, gasping for air. I want to go back down. It is crazy in this world.

"You scared me," he says, removing my snorkeling mask from my face. "I didn't think you were coming."

"I took a piece of the boat," I say. "It's in my pocket." I dig into my jean shorts looking for scrap wood.

"Show me tomorrow. It's late." He says this as he puts his finger through the loop of my jean shorts and starts to pull me toward the shore. A tugboat.

I am in awe of his mouth. How his words come out so perfectly even, his voice the same pitch as running water. I imagine he has saved my life, that I would have stayed in the open cabin, forgetting that I need air to breathe. There is nothing inside me but this warmth. We are under moonlight, drifted far from the beach. My sister is watching. Somewhere.

"Hang on," he says, pushing the hair from my forehead. "I'll get us there."

I float behind him, one hand on his waist, the other clutching my broken panel of wood. My mouth is open, pressing against the back of his neck. The blades of his shoulders part and his long arms cut through the waves like the crossed oars of the *Sister Mary*. This is all I want: to feel him under water, to be carried away by him. The water is not so deep anymore. I stand, letting my feet sink into the soft riverbed. My house is far away. We have drifted, and I'm unsure of the direction home. Abby is alone. I imagine she has fallen asleep under the yellow moon, her feet up on the old canoe, the sand giving way to her tired body.

"You know," Duncan says, dipping his head back in the water, "in this light, you don't look so ugly. You're almost pretty."

"What's that supposed to mean?"

"I'm saying you're not so bad but, then again, I whacked my head on the side of the boat."

I watch a smile come across his face—it is the only smile he could have. A broken smile with uneven teeth. It would not be beautiful on anyone else. A single bead of water rolls down my cheek. I feel the cold breeze against my chest. Duncan is treading water. It is as if I finally know how I am supposed to be. It is so easy to reach over and put my hands on his face. And before I kiss him, I know already that his kiss will be warm, and his mouth will open to me. Time does not stop. The fish swim. My fingers tremble. The backs of my knees itch. I don't count. It is my first kiss. One. Two. Three.

Something I mean to do all my life: swim the length of the river, shoot a crossbow, kiss the boy I love.

"Stop, Sarah," he says. His voice is gentle, a whisper. He holds my wrists, encircling them with his strong grip. "You don't mean to be doing this."

"Doing what?" I say, my voice going high. "It was an accident. I didn't know you were there."

"Come on," he says. "It's getting cold. We better get you out of here."

"We have to do it over again," I say. "That didn't count. I wasn't ready."

"You get big enough to see over the steering wheel of my Chevy and then we'll try again."

"It was an accident," I say. "That's all."

"I already forgot about it. Now let's go home."

"It was an accident," I say, filled with shame at his having seen me so closely. So close that he will always know that my eyes were open when I kissed him.

I hear the river crying again. It is how I feel, a part of the river, the part that is pulling back from the shore, leaving bits and pieces of itself scattered on the bank. Duncan goes underwater, closing his eyes, and smoothes his long hair back. I do not hold on to him. He swims ahead, every so often turning to look for me. I want to stay in the river, warm myself, hide in the black water. The night is hollow and lonely. The shore seems an unswimmable distance away. I am heavy. Duncan is like a razor. He zips forward, his large hands cutting through the water. It is easy to paddle in place, to put my feet down when I get tired, to decide that this is where I belong, floating just above the bones of a dead woman.

"Come on, Sarah," Duncan yells just above a whisper. He is waving his arm, pointing to the bank. If it were any darker, I wouldn't be able to see him. My chest is pounding. I run the kiss through my head a thousand times. I see his face so clearly I can trace the round of his ears, the smooth of his wide forehead. I can feel his thumb on my lips, the quiet hushing that burns my insides. The water is bubbling. Fish are coming up for air, breathing in the black night. Crickets frantically scrape their threadbare legs together. Waves lap over my shoulders, pooling pockets of white gauze. The girl is crying. My sister, on the shore, pale and white, nearly invisible under the tree cover, is calling softly.

"Where are you?" she asks, walking along the bank, her form liquid and disappearing. "Where are you?" she whispers.

She knows without seeing. I have the loudest head in the world. It told her last night about the kiss. I hide in the loft, the farthest corner of the house. I tell time by this room, measure the sunlight against the yellow walls, marking the shadows with a nubby pencil. The markings are slight, but I know they are there and it is calming. I am the only one in our family who doesn't wear a watch. Duncan is knocking on the screen door. My sister is clip-clopping across the room in her wooden shoes. I stand on the only chair in the loft until I am able to see out the porthole window. A beetle lies upside down on the sill. My fingers are covered with dust, sticky from tearing down spiders' webs. I am not wearing my soccer uniform but one of my sister's oversized T-shirts that hangs past my knees, covering me up.

The window is dirty, but still, I see everything. Duncan's truck is in our driveway, his tools spilled out of an overturned ice cooler; two bags of peat moss and a small sapling are stacked in the flatbed. The fender is dented. Windows are open.

"Come on, Sarah," Abby yells from the base of the stairs. "You know you want to come."

I pretend not to hear.

"Last chance," she says. "We're leaving."

"Go on," I say to myself.

The stairs creak under his heavy step. I count them. Fourteen to the top. I run in a circle counting, always counting, looking for a place to hide, but there is only a mattress and a sombrero on the floor with blue glitter spelling out the word "Olé." I consider placing this on my head but decide it is too obvious. There is only time to decide whether to sit or stand. There are disadvantages to both. It is with agonizing uncertainty that I sit, my knees curled up under my chin, my head turned to the side. Duncan crawls up the last step and peers around the corner. I yawn but he doesn't see me. I yawn again.

"You're tired today," he says.

"It's my stomach. Kept me up all night. Makes me do all kinds of things. That's what happens when you're sleep deprived. You do funny things."

"So that's what's wrong with you," he says. "Guess I'm sleep deprived too."

"It's not something that happens in one night," I say. "It builds and builds."

"Yeah, well, maybe you can nap after we get back from the tower."

"I'm not going," I say.

"Come on, Sarah. You know we can't go without you. Besides, who will break our fall in case we slip?" He says this smiling, as if his big smile makes all the difference.

"Abby's not going to climb that tower," I say. "Besides, it's not all that big. I could climb it with my eyes closed."

"You could climb all of three steps until you'd call me to come and get you." He smiles one of his bent smiles. "Come on," he says, grabbing my toe.

"You saved me, Duncan," I say. "I almost drowned."

"I didn't save you. Now come on."

He is not listening to me. He is wondering what Abby is doing downstairs. He is listening for her shoes. He follows the floor with his eyes, as if he were tracing her footsteps. He wants to know where she is, what she is doing. I want to make him listen. Listen to me.

"My sister has one leg shorter than the other." I tell him this with my head resting on my knees, eyes steady and voice calm. Matter-of-fact. Natural. I am reporting the weather. "She has to wear special shoes so no one will know." He is confused. His mouth sags, then it seems he is terribly disappointed. He stands, picking up his sunglasses from the floor. I am filled with energy. My mouth pours. The words taste like tar.

"She rode in the handicapped bus to school."

"You're lying," he says.

"I'm not lying," I say. "Ask her yourself."

"Are you coming?" he asks. "Because this is your last chance."

It is the first time I see him angry. His cheeks are flushed. His eyes hard. We are not the same. I know this now. This is when I know it. Duncan loves Abby. It is nothing to him, a short leg. He knows she's not going to climb the tower, or swim the river, or run across the road after his dog. We are not the same. I am nothing. I am nothing to him. Abby and I are not the same. She is perfect.

I stretch my legs on the floor of the loft. There is a bruise above my hipbone shaped like a hammer. I press on it. The wall says it is almost dinnertime. Abby is not home. A phone rings. The machine cuts on. It is my mother's voice, sweet as cake icing. "We're out and about . . . leave a message, please." Garage door opens. Ding Ding Ding. My mother does not close the car door. My legs, stretched out before me, do not look so even anymore. I put the sombrero on my head.

There is only one knock, but it is loud. There is only one voice, but it is loud. I don't hear how my sister dies.

*   *   *

The funeral is three days after the accident. I pull out drawers looking for panty hose with no holes. The window is open. My cousins from Brandon, Florida, are in the kitchen banging a wooden spoon against a glass pitcher, stirring out clumps of frozen orange juice. I'm wearing a purple sundress with tiny pink flowers and small antique amethyst earrings. The funeral is held under a pale green canopy. The flowers are wild, the kind that grow in cracks of sidewalks: cornflowers, dandelions, black-eyed Susans. My father tells the story about Abby learning to walk. At eighteen months she got out of her stroller and toddled across a crowded parking lot to a four-fifty-seven big-block Chevy and said, "Mine." He is laughing so hard I want to hit him. My mother rocks back and forth in her chair, her silk dress watermarked and wrinkled. She is crying in sheets. Her face is flat from the wetness. I don't cry with my eyes. My body holds water. I count blades of grass. Snap the heads off blooms. Make myself go in circles when nobody is looking.

"Abby," I whisper her name quietly. "Abby, Abby, Abby," I say softer and softer until it's just a whir in my mind, a frog in my throat.

It is all I can do. Listen to the river. Straighten my slip. Scratch a bug bite. It is all I can do. Duncan circles me in dark boots, talks to his fist. I lower my head. Talk to the ground. Peel my fingernails. He is crying. He makes noises only I can hear.

"Abby," he says. "I'm so sorry." His voice cracks. He says my sister's name without moving his lips. I long for water.

I imagine Abby behind the wheel of the truck, making doughnuts in the field, tearing up sod and slapping her hand on the dash.

"See that," she says, laughing. "See what I did."

I imagine one knee bent, foot resting on the hot vinyl seat and a bottle of root beer stuck between her thighs; the road open before her, a chalkboard for her scribbles. Duncan sits beside her, in my seat, swearing at the top of his lungs—the truck's tailpipe dragging over asphalt. They are wild with laughter, the seats sticky from perspiration. The truck is weightless.

My sister is weightless. She is happy like that, happy before she dies, feeling for the first time the freedom of letting go.

Two sisters wade in the same river, one tall and skinny, the other taller and skinnier. They hold hands, making a bridge with their arms, their hair tied in knots, shoulders brown as shoe polish. They hold hands until he comes. He says, "Go like this," wiping peanut butter from the corner of her mouth. He says, "I choose you." And the bridge falls down.

It is the last time I see Duncan.

I try to imagine him changed—a scar under the plaster cast, the seam running down his arm where the bone came out after the accident, his skin, puckered and damp. My own skin, pale and unmarked, tells no story of loss. And Duncan seems only vaguely familiar in my mind. I don't see him as he pumps gas or hammers a nail or loads his dog into the flatbed. I don't see him as walks down a tree-lined road in muddy, untied boots. I don't see him. I will never see him again.

My mother once told me the river was deep enough to house a whole city with skyscrapers and billboards and thousand-year-old trees.

"Open your eyes," she said. "It's another world down there."

"That's not all that deep," I had said to her.

"Well, I haven't told you about the mountain ranges, and the ruins—it's all there," she said, pointing at the water. "It's deeper than you think."

I say it is deeper still. There are places that have no bottom. I have dived straight down with my breath held for days and never seen the floor, though my fingers have grazed the water-logged planks of the *Sister Mary* and once, the handles of a wheelbarrow.

"The river is sinking," I told my mother, "unable to support all of these stories."

"It's not sinking," she said into my wet hair. "It just needs room to grow."

*   *   *

I am thirteen years old, sitting in my father's kayak, oarless, floating without purpose the afternoon my sister is buried. I am as tall as I ever will be. I know this now. Tall as the wiry stalks of midsummer corn. Tall as the first rung on the water-tower ladder. Through the trees, I can barely make out the people who are coming and going, wandering onto our deck, swishing their glasses of ginger ale, straightening their funny hats, tucking tissues into the sleeves of black suits. I am conscious only of my closeness to shore. I am not as far away as I want to be. I test the depth, shedding the tight rubber banding from my naked waist, and throw myself overboard, one hand firmly gripping the rim of the hull. My shoes sink into the unsteady bottom, filling my sneakers with sand and mud. The water is waist deep. Too shallow for boating, too deep for standing still. Waves spill over my shoulders, cooling the burn of the afternoon sun. I measure myself against the side of the kayak, making a watery mark with my finger at the very top of my head.

Peter Muñoz

University of Michigan

LATINNOVATOR

Delia first began to suspect a cosmic herpes conspiracy at the premiere of *Cesar Chavez: Su Manera*. It was one of those neighborhood fund-raisers she was increasingly asked to attend on the company's behalf: a converted firehouse, black-haired people in suits horseshoed around a plywood stage, strong coffee and homemade *pan de dulce* afterward.

She was sitting with Epi Ramirez, a graphic artist from work who had "organized" during the seventies. He still wore his gray hair in a ponytail, and during the first act he kept leaning over to say the actors were picking the invisible lettuce all wrong. By the second act, though, he was quiet, and Delia was staring at the top of the black canvas backdrop. She needed a catchy title for a handbook at work, but nothing was coming to her. Her leg was humming with low-grade pain, and in the semidark of the theater, she closed her eyes. Soon lights like the aurora borealis were undulating in her head like watery vertical blinds. In a moment the title came to her: *The Meaning of Demeaning*. It was a handbook on sexual harassment.

She heard clapping and joined in automatically, but Epi

grabbed her hand. She froze; no one else in the audience was clapping. People were looking at her and laughing or shaking their heads. Onstage, a young man wearing an incandescent white wig and a seersucker suit raised a finger. "As I was saying, these wetbacks have it too good here." The actors, all in suits, applauded again. She had clapped for the lettuce growers' consortium.

For the rest of the performance she was hyperattentive and nodded sympathetically during the closing soliloquy. She wanted to leave as soon as the house lights were up, but Epi said, "They still have the plane tickets to raffle off." He pulled his ticket stub out of his shirt pocket, and Delia fished hers out of her purse. They all held out their stubs as a short man with a face like a monkfish called out the number.

"It's me," Delia shouted in disbelief, and an odd, unhappy laughter rippled across the room. She had clapped for the lettuce growers, and now she was going to Cancún. Something was wrong about that, she knew. But there seemed to be a larger irony at work, one she couldn't quite grasp.

The fish-faced man beckoned her to the stage, and applause rose and then fell back like a groggy head. She felt queasy as she stepped onto the plywood platform. The man held out a white envelope that flared like a tungsten filament under the spotlight. She accepted it and a camera flashed, blinding her. In the billowing white, she awakened to the larger significance: something was wrong about her. As the cloud of blindness evaporated, the facts of her life condensed around her, clammy and crystalline. I have herpes. I am divorced. I attend functions with Epi because I don't date. I am an outstanding employee of the Cel-Pro Corporation. Sometimes the aurora borealis appears in my head.

Aurora borealis? Outstanding?

■

A YEAR before, she had been just the woman who put out the employee newspaper. She wrote articles on things like carpal tunnel syndrome, or the company's quarterly earnings, or some retiree's experiments with stained glass.

She had a hobby, but not a very original one: she collected souvenirs and trinkets. On vacation she loved visiting little stores where tarnished bells announced her arrival and the shelves were lined with macramé. On weekends she liked to visit flea markets and haggle over Christmas ornaments made of yarn or creamers shaped like cows. Her husband called them *chacharras,* and she displayed them around her apartment as if they were pieces of French crystal. Disney figurines, beanbag ashtrays, mugs from various kinds of parks—state, amusement, water. Back then the tacky mementos—and a strong resemblance to Natalie Wood in *West Side Story*—were her only distinctions. She was unremarkable and happy.

Then she caught herpes from her husband, and she became miserable—though she was still, as far as the company was concerned, unremarkable. And she remained so after her husband packed his bags and moved in with the woman who had infected him.

It wasn't until the aurora borealis started visiting her that she became outstanding. It arrived one night as she was writhing from the leg pain that had accompanied her first viral outbreak. The strange lights radiated brilliantly in her head, and ideas whispered themselves to her through the luminescent bars. The next morning, she stood in her boss's doorway looking like a thirsty child at two A.M.

"I have an idea," she said.

Soon she was spitting out ideas like watermelon seeds. She was a machine, an engine of creativity, a dynamo. She was—in other words—not herself.

She understood that now as she stood on the sidewalk and waved weakly to Epi as he drove off. When she entered her apartment, she felt like someone returning home after a long trip. A thick electrostatic fur coated the TV screen, Christmas lights still lined the living-room window, and the dining-room table was heaped with a cold bonfire of unread mail and catalogs. A whiff of something swampy reached her from the kitchen.

Where had she been? Who had been living her life? Her leg was throbbing. She sat down on the sofa and closed her eyes.

Instantly, slats of light fanned across the black space of her mind. Ideas for a video on workplace safety buzzed in her head like wasps in a jar.

She gasped and opened her eyes. Downstairs her landlord, Mr. Davies, was watching a late-night Western. Her eyes scanned the apartment wildly—where were her souvenirs? She stood up and began searching the apartment. She found them—chipped and unwrapped—in a cardboard box in the hall closet. A virus had taken over and packed her life away. She dragged out the box, and for the next hour she placed the trinkets around the apartment so that they looked like an army of household saints.

■

FIRST THING on Monday she attached a rubber Goofy and a rubber Donald Duck to the employee of the month plaque she had received in May. They looked like dogs in heat humping a leg, and she thought that sent the right message. To whom she wasn't sure (though she had decided over the weekend that something was behind the virus).

A single sheet of paper was sitting in her in-box. She recognized it as a memo she had sent to Epi the previous Friday (he refused—on some principle—to read or send e-mail). Her memo read: "Where's the August Missing Kids Poster?" Epi had circled the date, June 12, and attached a yellow Post-it note. "The August Missing Kid is still at home." She looked at the memo and at the now empty in-box. Where were the seminar brochures, the department copies of *Time* and *Newsweek,* the orange interoffice mailers?

During the day she made seven trips to the cafeteria to get coffee; the last three nights had been a struggle. In the dark of her bedroom, alliterative themes for the United Way campaign had circled her head like fat houseflies. It was all she could do to clutch a plastic glow-in-the-dark bust of Abraham Lincoln and will the thoughts away.

After work she went home and looked up herpes support groups in the Yellow Pages. She read her mail and discovered that two of her cousins had recently gotten married, and her best friend from high school had been a Hare Krishna since February.

She sat down in front of the TV and stared at the black screen, now dust-free. She could make out her reflection in the glass, but her features were muddy. She might be Natalie Wood or she might be Irma Peretti in payroll. She wished she were Irma, wished she were a woman who wore tie-dye T-shirts to work and read romance novels in the cafeteria while eating microwaveable casseroles. She had been Irma, minus the tie-dye shirts. But that was before the aurora borealis. Why had she been singled out?

■

THE NEXT morning Anne and Lil, her boss and her boss's boss, stopped by on their way to a meeting. Anne was a size sixteen and Lil was incredibly thin, but they both had pale blue eyes, button noses, and brown Dorothy Hamill hair. Epi liked to refer to them as Before and After.

"Did you come up with a title for the handbook?" Anne asked, eyeing Delia as if she were a goose from a fable.

"Um. Yes." In truth, she had forgotten the words. "*Keep Your Hands to Yourself*?" she offered, improvising.

The two women's faces went blank. Down the hall, a phone rang.

"Okay. Okay," Anne said after a moment, nodding slowly. She turned a tiny invisible screwdriver in the air. "Maybe tweak it just a little."

"Yes," said Lil, giving her own, larger screwdriver a quick twist. "Tweak it."

"We know you can make it special," Anne said. "We believe in you."

"Remarkable girl," Lil said.

Delia forced herself to smile.

■

AT THE support group everyone sat in a circle and took turns sharing five accomplishments from the past year. It was supposed to be an ego booster, but Delia ticked off hers like a list of sins at confession. The sock-hop to celebrate the company's fiftieth anniversary. The World War II–themed blood drive, with nurses dressed as WACs and a banner that read "Company Issues Call to Arms." Baskets of apples for employees with perfect attendance.

"I also took PageMaker classes so I could do ads in-house," she said, eyes downcast. "And the missing kids posters were also my idea."

"Well, that is something," said the group leader, a tall man with thinning blond hair and a pink scalp. "You see, folks, herpes is what you make it."

People looked from side to side and nodded, impressed.

"No, it's not a good thing," she said. "It wasn't me, it was . . ."

People waited for her to finish. The group leader looked down at his notes, as if she were straying from a script. "It was what?"

"Oh, never mind."

■

DURING HER outstanding period, Delia juggled assignments like some eight-armed goddess. She would type up articles for the newspaper while getting phone estimates on bulk paper supplies and eating vending-machine sandwiches. Now the jobs were falling around her like hail. She was constantly putting people on hold or telling them she'd call them back (which she never did). Meanwhile, the mail rose tsunami-like in her in-box. Deadlines were pushed back. Projects fell through the cracks.

"What's going on?" Anne asked. "The employee picnic's in three weeks and you haven't gotten the park permit yet. And the newspaper's late again. Is it burnout?"

Delia thought of the lights blazing in her mind.

"I wish."

A few days later, while dropping off copy in the graphics department, she saw Epi carving animals out of Styrofoam cups with his X-acto knife. His poster of Che Guevara had been put away. Things were returning to normal.

Pain was a problem, of course. When the aurora borealis was running things, her aches were always less a sensation than a noise, like the vibration of some internal machinery. Now she felt it loud and clear. At work she used an ice pad. At night she found it helpful to lie on the cool living-room floor and listen to Mr. Davies argue with his wife about baseball or who was the better fill-in for Ted Koppel—Peter Greenfield or Cokie Roberts. His wife had been dead for three years, and his one-sided debates made Delia feel not so alone. She began taking a new suppressive drug and gradually it took effect. The aurora dwindled to a pond shimmer, the whispers became incoherent.

Still she wished she could talk to someone about what she was going through. One day after work, she saw Mr. Davies standing in front of their building, watering grass in a plaid shirt and a White Sox cap. They almost never talked, but the winter after her husband had moved out, Mr. Davies had cleaned snow off her windshield in the mornings. He always pretended to be deaf when she said thanks.

"Hello, Mr. Davies," she shouted now. "Sounded like the missus was giving you a hard time last night." She was trying to establish just how sane he was. Not too sane, she hoped.

"What?" he said. He was frail and stooped and his teeth were long and yellow. "What did you say?"

"I said the wife was giving you a hard time last night. I heard you arguing."

He pursed his lips together angrily. "My wife is a saint. We never argue."

■

THROUGH someone at work, she heard that her ex-husband and his lover had started entering salsa competitions at Latin dance clubs around the city. They consistently placed third. This further supported Delia's notion that herpes, by itself, was not the driving force behind her once outstanding performance. The virus had merely primed her for the aurora borealis, which, in turn, was controlled by—what?

Anne began leaving notes on her desk saying things like "Are you OK? You don't seem like yourself." A twinge of pain would surface whenever Delia read these notes.

"This is my old self," she would say out loud. But even she had trouble keeping things straight. When she thought about it, her life broke down into three stages: souvenir, aurora, and neuralgia. It vexed her that no one had written little notes when she'd stopped being souvenir girl. Now that she had stopped being aurora woman, even Epi complained.

"What is up with you? One minute you're Mike Ditka and the next minute, you're—I don't know. Who? That Freddie Prinze character from *Chico and the Man.* Chico!"

"I'm just trying to get some balance back in my life," she said. "I thought you of all people would appreciate that." With a nod, she indicated the Styrofoam sculptures lining the front of his drafting table.

"I'm all for balance. Balance is good. Balance is what we had before you went and got religion. Now we have standards. Before and After keep coming by and asking me why I'm not busier. I tell them, I can't create my own work out of thin air."

"I'm sorry," she said.

■

SHE DECIDED to try working through her lunches for a week, just to ease the backlog. Eventually, the projects would get done or become obsolete. She was anxious, though; she didn't want to fall back into her old aurora self. The newspaper came out on time, and the lights remained weak. She worked through her lunches for a second week, and still nothing.

I'm winning, she thought.

Then the thick ecru envelope arrived in her mailbox. It had a classy ribbed stock, and printed in large blue type over her name and business address was a single word: *Latinnovator.* She thought it might be a new magazine for Hispanic professionals.

She ripped open the top flap and pulled out an ecru folder with an ecru letter attached to it. "Congratulations," the letter began. "In recognition of your career achievements, you have been named a Latinnovator." She looked up at Goofy and Donald, as if they had reneged on some agreement.

She took the letter to Anne and Lil, but neither of them knew anything about it.

"I didn't nominate you, that's for sure," Lil said.

Anne made an ouch face.

"I think what Lil is trying to say is that we miss the old Delia."

Delia rolled her eyes.

"What about the old, old Delia. The Delia of last year. What about her?"

Anne and Lil looked at each other.

"Well, she was nice," said Anne. "But the more recent Delia was better. Much better."

"I say we stay low-key on this one," Lil said. "No picture in the paper. I've received a number of complaints about the backlog."

Delia felt her leg begin to throb.

She took it upon herself to call up the award committee chair and tell her a mistake had been made. Her name was Elena Gomez, and she sounded like a cross between Mother Teresa and Delia's aunt who sold Avon.

"Don't worry, *querida*. I just spoke with your human resources director, and everything is fine."

Delia reached over to the plaque and squeezed her fingers around Donald.

"But if my company didn't nominate me, who did?"

"Oh, that's a secret, *querida*."

"What?"

"It's a tradition. The winners never know who nominated them until the award dinner. Then you'll be introduced by your secret sponsor. It's always a nice surprise. Lots of hugs and *besos, tu sabes*."

"But who could it be?"

"Well I can't tell you, but it could be lots of people. Vendors you've worked with, a community group you've helped out, a professional colleague. It could be any of them."

"Or none of them." She was certain now that some thing, some free-floating malevolence, was trying to claim her.

■

THE NEXT day was "beef" day at the support group meeting, and acyclovir side effects were leading the pack. When it was Delia's turn, she stood up to speak.

"Yesterday I found out I'm going to receive an award, and it's really making me depressed."

The group leader squinted at her and scratched his head.

"Delia, right? The overachiever."

"That's the problem," she said. "That's not me."

"What do you mean?"

"I mean—" She looked around the room and wondered if there were others like her. It was hard to tell. Some people wore business suits, but others wore sweats. It was the kind of heterogeneous mix you saw only at airport gates or on subway platforms in the Loop. "I just mean that an award is the last thing I want."

A skinny woman with long stringy hair raised her hand.

"Wouldn't it be nice, though, if an award was the last thing you got? Just a little something that says, 'Hey, nice life.' " She soured suddenly. "Not that I'd ever get one."

The group leader gave Delia a tired look.

"I'm sorry," she said. "I just mean that I don't want to be remarkable anymore."

"There's just no pleasing her," a white-haired man muttered to a woman in a pink velour jogging suit.

"Excuse me," said a husky man with dark hair and dimples that cut deep into his cheeks. "I work selling hospital supplies, and I know what she means. It's like your job just takes over your life."

She clasped her hands together and looked up at the acoustical-tiled ceiling.

"Yes."

■

A FEW days later Epi came into her office and pulled up a chair to her desk. He was smiling.

"What are you smiling about?"

"I hear you're a Latinnovator."

"Yes."

"Well, you're in good company." He handed her a glossy-covered booklet. "We've been asked to do the program book, and here's last year's. Look at the list of past winners." The name Jaime Quiñones was circled.

"So? What about him?"

"You don't know Jaime Quiñones? The guy on the wall of the Jimenez store on North Avenue."

She shrugged. He slapped his hands on the table.

"The mural of the guy who looks like the *Virgen de Guadalupe*."

She knew the one, a crude portrait of a man in a guayabera surrounded by a comic-strip aura. "Oh, yeah. What about him?"

"He blew himself up in his basement. Six months after he got his award. He was working on a bomb. Big FALN supporter, used to speak at colleges. Tried to put together these fancy slide presentations on American bombs washing up on some beach in Puerto Rico. But when you heard the tone between the slides, you could tell it was just a spoon against water."

"That doesn't sound good," she said. "Not the spoon, the bomb. The bomb." She was thinking about loopholes. Five minutes later she was on the phone with Elena Gomez. "I didn't know you had given this award to terrorists."

"Terrorists! Who are you talking about?" She was upset.

"Jaime Quiñones. He blew himself up."

"Oh," Elena said, her voice softening with relief. "That was an accident, *querida*."

"I know. The bomb was supposed to go off in the Dirksen Federal Building."

"No, I mean it was an accident on our part. Back then most of your high-profile Latinos were activists. Now we focus on professionals like yourself. Then we didn't have much choice. When we got Jaime's nomination, we thought it was risky, but . . . well, what's past is past. I should add that the person who nominated him is now a state congressman."

Delia pulled Goofy off her plaque and threw it against the wall. "Can you just tell me who nominated me?"

"No, *querida*. I can't."

"Of course, you can't."

■

SHE MET Josh for dinner at a fondue restaurant with royal blue upholstered banquettes and white enameled chairs. A little silver pot of oil sat between them on the table, heating over a Sterno flame. She told him a little about herself, and he told her a lot about himself—starting with his early "skinny" child-hood in Griffith, Indiana. She said uh-huh, uh-huh, and when the waiter interrupted with skewers of raw marinated meat, she went on the offensive.

"So tell me more about what you said the other night, about work taking over your life?"

"Oh, that." He smiled and invisible fingers pushed his dim-ples deep into his face. "Well, I just meant that I've been so busy lately. I've racked up more sales in the last six months than I have in the prior two years."

An overachiever, she thought. She leaned in. "Why do you think that is?"

"Oh, I don't know." He reached over to dip a skewer of meat into the boiling oil. "Focus, I guess. I'm much more focused now than I used to be."

Delia took a big gulp from her water glass. She felt like an orphan who was hearing her own early history repeated by a stranger—a stranger who would turn out to be her long-lost brother.

"When you say focused, do you mean that you're becoming more narrow, more single-minded?"

"Yeah, I guess."

"Okay. But do you feel that single mind is your mind?"

"What? Well, whose mind would it be?"

She hadn't figured that part out yet. An efficiency-minded demon? Aliens with mind-control beams and sizable invest-ments in her company's stock? The ghost of L. Ron Hubbard? She didn't care about that right now; she just wanted to know if he was enslaved by the aurora borealis.

"What I mean is, do you ever lay awake at night and feel the pain in your leg and suddenly there's this aura around you and the ideas keep coming, but they're coming from outside you?"

Josh looked down at his lap. "Actually, I'm an itchy, not an achy. I don't know which is worse. Some people are both, so I guess I should consider myself lucky."

She twisted her napkin in her lap.

"Listen. Do you ever ask yourself why we have herpes?"

"Well," he said, "maybe forces are at work that are beyond

our understanding." She smiled stupidly; he understood. Then he reached over and placed his huge hand over hers. He smiled back and his dimples dug deep into his doughy face. "Yeah, maybe it's Kismet."

She pulled her hand out from under his and let it fall into her lap like a dead bird.

"Seriously. Do you ever think maybe something was waiting for us to get this way? Waiting to use our pain?"

Josh exhaled and reached over to retrieve his meat skewer. "I'm not getting you." He bit a hunk of sizzling meat off the skewer.

"Listen, I used to be a good worker. Then after I got herpes, I became a great worker. And now I just want to be the regular me for a while, but I have this award hanging over my head, and I don't know who, or what, nominated me."

He chewed, occasionally sucking in air to cool off the meat. "Hot," he said, leaving off the "t" at the end. He took a drink from his glass. "We're not having sex tonight, are we?"

■

HE DROPPED her off in front of her apartment building. "Lighten up, sister," he said as he slammed the passenger door shut. She stood on the sidewalk and looked into Mr. Davies's living-room window. The lights were off, but the television was on. He was sitting in his recliner and his glasses glowed insect-like on his face. Suddenly she had the feeling that something was watching her. She rushed inside the building and ran up the stairs to her apartment.

She turned on her own TV and fell asleep watching *Nightline*. She dreamed she was sitting in a fur-covered room, and Ted Koppel was talking to her from the television screen.

"Now what's so wrong with getting an award? Lots of people like awards."

"But I'm not the same person anymore. That wasn't me."

"What's so wrong with working hard? Isn't hard work a good thing?" He was very good at playing devil's advocate, never curt or threatening.

"It wasn't me, though. Don't you understand?"

A new face appeared on the screen. It was a man's face, but it was covered in soot.

"I lost myself, too." Somehow, she knew it was Jaime Quiñones.

The camera switched to Ted. "You look burnt."

Jaime came on again. "They left me in the oil too long."

"You blew yourself up," she shouted at the screen.

"The oil came after. You'll see, you'll see." The scene changed, and she could see his whole body now. He was standing in front of an aura that had spines between the rays, like the bones in a bat's wing. In his hand he held a tall red candle in a glass, about the size of a tennis ball container. She could smell the wax. He began tapping the glass with a spoon. *Ting-ting-ting, ting-ting-ting.* "You'll see. After you become one, they boil you in oil."

She opened her eyes and a movie of the week from the seventies was on. She was holding a Precious Moments figurine in her hand. She looked down at the figurine.

"Oh, no," she said. "Is that what's happening?"

■

THE NEXT day she stopped by Epi's drafting table.

"Do you think Jaime Quiñones was a saint?"

He leaned back in his elevated drafting chair and twisted to face her.

"I didn't really know him personally, but no, I don't think he was a saint."

"I know he wanted to blow up that building, but I mean, there are other kinds of saints, don't you think?"

Epi screwed up his mouth and thought for a moment. "Here's what I think," he said. "A saint is someone who does something that's not really meaningful in an obvious way. They don't eat for weeks, they have visions, they cause flowers to bloom in the winter. That's what saints do. They don't campaign to get bombs off beaches."

"What about increasing blood-drive participation by thirty percent?"

He leaned farther back in his chair.

"That, also, would not qualify as a saintly act."

"Okay, but what if, just for argument's sake, the idea for increasing blood-drive participation came to you through a sort of vision?"

"Why are you asking these questions?"

"Oh, nothing," she said. "I had a dream."

He sat up and pointed a finger at her. "Martin Luther King! Also, technically, not a saint."

Later that same day Anne knocked on the wall just outside Delia's office. She approached the desk and placed one hand on the top of her in-box.

"Listen, I can't speak for Lil, but I want you to know that I'm still in your corner. I know what you're capable of."

Delia said nothing.

"Is it salary?"

"Oh no, no. It's not that."

Anne tilted her head to one side, trying to draw her out.

"It's just that I don't want my job to take over my life."

"Is that all? Listen, we don't expect miracles. We just want your best."

Delia put her hands on her desk to steady herself. "Anne, I know I've let you down, but I just want to be me. Not Aurora Ditka, not Freddie Prinze, just me. Just—" Her voice trailed off to a whisper.

"Freddie Prinze?" Anne stepped over next to Delia's chair and patted her on the shoulder. "Oh, sweetie. No one thinks you're Freddie Prinze. I believe in you."

Delia jerked her shoulder out from under Anne's hands. "But that's just it. I don't want you to believe in me."

Anne was stunned, but Delia didn't care. She wouldn't be a saint for Cel-Pro or any company.

■

AT THE support group meeting, a holistic nutritionist talked about herbs and teas that might help suppress recurrences. Afterward the group leader opened up the meeting to any questions or concerns or general sharing. Delia raised her hand and stood up. The white-haired man said, "Oh God, here we go."

"What do you want to talk about, Delia?" asked the group leader in a resigned voice.

"It's just that I feel like forces are trying to take over my life—does anybody else feel that way?"

"Take Prozac," someone said. She turned and saw it was Josh. He indicated her with tosses of his head and twirled a horizontal finger next to his ear.

"We all feel a little overwhelmed sometimes," said the group leader. The pink was seeping down from his scalp.

"I know that, but I'm trying to get my life back, and someone has nominated me for an award, and I don't know who it is. And I don't want it."

"Oh, poor baby," said a big-haired woman in a black caftan. "An award? Back in the Middle Ages, women like us were burned at the stake. And you want to complain about an award."

"Deal with it," Josh bellowed. "You're no better than the rest of us."

"Please," said the group leader, trying to look stern.

Delia turned to grab her purse and half ran out of the room, wiping tears from her eyes with the back of her hand. "I won't be a saint," she said as she pushed through the exit doors.

■

WHEN SHE got home from the support group, she made herself a cup of tea and sat shaking on the couch. Between sips of tea, she took deep breaths and held them for ten seconds. When she could hold her cup steadily, she looked around the apartment and noticed a mug from Ruby Falls sitting on a windowsill. She couldn't remember going to Ruby Falls, couldn't place it in her mind. Maybe that's why people bought souvenirs, she thought; so they didn't have to remember where they'd been. She looked at the other souvenirs and realized this was true, at least for her.

She missed having a husband, but she almost never thought of her ex. She had no strong memories, only mementos. She laughed into her cup when she realized that herpes was the ultimate souvenir of her marriage. Then she looked at the Precious Moments figurines on the television, and she became solemn again. She had never been serious—really serious—about anything or anybody. No wonder no one had cared when souvenir girl checked out and aurora girl checked in.

Maybe, she thought, being a saint wouldn't be the worst thing. There were saints for travel and for animals; why not a saint for employee communications? If her suffering served to increase United Way pledges, would that be such a bad thing? She imagined a statue of herself in a navy dress suit, with one beatific finger raised. Then she heard Mr. Davies downstairs shouting at his dead wife, and she hated the whole idea again. She didn't want to be Saint Aurora, but she didn't want to go back to being souvenir girl either. What did that leave her? A dull ache pressed against the small of her back like the barrel of a gun.

■

WEEKS passed, and the pain grew worse. "It's stress," her doctor said. "It won't let the medicine work."

She rarely left her office, and she kept the door closed so she wouldn't have to see Anne and Lil frown as they passed. Tickets to Latino functions started going to some systems analyst who had debugged a key accounting program three months ahead of schedule. The support group leader called and recommended she join Workaholics Anonymous. And a rumor began circulating around the company that she had nominated herself for the award, to save her flagging career.

She was miserable.

On the plus side, she had stopped obsessing over who had nominated her. Indeed by the night of the ceremony, she had abandoned any illusions about actually meeting her sponsor. It was some corporate animus, she assumed, and where would an animus find a decent tux anyway? When she and Epi arrived at Latino Fine Arts Center, she didn't even bother to scan the room for familiar faces.

The center had formerly been a park district gymnasium, and tables were set up on what used to be the basketball court. The floors still gleamed like honey, and a band of high windows lined the outermost wall. Shouts from a late-summer softball game could be heard over the din of the crowd and the guitarist strumming in the corner.

"Moving the center here was a bad idea, don't you think?" said a green-eyed woman as she seated herself across from Delia and Epi. She was with a shiny-faced man who wore a gold stud in one ear.

"Are you two Latinnovators, too?" Delia asked. "Two-too." She had been in and out of pain all day and was becoming giddy.

"I am," said the woman. "I'm Soledad and this is Harry. We work for the electric company. Has anyone ever told you you look like Natalie Wood? In *West Side Story*, I mean."

Delia nodded.

"Do you know who nominated you?" Epi asked Soledad, and Delia laughed.

Soledad pointed a thumb at Harry. "I'm not supposed to know, but who can keep a secret nowadays? We're in Jaycees together. Do you belong to Jaycees?"

"No," Epi said. "Delia?"

Before she could answer, a fist of pain clenched her tailbone and she grimaced.

"Are you okay?" asked Soledad.

"I feel shitty. Oh so shitty." She laughed and Epi laughed too. She had told him it was her time of the month. The sharp pain subsided to a general ache, and she smiled at Soledad. "Can I ask you something?"

"Sure."

"Have you ever made flowers bloom in the winter?" Delia started at her own question. The word "winter" made her think of Mr. Davies in his oil-stained parka and space boots.

"I don't understand," said Soledad, but she was looking at Epi.

Delia thought for a moment.

"Let me ask you this. Does the aurora borealis ever appear in your head?" Just then there was a dull pop, followed by cheers from the ball field outside, and then an explosion of glass.

"What the hell," Epi shouted amid a cacophony of screams and chairs scraping.

Delia turned to see several women dancing frantically beneath the windows as they tried to shake glittering shards out of their hair and clothes. In the middle of the room, a softball was bouncing high, then low. She glanced up at the shattered window frame, lined with a jagged set of glass teeth, and then looked down to see the ball wobbling toward her. It skittered weirdly beneath the table, and she smiled at the thought of it.

Without saying anything, she sank from her chair and began fishing for the ball under the table. When she found it, near Soledad's black pumps, she picked it up with both hands and immediately felt a stab of pain in her left palm. She backed herself out from under the table and stood up. A shard of glass lodged in the ball was glistening red as a ruby. She squinted at the ball, and then she squinted at her palm, which was coated with blood.

"Huh," she said, holding up her hand and watching the blood stream down her dress sleeve. "Well, what kind of saint would this make me?"

Later after Epi had driven her home from the emergency room, she stood outside Mr. Davies's door, holding the softball with her bandaged hand and ringing the doorbell with the other.

Kim Thorsen

Pennsylvania State University

ALIEN BODIES

You chalked it up to puberty, the way Chloe's hair swung in her plate at mealtimes, the way her voice lost its lilt, remained monotonous and monosyllabic whenever you could get her to employ it, which wasn't often. The way she stopped accompanying you on after-dinner walks or asking questions or playing the piano; all things she'd once done without prompting. She became finicky at mealtimes, a picker, edgy to be excused and return to her room.

You thought you knew her, that you'd have noticed if something was bothering her, if something was really wrong. *Yes,* you'd say, *Chloe and I are very close.* Until she was fourteen going on fifteen. That age all the books warned you about. You read the books. It seemed all the families in your circle of friends had an arsenal of parenting manuals lining the shelves of their den. *They're fine,* your friends might say when you asked about their kids, *playing lacrosse, dating so and so. . . .* But the bookshelves you spied surreptitiously during dinner parties told a different story: *Dealing with a Depressed Child, Grandchildren of Alcoholics (and the Problems They Face), Smart Parenting for the '90s.*

Chloe had recently begun high school, a private school in

another district. You thought she was probably just tired from leaving the house before seven to ride the hour to St. Joe's, exhausted from three-hour basketball practices and from not getting home most nights until after six. The team couldn't officially practice until November, but Coach Roswell had his girls lifting weights and running wind sprints around the red clay track every day after school. You told yourself it was the pressure of having to make new friends, to find her niche all over again, that had your daughter acting less than herself. In the end, you eased your worry by remembering you weren't the only mother who woke up one day without the slightest idea how to handle her teenage daughter.

And when Chloe abruptly quit the basketball team halfway through her freshman season and left St. Joe's for the neighborhood school, you supported her decision, though she refused to explain it. *It just didn't work out for her at St. Joe's,* you told people. You were sure she'd quit so that she'd be able to spend more time hanging out after school in neighborhood backyards or, on rainy days, playing board games in finished basements. That she'd quit to be a regular kid again. Maybe she wanted time for a boyfriend, you reasoned, and it was only hormones that had hold of your daughter. These explanations seemed false to you, though, even when you wanted so badly to believe them. Because Chloe had quit basketball altogether, refusing to play for the local high school or even to shoot hoops in the driveway. And she had been good at basketball. Really good, the way most people are never in their lives good at anything. Effortlessly, magically good.

She was so good, at nine years old and drowning in her jersey at the Y, that she'd been invited to play with the older girls. The program director called you to clear the change, to tell you to have her there at seven instead of six.

Why? you asked, almost as an afterthought.

He paused before answering. *Have you ever seen Chloe play?* he asked in a voice that made you feel foolish.

I guess not, you admitted.

She's dominating her age group, he said. *It's not fair to the other kids, not fun for her. We've got to bump her.*

You were sure he was exaggerating. Chloe had always been among the shortest in her class, and a little chunky. Never a standout athlete. Only an average tumbler. But, curiosity piqued, you skipped your yoga class and went to see her play. Nine years old. You hadn't been prepared for what you saw.

She played point guard, a term you learned only later, which meant she was in charge of bringing the ball up the center of the court. At the top of the key she'd dribble patiently, deliberately as the other girls pinwheeled around clumsily, calling for the ball whether they were open or not. Compared with Chloe, the rest looked like they were slogging through two feet of water. She would sense an opening and cut toward the basket. Then briefly, she seemed to be careening out of control, her blond ponytail flying in all directions at once, and you could almost feel her inevitable contact with the hardwood floor in the flesh of your own knees and elbows.

But she would stay in command: right herself, make the pass or hit the shot and keep her feet. Every time. She'd claim the lane and slip past bodies much bigger than hers. The ball looked huge in her hands, yet rolled off her fingers with such perfect trajectory you knew it was going in. The older girls were left slack-mouthed, their hands waving ineffectually in the air each time Chloe poured past them. Watching her play that day made you think of a nature special you'd seen about bats with echolocation so precise that a group of one hundred passed through a maple tree soundlessly. Not one bat brushed one leaf.

On the court Chloe seemed to leave behind the self-consciousness she carried everywhere else. Playing basketball she wasn't the girl whose face blotched scarlet as she rehearsed reading aloud a report on the emu she'd have to deliver to her fourth-grade class. Neither was she the girl who was often stricken with a mortifying, unshakable case of hiccups in the library or in church. On the court she was free to be utterly self-possessed, a genius, catapulted by gifts you hadn't given her. This, you found, perched in the stands that first day as the spectators encircling you commented on your daughter's impressive play, made you nervous.

You were in awe of her. That's the only word that fits. There were no grounds on which you could identify with this new daughter. You had been a cheerleader in high school, but that didn't compare. *It doesn't make sense,* you said to Phil that night the two of you sat at the kitchen table. *Basketball? Why didn't she tell us she was so good?* Phil gave an exaggerated shrug. He slid his knife through his reheated chicken cutlet. You were on your third glass of Chablis and he was only half listening. The kids had eaten and were watching a sitcom in the den. Canned laughter, sometimes accompanied by an abrupt guffaw from Ben, rolled into the kitchen every few minutes to punctuate your conversation. For some reason, what you'd seen Chloe do on the court that day unsettled you. You wanted Phil to see her play, to get a second opinion. *All right,* Phil said as he deposited his plate in the sink, *if this is something I've got to see, I'll be there next week.*

Three weeks later at seven, Phil showed up at the hot Y gym that smelled of chlorine and sweat. He sat down next to you on the hard bleacher, pulled his tie loose from his neck, and squeezed your hand. He kissed you on the cheek and waved to Chloe, who was lining up to take layups with her team. She saw him and waved shyly, a smile breaking across her full face. *Jesus,* Phil said. *Those girls are a head taller.*

Once the game started, your husband's eyes never left your daughter the whole time she was on the court. As you watched him watching her, you couldn't help thinking it was with new admiration. Like she was a painting he'd bought for ten bucks at a garage sale that turned out to be worth thousands. The next weekend Phil transformed your carport into a small practice area for Chloe, sinking a hoop and carefully measuring and painting court markings.

The rhythmic slap of ball meeting macadam became the pulse of your house, paced you as you prepared dinner each evening. Phil would linger out there on his way in from work, sometimes setting down his briefcase for a game of one-on-one. Some nights, still in his wing tips, he'd take the time to teach Chloe a drill or show her a new move. You got the feeling, watching the two of them through the broad picture window in your living room, that she was humoring him. Still Phil didn't say a word about the price of the sleep-away basketball camp Chloe's coach suggested she attend the following summer, just wrote the check. It had cost over two hundred dollars a week, and she'd gone for a month.

You can't remember what your biggest problem was then, when Chloe was nine and slicing through defenders in the Y gymnasium. Whatever it was, it seems minuscule now. You think of the mud. The way your lawn never drained properly and how the kids brought huge portions of the yard in with them when they plodded through your eight rooms, trampled over your light-colored carpets. Of course you had other problems. You suspected Phil was having an affair with Olivia, another agent at his office. You had no proof, but you never went looking for any either. It must have burned itself out after a year or two. But it's the mud you remember most. The everyday battle to keep the outside out and the inside in. That was your job. You shared a similar mission with all the middle-class mothers in the world: to keep the kids safe, to stay out of history.

Chloe's body, on the cusp of sixteen, is thick and soft again where it narrowed and hardened when she began playing ball every day. This is your best guess, though it's hard to know anything about Chloe's body because she keeps it veiled with big shirts, long-sleeved even in summer, and baggy pants as wide around each leg as they are at the waist. Shopping with her last week, you edged open the door of the fitting room where she was changing to show her a blouse, and she responded by slamming it back in your face, smashing your nose so hard your eyes ran with tears for an hour.

She hates you. She tells you every chance she gets, yells it in the mall when you refuse to purchase a pair of seventy-dollar jeans for her, just like she yelled at you when she was two and three years old and establishing herself as a separate person to begin with. The same fierce features, the same plaintive wail. Back then the tantrums passed quickly. This one has lasted for more than a year. Judy told you she might get stuck here for a while, in this phase. You need to think of this hatefulness as something Chloe's moving through, though. That helps. Still, only for so long when those three words are hurled at you on a near daily basis can you tell yourself, *No, it's not true.* Especially when every interaction you have with your daughter confirms her claim.

She hates you. You feel better accepting this, starting from there. She hates the way you talk and your stupid blue sweater and the green jeans you've worn every Saturday for as long as she can remember. She hates the hair you dye an unconvincing red and the way you punctuate everything you say with an apologetic giggle. She hates the chickens you cook and your large hooked nose and your loosening skin. She hates the fat of your hips and the curve of your lip and the wadded tissues you pull from your big granny purse. She hates the wine you drink from an economy-size jug and the stale, sweet breath it gives you. She hates the way you touch her brother lightly across the shoulders for no reason as you pass. She hates you because you're afraid to drive in snow and because you ask permission too often and because you beg her to drink a single glass of milk before she leaves for school in the morning, because it means so much to you. For this, especially, she holds you in utter contempt.

Chloe doesn't hate Phil. Alternately you're grateful for this and resentful of it. It's true, she's rude and snappish and short with him. But she doesn't hate him. You try to work out the reasons for this in your head. Phil makes her laugh when he trashes the kitchen as he makes Sunday dinner, goofing off in a silly apron while whipping up a tasty stew without the aid of a recipe. Chloe eats three helpings. Phil slips her folded tens and twenties so she won't have to get a job, though he'd demanded more of Ben, taking him off allowance as soon as he was old enough to solicit the neighbors for yard work.

You think working would be good for Chloe. After the disastrous shopping trip, the two of you worked out a tenuous truce and went for cones at Sweet Dreams, an old-fashioned ice-cream parlor you chose especially because you'd spotted a "Help Wanted" sign in the window the week before. It was still there. The girls mixing shakes and wiping down sticky tables looked to be about Chloe's age, and they were so lovely in their red pin-striped smocks that you immediately pictured Chloe among them. Their open, relaxed faces made them seem pleasant and optimistic, like they could have fun doing just about anything. They reminded you of the crowd Chloe had been a part of in junior high. *How do you suppose they keep their figures, working here?* you asked, by way of broaching the subject.

You had said the wrong thing, it quickly became apparent. Again. Chloe gave you a disgusted look, then slid from her wrought iron chair and tossed her half-eaten cone in the trash. She pushed on the door to leave, jingling the bells that hung from the hinge, then turned and called across the store, *They puke, Mom.*

The voices of your husband and daughter reach you sometimes late at night as they talk in front of the television and you read in bed. Some days this is as civil as her voice gets. They never discuss anything real; you've listened at the top of the stairs. Just chit-chat about which team has clinched the play-offs and why tall players can't shoot free throws. One night in bed as you lay next to Phil in the perfect darkness, you asked why he didn't try to get her to open up a little bit, to ask her how it was going with the therapist she'd been seeing weekly as part of her aftercare. To talk about it. *Since she talks to you at all,* you said.

What do you want me to say to her, Evelyn? Phil answered flatly. *That there are bad people who will hurt you for reasons you'll never in your life understand? That sometimes your parents deliver you handwrapped to the monster under the bed? Guess what, Evelyn? She knows that. And all the therapy in the world isn't going to change it.* He rolled over and went to sleep, his body cooling and hardening like wax. You didn't bring it up with him again.

You don't suppose Chloe has picked up a basketball since she got out of the hospital, just over a year ago, or that she's spoken with any of her friends from junior high. Not that she'd share it with you if she'd done either. What she *has* been doing is God-knows-what with a skinny Italian kid who recently moved into the house up the street. Victor. She spends the bulk of her time in his company. The parents rarely seem to be home, you notice, just Victor and his creepy older brother, whose entire wardrobe seems to consist of hooded sweatshirts. He's rumored to sell marijuana to the kids who gather in loose knots at the neighborhood park.

Victor wears a denim jacket even on the coldest days and doesn't appear to own a pair of gloves; he stuffs his hands deep into the front pockets of his jeans when they get cold. They always look raw and chapped. His hair is clipped short and looks freshly combed at all times. You sense this is a priority for him. He's a year ahead of Chloe in school and has just gotten his driver's license. You liked him slightly better when he rode his BMX bike to your house. Some days now he rolls up to the curb, suspiciously slowly, in his brother's Mustang. Chloe sprints across the lawn like it's a jailbreak, hops in, and they race off.

Victor. You smell Marlboros all over him and see the imprint the pack wears in the back pocket of his Levi's. But he's always very polite. *Hello, Mrs. Shepard. Thanks for dinner, Mrs. Shepard,* he says with the trace of a Brooklyn accent. It irks you, how polite he is, but that isn't really cause for complaint. You heard that his father is semiretired, that the parents spend a lot of time in Florida. No one seems to know much about them. They talked to Phil once about buying a house, but eventually went with another Realtor. He doesn't quite remember them, though you've tried to jog his memory on this subject more than once.

The kids' report cards, you got them in today's mail, preoccupy you as you fold laundry in the basement. Ben's is full of B's and even an A in history, though he's already secured admission to Rutgers and can afford to relax a little. Chloe's missed eight days of school this term, but you only remember okaying two. Her grades are holding at C's, though she can do better. She made straight A's through junior high. *Not the same kid,* you remind yourself. You're planning gently to bring up the absences with her when she gets home from school. Somehow she'll get through her sophomore year intact, then make a run at preparing for college. Like Ben.

You're relieved to hear her footfalls overhead in the kitchen. She's alone, and home right after school. Some days you have to send Ben over to Victor's at dinnertime to retrieve her. Today she tromps loudly, carelessly down the basement stairs, seeming sunny and carrying a big handful of Oreos. You never know what the hour will bring with Chloe, but today she's talking about school, a geometry test she thinks she did okay on. Just as you're working up the courage to ask her about her attendance, she presents you with a more pressing question.

It seems Chloe would like to spend the upcoming winter break in Myrtle Beach with Victor and Victor's older brother and a friend of Victor's brother called "Pizza." She wants to drive the thirteen hours south in Victor's brother's red Mustang convertible, *top up* she assures you, so that they can "crash" at the beach house of a guy Pizza knows from rehab. You keep your hands busy shaking out and folding towels as she speaks, but your eyes enjoy taking her in. She looks so hopeful and calm, twisting the Oreos apart and licking the filling, that you want to say yes. You want to tell her to go upstairs and pack her bag. You want to take her shopping at Walgreens and buy her a beach towel and a travel toothbrush and some condoms. The week of peace it will bring to the house tempts you. Phil and Ben could use it. You could use it. Even Chloe could use it, you're sure. At this point you're desperate to see her content for ten minutes. You want this so badly that *yes* almost flies out of your mouth.

Absolutely not is what you say instead, as you pluck one sock randomly from the pile and begin rooting for its mate. *You're fifteen years old, Chloe.*

Victor's brother will be around, she says.

You can't begin to tell her how little this fact reassures you.

He's nineteen, she says. *He's an adult.* It occurs to you that she'd had herself convinced you might say yes.

Stop, you say, *just stop.*

What do I have to lose, Mom? Chloe says, dropping her last Oreo on the basement floor and dusting her hands off coldly, as though she can't believe she's been eating them. *My virginity?* Her face twists as she says this. For a moment you're relieved to glimpse the pain that drives her, though it kills you too. She's still in there somewhere, behind the dirty, dredded hair and the stud piercing her eyebrow, behind the pale pink scars that spiral from her inner elbows to her wrists, beneath the six-inch-long question mark tattooed in indigo ink between her breasts. She's still in there.

That's not the issue, you say quietly, folding Phil's boxers in half and stacking them on the table, glad its width gives you a buffer from your daughter. Before you can say more, she's gone like a gale up the stairs, slamming cabinets in the kitchen. Then the house gets so quiet you think she must have left, but a few minutes later you hear her talking on the phone, though you can't make out the words.

Your eyes sting with tears that surprise you. So much to cry over, yet you so rarely do. It's not this fight, or any fight, really. It's stupid. Stupid stupid you. You had thought that over winter break the four of you could take a long ski weekend in the Poconos, rent a suite with a kitchenette like you did the winter Chloe was ten and Ben twelve. Before basketball seasons demanded all of Chloe's time and grounded the entire family for most of the school year. You were going to propose the idea to them that evening over dinner.

Sure, it was last minute, but what was wrong with a little spontaneity? The slopes would be crowded, but the sun would be warm and the snow soft and forgiving. Phil could take a few days off and you could ski until your legs were sore and your digits numb. At the bottom of the hill you'd fall easily by twos into the lift line, not caring who got paired off with whom. Now it was ruined. Even if you could make Chloe go, which you can't, she would rage or pout the whole time.

You finish folding the laundry and cart it in a wicker basket up the stairs. In the kitchen the phone is on the hook and the cord is still swaying, but Chloe isn't to be found. As hard as all this is, you suppose it's preferable to her silent descent of last winter. When, after Easter, you finally developed the pictures you'd snapped on Christmas morning last year, they frightened you. Chloe smiling woodenly for a gift, then turning dutifully toward the camera and smiling again for the flash. That's what four months of Roswell had done to her. If he has a first name, no one ever uses it. In your house he was always *Roswell,* or *Coach,* both before and after. His name used to be spoken neutrally, like a fact. He was common knowledge. You decided not to bring the pictures with you to show Chloe during hospital visiting hours after all.

This year on Christmas morning Chloe regarded all her gifts with open scorn, first listlessly ripping the paper, then tossing aside plaid sweaters or paperback books after only half a glance. She smiled sarcastically at the video camera Phil circulated with, flipping her middle finger in the direction of the lens when he looked away. You badly wanted her to behave for just one day, at least until your parents left after dinner. You felt a hard knot of resentment catch in your chest as she glared at you. Judy warned you against comparing this Chloe with the one you used to enjoy. *If she broke both legs in a car accident, would you expect her to get up and dance?* she asked.

But you can't help thinking of Chloe the year she was twelve, not so long ago, throwing her arms around you when Phil brought out the Christmas present she didn't think you could afford. Your luminous, sleepy daughter, hoisting her new skis over her shoulder before even eyeing the rest of her gifts, going out the door to break them in on the slight slope and a crust of old snow your backyard provided. In the memory Chloe's an apparition, as fuzzy around the edges as someone dead. Your daughter finds ways to remind you every day how much has changed. One evening last month she announced emphatically that she'd be changing the spelling of her name to K-l-o-w-e-e, effective immediately.

Weeks after she quit St. Joe's, you found your daughter in the childhood playhouse Phil had built for her in the backyard when she was four. It had been years since she'd used it, and you'd been meaning to convert it to a gardening shed. Chloe was slumped on the floor, absentmindedly carving shallow swirls in her left forearm with the Swiss Army knife you'd bought her for Girl Scout camp years before.

It's okay, Mom, she said as you wrapped your powder blue sweatshirt around her arm and her blood seeped through almost immediately. *I don't feel this.* It was cold in the playhouse and you could see your breath coming fast in front of your face. Her blood was bright against the butter-colored linoleum. On the way to the hospital with Ben driving and you in the back curling Chloe in your lap, she kept assuring you it didn't hurt.

All you could think of, as you alternately implored your son to go faster and insisted he drive carefully, was the day that Chloe was seven and playing in the yard when a lawn dart came crashing down on her head. You didn't see the accident happen, but she came walking into the kitchen a minute later holding her head, blood seeping between her fingers. *I'm bleeding, Mommy,* she said matter-of-factly. She never cried, not in the kitchen, not at the hospital when they laced her scalp with fourteen stitches and X-rayed her skull for a hairline fracture that, *Thank God,* you had said, was not there.

On the way home you admired aloud Chloe's capacity to endure pain without a fuss. Your quiet little girl. It was, you had to admit, how you liked her. It didn't occur to you to wonder how you'd raised a child who could be so unsurprised that a pleasant afternoon in the yard could end in such violence. The immediate acceptance on her face that you mistook for shock would have been tears of incredulity on Ben's, you are sure. How did she come to expect no more from the world?

I never worried about this kid. It was Ben who came home crying from elementary school, smarting from some slight. Ben caught stealing. Ben joyriding in the car at thirteen. Chloe learned to tie her shoes when she was three. She wrote her name in neat little cursive letters when she was only five. I worried a little about her weight, that she would be rejected for that later on. She got Phil's build and his poker straight hair, while Ben is slim like me, with my curls. Other than that, though, she was perfect. These are the things you told Judy, the therapist in charge of Chloe's case in the private hospital where she'd spent six weeks after they knitted up her arms in the emergency room. The two of you were trying to figure out what had gone so horribly wrong with your daughter.

Judy had mangled hands from some sort of congenital defect. Her fingers swirled around each other, looking more like the branch of a tree than a hand. It was difficult at first for you not to stare at her hands. You didn't want to ignore them completely either, so you had to find the proper balance. When you think back to the dozen or so sessions you had with Judy, it's her hands you remember most vividly. Her grotesque hands hovering and swooping through the air as she gesticulated and spoke.

It was Judy whom Chloe would eventually tell about Roswell, and Judy who had, with Chloe's permission, told you some of the story. Judy didn't usually want to talk about Chloe, though. She wanted to talk about you. You went to see her twice a week during the time that Chloe was in the hospital. Phil was supposed to go too, but usually he went to work instead. You didn't want to talk about yourself then. You were afraid you'd bore Judy, or that you wouldn't be able to stop talking once you started. So you stonewalled her by telling her you were concerned with your daughter, and that you didn't see what any of it had to do with you.

Lately you've been thinking you might call Judy again. Especially on days you find it all too much. The terrible truth is that you're beginning to hate your daughter. You hate the hooded look in her eyes and hate her for thinking you're stupid. You hate her for tromping through your dinner parties in her big shoes, dragging the smell of marijuana through the dining room. You hate her for thinking you don't know what marijuana smells like. You hate her for noticing that your husband never touches you anymore, and for the smirk she wears to let you know she's noticed. You hate her wrecked room and the way she goes through your drawers and closets when you're not home. You don't know what she's looking for. These intrusions would be more tolerable if you understood her snooping, if she were scrounging for something valuable she could pawn for pot or blue jeans. But she leaves thousands of dollars' worth of jewelry untouched, then disturbs your lingerie and your old diaries from high school just enough to let you know she's been there. It's as though she's ransacking you for yourself.

You hate her for not coming to you, for not giving you the chance to help her. You hate her for the many whispers and nudges her altered appearance inspires. Some days you have to admit you wonder what her part was, in the thing with Roswell. If she has nothing to be ashamed of, why won't she talk about it? Why can't she be more resilient, and realize that one bad turn doesn't give her an excuse to make everyone's life miserable? Maybe you hate her for being chosen. She's not even that pretty, you catch yourself thinking. Then you hate yourself for that. Some days a black and bitter feeling rears up in your throat when Chloe's not even at her worst, when she's just sitting across the breakfast table looking especially stoned or sullen or damaged. And you want to reach out and give her face a slap, a hard slap you can never take back.

But it all comes back to Roswell, or should. Roswell, who'd gotten himself invited into your home, who wiped his size-twelve sneakered feet on your doormat perfunctorily. This time of year, late February, the year Chloe was in eighth grade. Thirteen. The yard had been muddy. He stood in your foyer wearing a navy nylon warm-up suit with "St. Joseph's" embroidered across the back, his hair cut into the shape of a box on the top of his head. His razor-burned neck, his sporty cologne. You put his age at around thirty-five, though there was something elusive about him.

When he said his name and enfolded your hand in his much larger one, you saw a mental image of the desert floor and the broken alien bodies they'd supposedly found sprawled near Roswell, New Mexico, in the fifties. *Chloe is very talented,* he said as he sat on your couch sipping tea from an intricate bone cup that looked out of place in his big, blunt hand. He'd seen her play when her junior high team matched up against his JV. Phil cracked his knuckles. Chloe sat quietly in the other corner of the couch, her legs tucked into her sweatshirt. *At St. Joe's she can get the exposure to top colleges she won't get at the public school. A scholarship.* The word hung in the room. First to cover the pricey tuition at St. Joe's, and later to a top college program, he was sure. Chloe would have her pick, Roswell seemed to think. He'd looked so authoritative, making promises, speaking sport, that you believed everything he said. When the only remaining hitch was getting Chloe two towns over to St. Joe's every day, he'd volunteered to pick her up in his Blazer and take her to school every day. *It's only ten minutes out of my way,* he said. *Not a problem.* For days afterward you'd ask Chloe, *Do you* want *to go?*

I guess, she'd say. Then, more certain, nodding as if trying to convince herself, *Yes.*

As many times as you've retraced that visit in you mind, the truth is there was nothing. No vibe, no way for you to know this was the one, this was the man who you'd always known was out there, the man who would hurt your daughter beyond anything you could comprehend. You thought you knew what to look for, but you had it all wrong. You were afraid of the polyester-clad stranger at the bus station whose face you could conjure only in a blur, of the shoe salesman whose eyes lingered on your daughter's face for an instant too long as he laced her sneakers. Roswell was sanctioned. Chloe had a dozen coaches before him who had nurtured her gift. And since Chloe isn't willing or able to talk about him much less testify against him, Roswell is still coaching. St. Joe's record, you read in the paper today, is twelve and four.

A few hours pass as you leaf through magazines on the couch when your mother calls. She tells you on the phone that Chloe has been to see her. *Really?* you say. *Today?*

Uh-huh, she says. *They left a little bit ago. She brought that young man, what's his name? Terrence?*

Just then the front door opens and Chloe drags Victor by the hand through the foyer and up the stairs to her room. They are both laughing. You hang up with your mother and start dinner. When neither Ben nor Phil is home when it's cooked, you call Chloe and Victor down from her room and, to your surprise, they appear right away.

Victor eats three pork chops and two helpings of noodle casserole. You contemplate saving some chops for your husband and son, but mostly you feel glad that someone is eating them, that they won't be left to stiffen and congeal in the fridge until you find them in three weeks and toss them in the trash. You're asking him what his father does. *It's complicated,* he says, shoveling noodles into his mouth. *He never talks about work, but he makes good money. Something with shipping.*

You turn to Chloe and inquire about the visit your mother mentioned on the phone, but she doesn't respond. Instead she pushes cut green beans from a can around her plate. You assumed it was making her happy, the way you were talking to

Victor, drawing him out. She's constantly accusing you of not liking him. But one glance at Chloe tells you you're wrong again. She's tucked her curled fists inside her sleeves and pointed her dented chin toward her chest. Soon she pushes back from the table and goes upstairs. After a minute Victor gingerly excuses himself and follows her up. As you load the dishwasher, you can discern the cadence of her sobs through the ceiling.

You finish the dishes. Without a real sense of destination, you head quietly up the carpeted stairs. When you reach the top, you don't turn on the overhead hallway light. You pause in the doorway of Ben's room, which lacks both the chaos of Chloe's room and the comfortable clutter it once contained. The bed is neatly made. Your son took the initiative, just before Christmas, to load the toys and sports equipment he'd outgrown into boxes and take them downtown to the homeless shelter. He's paring down his belongings to what he'll take to college in the fall. These days Ben even hangs his damp towel evenly on the rack every morning like a guest.

You move to the end of the hall and stand at the door to Chloe's room. You can see into her room through the door left slightly ajar. She and Victor are sitting on her bed, their backs braced against the far wall. She's stopped crying, but he's still comforting her: holding her in his arms, rocking her almost imperceptibly, kissing the fused bones of her head.

Suddenly you feel like a voyeur, an intruder in your own home. The few bites of dinner you'd gotten down before Chloe got upset rise to the rear of your throat. You want to reach for the doorknob, to burst in the room and catch them doing something, but you can't think of what you'd accuse them of. Instead you pad away quickly and retreat down the stairs.

You finish your second glass of wine as you sit with Ben while he eats his dinner. Phil calls to say he will be late. At some point Victor goes home and the house grows very still. You sit on the couch and stare at the reflection of your living room in the darkened window.

Chloe comes in, her face still blotched and patchy. She sits on the leather recliner and puts the footrest up, laces her hands behind her neck and crosses her legs at the ankle.

Changed your mind yet? she asks.

No, you say.

I'll go anyway, she says, and collapses the recliner so forcefully it propels her toward the front door. You think she'll slam it hard enough to shake the frame of the house. Your body braces for this. But instead she closes the door softly behind her and walks toward the garage. She snaps on the floodlight that illuminates the carport, then retrieves a basketball from somewhere deep in the garage and begins to dribble in lazy circles in the driveway. Once again your house is filled with the bladdery sound of the ball smacking the pavement.

Chloe dribbles around her back, cutting sharply toward the hoop with the weathered net, making one layup after another. Then she tries some hook shots, lefty, over her shoulder. When she makes three in a row, she begins tossing up purposely errant shots so that she can tap them back in or pull down her own rebound with fiercely flailing elbows. Each time she leaps, she gets so much air beneath her you lose your breath until she's on the ground again.

After a few minutes your daughter stows the ball back in the garage and heads out the driveway, stopping at the seam where the blacktop meets the street and hesitating for the briefest moment before heading away.

Julia Tonkovich

University of Washington

SEDUCING MRS. ROOSEVELT

On the night before the consummation, it is necessary to make my case clear. To state my argument if you will. I will begin by saying that none of it happened the way I'd intended. In fact I still maintain that the telephone was responsible. A seductive instrument in itself, black and sleek, cool at first in the palm and against the ear, then warming with pulse and breath; eventually its shrill ring becomes a trigger of sorts. How I've brought Eleanor around is a miracle of electricity and copper filament, wedded to a bit of incidental deception, no more than sleight of hand, really. I haven't had to work that hard myself. For as much as she's revered the institution of marriage, Eleanor has never been happy in hers; this is evident not only in her ragged letters to her mother-in-law about duty, in the barbs she's slipped to the press, in the two A.M. pillow fights she's had with women who look like William Burroughs. My knowledge of her discontent has been made clear by her tacit acceptance of my logic, to the case I've presented in favor of myself and my desire. It's been through Eleanor that I've learned a well-formed argument can be as potent an incitement to the Act of Love as fingers curling under the hem of a skirt. Though my argument has taken seventeen years to complete, I've got it watertight now. She can't resist it. I've all but made her mine.

Of course, in the dismantling of any woman's resistance there are things which must be addressed before the telephone. Desire, after all, is not just transmitted; it is compiled. And that means research. Books, classrooms, names, dates. It is 1978 and Ken Maddox asks his fifth-grade class to write an essay on role models. He stands up, six-foot-five, in front of the class, and writes on the board: "Who's yours, and why? Three pages." He wears cream-colored polyester trousers and a satin-backed vest, and has the only Afro these children in their Wranglers and Toughskins have ever seen up close. Knowledge of the language of hair is just beginning to sift down to them; it is on the verge of becoming a preoccupation. Banana-combing it, parting it in the middle, layering it, feathering it, braiding it, perming it, curling it, examining the triangulations it's just now starting to sprout from. The girl in the last row near the windows stares at the hair of the boy in front of her. It is blond and belongs to freckled Shawn Urbanski of the Chief Joseph Apartment Villa, the one-story units right across the playground from school with the rusted green Dumpsters that never seem to get emptied. He touched her hair in the lunch line yesterday. Didn't tug, just touched it.

Ken Maddox paces the aisles between his students, their pale hands guiding rows of fattish, uncertain blue script across their notebook pages. He looks at the girl's blank paper, indicates she is taking a long time indeed to think. Surely thinking can't be so difficult an endeavor, he says. She writes, dotting the *i*'s with circles, "Why Eleanor Roosevelt is My Heroin." But what she's thinking is: Rizzo. Why Rizzo is who I want to be. Not the blond lead but the dark bad one, the one who teaches Sandra Dee to be a real woman. To smoke, to wear a leather jacket and hot pants, to be so tough that even the fast-driving, taut-mouthed Kenickie wants to get in the backseat with her. To be the one who shouts from the Ferris wheel the mystical phrase, "I'm not knocked up!" Meaning, the girl knows, I'm not afraid—or perhaps, I didn't fail after all, I will graduate, I told you so. Rizzo, smiling in the sun with a cigarette, girlfriends all around her. The girl knows that writing about Rizzo would be F-city. But who could go wrong with Eleanor Roosevelt?

Two o'clock is library hour, and the girl is doing research for her essay. She finds the biography section and learns that even in black and white Eleanor is not beautiful. The girl knows she is not supposed to notice this. If Mrs. Roosevelt came into their classroom and spoke, the girl knew she would feel embarrassed for this big woman in the block-cut suit. The woman who would grip the podium with authority (so her hands wouldn't tremble) and speak about the rights of the poor, rising opportunities for women, and the need for public commitment to social justice with her steel-shanked down-curving sentences (the fruit of hour upon hour of training with her husband's spectacled assistant who'd rap the table if her voice rose timidly where a period should have been). The girl would notice none of this. If Mrs. Roosevelt were standing in front of their class, Shawn Urbanski would look at the girl, stretch his mouth wide, stick his tongue out, and roll his eyes so the whites showed, mouthing *uuuuuh-gleee!* like he did when the art teacher came on Wednesday mornings; *this* the girl would notice. The book says it is one of the things people liked about Eleanor, her plainness. It proved she was a woman of the people, that she was warm and human. It proved, the girl thinks, that she had to get out of the house because there were mirrors everywhere she turned.

The girl reads on. She learns that when Eleanor was fourteen she stood in a short schoolgirl dress at a cocktail party, her hands laced together to keep them from moving to cover her uncommon mouth. That was what her grandmother called it; a mouth with character, a mouth that told of strength as much as beauty. The other girls called it the Hamster Pout, the girls who wore long gowns and moved with refinement running through their limbs like glycerin. A boy named Franklin asked Eleanor to dance. He said she had beautiful hair, thick and long, not bobbed. Girls should look like girls, he said, not squires. Eleanor was grateful. The girl remembers that Rizzo had short hair like Peter Pan, elves, pixies, and other make-believe creatures; Rizzo never seemed to be grateful for anything. In fact she seemed angry most of the time. Perhaps this is the key to Eleanor, the girl thinks. She is grateful for what she gets, and this gratefulness in turn gets her married to a president.

The girl takes Eleanor's gratefulness, draws three pages out of it. "A strong grateful woman who was committed to democracy, family, and President Franklin D. Roosevelt. She can be an inspiration to any girl today. And to boys even." The girl's essay is deemed good, A-level, by Ken Maddox; it is framed and hung up in the glass case by the principal's office. On Chief Joseph Carnival night Ken Maddox introduces the girl to a tall blue-eyed woman named Diane whose eyelashes are lacquered into points; he is holding Diane's elbow. She leans down to where the girl is waiting her turn at the cakewalk and says, "I think you will make a very good feminist." Ken Maddox laughs and the adult smell of his mouth touches the girl like a finger. Diane is wearing the shoes the girl's mother has forbidden her older sisters to wear: white straps, open toes, cork wedge soles, heels so high the feet arch off the ground like an antelope's dainty hooves, the ankle leading the way right up to the thigh. And though a real antelope wouldn't need them, red toenails to get the eye started.

The girl takes the alleyway home, even though she has been warned about vague things that can happen to girls who walk by themselves in the dark; with Eleanor in a frame and Diane the blue-eyed antelope behind her, she is protected. Part of her wants still to be Rizzo, who wasn't a woman at all but a girl (and a bad one at that), but she is grateful that Diane has recognized enough womanliness in her to say that she would make a good woman.

Four years later when she is a year older than our young dancing Eleanor, the girl will meet a boy named Matt, who drives a Datsun pickup with a stick shift. She is grateful he recognizes something in her that he wants to kiss, and she lets him, and when he does she feels her gratefulness take shape in her mouth and wend its way down her body and ring softly there so that she hollows like a bell. It is nothing like kissing her own hand. It is so much better, this whole-body gratefulness, that four weeks later she will close her eyes and try to move with him there in his Datsun on a Saturday night that is so cold it makes the inside of her nose prickle. Because the cab is too short he will open the passenger door; because the truck is old, the door won't stay put. His feet will push it and then push again as it swings back; the overhead light will send garbled Morse code to anyone who might be driving east on that particular highway:

dotdot.dashdashdashdot.

Dot.

Unlike Matt's girl, Eleanor most certainly did not have carnal knowledge before her sixteenth birthday. And Eleanor never took a lover, as far as anybody knew. At least nobody imagined she would, looking like she did. The society pages said once that though she was an intelligent woman and quite fit to be the wife in the White House, her teeth and lips were never to recover from the seemingly overwhelming shock of her birth. I imagine her seeing her own name in the *Post*—perhaps even the *Times,* in its yellower days—one strong finger looped inside the handle of her bone china teacup, Darjeeling steam rising, her spine straightening away from the back of her cherrywood dining set chair, laughing nervously and then stopping herself from laughing, turning the page with a dry, shouldery reserve though her hands tremble like milk. Learning how to shrug off the guilt the papers wanted to place on her for committing that greatest of womanly sins, ugliness. Before infertility, before shrewishness. Infidelity was off the scale in those backward days, unimaginable, at least for a woman.

I think of the shrug as the ultimate adult gesture; it's difficult to perfect, and timing is important. It was something I never did as a child. But now that I'm thirty I shrug often. Perhaps too often, according to my best friend, Teresa Geske. She says maybe I put up with too much, and that this is the part of adult life she'll never get used to—the amount of garbage we put up with growing and growing until it's as large as we are. Maybe larger. "It's like Sisyphus and his rock. Except forget the rolling-up-the-hill part. This crap doesn't even budge." This is what she said when

I told her that the lab tests came back reading "abnormal." Cells behaving improperly, not yielding, not stopping, multiplying far above the speed limit, breaking all sorts of traffic regulations. They are outlaws, the lab said; they must be stopped. Teresa asked if I'd told my husband, and I said, not yet. And she said he had to know, that I shouldn't try to go through any of it by myself. That was when I shrugged. Quiet resignation being the proper response to things beyond my control, this shrug didn't even warrant a dramatic turning out of the hands.

My husband is nothing like Matt. He is even less like Franklin D., and he rarely shrugs. He is confident and caring, and in control of most situations. He is dependable, he smiles at me in the morning when he puts the knife into the grapefruit, he still asks if he can hold my hand after five years. I don't always know what he is thinking and that pleases me. He doesn't usually ask what I am thinking, and that respect pleases me also. When I returned from the doctor's, I looked at my husband's hair, curling around his ears like a child's, and I didn't want to tell him what I was thinking, which was what the doctor had said. Cancer. Maybe. I'd spent the drive home practicing those two syllables with various intonations. Swooping upward like a question, as in: Who, me? And then like a statement: Yes, you. And then in a monotone: Not me, not now, not yet. Not conclusive, I reminded myself as I pulled into the driveway. For I didn't feel any different; I certainly didn't feel like anything malignant or even unusual was taking place in my body. For a week I kept the news and the brochures from the doctor's office to myself, stashed away in my purse, before sitting down with my husband at the kitchen table and going over my options. I felt like we were planning a trip, looking at possible destinations. Bermuda, Tahiti, Portugal. Exploratory, partial, radical. I don't fault him for where he has decided to go instead. Even if it is a place where they listen to the kind of country music that has started appearing in our cassette deck.

Though it was not a thing that married women did, who would blame Eleanor for taking a lover herself? Her husband, after all, had his Lucy—though the court barred him from all contact with her, Eleanor must have known he lay in bed nights thinking of Lucy's wrists, Lucy's soft laugh, the way Lucy's teeth shone when she opened her mouth in the dark. And after Lucy came polio. How strong Eleanor must have been, how true, not caring that helping him in and out of his chair would amplify her stoutness. Not knowing that spending so much time on her knees massaging the useless legs of one of the Great Men of History would launch her into weeping fits as she told her young boys their after-school stories, sending them soft-footing it back to their bedrooms, glancing at one another, saying nothing, mastering the shrug ten years too soon. At least there are the boys, Eleanor might have said to herself, at least I have succeeded in that. Eleanor has one over on me in that respect.

It is Saturday morning, and in the midst of cleaning the bathroom I survey the various latex child-proofing barriers sitting alertly in our medicine cabinet, mine in its inglorious pink box and his in their bright Christmas-colored wrappings. Kimono. Trojan. Saxon. And now Sheiks, those are new. Japanese robes, Greek instruments of deceit, squat bearded Germanic conquerors, Lawrence of Arabia extras. But mine humbles even those infidels with its hidden resilient spring, its flesh-toned durability. "So what if you don't have a decent name," I say, holding it up to the light, looking for weak spots or tiny holes. A rather useless ritual at this point, considering the dubious prospects outlined by the doctor's brochures, but one which is impossible to discard. Because it makes counting the condoms seem more natural, and less the petty fishwife's habit I know it is. "You've come up short again, troops," I say to the Trojans. Someone's indeed gone AWOL, but how is that possible, after all here he is, my husband, across the hall, asking me who I'm talking to. "Myself," I say. He glides across the carpet with his perpetual cup of coffee. Alert at all waking hours is the man I love. Here, next to me, like always.

"What is that?" He peers at the diaphragm and his chin sags a bit.

"You've never seen it?"

"I guess not. It's bigger than I thought."

He looks at me, and I see the sizing up taking place before he holds out his hand. When I place it in his palm, it looks big to me too, and I know we are both thinking about what it covers. But I doubt my husband is thinking that it is the shape of the ghost town saloon where the outlaws have holed up, and I can't help smiling. He looks serious. He weighs the diaphragm, puts a thumb and index finger around its sallow edges and tests its resistance before putting it back in its box. One firm snap, and its sturdy domed emptiness is out of sight. He picks up his cup of coffee as I leave the room. Then I hear the cup set quietly down on the counter, the sink taps running furtive and slow. Though the doctor has said of course it's not contagious, don't worry, my husband does nothing in bed now but place his beautiful drafter's fingers in the hollow above my hipbone and pat me lightly once or twice before he falls asleep.

"Are you working today?" I call from the kitchen. He comes around the corner, dry-handed already.

"Yep. Unfortunately. All these new clients."

He smiles wistfully and touches my elbow, then my neck. He is a man of certainty and responsibility, and I know that while I might not be married to a Great Man of History, I am married to a great man of normalcy. And at the same time a man who works magic. I want to tell him I know. I want to ask how he does it, how he can change Trojans into Sheiks, pull projects from his sleeve, say a couple of conjurer's words and suddenly fit us into those doin' wrong, been done wrong slots his newfound country singers bark and whine about. But at the same time I want to believe him. "And I guess you have the headquarters transfer coming next year too," I say. "Just don't work too hard." He kisses my forehead and drifts out of the room, his grace restored. From a great man of normalcy it may be possible to accept this too as normal, suck it up, shrug it off. Rizzo wouldn't; she would scream and curse, she would fight. But Eleanor would put up with it. So I will, I do. Teresa Geske agrees that a confrontation would do me no good at this point, and says she'd wait a bit too, and that yes, men can be horrible. Though I never said my husband was horrible, I want her to understand me, so I nod.

*　　*　　*

"GodDAMN, that's harsh," says Teresa. We're having our once-a-week martinis at the Bar-S Grill. Teresa puts a black licorice twirl in her mouth, which is lean like her body and glossed with lipstick the color of raw liver. I can't wear it with the same authority; she says it's because I buy only what's on sale. This afternoon we have sworn not to talk about husbands. I have just told her the cell rebellion in my body may have started back in the Morse code days, thirteen years ago, from doing things too soon. Teresa's indignant. "Why didn't they tell us this when we were fifteen and wanted to have sex? They told us about syphilis, but that's just a penicillin thing. And they didn't know about AIDS yet. But they should've told us about this."

I tell her smoking causes cancer, and that doesn't stop many fifteen-year-olds from trying cigarettes.

"But it's not as if having sex when you're that young is a cause per se. It's a factor, right? Your great-aunt had something like this too, right?"

Teresa is worried; I haven't told her about the interim illness I've been told I carried around like a stashed red pomegranate seed for years, about how when the doctor found it he hadn't bothered to hide his reproach, as he hadn't bothered to remove his class ring. It may have come from Matt and his Datsun, it may have come from my husband working Saturdays. But talking about other people's diseases is tiresome and I want, above all, to be kind. So I change the subject. I tell Teresa I am about to have my first affair.

"You're kidding." She looks at me and stops chewing. This is a sign that she is truly riveted; like many smart people, she is also impatient and can't stand to do a simple thing like talking without also doing another simple thing, like eating or smoking. And then she says, "Isn't this kind of a bad time to do that?"

I ask my friend, when is it a good time?

Now Eleanor knew that an affair couldn't cure a disease. Her husband, the future president of the United States, tried to cure polio through swimming and a girl named Missy. But although Missy called him Eff-Dee and looked great in a bikini as she frolicked in the waters beside the good ship *Larooco*, she couldn't get him out of his wheelchair. If Rizzo were married to Franklin, she would've kicked him out of the house, disease, presidential aspirations, and all. She would've gone out on her own, taken a job as a secretary. No, a waitress. F-city. But Eleanor also knew that a disease could make you do all sorts of things you never imagined possible, in spite of it, not because of it. She learned to drive. She spoke in public, she wrote books, she dealt with the Tennessee Valley Authority. She set up a factory. Of course the factory failed, but that's not central to my argument. She learned to believe in not knowing things your husband did not wish you to know. So in spite of, not because of, I speak to my boss, as usual; I write service orders; I deal with the guys in maintenance when a new line has to be put in. I learn to believe in not knowing; I also learn to believe in not telling. Not that I have anything to tell, yet. Except that I have earned the great prize of secrecy. And even this is something I tell only myself, because it would be difficult to convince anyone else that it is something to be desired, let alone won.

Teresa wants to know details as she resumes her licorice. Her eyes are bright on me. Who, how? Over the phone, I say. A new customer, just switched companies, wanted all this stuff added. Call waiting. Caller ID. Two lines, one with distinctive ring. New jacks. The whole bit. Four times I talked to him; the third time he said I had a nice voice. The fourth time, he asked me out for coffee. "Is he married?" she asks.

I tell her, everybody's married. At our age. Be realistic. This time, it's Teresa who shrugs. She says, "But you haven't done anything yet, really." I say no, not really. She says, "Come on. You can tell me. Have you kissed him?" I say no, not in person. "What are you talking about, not in person?"

I tell her I've kissed him over the telephone. And more. I try to tell her about how arousing it is, hearing the voice and knowing what it goes through to reach me, how it burrows through Sheetrock and pine studs, slithers underground through dark cool soil, shimmies up a metal pole and hums along a wire faster than traffic, slices through the atmosphere and careens off a satellite, how it whispers from a car on a radio frequency, naked and artless as a kid on a walkie-talkie. How it makes all my nerve endings curl up into my ear so that my eyes stop focusing. Teresa can't stop laughing. "You're having an affair over the goddamn telephone! I was actually worried about you for a minute." She laughs and picks up her drink.

"To infidelity," she says, still laughing.

"And cowards like us," I say. We clink the glasses together, tap the bases on the table and drain them. She tells me her second anniversary is next week. "I think we'll order take-out, leave the cartons on the table, fall asleep with the TV on. Something romantic like that." Peace falls delicately over the table as the waiter brings us the third round. We talk for a half an hour like girls about things we can do nothing about: shaving versus waxing, the mayoral election, insurance brokers, spider veins, property taxes. As we're getting ready to leave, Teresa says, "You're not going to go through with this for real, are you?"

I raise my eyebrows at her; I tell her I don't know. But I do. I will.

I drive home with the radio on. Something urban and mechanical and loud, the loathsome George Jones tape now under the seat. I sing, feeling dangerous and wise, feeling like I've won, like I'm standing underneath the Ferris wheel in the sun and shouting. I let myself into our apartment; it's ten o'clock on a Wednesday night and nobody is home. I make myself another drink and stand in our bedroom in the dark, waiting for the telephone to ring. And it does. He calls from somewhere inside his own house, where his wife cannot hear, where his children cannot hear. He has said to open my legs twice before on the telephone, and I have done as I have been told, and the wonders of the copper filament have made their isolated pleasure manifest in hair and darkness. As I pick up the phone, I know this will be the last rehearsal. My research is complete. There is a hotel waiting, and I've won it.

He says he hears a smile in my voice. Why are you laughing? he asks. Just because, I say. I don't tell him it's a victor's laugh. I don't tell him I've just proven true what I've been told all my life. That even if your path is difficult, you must honor your responsibilities and endure the necessary. That if you choose the right guide, your strength will multiply and you will reap great rewards. Like Eleanor and me. It is the night before the consummation and I've won her too. Our argument is complete. We are taking responsibility, we are determined to be the agents of our own fates. We are not undone, not yet.

Jill Kronstadt

University of Washington

WHITE SPACE

Photograph: Grandmother on her wedding day, the web of lace and satin that forms the bodice of her dress, the heart-shaped map of skin above her breasts. She has sprigs of baby's breath braided into her veil. In the photograph my grandfather stands next to her, his hand stiffly gripping her waist, his clothing angular, like boxes.

I am not looking at the photograph, but at my grandmother's face: her skin cool as river stones and her cheeks always the same flat gray.

Portrait: Grandmother holds her wedding flowers. The sun streams through a window on the left, leaving an overexposed diamond of light above her cheekbone. When I was in art school, the smear of light seemed slovenly and garish, a mark of professional inadequacy. Again and again, I wiped it away in my imagination.

I am looking at the photograph, not my grandmother.

Grandmother kept the portrait in a hand-carved frame, propped up on her walnut vanity in the guest room with the chintz wallpaper so old it had yellowed at the edges. She wanted her guests to see the portrait. Grandmother with a bright hole in her face. The blotch of light assumed the effulgence of a precious gem, a dot of flushed young bride that had clattered from its prongs.

Every year I spend the month of September taking portraits of high school seniors at the studio where I work. I powder their noses and cheeks, safety-pin navy satin drapes over the shoulders of the girls, and button pressed white chokers and bow ties around the necks of the boys. In the final photographs, they will look as though they're wearing formal clothes. Under the swathes of dark fabric are halter tops, T-shirts and shorts, sandals with thick rubber soles. I smile sympathetically when they cough at the cloud of face powder, and I compliment them on their graduation so that they feel more comfortable in front of the camera. All their lives they will point at these photographs like icons, saying, *those were the good times* or *never again.*

I am still baffled by new faces. Their expressions are always a foreign terrain, pitching me into a stranger's odd hopes. I have a reputation for quiet and even shyness. Sometimes the clients worry that I'm uncomfortable and they forget to be self-conscious. They talk about their jobs and families, or they ask me what I'm doing for the holidays.

"Julia," Adam said. "Earth to Julia."

There is after all, as I pointed out to Mother before I moved to Snoqualmie, there is after all the telephone. When I call, I can hear her pots and pans clattering over the telephone line, and the sounds of water being turned on and off. She will have the phone tucked under her chin as she talks to me, and as she washes the dishes she will be wearing rubber gloves, bright yellow, part of her latest crusade to grow her nails. The afternoon light will filter through the windows and fall on a vase of flowers on the table, or a stack of newspapers lying on one of the chairs, open to the crossword section.

I can see myself sitting at the table and considering the spiderweb stains at the bottom of my mother's coffee mug while she speaks on the phone, the cord zigzagging dangerously around glass bowls, a dozen eggs, open bags of flour.

"Julia," my mother always says when I call, "come home."

"I can't," I say, adding the excuse of the moment. She is waiting, I know, until I have exhausted all my arguments against visiting, as if my words are ballast and when I have cast enough of them away she will be able to lift me up and carry me home.

The August I was seven years old my grandmother took me to the natural history museum in Santa Barbara. I sweated and fidgeted, my thighs making sucking sounds when I shifted on the seat. Grandmother made me look out the windows to keep from getting nauseous, and for the whole ride I stuck my hand into the blowing air and wished I were barefoot and running through the sprinklers. Grandmother wore a tailored linen dress and an outdated pillbox hat, pumps and gloves, because we would be riding the bus. Her gloves were white, like a first snow without footprints in it, and they fit her hands: not strained between the fingers, or worn at the tips, or creased at her wrists.

Grandmother took me to an exhibit on the human body, a ten-foot man made of clear plastic, standing on a slowly rotating obelisk. A commanding voice boomed out the strange names of the man's internal organs: medulla oblongata, diaphragm, spleen. "There are twenty-seven bones in the human hand," the voice intoned. "The body's largest organ is the skin." Grandmother was still wearing her gloves. I scanned the other people around me, suddenly suspicious of their opaqueness. The crowd dispersed as families carted off their bored children.

"Ready to go?" Grandmother asked. I stayed, watching the plastic man hum out the secrets of his internal life again and again.

"Let's go now," Grandmother said, finally pulling me away.

"Grandmother," I burst out, yanking at her hand, "do you have organs? Like that man in the museum?"

"What man?" she said vaguely.

"Do you have stuff inside of you?"

"Everybody does," she said. "It's science."

*   *   *

Grandmother stayed married until Grandfather died of a heart attack. He was fifty-seven; I was eight. His hands were always in motion, always sifting through the things around him. When Grandmother sold their house, it was marked all over with his restlessness—the mended cabinets, hand-carved boxes, fitted bookshelves, piano and its chipped keys. When Grandmother forced him to sit still, he smoked.

I still have the three-legged stool he built with me. One night when I was visiting, a thunderstorm filled my room with flashing light and sent the window shades flapping up into their rollers. Rain hammered against the panes and seeped under the molding, spilling onto the floor. I crept down the stairs for a towel, keeping my hand fastened on the banister so I wouldn't make any sound. Light and heat came from the kitchen, along with thick smells of baking bread. From the doorway I could see Grandfather's cigarettes stumped out in his ashtray. Grandmother was in her bathrobe, her head tossed to the back of her chair, Grandfather perched on my new three-legged stool like he was kneeling for a fairy princess. In his hands he held Grandmother's feet, and he was rubbing them steadily, playing their knobs and veins like a serenade on the old piano in the living room.

I am not married.

I spend most days in the darkroom poring over the circles of light under the enlarger, my hands stinking of stop bath and fixer. I tug images through water with wooden tongs; they wave at me from their trays. It's the small events I've documented, the way lines on a face in conversation become their own kind of sloppy handwriting, shape and color shifting on a doorway. It's a sort of intimacy. I admit it.

My grandmother divided crises into two categories: those that could be washed away with water, and those that couldn't. A skinned knee or spilled cereal would draw her, her face working with rage, and her hands when they touched me were fast and painful and accurate. She tore away clothing and plunged it into the sink; she covered me with sprays of water; without mercy, she rubbed soap into a wound. "Bite your lip," she would say when I screamed. She had always just given me the warning that would have saved me, and she gloated once disaster occurred: "That's what you get for playing with your food" or "The way you've been carrying on I'm surprised they don't send you to the asylum." Her tongue grew wilder with each pronouncement, as if a show of fury could vanquish chaos.

The other things, the insoluble ones, brought quiet. I remember breaking Grandmother's wedding vase one morning while she was scrambling eggs at the stove. I couldn't have been more than five years old. I was dancing and singing, swinging my arms in wide angel-arcs and bounding on and off the chairs when I took it down. It seemed to float, like the soap bubbles I'd been blowing the afternoon before, and then it plunged onto the kitchen tile. Just as it struck, it made one of those sudden, crooked shrieks that glass makes when it falls, and then it crumpled and shot outward at my bare toes. It was a sound that turned my grandmother. She stared at me, her lips pressed together and her eyes squeezed narrow, and then she showed me the stretch of her back as she finished the eggs. "Don't move," she said, not looking at me. Her fork scraped the pan and her elbow carved circles in the air around her hip. The butter hissed. Her feet nudged the floor. Her blue robe hung square over her shoulders without shifting until she finally shut off the burner and slapped the lid on the top of the pan.

She mentioned it sometimes over the years, my having broken her wedding vase. Now that I am older I wonder whether, when she went back to her room to dress for the day, she looked out the window, down over the front yard, toward the garden where my grandfather was hammering a bean trellis or putting down manure. I wonder if she knew, then, somewhere in her chest, that in three years her husband would be dead. I didn't hear her crying. She walked down the hall as soon as I'd finished my eggs, her slippers whispering on the carpet, and I heard the soft click of the tongue of the door in its latch, and then silence.

Listen to the way sounds change things.

*   *   *

Adam is an ornithologist. I met him in the woods. On weekdays I worked at Jack Flash Professional Photographic Studio; on weekends I crawled through mud and under fallen trees, shooting pictures until the last daylight. This is what I remember: the sharp stinging smell of wet clay soil, soggy from the first rains, the firs and hemlocks painted green and aqua with moss and lichens, their arms held lacy against the sky. My shoes heavy with water, my hair threaded with bark and the broken edges of dead leaves. I knew the heavy presence of stones, the gulping sounds they made when I struck them, the give of ferns around my legs where I moved, the sudden explosion of wings when I found water.

There was a man watching me without moving, not twenty strides from where I stood. We looked at each other. I thought about the film in my camera and remembered stories of fugitives who had been photographed accidentally, had ripped film out of cameras, smashed thousands of dollars of equipment and attacked the photographer. I studied him, carefully listing the details in case I had to repeat them later. Brown hair, untrimmed. Tall. Green ski jacket. Jeans. No gloves. Binoculars. Clean shaven. Glasses. Brown duck boots. Blue daypack.

"Hi," he said.

No visible weapons.

"I'm Adam," he said.

"All men in the woods probably call themselves Adam," I said.

"I didn't mean to scare you," he said. "I'm bird-watching."

"And I'm the bird?"

He laughed.

Biography: A generation after my grandmother's wedding I plummeted heedlessly out of her daughter's womb, beating the air with my fists. My father bought a box of cigars to celebrate my birth, and he endured eight months of dirty diapers before he left my mother. My parents' wedding photograph hung on the wall at Grandmother's. My father had looked at the camera with intense curiosity, it seemed; I've got his hazel eyes.

The story of his abandonment changed shape and weight according to Mother's evaluation of my character. At eight, when I was racked by fierce cravings for candies and toys, he'd gone because of the demands of fatherhood; at eleven, when I wrote impassioned, homesick letters to imaginary friends, he'd been too much of a dreamer to stay put; when, at thirteen, I'd wept over my first crush at the dinner table, she said they were just foolish children, too young to know better than to marry.

Mother listed her memories in terse adjectives: "Grandmother was strict," "Grandfather was popular," "Your father and I were wild." Whenever I asked her to explain, she would concoct a chore that had suddenly become urgent. Sometimes, without warning, the phone would ring and she would send me to my grandmother's. Business trips, she said. When I came home she was tanned and smiling, or she'd bought new clothes.

"Grandmother," I said once, "I'm bored."

She looked at me in disappointment. "If you're bored," she said, "you must not be paying attention."

Photograph: Me, Julia, as an infant, my eyes pink and swollen and my head propped from behind with a crocheted blanket.

Real life: Me, Julia, ten years old, standing on the stairs, removing the photograph of baby Julia from Grandmother's wall, turning the frame to look at the backing, hoping to find something written about me—my name, the date, anything.

Instead I found a classic old-fashioned snapshot, Grandmother in a cotton sundress and a man in a striped shirt, both of them squinting impatiently at the camera with plenty of airspace between their elbows. There was a valentine, a scrap of a lace heart, that said simply, "Yours, G."

I took the photograph straight to my grandmother. "Grandmother," I called, "who's this?"

Grandmother stared at the picture for a minute as though she couldn't remember who I meant. "Oh," she said, letting her breath out slowly, "that's Gerald."

"Was he your boyfriend? Did you go on dates?"

"He was a neighbor of ours," she said.

"Were you in love?" I persisted.

"I don't think so." She handed the picture back to me. "Why don't you go put this back where it belongs," she finished.

In my baby picture I was an upended pink beetle. My features were little and dumb, my body pampered and helpless. My baby mouth was cracked slightly open, as though I'd meant to explain something. Now even I didn't remember what. Gerald and Grandmother smiled in the sun, content to say nothing.

I kept the picture. I left my baby picture and the valentine for Grandmother, slipping them both under the backing, being careful not to tear the yellowed lace. My fingers moved expertly, as though they already understood deception. I tucked the photograph under my shirt, emulsion facing out, and later pressed it between the pages of one of my coloring books.

I told Mother I had met Adam in a diner, because we went to one afterward. This was the first of the diners: a row of khaki vinyl-covered booths, arranged like the seats on a train, looking out at the dark and the sets of headlights passing on the road. Across from us the cook shoved chicken-fried steaks onto plates, scooped French fries into the air with a metal basket. A TV blasted news of an unexplained plane crash in Colorado. Two women shouted at each other through veils of smoke, blotting spilled coffee with paper napkins. I had my arm pressed against the wall and I could see the reflection of half my face in the window.

A man passed our table with a baby in a shoulder pack, resting its face and doughy fists on a towel at the back of the man's neck. His wife followed, her body swaying from side to side as she walked, her limp blond hair pulled back in a hot pink clamp.

Adam had brown eyes. In his daypack he had an actual ornithology manual, and he wore rubber duck boots that flapped against the legs of his jeans. He groped between a windbreaker, a notepad, and an extra pair of socks to produce his wallet and offer to pay for the coffee.

"I've never seen anybody else out there," Adam said, his gaze indicating the woods we'd left a half hour ago.

"I come here a lot," I said. "I've never seen anybody either."

We studied each other from across the table, our muddy clothes and dirty fingernails. He bowed a little bit in the middle, and his joints looked too big for his bones; his buttonholes and sleeves were frayed and unraveling. I glanced at his face to find him looking at me intently, as though I were one of his subjects and he had to describe the precise line of my skull and the pattern of my feathers. We each make a living looking at things. Suddenly we both broke into cascades of nervous laughter.

"You caught me," he said.

"Me, too," I said. "Well."

"Maybe we'll see each other again," he suggested.

"Is your name really Adam?" I asked him.

When Mother took business trips and sent me to Grandmother's, I stole pictures.

Grandmother had no discernible system for deciding where to put her photographs. Some hung on the walls, some filled bulging albums, some were stacked in shoe boxes or left with their negatives at the bottoms of drawers. Often the most nondescript photos—say, of a woman showing her teeth to the camera, a peach blob of fingerprint aimed at her right ear—were in the most elusive places. I found a snapshot of myself loping along with a beach ball half my size; there was a man I couldn't recognize in the corner. I had no idea what mattered and what didn't. I looked at the photographs so intently I felt I knew my way through the homes of people I'd never seen in life, knew the cracks in their walls and the worn patches in their linoleum. There were pictures of me, always looking infuriated and trying to dodge the camera.

But Grandmother's photographs began to disappear. One day I went to her armoire, expecting snapshots of Grandmother and Grandfather on vacation at the Grand Canyon, but I found a blurred series of wildflower still lifes instead. Grandmother and Mother in their vegetable garden had been replaced by a box of paper clips and half pairs of earrings. Finally, after a day of searching, I stood in the doorway of her kitchen and swallowed. She was washing dishes, and she turned.

"Grandmother," I said, "some of your pictures are missing."

"Yes," she said.

I tried again. "I think someone's been stealing them."

"Yes," she repeated. "I think so too." She faced the sink and turned on the water again before I could say anything more.

The autumn I began fifth grade, Grandmother announced that she was selling her house and coming to live with us. The house, she complained, was too large: too much dusting, too much wood and worry about termites, too much space, too much clutter, too hot in summer, and too chill in winter. "I'm old," Grandmother said. "My feet hurt."

"We'll hire a cleaning lady," Mother suggested.

"I'm not having strangers in here."

"Maybe Ruby's daughter could stop by a couple of times a week to—"

"No."

"—and she needs the work, home from college and couldn't find a summer job."

Grandmother didn't answer.

I took pictures of our sandwiches, the thermos, his belt buckle, the wallet-sized pad of paper he kept in his shirt pocket to record the number and location of the birds. Ridiculous pictures. I photographed him crouched behind moss-covered logs while he waited for birds to return to their nests, sitting in practiced silence and stillness, his eyes fixed on the treetops, barely flickering when I raised the camera. I felt the heat of our bodies and the textured soundlessness of the air, taking care not to touch anything solid.

Most often we hiked, saying I would take photographs and he would make field observations, but I was inexpert at being silent in the woods, getting snagged in brambles or cracking branches under my feet unless I had time to settle into a comfortable position, and having him there while I was working made me too nervous to get any worthwhile shots.

"Maybe we should just call it a day hike," I said finally on Mount Si when the click of my shutter frightened away a flock of quail, sending them noisily into the air.

"Yeah, I just came up here with you so I could ruin all your pictures," he teased. "At least now I'll have a sense of purpose."

We followed a steep switchback and leaned into the hill. When we reached the narrow part of the trail, Adam climbed ahead of me. He wore khaki shorts, a faded YOSEMITE T-shirt and a worn leather hat with a brim that bobbed up and down when he walked. "All you're missing is the butterfly net and you'd look like a mad naturalist," I'd laughed earlier. I imagined years of hiking with him, just like this, rocks and leaves and feathers accruing in his pockets, pine needles burrowing into his hair; and a secret tunnel began to construct itself in the hollows of my chest, a cave, a cavity filled with murmurs and whispers and the sound of water. I watched the play of muscles in his legs, his calves dividing and combining with each step, the sway of his torso as he climbed. My arms prickled and my eyes burned. I loved him.

When we came to a wider part of the trail, I caught up with him and reached for his hand. We walked for a while that way, not speaking.

"If you don't tell me what you're thinking, I'm going to have to ask you what you're thinking," Adam said, "and then I'll sound like the moron boyfriend in a lame movie."

I hesitated. "I'm trying to be quiet so I don't scare the birds," I said, blinking.

"What's wrong?"

"I think I've got something in my eye," I said. I rubbed my arm across my face. "There, it's gone." I swallowed. "There's something I've been wondering," I began.

"What?"

I turned my face away from the trail. There had to be something I could ask, or say. I felt like words were being sucked out of my throat. "How do you tell the difference between a crow and a raven?" I finally asked.

"Crows are smaller, with straight beaks. Ravens are mostly solitary and much larger, with a wingspan of a couple of feet, and their beaks are hooked."

"Thanks."

We climbed in silence for several minutes, picking our way

through a section of trail blocked with fallen hemlocks and cedars.

He poked me between the shoulder blades. "You're beautiful," he said.

"What's that got to do with birds?"

"A lot," he said.

The real estate agent told Mother that Grandmother's house would sell quickly, large and solid as it was, and close to the coast besides. Mother kept the armoire and an antique desk she'd coveted for years; I packed small boxes of books, which would be donated to the county library. Room by room the photographs were roused from their hiding places.

"What," exclaimed Mother, "is this junk?" She rattled a drawer full of old coupons, rubber bands, and photographs. "Do you want to put the pictures in an album, or should we just throw them out?"

"Oh, just leave them for now," Grandmother answered.

"I want them," I said.

Grandmother met my eyes, giving me a raw look of amusement.

"What do you want them for? You don't even know most of these people," Mother continued.

"I just do," I said.

"I hope you have a place to put them," said Mother. "Why don't you sit down," she said to Grandmother. "You look tired."

Photograph: Grandmother's house in Ventura, seen from the long flag-shaped driveway that wound between the cypresses and elms. Its windows are empty and stripped of curtains, the furniture sold at auction, the knickknacks wrapped in tissue paper and put away in boxes, the picture frames unclasped from the walls.

Grandmother stayed in what had been our guest bedroom. She arranged her things in jarring and unexpected combinations, producing objects we had never seen in her house. A livid green cherub appeared in the center of the dining-room table where a vase of dried flowers had been; she replaced our bookends with lumpy wax candles of spontaneous design; she hung a gaudy orange-and-purple towel on the rack next to ours. Mother insisted that Grandmother had brought them with her to be aggravating. Each morning she appeared coiffed in her usual style, wearing clothes heavier than perhaps seemed necessary for the weather.

After dinner Grandmother rubbed her feet while we watched television, making sounds of pleasure or discomfort. Finally Mother bought her a pair of oxfords, soft brown leather with rubber soles and dime-store laces.

When she opened the box, Grandmother held the shoes in her lap for a full minute before anyone said anything.

"Do you like them?" Mother asked. "I thought they looked comfortable."

"You'll make me feel like an old lady," Grandmother said slowly, "going around in those things."

"You'd think you'd feel younger if your feet didn't hurt," Mother retorted.

"I thought I raised you to have better taste."

"Oh, Mother, why can't you just keep them and say thank you instead of making it into a whole parenting issue?"

"Okay," Grandmother said. "I'll keep them." She stood up and walked to Mother's china cabinet.

"What are you doing?" Mother asked.

Calmly Grandmother shifted plates and figurines, then dropped the shoes in the center of the display.

"Get them out of there!"

"If they're such nice shoes," Grandmother said, "you won't mind keeping them with these other pretty things. Surely not."

"Mother—"

"What's wrong? Don't you like them?"

Mother walked out of the room and slammed the door.

Photograph: Adam and me, holding hands in front of the diner where Mother thinks we met, Adam smiling into my hair, me glaring glassy-eyed at the camera. A waitress took the picture when we told her we'd just become engaged. Afterward we ate, extracting eggs and potatoes from pools of grease, pouring sugar into lukewarm coffee and sharing rice pudding.

"I knew there was a reason I stay on the other side of the camera," I quipped when I'd processed and printed the film. We sat on the bed looking at the picture. "Do I really look like that?"

"Yes," Adam said, kissing me.

"Don't you think we look like we've just lost the lotto?"

"Marry me," he said, for the second time that day.

I ducked under the blanket, like a ghost, and grabbed him behind the neck with fuzzy fingerless hands. "Boo-oo, whoo-oo!" I laughed, pulling him down with me.

The ascetic scientist and the starving artist, that's what we said. We were bones groping for other bones, skin tangled in other skin, and cold.

One afternoon I came home from school and found Grandmother in the kitchen, her face puffy and blotched with tears. She was surrounded by vegetables in plastic bags. There she was, her face wet. I hovered in the doorway, laboring over the connection between crying and my grandmother.

"Hi," Grandmother said.

"Hi."

"Have a good day at school?"

"Yes." I hesitated. "Are you homesick?"

"Sometimes. Not right now."

"Why are you crying?"

"I'm not crying," Grandmother said. "I'm chopping onions."

"What?"

"Onions make you cry," she declared. "Here, try it. I'll show you."

"What are you making?"

"Tonight," she said, "tonight I was thinking we would have spaghetti." She handed me an onion. "Now. You're going to make a checkerboard. Be sure you keep your fingers away from the knife."

Obediently, I started cutting. "There, that's it," Grandmother said. "Now, cut like this—" She demonstrated. "Are you crying yet?"

"A little," I admitted. It wasn't much of a cry, really, little more than stinging eyes.

In December Adam went to a weeklong ornithology conference in Alaska. He called me after two days. "The sun never comes up, and I miss you," he said.

"Me, too," I said. "Can you see the northern lights?"

"Not from where we are."

When we got off the phone, I cradled the receiver without hanging up, an old habit. Maybe I'm waiting, I thought, as if the phone could suddenly turn warm and become alive—like a turtledove, in the hands of a magician, arising from the folds of a white handkerchief.

I'd wanted to say *I love you* but I couldn't.

In reality I was only sitting.

Grandmother began to wear large clothes, getting up later and sipping cups of tea. "A little stomach bug," she said. The bug persisted for weeks, Grandmother denying it with measured determination.

"Have you been to a doctor?" Mother kept asking her.

"He says it's a touch of the flu," Grandmother said. But she began to change shape: her body bent and billowed under her tailored suits; her face closed in on itself and took on the dry cast of peeling paint. She made strange sounds when she sat, and she played records loudly, at odd hours. For days she would refuse to eat anything but saltines and ginger ale, and then we would find her in the kitchen cooking something elaborate, reading out loud from the cookbook as she grated and stirred.

Finally Mother called Grandmother's doctor. "She's not young, you know. And you think she should what? Any fool can see it's not a touch of the flu! Start acting like someone who has a license to practice medicine!"

"Flu," the doctor said. "Is that what she told you?"

That's how we found out about the cancer.

Grandmother loved me very much, Mother told me when Grandmother died. I was eleven years old, my body outsized and jittery, my legs tanned and scraped in their shorts. Love was something preposterous and unknown, something you echoed back to others when they said they loved you. Love, or as much as I knew of it, was something for Barbie dolls, film stars, and bronze monuments in the park—looming, improbable, and brittle—something that didn't yet fit the shape of my body and wouldn't lie close to my heart.

One day Grandmother appeared at breakfast in her bathrobe instead of her usual tailored suit. She'd lost weight, but in her blue robe she looked padded and cylindrical. Now and then her lips pinched together, as if she'd been sucking a persimmon, and she swayed a little in her chair.

I still had the photographs I'd stolen from her. Collected in a shoe box and stored in one place, the pictures were disappointing. There were enough of them to make a time-lapse film where everyone smiled and stared hollowly at the camera, occasionally shifting their feet and smoothing their clothes as they grew older.

I decided I had to give them back. I wrapped the shoe box in aluminum foil and carried it downstairs to the room that had become Grandmother's. She sat in a rocker in the corner, staring at the wall as though she were watching television.

"Grandmother," I said. "I have something to give you."

"I've heard those stories," she said.

Somehow this didn't make sense, but nevertheless I persisted. "I have your photographs," I said, swallowing hard. "I took them. From your house."

Her face twisted into an odd shape and she looked at me, confused.

"Please, Grandmother," I said. "I want you to have them back." I tried to put the box on her lap.

"Don't you touch me," she said. I jumped back, terrified. "You know," she began, and grimaced, "the Angel of Death sometimes comes in the guise of living relatives. Instead of dead ones."

"Please just *take* them," I pleaded.

She looked at me and covered her face with her hands.

*   *   *

The dead still walk, Adam said once, only more slowly than they did when they were younger, and in quieter places.

I could see that he was surprised to have said it. He raised his chin a fraction and looked at me to measure my response. A moment later he was a scientist again, telling me that he did not believe in ghosts. He had read—though I certainly shouldn't consider him an expert on this subject—that the subconscious mind was capable of producing a wide variety of hallucinations in order to help the conscious mind come to terms with death. There are synapses in the brain that fire when people see their loved ones, he said, and there is no reason to believe that these neurons become inactive just because the loved one is gone.

During the last weeks of her life Grandmother liked to sit outside in her rocker, and when she would let me, I pulled up a chair and sat next to her. Our house had a view of the cliffs and hills, ragged with sagebrush and yucca, the sky cupped over us like an inverted bowl of clear blue glass. She never rocked; she said she was saving her energy.

This is what I remember: an afternoon in late summer, Grandmother sitting and not rocking, me swinging my feet, kicking restlessly at the vast blank of the sky. My clothes had stopped fitting me. Every day I seemed longer, my bones jutting out at odder angles. It's August, I thought. We'd all stopped tracking the days.

That was when the hawk came. It rose from behind one of the hills and settled briefly in a scrub oak. I looked at Grandmother to see if she saw it. Her eyes from the side were hard and glassy, her breath shallow and loud, like a failing engine. "A month or two more," Mother had said. Until Grandmother died, she meant.

"Look," I said, "a hawk."

As if in response, the oak branch bent and the hawk lifted into the air. Its wings scarcely flickered as it flew. The hawk circled, its head jerking slightly from side to side as it scanned the ground. It found a current of air and drifted, spiraling away toward the rocks. "Do you see it?" I asked, turning to Grandmother.

She was following the hawk with her eyes. Its wings stretched tight as metal. As I watched her, her mouth shifted with the curve of its flight, her shoulders slumping right and then left. She watched the hawk for a long time; her breath rose and fell with its lifting and sinking. I expected it to dive toward the earth, surfacing again with something bloody in its beak, but the hawk was patient. The sun painted orange and red on Grandmother's face and hair as it sank toward the cliffs, and she pulled her robe closer, but still the hawk circled and she watched. Her face carved its silhouette into the air around her. Finally she sighed, a sigh so deep it made her shudder, and she blinked.

"I want to go inside," she said.

I helped her out of the rocker, leading her through the sliding glass doors and under the blankets spread out on the sofa, and then I sat down at the kitchen table. "Did she say something to upset you?" Mother asked me.

"She didn't say anything," I said.

Mother was cooking dinner, clanking saucepans and running water. She'd been setting the table when I came in. I looked at our two place settings, at the nail coming loose on one of the chairs, at the sky, which had become a deep crystalline blue.

"What happened?"

I shook my head. My chest filled with something stark and immobile. "Nothing," I said. "Nothing happened."

Photograph: Adam and me in the parking lot at the Deception Pass picnic site, with a quarter pound of cooked shrimp and scampi we bought from a fisherman at Anacortes. Our faces are shaded and blurred. I've set up the tripod but the film isn't quite fast enough to compensate for the low lighting under the trees. Why I've made such an amateur blunder, I couldn't say. I take my camera and leave the tripod in the car.

Adam and I took an easy hike around the picnic area. The trail threaded through blackberries and Douglas firs, spilling into a small clearing where the foliage thinned to reveal a hilltop and bare white rock. From where we stood we had a plain view of the water.

Unexpectedly, Adam sat down on the rock. "I don't know," he said.

I stared at him.

"I don't know," he repeated. "I don't know if we should get married." He smoothed his palms over his knees. "Do you want to sit down?"

"I'm not sure," I said, but I sat down next to him.

"I love you," he continued. "But sometimes I don't feel like I know you. It's always like I'm watching you through binoculars, from a distance."

"I can't help it," I said. "It's just me."

"I know," he said. "I'm sorry."

I looked at him now, his bony legs in their jeans, the T-shirt stretched across his shoulder blades, his arms, folded protectively around his abdomen.

"This can't be happening," I said, but he didn't contradict me.

We walked downhill toward the picnic area and the car, cedars creaking around us, creating a canopy so thick that the ground was still muddy from last week's rains. Beyond the trees, sprays of finches rose from the blackberries; two gulls flew now over the lake. I took Adam's hand and forced my fingers through his, the camera still swinging around my neck.

It was a few months after we met that Adam first brought me to the lake. We went there in the middle of the week, after the schools were in session, and despite the clear sky and late-summer heat the park was eerily empty of hikers. A lone boat struggled across the lake's surface, its sail flapping repeatedly into the water. "They must be learning," I said.

"The hard way," said Adam.

He led me along a path that skirted the west shore of the water, rose to avoid an outcropping of rock, and then dipped down toward a curl of trail where the lake bulged inland, forming a small cove overshadowed with maples and hemlocks.

"My swimming hole," he announced.

We undressed down to our bathing suits and eased our bodies into the water, our legs twitching from the cold. "It's not so bad in this part of the lake because it's so shallow," Adam said. He dove underwater, emerging with his hair slicked over his forehead.

I kicked my legs in front of me and bounced off the lake bottom, then did a handstand underwater before I came to the surface. "It'll feel good after a couple of minutes," I agreed.

"It's a little deeper out in the center," he pointed. He flipped over on his stomach and paddled away from shore; I followed, pointing my toes to test the distance to the bottom. When we reached the deeper water, we floated on our backs, drifting. Above us the sky filtered through a net of trees, dappling the water and creating a haze of light in the treetops. "Did you ever notice," Adam said, "that when you float you go up and down when you breathe?"

"No," I said.

"It's the air inside us, in our sinuses and lungs, that keeps us afloat, and it's why people sink when they drown—no more air. Try it."

I closed my eyes and inhaled. As I did, the water peeled off my skin and I rose; and when I exhaled the water lapped back over my stomach and legs. I imagined myself filled with gaps and holes, my organs slipping and pressing against air and space, wet, red blood swimming toward the oxygen in my lungs and through the tunnels in my bones. I rose and fell, rose and fell, letting the water pool in and out of my ears as I breathed.

When I opened my eyes, Adam was treading water about fifteen feet away, his head an oval framed in shadows. I watched his lopsided smile slowly spreading as his eyes met mine.

There, among the trees and birds and the image of trees and birds, there we wore the faces of children.

PARTICIPATING
WORKSHOPS

UNITED STATES

American University
MFA Program in Creative Writing
Department of Literature
440 Massachusetts Avenue NW
Washington, D.C. 20016-8047
202/885-2972

Arizona State University
Creative Writing Program
Department of Literature
Tempe, AZ 85287
602/965-3528

Bennington College
Writing Seminars
Bennington, VT 05201
802/440-4452

Boston University
Creative Writing Program
236 Bay State Road
Boston, MA 02215
617/353-2510

Bowling Green State University
Creative Writing Program
Department of English
Bowling Green, OH 43403
419/372-8370

Brooklyn College
MFA Program in Creative Writing
Department of English
2900 Bedford Avenue
Brooklyn, NY 11210
718/951-5195

Brown University
Program in Creative Writing
Box 1852
Providence, RI 02912
401/863-3260

California State University,
Fresno
Creative Writing Program
English Department
5245 North Backer Avenue
Mail Stop #98
Fresno, CA 93740-8001
209/278-3919

California State University, Long
Beach
English Department
1250 Bellflower Boulevard
Long Beach, CA 90840-2403
562/985-4223

California State University,
Northridge
Department of English
18111 Nordhoff Street
Northridge, CA 91330-8248
818/677-3431

California State University, Sacramento
Department of English
6000 J Street
Sacramento, CA 95819
916/278-6586

Chapman University
Department of English and
Comparative Literature
333 North Glassell
Orange, CA 92866
714/997-6750

City College of the City University of New York
138th Street at Convent Avenue
New York, NY 10031
212/650-6694

Cleveland State University
Department of English
Creative Writing Program
Euclid Avenue at East 24th
Street
Cleveland, OH 44115
216/687-3950

Colorado State University
Department of English
Fort Collins, CO 80523-1773
970/491-6428

Columbia College Chicago
Fiction Writing Department
600 South Michigan Avenue
Chicago, IL 60605
312/663-1600 (ext. 5611)

Columbia University
Writing Division
School of the Arts
Dodge Hall
2960 Broadway, Room 400
New York, NY 10027-6902
212/854-4391

DePaul University
MA in Writing Program
Department of English
802 West Belden Avenue
Chicago, IL 60614-3214
773/325-7485

Eastern Michigan University
Department of English
612 Pray Harrold
Ypsilanti, MI 48197
734/487-4220

Eastern Washington University
Creative Writing Program
705 West First Avenue
MS #1
Spokane, WA 99204
509/623-4221

Emerson College
Writing, Literature, and Publishing
100 Beacon Street
Boston, MA 02116
617/824-8750

Florida International University
Creative Writing Program
English Department
3000 NE 151st Street
North Miami Campus
North Miami, FL 33181
305/919-5857

Florida State University
Department of English
Tallahassee, FL 32306-1036
850/644-4230

George Mason University
Creative Writing Program
MS 3E4
Fairfax, VA 22030
703/993-1185

Georgia State University
Department of English
University Plaza
Atlanta, GA 30303
404/651-2900

Hollins College
Department of English
Box 9608
Roanoke, VA 24020
540/362-6317

Indiana University
MFA Program
English Department
Ballantine Hall 442
Bloomington, IN 47405-6601
812/855-8224

James A. Michener Center for
Writers
FDH
702 East Dean Keeton Street
Austin, TX 78705
512/471-1601

Johns Hopkins University
The Writing Seminars
135 Gilman Hall
3400 North Charles Street
Baltimore, MD 21218-2690
410/516-7563

Kansas State University
Creative Writing Program
Department of English
Manhattan, KS 66506
785/532-0384

Long Island University
Brooklyn Campus
University Plaza
Brooklyn, NY 11201
718/488-1000 (ext. 1050)

Louisiana State University
English Department
213 Allen
Baton Rouge, LA 70803
504/388-2236

Loyola Marymount University
Department of English
326 Foley
Loyola Boulevard and West 80th
Street
Los Angeles, CA 90045
310/338-3018

Manhattanville College
Office of Adult and Special Programs
2900 Purchase Street
Purchase, NY 10577
914/694-3425

Mankato State University
English Department
Box 53, Mankato State University
Mankato, MN 56002-8400
507/389-2117

McNeese State University
Program in Creative Writing
Department of Languages
P.O. Box 92655
Lake Charles, LA 70609
318/475-5326

Miami University
MA Program in Creative Writing
Department of English
356 Bachelor Hall
Oxford, OH 45056
513/529-5221

Mills College
Department of English
5000 MacArthur Boulevard
Oakland, CA 94613
510/430-2217

Mississippi State University
Drawer E
Department of English
Mississippi State, MS 39762
601/325-3644

Naropa Institute
2130 Arapahoe Avenue
Boulder, CO 80302-6697
303/546-3540

The New School
Office of Education Advising
and Admissions
66 West 12th Street
New York, NY 10011
212/229-5630

New York University
Graduate Program in Creative
Writing
19 University Place
New York, NY 10003
212/998-8816

Northeastern University
Department of English
406 Holmes Hall
Boston, MA 02115
617/373-2512

Ohio State University
Department of English
164 West 17th Avenue
Columbus, OH 43210-1370
614/292-6065

Oklahoma State University
English Department
205 Morrill Hall
Stillwater, OK 74078-4069
405/744-9469

Old Dominion University
Department of English
BAL 220
Norfolk, VA 23529
757/683-3991

Pennsylvania State University
Graduate Admissions
MFA Program in Writing
Department of English
University Park, PA 16802
814/863-3069

Purdue University
Office of Admissions
1080 Schleman Hall
West Lafayette, IN 47907-1080
765/494-1776

Rivier College
Department of English
South Main Street
Nashua, NH 03060-5086
603/888-1311

Rutgers University
Writing Program
Department of English
Newark, NJ 07102
973/353-5279

Saint Mary's College of California
MFA Program in Creative Writing
P.O. Box 4686
Moraga, CA 94575-4686
925/631-4088

San Diego State University
MFA Program
Department of English and
  Comparative Literature
San Diego, CA 92182-8140
619/594-5443

San Francisco State University
Department of Creative Writing
College of Humanities
1600 Holloway Avenue
San Francisco, CA 94132
415/338-1891

Sarah Lawrence College
Program in Writing
1 Mead Way
Bronxville, NY 10708-5999
914/337-0700
The School of the Art Institute
  of Chicago
MFA in Writing Program
37 South Wabash Avenue
Chicago, IL 60603-3103
800/232-7242 or 312/899-5219

Southern Illinois University at
  Carbondale
MFA Program in Creative Writing
Department of English
Carbondale, IL 62901-4503
618/453-5321

Southwest Texas State University
MFA Program in Creative Writing
Department of English
601 University Drive
San Marcos, TX 78666-4616
512/245-2163

State University of New York at
  Stony Brook
Creative Writing Program
Department of English
Stony Brook, NY 11794-5350
516/632-7373

Temple University
Graduate Creative Writing Program
English Department
Philadelphia, PA 19122
215/204-3014

Texas Tech University
Creative Writing Program
Department of English
Box 43091
Lubbock, TX 79409-3091
806/742-2501

University at Albany, SUNY
Writing Program
Department of English
Humanities Building 333
Albany, NY 12222
518/442-4055

University of Alabama
Program in Creative Writing
Department of English
P.O. Box 870244
Tuscaloosa, AL 35487-0244
205/348-0766

University of Alaska, Anchorage
Department of Creative Writing
    and Literary Arts
3211 Providence Drive
Anchorage, AK 99508
907/786-4330

University of Alaska, Fairbanks
Creative Writing Program
Department of English
P.O. Box 755720
Fairbanks, AK 99775-5720
907/474-7193

University of Arizona
Program in Creative Writing
Department of English
445 Modern Languages Bldg.
P.O. Box 210067
Tucson, AZ 85721-0067
520/621-3880

University of Arkansas
Department of English
333 Kimpel Hall
Fayetteville, AR 72701
501/575-4301

University of California, Irvine
MFA Program in Writing
Department of English and
    Comparative Literature
435 Humanities Instructional
    Bldg.
Irvine, CA 92697-2650
949/824-6718

University of Central Florida
Department of English
P.O. Box 161346
Orlando, FL 32816-1346
407/823-2212

University of Cincinnati
Creative Writing Program
Department of English and
    Comparative Literature
P.O. Box 210069
Cincinnati, OH 45221-0069
513/556-5924

University of Denver
Creative Writing Program
Department of English
Pioneer Hall
Denver, CO 80208
303/871-2266

University of Georgia
Creative Writing Program
English Department
Park Hall 102
Athens, GA 30602
706/542-2659

University of Hawaii
Creative Writing Program
English Department
1733 Donaghho Road
Honolulu, HI 96822
808/956-8801

University of Houston
Creative Writing Program
Department of English
Houston, TX 77204-3012
713/743-3015

University of Illinois at Chicago
Program for Writers
Department of English MC/162
601 South Morgan Street
Chicago, IL 60607-7120
312/413-2229

University of Iowa
Program in Creative Writing
Department of English
102 Dey House
Iowa City, IA 52242
319/335-0416

University of Kansas
Creative Writing Program
Department of English
3116 Wescoe Hall
Lawrence, KS 66045
785/864-4520

University of Maine
English Department, Room 304
5752 Neville Hall
Orono, ME 04469-5752
207/581-3822

University of Massachusetts,
  Amherst
MFA in English
Bartlett Hall
Box 30515
Amherst, MA 01003-0515
413/545-0643

University of Memphis
Creative Writing Program
Department of English
Memphis, TN 38152
901/678-4589

University of Michigan
The Hopwood Room
1176 Angell Hall
Ann Arbor, MI 48109-1003
734/763-4139

University of Minnesota
MFA Creative Writing Program
English Department
207 Lind Hall
207 Church Street, SE
Minneapolis, MN 55455
612/625-6366

University of Missouri, Columbia
Creative Writing Program
English Department
107 Tate Hall
Columbia, MO 65211
573/882-6421

University of Missouri, St. Louis
MFA Program
Department of English
8001 Natural Bridge Road
St. Louis, MO 63121
314/516-5541

University of Montana
Creative Writing Program
Department of English
Missoula, MT 59812-1013
406/243-5231

University of Nebraska, Lincoln
English Department
202 Andrews Hall
Lincoln, NE 68588-0333
402/472-3191

University of Nevada, Las Vegas
MFA in Creative Writing
Department of English
4505 South Maryland Parkway
Las Vegas, NV 89154-5011
702/895-3533

University of New Hampshire
Creative Writing Program
Department of English
Hamilton Smith Hall
95 Main Street
Durham, NH 03824-3574
603/862-1313

University of New Orleans
Creative Writing Workshop
College of Liberal Arts
Lakefront
New Orleans, LA 70148
504/280-7454

University of North Carolina,
  Greensboro
MFA Writing Program
English Department
134 McIver Building
P.O. Box 26170
Greensboro, NC 27402-6170
336/334-5459

University of Notre Dame
Creative Writing Program
Department of English
Notre Dame, IN 46556-0368
219/631-7526

University of Oregon
Program in Creative Writing
Box 5243
Eugene, OR 97403
541/346-3944

University of Pittsburgh
Creative Writing Program
526 C.L.
4200 Fifth Avenue
Pittsburgh, PA 15260
412/624-6549

University of San Francisco
MA in Writing Program
Lone Mountain 340
2130 Fulton Street
San Francisco, CA 94117-1080
415/422-2382

University of Southern Califor-
  nia
Professional Writing Program
Waite Phillips Hall, Room 404
Los Angeles, CA 90089-4034
213/740-3252

University of Southern Missis-
  sippi
Center for Writers
Box 5144
Hattiesburg, MS 39406-5144
601/266-4321

University of Texas at Austin
English Department
PAR 108
Austin, TX 78712-1164
512/471-5132

University of Texas at El Paso
MFA Program with a Bilingual
  Option
English Department
Hudspeth Hall
El Paso, TX 79968-0526
915/747-5731

University of Utah
Writing Program
English Department
Salt Lake City, UT 84112
801/581-6168

University of Virginia
Creative Writing Program
Department of English
Bryan Hall
Charlottesville, VA 22903
804/924-6675

University of Washington
Creative Writing Program
Department of English
Box 354330
Seattle, WA 98195-4330
206/543-9865

University of Wisconsin, Milwau-
kee
Creative Writing Program
Department of English
Box 413
Milwaukee, WI 53201
414/229-4243

Vermont College
MFA in Writing
Montpelier, VT 05602
802/828-8840

Virginia Commonwealth Univer-
sity
MFA in Creative Writing Pro-
gram
Department of English
P.O. Box 842005
Richmond, VA 23284-2005
804/828-1329

Warren Wilson College
MFA Program for Writers
P.O. Box 9000
Asheville, NC 28815-9000
704/298-3325

Washington University
Writing Program
Department of English
Campus Box 1122
One Brookings Drive
St. Louis, MO 63130-4899
314/935-5190

Wayne State University
Creative Writing Program
Department of English
Detroit, MI 48202
313/577-2450

West Virginia University
Department of English
230 Stansbury Hall
P.O. Box 6269
Morgantown, WV 26506-6269
304/293-5021

Western Illinois University
Department of English and Jour-
nalism
Macomb, IL 61455-1390
309/298-1103

Western Michigan University
Program in Creative Writing
Department of English
Kalamazoo, MI 49008-5092
616/387-2572

Wichita State University
MFA in Creative Writing
Department of English
Wichita, KS 67260-0014
316/978-3130

CANADA

Concordia University
Department of English
Creative Writing Program
LB 501
1455 de Maisonneure Boulevard
  West
Montreal, PQ H3G 1M8
514/848-2340

University of Alberta
Department of English
3-5 Humanities Center
Edmonton, Alberta T6G 2E5
403/492-3258

University of British Columbia
Creative Writing Program
Buchanan Building, Room E462
Vancouver, BC V6T 1Z1
604/822-0699

University of Calgary
Creative Writing Program
Graduate Studies
Department of English
Calgary, Alberta T2N 1N4
403/220-5484

University of New Brunswick
Department of English
Box 4400
Fredericton, NB E3B 5A3
506/453-4676

FICTION

Selected by bestselling author and American Book Award–winner Sherman Alexie, the freshest and most innovative voices in North American fiction today

This third volume in the acclaimed Scribner's Best of the Fiction Workshops series contains stories culled from over one hundred prestigious writing programs around the United States and Canada. These nineteen ingenious stories, selected by guest editor Sherman Alexie, are a must-read not only for students and teachers of writing but for all short-story lovers who are looking for original, stimulating, and unpredictable storytelling.

"A good antidote to the somewhat clubby selections that appear in the annual O. Henry and Best American Short Stories anthologies."
—DAPHNE MERKIN, *The New Yorker*

SHERMAN ALEXIE is the bestselling author of ten books, including the American Book Award–winner *Reservation Blues*. Chosen by *Granta* as one of the twenty best American novelists under forty, Alexie is also the screenwriter and producer of *Smoke Signals*. He lives in Seattle. JOHN KULKA is a bookseller in New York City. He is on the advisory board for Dalkey Archive and is currently at work on a novel. NATALIE DANFORD is a seasoned writer and book critic whose work has appeared in *The Boston Globe*, *The Washington Post*, and other major newspapers. She lives in New York City.

SCRIBNER PAPERBACK FICTION
Published by Simon & Schuster New York

Cover design by Richard Prachot
Cover photograph by Lars Klove

04991400

U.S. $14.00
Can. $21.00

51400

9 780684 848297

ISBN 0-684-84829-5